UNCOVERED PASSION

"You're a cop with a heart, Dory, and it makes you human. I guess that's why I . . . well . . . like having you as a partner. I've seen many cops become hard and calloused by what they've experienced in this job. You've been on the force for ten years, and you're still untouched. Stay that way, Dory. It's what makes you a good cop. You care, and you try to do your best to end the suffering. You're good people. Don't let this get you down too much. I know we'll solve this case soon. The perp has already panicked once when he went after Paul. He'll slip again, and when he does, we'll catch him," Tom counseled as he looked deeply into her eyes.

The moonlight cast shadows on his face, highlighting the hollows and crags and making his eyes shine warmly. A few strands of gray hair played on his temples as he hoisted his frame from the bench and extended his hands for her to grasp. With one quick motion, he pulled her to her feet and into his arms.

"You'd better not hold me so close," Denise whispered as she melted into the warmth of his arms. "People will think we're in love."

Smiling into her upturned face, Tom replied, "We are."

BOOK YOUR PLACE ON OUR WEBSITE AND MAKE THE ARABESQUE ROMANCE CONNECTION!

We've created a customized website just for our very special Arabesque readers, where you can get the inside scoop on everything that's going on with Arabesque romance novels.

When you come online, you'll have the exciting opportunity to:

- View covers of upcoming books

- Learn about our future publishing schedule (listed by publication month and author)

- Find out when your favorite authors will be visiting a city near you

- Search for and order backlist books

- Check out author bios and background information

- Send e-mail to your favorite authors

- Join us in weekly chats with authors, readers and other guests

- Get writing guidelines

- AND MUCH MORE!

Visit our website at
http://www.arabesquebooks.com

UNCOVERED PASSION

COURTNI WRIGHT

ARABESQUE

★BET★

BOOKS™

BET Publications LLC
http://www.bet.com
http://www.arabesquebooks.com

ARABESQUE BOOKS are published by

BET Publications, LLC
c/o BET BOOKS
One BET Plaza
1900 W Place NE
Washington, DC 20018-1211

All Kensington Titles, Imprints, and Distributed Lines are available at special quantity discounts for bulk purchases for sales promotions, premiums, fund-raising, and educational or institutional use. Special book excerpts or customized printings can also be created to fit specific needs. For details, write or phone the office of the Kensington special sales manager: Kensington Publishing Corp., 850 Third Avenue, New York, NY 10022, attn: Special Sales Department, Phone: 1-800-221-2647.

First Printing: February 2002
10 9 8 7 6 5 4 3 2 1

Printed in the United States of America

PROLOGUE

The pile on the thick carpet showed the crisscross pattern of weary footsteps as the senator paced beside the heavy mahogany desk. His energy appeared to flag with each step. His shoulders bent under the strain of the decision that rested firmly on him. In his hands lay the fate of his fellow members of Congress. To decide incorrectly meant that more men might die.

"But, John, a woman detective!" Senator Edwin Robinson repeated as he stopped in front of the chair in which the saddened leader of the United States Senate sat hunched from fatigue and worry. "Such a thing is unthinkable. The chief of our police department is already upset at our decision to bring in outsiders, but to bring in a female would only compound matters."

"I do not understand why he has taken offense. We are building a multistate team and need someone from Maryland. We cannot simply rely on the Capitol police department when we are trying to quell the concerns of all of our constituents. The fact that this detective is female is of no consequence. The objective is to staff the unit with the most qualified people," Senator John Moore replied as he distractedly fingered the tie his wife gave him for Christmas. They had been arguing this point for what seemed like hours, and he felt drained of the last of his reserves. On days like this, he felt every one of his eighty years.

"I am very familiar with our task, John, but I don't understand why we can't ask the state to nominate a man. I know it sounds sexist, but, despite the increased number of women on the Hill, the men here might feel more comfortable talking with another man," Senator Robinson rebutted as he sank into the comfortable leather of the chair nearest the door. "I was of the impression that our first charge was to find personnel with whom our people would have the most ease of conversation and who were simultaneously the best qualified."

Straightening his weary body, Senator John Moore responded slowly, "Not at all. We need the best possible team of detectives; our Capitol police force is too small to handle the magnitude of this assault on us. This woman is the best Maryland has to offer. Therefore, we must invite her. I don't see why we need to continue arguing this point. I am very tired. This whole business has exhausted me emotionally and physically."

Perhaps it was time for Senator Robinson to acquiesce to the majority leader's wishes to save the gentle elderly man further discomfort. Senator Moore's lined face certainly indicated that the leader of the Senate had almost endured more than his fragile constitution could stand. As the oldest man on the Hill, he had survived more political upheaval than anyone else. He had served under countless presidents, stood beside untold numbers of legislators, and fought countless battles. Perhaps someone else needed to carry the weight of this latest assault on Congress for him.

Senator Robinson replied slowly as he thumbed the contents of the file, "From all reports, she is the most logical candidate. The file provided by the Maryland governor's office contains glowing accolades, recommendations. The newspaper accounts were glowing.

She has won more recognition and awards than any other police officer in the United States. According to this dossier, she spends almost as much time working in other jurisdictions as in her own; the Maryland police always lend her to other jurisdictions for cases. She has lectured on the university level and is an expert at solving impossible cases. Her credentials are far superior to those of the other candidates."

"Then, why do you hesitate to extend the invitation? Let's finish this task. I'm tired. All of this excitement has been too much for me. I'd like to get a little rest before the evening session. I doubt that every state will send someone, but I hope that the Montgomery County police will release Detective Dory. Her reputation and expertise would add so much to this investigation," the statesman replied as he stretched his shoulders. He had endured meetings all afternoon and could feel crankiness beginning to descend on his otherwise cheerful personality.

Edwin Robinson watched as the obviously exhausted elder senator carefully rose from his chair and headed toward the door that opened into the usually noisy hall. At this hour, almost everyone had gone home for the weekend, leaving the two men to feel very much alone with their heavy responsibilities. John Moore had become so frail in the last year that everyone wondered about his ability to carry on his demanding schedule. Unlike the days of his early tenure as the senator from Missouri, he no longer walked with a jaunty stride but shuffled like the elderly statesman that he had become. His thick, dark hair had thinned and turned to silver. His hands shook almost constantly and his head bobbed slightly when fatigued. Still, the senator's mind was keener than that of most men half his age, and his ability to see into the most complex issues had not diminished. Everyone said that if John Moore ever retired, he would go down in the history of the Senate as the most competent, politically astute man ever to walk the halls of power.

Smiling, Edwin Robinson stuffed his papers inside his briefcase as he prepared for the short walk down the hall to his office. He and John had become fast friends in the ten years they had worked together. He knew Senator Moore's quirks and could anticipate his reaction to most topics. The elderly statesman trusted him implicitly and knew that, despite Robinson's quirks and prejudices, he was a bighearted man who always tried to be fair.

Looking back over his shoulder, Senator Robinson scanned the spotless office. Moore's favorite pen lay across the sparkling crystal inkwell and his gold-embossed copy of the Constitution rested on the stand to the right. Everything was in its place and ready for his return. Edwin Robinson would be waiting, too. He had much to learn if he ever wanted to be as productive and astute a politician as his friend and mentor.

ONE

The detectives in the busy police station sat hunched over their desks as the telephones rang and the radios blared. Keyboards clicked as the detectives pounded out reports and transcribed eyewitness testimony. The smell of burned coffee filled the stale air of the squad room. Officers trying to cut back chewed gum and tried to control their tempers while their heads ached from the effort. Handcuffed prisoners waited for booking while gruff, tired officers filled out the necessary paperwork and stored their personal belongings in carefully marked bags. Some of them looked frightened, but most only wore expressions of arrogance and indifference as they glared at their captors. It was a routine day in the police station.

"I sure am glad that I don't have to work that detail," Denise Dory said to no one in particular as she watched the crowd of mourners on TV standing in front of the Capitol as they waited to enter the rotunda. "I'd hate to be the one to investigate that murder."

"What makes you think it's a murder, Dory?" Tom Phyfer asked without looking up from his work. "He was an elderly man with a history of health problems. He could have died in his sleep."

"I just have a gut feeling about this. Sure he was old, and I think that's what the murderer was counting on, especially since he was just reelected despite concern over his age. I remember reading that he had a physical before the grueling campaign began to assure his constituents that he was fit for reelection. His death looks too planned for me," Denise rebutted as she sipped her coffee.

"Look, it happens. The stress of running the campaign against young competition was probably too much for him. His heart just gave out. Don't make too much out of it," Tom added as if to end the discussion.

"Maybe you're right, but it just seems too convenient to me. After all, he was the second newly elected member of Congress to die. How many sick old politicians can they have at the Hill, I ask you? The first one died of kidney failure, and now this one dies of a heart attack. I'm just glad to be here in Maryland and not on the police force at the Capitol. Something doesn't sit right with me about this case," Denise muttered as she returned to her cluttered desk.

"You're becoming too cynical in your old age. Who would off a senator as well loved as that old man?" Tom queried as he peered at her over his glasses.

"Stranger things have happened. Besides, I'm not getting old. I just remember my history lessons, that's all. This kind of thing happened all through the ages to Roman senators and kings. I don't see why it can't happen at the U.S. Capitol," Denise responded as she cast a sidelong glance at her partner of five years.

Changing the subject, Tom snarled as he unhooked the chain of paper clips the office prankster had made of his supplies. "If I ever catch the asshole who does this to my paper clips, I'm going to tear him a new one."

"You're such a sexist. What makes you think that only a man would knot up your paper clips? A woman could have done it. There are a few of us on this police force, you know." Denise chuckled merrily at his anger.

Tom glared at her silently for a moment and then said with a growl, "Let me correct myself for your benefit, Dory. If I ever catch the wise ass who did this, I'll tear him or her a new one. Are you satisfied? Geez, of all the cops I could have been assigned to work with, I get you. Joan of Arc in a patrol car."

Laughing at his distress, Denise replied, "You know you love it when I give you a hard time. You've been the happiest man on this force with me as your partner. Don't try to deny it. We're a great team, and you know it. We wouldn't have been voted the couple most likely to succeed if we weren't the best."

"Humph!" Tom snorted as he turned his attention from Denise to the mass of rubber bands in his top drawer. Whoever played with his paper clips had also tied his rubber bands in a knot. Denise would never be the one to disclose the identity of the joker, and she knew that Tom would never guess. He had put her on a pedestal above the mundane activities of office highjinks and made himself the butt of many of her harmless little pranks.

Smiling, Denise strolled across the office for another cup of coffee and a better view of the television. All three channels carried the news of the latest death on the Hill. The dearly loved and revered Senator Armstrong had died of cancer six months ago after suffering for many years. Denise had not been surprised when he passed away in his sleep. Like most people, she felt relief that his suffering had finally ended. However, when first one newly elected senator and then another died so suddenly, she had become suspicious.

Mourners packed the square in front of the U.S. Capitol as they waited in the sunshine for the Capitol police officers to announce their turn to enter the building's shelter from the hot early Washington D.C. summer. Sorrow hushed the voices of the people as fresh tears washed their faces. The political crowd of Washington had mourned the loss of one beloved friend only a short while ago; today they prayed for the soul of yet another.

Watching the coverage of the crowd, Denise thought about the mood of the people who had gathered on the same steps only a short while ago. Their faces had reflected the mixed feelings of sorrow at the death of one of their own and curiosity as to his successor on special-interest projects. She recognized many of the same faces among the mourners waiting in the hot sun.

"An incredibly sad sight," Denise muttered to no one in particular.

"This is the part of working in this area that I don't like. The networks don't hesitate to broadcast human suffering . . . too much if you ask me," Captain Morton commented as he sipped the thick, strong police station brew. By the afternoon, the coffee was so dense that it could almost stand without a cup.

"You're right. Makes me long for small-town life, or at least what I understand of it," Denise replied as she accepted half of his sticky, slightly stale, honey-glazed doughnut.

"I grew up in a small town. It's quiet and peaceful most of the time, not like this area where something's always happening. However, when a single kid falls down, all the mothers go nuts. That's good and bad, I guess. You'll have to give it a try one day," Captain Morton responded as he licked the sugar from his fingers and poured another cup of the precinct's sludge.

"I might just do that. My main objection to small-town life is that everyone knows everyone else's business. I like my autonomy. I guess I've talked myself out of it," Denise explained with a shrug.

"Whatever. By the way, the chief wants to see you.

We're due upstairs in fifteen minutes," Captain Morton added in an offhand manner.

"Why does she want to see me? I haven't stepped on anyone's toes lately," Denise asked as she turned to study the captain's face for the answer.

"Hey, don't ask me. She called, and I said we'd be there. She didn't offer any explanations, and I didn't ask for any. We'll find out soon enough," Captain Morton replied with a shrug as he drained his cup down to the dregs.

About fifteen minutes later, Denise placed her half-full cup on the table beside the steaming pot and followed Captain Morton out of the police station and onto the elevator that would carry them to the fifth floor and Chief Grant's office. Denise was not a stranger to the chief and had been upstairs many times in her ten-year career on the force. Most of the occasions had been pleasant ones. However, Denise had done her share of standing at attention on the carpet. Whatever came from this meeting, she was woman enough to take it.

"Captain Morton and Detective Dory, come in, please. It's good to see you again. Have a seat. Coffee?" Chief Grant asked as she ushered them into her office.

"No, thank you, ma'am, I've reached my limit for the day," Denise replied, taking a quick look at the view from the wall of windows and settling into the offered chair. The chief was smiling, and the sun was shining. These were good signs.

"Before we get started, I'd like to congratulate you, Detective Dory, on the fine work you've been doing. Believe me when I say that it's officers like you who make this police department what it is. The Montgomery County Police Department would not have the success rate in solving cases it does if it were not for the hard work of our dedicated officers," Chief Grant said with a broad smile.

"Thank you, Chief Grant, I appreciate the kind words. I'll be sure to convey your message to my partner, Tom Phyfer," Denise replied. She wondered why the captain had not invited Tom to join them. He had been sitting at his desk when the captain entered the room. She could smell a setup.

"I'll get right to the point of this meeting. The President of the United States has established a task force composed of police officers from every state in the Union to investigate the recent deaths on the Hill. As one of the premier police forces in the state, we've been selected by the governor to represent the State of Maryland. We've decided to send you as our representative," Chief Grant explained slowly and carefully. From the expression on the chief's face, Denise knew that she was supposed to feel highly flattered by this honor, but she did not. Instead, she felt as if someone had just hit her in the middle of her back and knocked the breath out of her.

"Chief," Denise blurted, sitting on the edge of her chair, "I can't go to D.C. I have a ton of work on my desk. My partner and I are within days of solving a case we've worked on for three months. I can't leave him now."

"Your dedication to duty is commendable, Detective. However, your acceptance of this assignment is not open for discussion. You have been selected, and you're going," Chief Grant responded forcefully. She appeared highly offended that Denise had not thanked her for the opportunity to join the other handpicked officers.

"Chief, I thank you for your support and confidence in my abilities. You've been behind me every time I've been called into this kind of action, but I really must decline. I've put too much effort into these projects to turn away from them now," Denise repeated as she tried to take a different approach to the matter after deciding that a softer one might get around the chief's irritation at her first refusal. "We have worked countless hours on these cases. If I leave now, my partner will have to carry the load alone and that wouldn't be fair to him. Would it be possible for me to join the others in a week or two? I will have closed many of my cases by then."

"That's enough, Detective," Captain Morton interjected in his most authoritarian voice. "I'll assign someone to work with your partner in your absence."

"But, Captain, I can't dump all that work on Tom—" Denise started to explain but was cut off by a swift, impatient wave of the captain's hand.

"I said, that's enough," Captain Morton hissed through lips that barely moved. He was no longer the easygoing captain that Denise knew so well; he had become a commander, something he seldom did. Denise could feel his need to impress the chief and his disappointment that she did not share the desire.

Realizing the futility of her efforts, Denise closed her mouth with a snap and listened. She had no choice except to follow his directions, but she was not happy about it. She preferred management by objectives rather than by the boot-on-the-buttocks approach. Since she could feel Captain Morton's heel imprint on her fanny, Denise decided that she had lost this battle even before the war started.

Reaching into a folder on her desk, Chief Grant pulled out an official-looking leather-bound portfolio and tossed it to Denise. She folded her hands on top of her massive appointment calendar and said, "You leave tomorrow and remain in the company of the other officers until such time as you solve this crime. Have I made myself perfectly clear, Detective Dory? This is a great honor for the State of Maryland, Montgomery County, this office, and yourself. There is nothing more to discuss. Enjoy your time in D.C. and make us proud. You're dismissed."

Rising, Denise breathed a sigh and said with a sharp salute, "Thank you, ma'am, for this honor. I'll do everything I can to be worthy of the trust you have placed in me."

Denise followed Captain Morton from the chief's office into the elevator. Neither of them spoke on the ride down to the first floor. However, as soon as the door opened, she said, "Captain, I don't know what to say. I simply cannot leave all this work. I've spent too many hours on these cases to walk away from them now. I need to see them through to the end. This isn't fair to Tom or to me."

"Denise, this is out of my hands," Captain Morton replied with a big shrug of his shoulders as he handed her the preliminary instructions. "I agree that the timing is bad. I understand your need for closure on your cases, but there's nothing I can do. The chief has made it perfectly clear that everything about this matter is special and beyond our control. You'll have to suck it up and roll with it.

"I know that you and Tom are a top-notch team, but Tom's a big boy. He'll get along just fine. This isn't the first time that an officer has been pulled off a case before it was solved. Cops are transferred and promoted every day. I'll find someone to work with him while you're away. It won't be easy because Tom's rather set in his ways, but I'll assign someone to be his partner. I suggest you get busy. You have some loose ends to tie up before your flight. As of the end of your shift today, you're on special assignment to the U.S. Capitol. I don't want to see you in this office tomorrow. Make us proud."

"Yes, sir." Denise smiled bravely. She walked a few paces away, turned, and said, "I'd like to be the one to tell Tom, if it's all right with you."

"No problem. He might take the news better if it came from you. Now, get to work," Captain Morton replied with a sympathetic smile.

Returning to her desk, Denise pulled out each of the twenty cases on which she was currently working. Turning to her computer, she updated the detailed logs she kept on them and printed out the necessary copies. She inserted the update into the front of the folders and tossed her disc into an envelope. Then she made a list of all the things she had to do before she could leave for D.C. At the top of the list was the talk she needed to have with Tom.

"You've been hard at work for the past hour. What did the chief have to say?" Tom barked from his desk behind her.

Tom was a fifteen-year veteran of the force with a reputation for being hard-nosed and difficult. While others had shied away from being his partner, she had requested that the captain pair her with him. Something about Tom's tough demeanor and loud voice had told her from their first encounter that he was a man she could trust to lay down his life for her if necessary. From the first time he had shared his doughnut with her, she had known that she would do the same for him. Their partnership had been filled with a deep affection and mutual respect. They never discussed it, but she felt that they shared an unspoken affection but they were both too fearful of being hurt again to mention it.

"I have something to tell you, and you're not going to like it one bit. As a matter of fact, you're going to hate it. I'm not too fond of it myself," Denise said as she turned her chair until she could share Tom's desk with him. Over the years, they had discussed many cases this way. She would miss having him at her back and already felt vulnerable without his strong right arm and steady aim.

"Okay, now that you've told me how I'm going to feel, would you mind telling me what this is that I'm reaching for?" Tom asked as he leaned forward. His shirtsleeves were rolled up to expose his muscular hairy arms and deep brown skin. As usual, Denise felt secure knowing that he was only inches away. She quickly forced her mind to focus on the news and not the closeness of his warmth.

"I'm leaving for D.C. tomorrow. It seems the U.S. Capitol has decided that it needs help in finding the murderer of the senators. I don't know when I'll return. The captain will assign someone to partner with you while I'm away. I tried to talk the chief out of sending me, but she wouldn't listen. She said that the governor's office had made all the arrangements, and that it was beyond her control," Denise stated after taking a deep breath. She had learned that Tom liked to have his news, both good and bad, straight up and direct.

Without blinking, Tom asked, "Exactly when tomorrow will you leave?"

"I report there at eight in the morning. I'll even have to live in town for the duration of the case. They've made all the arrangements," Denise replied without taking her eyes from his tight face.

Tom's brown eyes flashed the anger that he kept inside. "Damn," he spat without looking away from her. "That doesn't give us much time. Let's go. We'll have dinner together and go over our cases. I'll take care of that nasty cat of yours while you're away if you'd like."

"I'd appreciate it. You're the only one of my friends that Tony hasn't clawed. He likes you for some reason. Maybe it's because of the similarities between you two. You're both street savvy and real scrappers. I'll miss you while I'm away. I won't find anyone like you in D.C. I never have to worry about saying the wrong thing when we're together. You're one of the few people I have ever known who doesn't look for an underlying meaning in every word I say. You're a good partner despite what everyone says about you being a tough nut and a badass," Denise commented as she swallowed hard.

"Don't get mushy on me, Dory. Get your coat. Let's get out of here," Tom bellowed as he threw his jacket over his shoulder and strode out of the police station. His broad back vanished through the door before she had a chance to move.

"Hey, wait for me! You're walking too fast as usual," Denise called as she tossed her desk keys into the top drawer and turned out the little light with the dented green, metal shade. She threw her old comfortable tennis shoes into her briefcase and shoved in her chair as she listened to the sound of his footsteps blending with the others in the busy hall.

Giving the desk one last going-over, Denise picked up the photograph of the captain, the chief, and herself as they stood together during a ceremony at which she had received special commendation for solving an especially intricate murder case. That had been the happiest day of her career. It had also been the one that had firmly placed her among the ranks of outstanding United States police officers. She wrapped the photo carefully in an old scarf and placed it in the pocket of her briefcase. With a smile, she picked up the photo of Tom leaning on their new brown patrol car and included it with the other. It nestled safely among the case folders.

"Are you coming, Dory?" Tom shouted impatiently from the door. "I'm starving. Get the lead out!"

"I'm coming. Keep your pants on," Denise retorted as she slung her jacket over her arm and trotted from the room. No one noticed as she hurried past; their buddies in the police station had gotten used to their routine. Not once in their long partnership had Tom waited for her. He was always the first out the door with her bringing up the rear when it came to meals or quitting time.

Tom picked the restaurant as usual, but it really did not matter since they both loved Italian food. Over dinner, they discussed the cases, but mostly they ate in comfortable silence. Tom was a man of few words, but his actions always spoke for him. He barely touched his lasagna and did not order dessert. He looked uncharacteristically glum when he added the folders to his briefcase. When he walked her to her apartment door to pick up Tony, his mouth wore an endearing turned-down expression. Denise could tell that he would miss her, too. She would try to grab a weekend or two to meet him for dinner, if her schedule allowed the time. If the actual schedule were as demanding as the preliminary one, she would hardly ever leave the Capitol grounds except on official business.

Before he left with the loudly complaining cat in his carrier, Tom said, "Don't forget to buy bottled water since you're not used to Potomac punch. You don't want a case of the trots."

"Thanks for the advice. Take good care of yourself and my cat," she replied in the open door.

"Yeah, you, too," Tom responded with a lingering gaze. Forcing himself to leave her, Tom vanished around the corner. Denise listened until she heard the elevator bell, and then she closed the door.

The next morning Denise threw the essential business suits, blouses, and comfortable shoes into her suitcase. She did not know exactly which items to pack because she did not know the length of her stay in D.C. If necessary, she could always sneak back to the apartment for more or have Tom bring her whatever she had left behind. She hated the thought that she might be stuck in D.C. for months without a chance to come home.

The next morning before walking to the subway stop around the corner, Denise called her sister. As children, Ria had been a major pest and the bane of her existence. Now, however, age had caused their relationship to mellow, and she counted her baby sister among her friends.

"I'm so proud of you that I could just burst," Ria gushed. "I know you'll soon become the leader of the investigation. You'll take over just as you've always done here. All of those seasoned veterans will look to you for guidance. Your ten years on the Montgomery County force and master's degree in criminology will pay off handily. Your five years as Tom's partner are enough to earn you a distinguished service metal."

"Would you mind leaving him alone? Tom's a good guy. We get along just great. He's a wonderful partner. I couldn't have solved any of those cases without him," Denise replied sharply although she did not want to start a fight before leaving home. She had learned not to let the sun set on family disturbances.

"I don't know why you're so fond of that grumpy, unpleasant man. He gives me the creeps. He's as hard and scary as the criminals. You have a soft spot in your heart for hard-luck stories, that's all. That's why you picked up that terrible cat. No one else cared enough to feed him. He was a mangy stray until you gave him a home," Ria concluded as she clucked her tongue in an unflattering motherly way.

"Get off his back," Denise rebutted. "Tom has had some problems, but he saved my life more than once. I wouldn't have any other partner. Regardless of what anyone says about his gruff exterior, he has a heart of gold. He would do anything for me. Many times he placed his own life in danger in order to protect mine. That's what good partners do for each other. In D.C., I'll be alone without someone to protect my back. I'll have to fend for myself. And don't dump on my cat!'' Denise's protective instincts went into action whenever anyone attacked either Tom or Tony.

"Yes, and you'll do just fine. I seem to remember that every time he has done something for you, you've done five things for him. Changing the subject to something more pleasant, bring me back something interesting. A lace shawl from that new shopping mall would be nice," Ria added as she thought about the riches of the District's many eclectic shops.

"No problem. I'll see you whenever I come home. Stay out of trouble while I'm away," Denise advised, taking the big sister role.

"I don't have time or energy to get into trouble. I have three kids and a husband, remember?" Ria replied as she hung up the phone with a chuckle.

The ride to D.C. on the subway gave Denise time to review the profiles of the deceased senators. They had lived exemplary lives in the political limelight, risen to positions of power, and been elected according to the rules of the Constitution. She did not see anything unusual or suspicious in any of the material. The photographs that smiled back at her were of elderly men of serious, almost academic dispositions, making it hard for her to imagine anyone wanting to kill them, although someone had.

Stuffing the folders into her briefcase, she brushed her fingers against the picture frame. Lifting it carefully, she gazed into Tom's unsmiling face. He tried too hard to look mean and usually succeeded in convincing everyone that he was as tough as he appeared, but she knew differently. He was one of the nicest men she had ever known. She would miss not sharing the next weeks and maybe months with him.

Returning his photograph to her briefcase, she watched the suburban neighborhood whiz past until they finally reached the D.C. line. The landscape had changed from sprawling to heavily populated in a matter of minutes. People filled the once partially empty subway car as it sped toward Metro Center, the transfer point to the blue and yellow lines. From there, she would take a short ride to the U.S. Capitol. She closed her eyes and enjoyed the unfamiliar leisure. It was a pleasure not having to fight the traffic while leaving the driving to someone else.

"Do you mind?" The voice intruded into her contentment as the train slowly began to pull away from the station.

"Oh, no problem," Denise replied as she moved the folder containing the Capitol case information. Thinking she would have the two seats to herself, she had spread her things into the empty seat when she had been virtually alone on the train. Now that riders had filled it to capacity, her fellow commuters needed every available seat.

"I had trouble getting out of bed this morning and almost missed the train from Grand Central. I wouldn't want to be late on my first day at work," the gentleman sputtered, telling her more than she needed to know from a stranger.

"Um," Denise replied as she turned her attention to the landscape that whizzed past her window.

"How do you do? Richard Evans is the name," the gentleman introduced himself as he slipped into his seat. He wore a well-tailored lightweight wool suit, cream shirt, and striped tie. His neatly trimmed hair and highly polished shoes said that he was a banker or stockbroker.

"Denise Dory. Nice to meet you," she replied as she slid closer to the window to give him extra space.

"I love this area. My wife and I visit Washington every chance we get," Richard Evans commented as the train stopped at the Fort Totten station and more people squeezed into the crowded car.

"I was born and raised here, Mr. Evans," Denise replied absently, hoping that he was not the type who liked to strike up a friendship and talk for the entire ride into town.

"Call me Richard. Everyone does."

"In that case, I'm Denise."

Flipping through the folder on his lap, Richard asked, "What's your line of work, if I might ask?"

"I'm a police detective," Denise replied as she tried to read over his arm.

"The world just became even smaller. So am I. I'm on my way to the U.S. Capitol for some rather beastly business," Richard stated as he scanned the pages of the report.

"So am I," Denise commented, wondering if they had the same destination.

"Could we possibly be in the same business?" Richard asked as he leaned closer and lowered his voice to a whisper. "Are you by any chance joining a group of law enforcement officers at the request of the U.S. Capitol?"

"Yes, I am," Denise whispered as she matched the volume of her voice to his.

"It's a small world indeed," Richard said heartily as he once again pumped her hand. "The U.S. Capitol very wisely invited a representative from every state to help in this investigation. It will be sensational seeing all of us work as a unit to uncover the perpetrator of this dreadful deed. I'm from New York."

Massaging her bruised knuckles, Denise replied, "I

think it will be a very impressive group if everyone arrives. At least no one will be able to accuse us of bias with police officers from so many states on the team."

Settling into his seat with a stretch of his long body, Richard continued, "I've been mulling over this case ever since I read the dossiers on the two recently deceased senators. They were both well loved and respected men in their states and on the Hill. Senator John Brown was from a family whose history involved prominent positions in the church as well as state politics. His humble beginnings as a coal miner's son endeared him to the hearts of most of his constituents."

Denise interjected from her readings, "I remember that he earned a full scholarship to study at Princeton, played football for four years, and graduated magna cum laude. His law school record was just as impressive. By all accounts, he worked tirelessly for educational issues and health care."

Nodding enthusiastically, Richard commented, "His wife was equally dedicated to his causes. I can't imagine who would want to harm him."

Denise expertly added the information that she had gained about the most recently murdered senator. "According to the U.S. Capitol's information, William Thomas was born in the Chevy Chase section of D.C. and from a devoutly religious family. His father had hoped that his son would join him in the banking business. However, William had a different idea and chose politics."

Nodding again, Richard continued, "Although both of the men were in their late fifties, neither had a history of serious health problems. They were trim and as athletic as their hectic schedules would allow. According to their medical reports, they drank moderately, exercised daily, slept without sedatives, and had never experienced more than the usual annoying cold and flu."

Warming to Richard's quick mind and the pleasant competition that had arisen between them, Denise said, "However, according to the coroner's reports, they died of heart and kidney failure. The first death did not cause the medical examiner to become suspicious, but the second one did. That's when he began to suspect foul play and perhaps poisoning. Strangely, he could not identify any traces of it in the stomach contents, yet both men had complained of extreme intestinal discomfort, flulike symptoms, and high fever the day after attending elaborate dinners in their honor. Even though they both went to the hospital, nothing the physicians did could alleviate the symptoms or slow the progress of the organ failure. As soon as we get the toxicology reports, we'll know conclusively. For the time being, the official word from the Capitol is that the two senators died from natural causes."

Returning the folder to his briefcase, Richard said, "We have our work cut out for us. I have several theories about the events that surrounded the death, and I'm sure that you do, also. I'll share mine, if you'll share yours."

"I'd love to hear them. However, I don't have anything to share yet. I have too many unanswered questions," Denise replied graciously and listened as Richard's voice joined the sound of the wheels on the track as he droned out the details of his suspicions.

Although his speculations had merit, Denise could not embrace them and thought that it was premature for her to come to any conclusions. They still did not know many elements of this case. Until she had more hard evidence, Denise would reserve judgment. She needed to interview the people who had access to the senators, review their political leanings, and learn more about the composition of the various subcommittees before she made up her mind. She did agree, however, when Richard said that they definitely had their work cut out for them. The fact that the U.S. Capitol had gone to such expense to assemble a staff of detectives when it had its own police force was indication enough to her that this would be an intricate and perhaps delicate case. Somehow Denise sensed that she would be in D.C. far longer than she had originally hoped.

TWO

The walk from the Capitol Hill subway stop on C Street was hot and harried, as Denise pushed and shoved among the many government workers headed to their offices. Denise waited on the corner for the light to change as sweat beaded on her forehead. She watched as taxi drivers attacked the traffic as if they were participants in a demolition derby. They wove in and out of cars and between buses and trucks as horns blared and tires squealed. Many appeared oblivious to the cursing and hand gestures that greeted them and continued to demonstrate the penultimate in road rage. The heat from the humid summer morning blew into their faces as Denise and Richard squinted against the swirling dust and debris.

"What's the speed limit around here?" Denise leaned forward and shouted above the noise.

"I can't tell. I thought it was only in New York that cabbies drove like this," Richard replied as they picked their way across the pedestrian-clogged intersection.

"We don't have traffic quite like this in the suburbs. This is a mess. Imagine having to face this congestion every day. No wonder so many people ride the subway," Denise commented as she transferred the bubble gum from the bottom of her shoe to the closest patch of dry grass.

"I was thinking about New York City, too, only I think

this is worse," Richard commented as they approached the majestic structure that stood as the symbol of American politics.

The massive marble building with the imposing dome nestled among the museums of Washington while still managing to cast a striking profile. Its sweeping stairway led to the halls of power of the United States. Dignitaries, lawmakers, students, and visitors passed through its doors daily to catch a glimpse of democracy in action.

"Let's join a tour at lunchtime. There's a wonderful one of the grounds," Denise suggested as they showed their identification to the Capitol Hill police officers at the massive doors.

"Outside? The forecast is for eighty-five degrees and one hundred percent humidity. I gave up walking a beat so that I could stay indoors on days like this," Richard exclaimed as he passed through the metal detector.

"Far be it from me to drag you anywhere you don't want to go. My partner says that I'm too bossy and made me promise not to force my new associates to do anything that goes against their wishes while I'm here. I'm more than capable of seeing the sights of D.C. by myself. You don't have to feel obligated to accompany me. However, I understand that there are some really good restaurants around here," Denise commented with more than a hint of sarcasm in her voice at his reluctance to explore the wonders of D.C. on a warm day.

"Well, if you put it that way, I suppose I'll have to do the gentlemanly thing and accompany you. I'd hate for you to wander the streets lost and alone," Richard quipped with a grin.

"I spent almost every summer downtown as a kid. I probably enrolled in every program the Smithsonian sponsored. I think I can find my way back, but sightseeing would be more fun if I had someone with whom to share it," Denise rebutted with a big grin as the new association quickly turned into friendship.

Laughing, Richard acknowledged, "Okay, you talked me into it. We'll ease out as soon as the session ends, but on one condition."

"Name it," Denise accepted gleefully as they followed the signs that pointed the way to the conference room.

"You have to accompany me to the Botanical Garden before we finish our work here. My wife made me promise to pick up an exhibit schedule. I'll have hell to pay if I don't bring it home," Richard replied as they peered through a window at the crowd on the Washington street.

Their friendly banter stopped as they stepped into the handsomely decorated halls of the Capitol Building. Portraits of former senators lined the walls as green plants softened the sharpness of corners. Its thick leather seats and poster-filled walls made the briefing room of her precinct look drab by comparison.

"It's good to be a senator," Denise muttered.

"It is if you're not murdered for the honor," Richard whispered wickedly.

"You certainly believe in looking on the darker side. Well, at least we won't have to worry about feeling cramped. There's certainly enough space for all of us," Denise commented as she watched the others enter.

"I would say from the heavily guarded appearance of this place that they'll be completely sheltered from the press. No one could find us within these walls unless they had a map," Richard said as he peered at walls of priceless art and huge statues.

"I wouldn't get too cocky, if I were you. Someone got to the senators. Remember?" Denise responded with raised brows.

Opening her sketchbook, Denise made quick drawings of the Capitol's architecture to include in her expanding binder of the places she had visited and the faces of the people she had met. She always regaled Tom with her exploits when she returned to their office by sharing her sketches with him.

"It will take us forever to learn our way around here. I hope the planners of this little gathering remembered to provide us with a guide," Denise remarked as she marveled at the architectural details that made the Capitol like no other building she had ever visited.

"If my hunch is correct, we won't see much of anything other than this area until it's time for us to return home. We'll probably spend our days in a very small section of the building. I'm sure we won't be allowed to wander freely. I don't think they would trust even a group of police officers that much; there're too many top-secret negotiations happening in this place to turn us loose," Richard observed as he pointed to a well-recognized painting that hung on the wall amid others of equally irreplaceable value.

"It's like working in a museum. Do you think the senators stop on their way to committee meetings to appreciate all of this?" Denise inquired as she sketched yet another impressive masterpiece of art.

"I would imagine that they wouldn't even notice their surroundings after awhile. No one would ever get anything done if they stopped to study each painting or admire the sculptures. Perhaps someone on the staff gives the new senators a guided tour during the first few weeks of their tenure," Richard suggested with eyes as wide as a schoolboy's.

"The sale of any one of these treasures would net a fortune," Denise mused as they entered the conference facility.

The room was much less ostentatious than the halls of the Capitol although equipped with every possible necessity and a few items that she did not even know she

needed. Comfortable leather chairs, state-of-the-art
video equipment, and strategically arranged tables created a very pleasant and professional environment. On
one table, their host had placed an array of food to
tempt them. Built into another was the largest wide-
screen television she had ever seen, which their guide
said would provide them with access to cable television
from every state so that they could watch the news from
home.

"Tea," Richard whispered gratefully as he nodded
toward the table. "Would you care for a cup?"

"I'd love a cup. Thanks," Denise replied as she accepted a steaming cup from a member of the unobtru-
sive catering staff.

"I think we're the last to arrive. Let's join the others,"
Richard observed as he motioned toward the front of
the conference room where the other detectives had
already taken seats.

Before Denise could introduce herself to the heavyset
gentleman seated beside her, a spokesman for the U.S.
Capitol stepped forward. In a weary tone, he greeted
the group saying, "Ladies and gentlemen, on behalf of
the senators and congressmen who work here for the
good of the nation, I would like to take this opportunity
to thank you for accepting the invitation to help us solve
these crimes. I am Anthony Salermo, one of the senators from New York. I will be your intermediary in all
dealings with the U.S. Capitol as you work to find the
person behind these dreadful events. I am at your service day or night.

"Each of you received a portfolio containing a map
of the Capitol, your room key in the Page School, and
an identification badge. You are free to stroll these corridors at your leisure, but I must ask you to refrain from
leaving this designated area without the benefit of an
escort. My request is for your own protection. You will

become lost in the hallways if you try to venture out independently. Someone from my staff will always be available to escort you and see to your needs.

"As you can see from your map, we have opened the Page dining room to you while they are on break. This conference room will be your command center. Additional breakout rooms are adjacent to this one. While you are working, you will not be disturbed by anyone, including my staff. If you require service, simply ring the bell and someone will come immediately.

"As you can see from your itinerary, early this afternoon we will take you on a tour of the Capitol, Senate Office Building, and Library of Congress. You will then have a briefing session with the medical examiner and members of the various Senate and House staffs, followed by dinner and a leisurely drive through the city. I have been told that visitors especially enjoy seeing D.C. at night when spotlights illuminate all of the monuments. Now follow me please. I will escort you to your rooms. I am sure that those of you who have traveled a great distance to join us would like the opportunity to freshen up a bit."

As Richard and Denise joined the line of detectives representing over forty states, she whispered, "He thought of everything, didn't he? The only thing he didn't arrange for us was the identity of the murderer."

"Is this the biting wit your partner complains about all the time?" Richard moaned.

"No, not at all," Denise replied with pretended offense, "I prefer to call it realism. A little smoke, some lights, and no doubt the necessary mirrors, and we'll see whatever they want us to see."

"What exactly do you mean by that?" Richard asked as they slowly followed the others down the hall.

"Only this . . . we're invited here to do a job that their own Capitol Hill police couldn't do. The appearance is that we'll have all the support we could possibly need. However, we're virtually prisoners here because of the massive size of the structure. We can't wander about gathering clues the way we do at home without the ever-present eyes of our hosts. I bet that while we're going about our investigation, someone will be watching us and recording our actions. We'll be allowed to discover whatever they want us to know. If by some chance we stumble into sensitive areas, the dedicated Capitol Hill staff will see to it that we're redirected. I say it's an ingenious way to conduct the investigation of the murders. We do all the work, and they get all the credit."

"Are you saying that the people here on the Hill don't want us to discover the identity of the killer?" Richard asked as he turned his attention from the building's structure to Denise's face.

"No, not at all. I'm saying that they don't want us to uncover any other dirty laundry in our pursuit of the truth. All kinds of underhanded, shady dealings might be going on right under our noses. That's what they don't want us to expose. We might discover more than one plot afoot to kill the two senators. Maybe this was the one that succeeded," Denise said.

"Amazing. You figured out all of this by simply reading the itinerary and looking at the map," Richard commented sarcastically in the same tone that Tom so often used with her.

"You're absolutely correct. Look at the itinerary. With the exception of the next few hours, we will be together without interference from the outside every day. I'm sure you've noticed that our hosts have posted helpful assistants randomly along this corridor. Ostensibly, their job is to make our stay more comfortable. However, they will also serve to keep us from wandering around without guides who will observe everything that we learn. Should we venture out of our rooms, the guides will be there to redirect us. The access to information seems pretty controlled to me, too. Don't forget, the coroner is coming to us; we're not going to the morgue to view the bodies. I actually thought that I saw little curly wires behind that last guy's right ear. Makes me wonder if he's Secret Service or simply hard of hearing."

"That's certainly an interesting theory you've cooked up, Denise," Richard scoffed. "However, you've forgotten something. The deceased senators have already been buried. There's nothing to see in the morgue. I watched the televised funeral for both of them myself."

"You watched what the Capitol wanted you to think was a funeral performed in the company of the corpse. According to the medical examiner's report that a friend of mine smuggled to me, the coroner had not finished the autopsy on the last senator until the day after the funeral. If the body was present for the service, then whose information is included in the autopsy report? I say you watched a conveniently staged theatrical performance designed to maintain the integrity of the Capitol during this difficult time. It certainly wouldn't do at all to scare the electorate into thinking that its government is in chaos. If the political powers would do that for a funeral that could have been postponed for a few days, just think of what could happen to more important matters. I think that it would be to their advantage to rely on outside sources whenever possible," Denise commented in a very low whisper in case the walls and vases had ears.

Richard looked at her as if she had spoken treasonous thoughts. "You don't really think that the government would do anything underhanded, do you? I refuse to adapt your skepticism. I prefer to believe that we will have free access to everything until I learn otherwise."

Stepping into her room in the Page housing, she replied, "And God didn't make little green apples. I'll see you later." Leaving Richard to reflect on her suggestions, Denise closed the door. She looked forward to time to think without the influence of his sunny disposition.

Tom, her partner, always complained about her skepticism, but he had learned to accept it as one of Denise's gifts. Opening her sketchbook, Denise took a few notes and made quick drawings of the faces of the people she had met. Often she forgot a name, but Denise never lost track of a face. Her sketches were a more accurate recording of cases than any diary. She knew that her drawings would come in handy in this case, too.

THREE

The sun streamed through the windows of the rotunda as the police detectives stood with their guides. They felt like tourists as they studied the famous ceiling. Strangely, Denise could feel someone watching her. Turning, she gazed into the earnest face of a young aide. The woman quickly diverted her eyes and eased away. Shrugging, Denise thought nothing more of the young woman's curiosity and returned to her admiration of the architecture.

"Fabulous, isn't it? It's hard to believe that these are not living beings. The bodies are so well formed and expressive. If you stare at this one long enough, you can almost see him breathe," Denise commented to Richard as the statue appeared to beckon to them.

"This building is an absolutely astounding tribute to man's artistic abilities and his dedication to the cause of justice," Richard replied in a deep, resonant voice.

"It certainly is a good representation of the founding fathers' tribute to themselves and a reminder of promises they didn't keep," Denise voiced as she tried to share Richard's enthusiasm.

Richard countered as he peered over his reading glasses at her, "Yes, that's true, but I would like to think that the advancements of modern times have compensated for the oversights of the past."

"I wonder if the person who murdered the senators

feels that he or she had been vindicated or misused by the present?" Denise mused, ignoring his thinly veiled challenge.

"Are you implying that the perpetrator might have been some kind of zealot rather than the killings being purely random acts of violence?" Richard asked incredulously.

"Sure, that thought had crossed my mind," Denise replied. "Not all Americans are of one mind, you know, any more than two new friends must be. For instance, you look at this structure and see a symbol of democracy and a long heritage of sound government. I, however, see a monument to good intentions that failed to embrace all of the people. I'm simply suggesting that the different factions within the country might not have been impressed by the résumés of the new senators. They might have taken steps to eliminate them in favor of people whose philosophies they preferred."

"It's an interesting and controversial theory that certainly warrants consideration. Did you have any particular groups in mind?" Richard asked as he continued to marvel at the architecture of the Capitol, undaunted by her more cynical outlook.

As they walked with the others, Denise replied, "I don't think we should rule out the people who favor less federal government interference in state affairs, those who are against a woman's right to choose abortion, and those who oppose further tax cuts and welfare. All of them and probably others had reason to commit murder. I think the question centers on the means. Who had the opportunity and the access to the senators to pull off the deed? When we have the answer to that, we'll have our killer."

"Hundreds of people, not including tourists, have access to the senators during the course of the day. If we interview all of them, we'll be here forever. We have to find another way to narrow down the list of suspects," Richard retorted as he gazed at the magnificent bas-relief ceiling.

"That's true, but I don't think we'll have too much trouble finding our perpetrator if the U.S. Capitol wants us to uncover his or her identity. I think that as soon as we show our ability to sift through the polite rhetoric of government sheltering itself and get down to the real issues, our hosts will become considerably less guarded. Any one of the senators or congressmen might be afraid that we'd point in his direction as the possible murderer. The police force might itself be tainted with bad cops who are protecting the senators' assailant. It has been known to happen, you know," Denise replied as they caught up with the others during the tour of the reception rooms under the ever-watchful gaze of their guides.

"You use both third-person pronouns. Do you really believe that a woman might have murdered the senators?" Richard asked with amusement in his voice.

Laughing, she replied, "I'm not ruling out anyone as a suspect. Women are equally as capable of committing murder as men. We're just not usually pressed to do it as often, that's all."

"Until a few years ago, I would have said that this is definitely a man's world. Now, however, I agree that we can't rule out anyone. Women are still in the minority, but they're more visible than when I was a kid," Richard agreed as they strolled through one expansive room after another.

"You're right about the gender imbalance here, but don't forget that men in sympathy with women's causes might be willing to act on their behalf. I don't think that we can rule out anyone especially since women do work here in support services and always have. One of them might be trying to make a statement for better conditions or more recognition," Denise replied with a half smile.

"You're considering the possibility of a fairly well structured plot, aren't you? Well, I suppose that a militant group could accomplish what would appear on the surface to be the impossible in this fortress. Since the shooting on the Hill, security has really increased," Richard stated.

"I've learned to be very suspicious of impenetrable fortresses. The challenge of breaking the code often provides the needed impetus for committing the crime," Denise replied as they entered the private chambers of a senator who had already returned to his home state to campaign for reelection.

The group of detectives slowed to a crawl as they toured the photo gallery. Photographs of heads of state mixed with those of senators and congressmen. Each print showed the unmistakable similarity between the elected officials of the U.S. and the crowned heads of other countries.

Overhearing their conversation, their guide, the freshman senator from Tennessee, interjected, "It would not be appropriate for the leaders of the free world not to associate with other heads of state. We'd look like separatists."

"Really? I wasn't of the impression that the U.S. cared too much about the impression of other countries," Denise responded with a slight smile.

Senator Price's shoulders straightened as he looked down his long regal nose and replied, "You are entitled to your opinion, Detective Dory."

"You've made an enemy, I see," Richard interjected with a wink as Denise almost laughed out loud while the senator walked to the head of the line, leaving them to wallow at the rear in his personal ostracism.

"Serves him right for eavesdropping on our conversation. He's one of those senators with old money backing him. He undoubtedly feels that he's entitled to this style of living or even better. Perhaps Senator Price should be on our list of suspects," Denise commented hotly. She was not in the least bit put off by the senator's reaction. In fact, it provided her with even more reason to suspect an insider of murdering the senators.

"Has anyone ever said anything about your fiery temper?" Richard chuckled.

"Yes, Tom does . . . all the time, but I ignore him," Denise replied with sarcasm as they returned to the conference room from which their day had begun.

The detectives reassembled to listen to the coroner's report on the autopsies. Sitting on the last row against the wall, Denise noted that another woman had joined their ranks. She was tall, blond, tanned, and spoke with a southern accent. The woman sat with the detectives from South Carolina and Georgia.

"Where are the slides?" Denise whispered to Richard as the coroner droned on about the poison that had killed the senators.

"There aren't any. Why?"

"Don't you think it's strange that not only are there no bodies for us to examine, but we can't examine autopsy slides of the deceased? I'm going to ask about this oversight," Denise whispered as she raised her hand.

"Yes, Detective?" the coroner said as he paused in his discussion.

"Although I appreciate the invaluable information you're sharing with us, Doctor, I'd like to see slides of the bodies, please," Denise requested as she stood to the side of her seated comrades.

Glancing uneasily at Senator Salermo for direction, the coroner replied, "I don't have any to show you, Detective."

"You have no photographs of the bodies? How will we be able to conduct our investigation without the evidence? I had hoped to see the bodies or at the very least the slides for any signs of violence and trauma," Denise complained as the others shifted uneasily in their seats.

Stepping forward, Senator Salermo motioned to the coroner to step aside. Taking the podium, he replied to the assembled detectives, "The good doctor and his people have conducted a very thorough examination of the bodies. We felt that it was imperative to give the senators a timely burial because of the upcoming elections in the fall. Therefore, we cannot show you the corpses. You will have to rely on the reports Doctor Smith has prepared. You will find that he has anticipated all of your questions in his analysis of the cause of death. If you have no further questions, Doctor Smith will continue."

"Another enemy. You don't care whose toes you trod on, do you?" Richard whispered as Denise sat down amid the silence of the room.

"I'm flabbergasted," Denise fussed quietly. "This is the most unprofessional investigation I think I've ever seen. The bodies would have kept until we arrived. We could have learned so much from seeing them. You're right about this place being a fortress. The good senator certainly wants to control the dissemination of information."

"Well, we can't see them; therefore, you'll just have to trust the coroner's report. Were you this suspicious in Maryland?" Richard whispered behind his hand.

"Definitely and more. I've only just begun to overturn stones," Denise replied confidently.

Denise listened quietly as the coroner continued to impart the information from his copious report. He still could not identify the specific poison and had sent tissue and stomach-content samples to the Center for Disease Control for further analysis. The results would return in about a week.

Animated conversation sprang up throughout the room as the detectives digested the information. Richard leaned over and commented with a chuckle, "Until now, it looked as if we'd have a nice little holiday. Looks like we'll have to work for our money. I'm surprised at the shoddy police work, too."

"I'm glad Tom isn't here," Denise added with a shake of her head. "He'd really lose his cool at this waste of our time. Looks like they would have had all the information ready when they called us here. I have cases that need my attention on my desk. Poor Tom has to handle all of them for me. I don't like sitting and waiting."

"You need to learn to relax. A little sitting can be good for the soul," Richard replied with a chuckle.

"One more question, please, Senator," Denise asked as she stood once again, catching the senator on the verge of leaving the room.

With an obvious expression of displeasure on his face, the senator turned and quipped, "I'm at your service, Detective Dory."

Over the subdued mutterings of her colleagues, Denise asked, "Has the mourning period ended for the deceased?"

"Why, yes, it has," Senator Salermo replied quickly as he looked around the room at the animated faces of the detectives.

"Then, sir, I suggest that you make arrangements for us to interview all the members of the House and Senate and especially those whose names appeared on the short list of those with causes to advocate. It's imperative that we know their political leanings and their enemies," Denise responded as the noise volume subsided.

"I'm afraid that I don't understand the request.

Please explain, Detective Dory," Senator Salermo responded coldly.

"Senator, it has been seven days since the most recent death of a senator. I strongly suggest that you make the arrangements I have requested if you wish to prevent another murder. If someone is murdering colleagues for a cause, we cannot assume that the person has satisfied his ambition. If he hasn't, he might strike again. If he's murdering because of a grudge against people on the Hill, no one will be safe until we discover his identity," Denise responded sternly with the hopes of forcing him into action.

"As much as I hate to think that any of my colleagues would be capable of murder, I must agree with you that we need swift action in this election year. A number of my colleagues have postponed much-needed trips to the constituents because of these attacks. Surely you do not believe that the murderer will strike again with so many police officers on the job," Senator Salermo replied stubbornly as he tried to resist the thought that a senator might mastermind the murder of a colleague.

Unable to tell if he was being cunning, deceptive, naive, or ignorant, Denise stated, "I will be blunt, Senator Salermo. These are politically charged times in which we live. If someone can tamper with hanging, dimpled, and pregnant chads in Florida, anything can happen. Therefore, let me say emphatically that unless you provide us with the list of senators who are advancing the most sensitive and controversial topics, no one is safe or above suspicion. Unless you arrange protection for them, you will have the blood of another senator on your hands. Even with precautions, we might be too late to prevent another attack."

Denise watched as the senator's expression changed from confident and somewhat irritated to frightened. "I will arrange for the ten most outspoken and active senators to be at your disposal tomorrow morning at nine. The rest of my colleagues will be available as you need us," Senator Salermo replied shakily and without further hesitation. "If there are no further requests, we've arranged a welcome dinner in your honor."

Realizing that she had scored a small, reluctant victory, Denise did not press her case further by stating all of the scenarios that ran through her head. Instead, she picked up her things and followed Richard and the others into the makeshift dining room, surrounded by priceless paintings, sculptures, and tapestries. Conversation was animated as they digested their thoughts along with the roast duck and vintage wine. As usual, their assistants were on hand to provide them with whatever they might desire and find missing on the table. Aware that the room had ears, the detectives proceeded cautiously with their discussions.

Leaning closely, Denise commented to Richard, "From the way Senator Salermo's expression changed, I'd say that his name is on the short list. Tom would say that he's a man with fear written on his face."

"I had noticed the reaction myself. I would say that he's a bit worried not only about his safety but about what they'll uncover," Richard replied as he slathered butter on his hot roll.

With a chuckle, Denise replied, "Perhaps Senator Salermo had thought that with the others out of the way, he would be able to advance one of his favorite causes. He might have felt that he was invincible, but I doubt that he does anymore."

"I'm surprised that he ever would feel that cocky, unless he had something to do with the murders," Richard suggested with a lift of his thick, black caterpillar brows.

"That's possible, of course, but I don't think that's it. I think he is simply one of those people who believes that he is above the reach of others. He's the head of many powerful committees. According to his dossier, he fancies himself an unquestioned authority who has the ear of the president. It must have been quite a shock to him when the realization of vulnerability struck him," Denise stated without embellishment.

"Well, Denise, since you've thrown down the gauntlet before this group, who do you think murdered the senators?" Richard asked as they were leaving after the dinner.

"I don't know yet. I was hoping for a complete forensic report on the poison, but it appears as if one won't be coming. It would have helped clear up so many questions. Until we can conduct our own investigation of possible toxins, I'm open to all possibilities," Denise replied without committing herself to anything definitive. She matched her stride to Richard's as they followed the others into the humid night.

"Without a doubt, we must move quickly on this one. The senators need protection from whoever might still be waiting for them. Their lives are very much in danger if your hunch is right that the murders were an inside job," Richard concluded as he helped her board the bus for the tour of the city.

"If the killer has a political motive that continues to be unsatisfied, and if the same person committed both murders, we have no time to waste. If the assassinations were simply random acts of violence perpetrated by someone who has a grudge against senators, then all of them are in danger," Denise replied as she scanned the night for signs of the famous landmarks.

"You certainly have set the tone for this investigation. I wonder if the U.S. Capitol expected us to make so many demands from the onset of our inquiries. They might have expected a more laid-back approach. You've upset a few of these complacent senators, too. I have a feeling that this might be our last night at leisure," Richard stated as the lights of the Washington Monument came into view.

"You've heard the saying that there's nothing worse than an educated black woman. I guess the U.S. Senate is about to find that out, too," Denise responded as she snuggled into the upholstery.

Despite the magic and majesty of D.C., Denise barely noticed as they drove through the night traffic. Her mind swirled with possibilities and questions. Although not as trusting as Senator Salermo pretended to be, she also wondered what would motivate a senator to kill one of his own. Although Denise had raised the issue that now burned in all their minds, she preferred to believe that someone from outside the Capitol had orchestrated the killings. However, until they had gathered more evidence, the only people who were not suspects were the members of their little group of detectives. If only Tom were at her side instead of Richard, she could bounce her half-formed thoughts off his broad shoulders. He would tell her in no uncertain terms whether her thoughts were too extreme. Without him, she felt empty and only partially herself.

Shrugging her shoulders, Denise mused into the darkness at the strange turn of events. Only a few days ago, she and Tom were fighting like cats over the last honey-glazed doughnut. Now she would gladly share one with him for the chance to spread her thoughts on the table before him. Denise decided that as soon as she had more than half-baked notions, she would give him a call. He might just miss her as much as she missed him.

FOUR

The next morning, the senators sat in the breakout rooms with their hands folded serenely on the tables in front of them. They waited patiently as a spokesperson from each of the groups of detectives interviewed them using a standard set of questions designed to extract the desired information from their reluctant interviewees. They answered truthfully and accurately with only the occasional tapping of manicured fingertips to belie their calm demeanors. The years in front of the camera had prepared them well for interrogation.

Denise was the interviewer for their team as Richard sat at her side observing any change in the senators' facial expressions. As luck would have it, they had to interview Senator Salermo, whose confidence had returned following a good night's sleep. Senator Salermo sat with his back straight and his voice contained as he responded to their questions. Surrounded by priceless works of art, they looked more like adversaries than three people on the quest for the identity of a ruthless murderer. Denise could see that Senator Salermo was not used to having his authority challenged by anyone and especially not by a black female. Denise did not allow the constant flexing of his jaw muscles to interfere with her work. Her job was to protect him, not to win his friendship.

"Senator, your dossier states that you are fifty-five,

grew up in one of the rougher neighborhoods, and a proponent of maintaining the status quo on abortion. Have you found that your political leanings have in any way made enemies for you?" Denise asked as she studied the senator's composed expression.

"Coming from D.C. can always give one a handicap and at the same time an advantage; people try hard to cover their dislike for the city's former political leader. Some of them go out of their way to be welcoming, and others have turned away, thinking that I'm as corrupt as others from that government. When they learn that I'm not the nonvoting representative from D.C., but that I represent another jurisdiction, they change their minds. As I am sure you are aware, I have served our country in the Senate for the last twenty years. My concerns over that time have centered on national issues . . . education, women's rights, and such. I don't see that any of my political activities should have put me in danger.

"As to my views on any controversial issue, I believe that open discussion rather than radical action is the preferred course. I would hate to think that exercising my freedom of speech could lead to my death. I've always taken a fairly traditional path."

Making careful notes to share with the others, Denise asked, "Are your views on most issues the same or different from those of the murdered senators?"

Tapping the tips of his long fingers together, Senator Salermo replied, "My deceased colleagues believed the same as I do on most issues although we selected a different path for accomplishing our goals. While the others chose causes to espouse, I preferred to champion none. You will find that there is little dissention among my fellow senators once you scrape away the partisan lingo. We're mostly interested in the same issues. I have found that it is largely the junior senators who lean favorably toward liberalism. The ones of my generation see the need for traditional values."

"Then, Senator Salermo, I think it would be safe to say that your life is in danger if the murderer killed to make a statement in favor of radical change, such as the issue of school vouchers," Denise stated as she studied his face.

"I suppose you could be right, but I'm not worried. My constituents elected me to represent them, and that's what I intend to do," the senator responded with an almost smug belief in his invincibility.

"I can only assume that the two murdered senators felt the same way," Denise commented sarcastically as she sketched the change in Senator Salermo's passive face to one of haughty piety. Then she continued, saying, "I would appreciate hearing your views on school vouchers. I understand that this is a hotly debated topic at the moment."

"As you know, there is a movement afoot to use federal funds to help parents enroll their children in private schools. It's not a new idea and will undoubtedly be an issue for some time. Many people feel that public school education has slipped drastically. They think that fleeing the systems for private schools is the only way that their children will receive quality education in this country. I say that we don't need vouchers and flight; we need people who will fight for reform. The entire education system in this country, public and private, is antiquated. We need to bring education into the twenty-first century. Leaving public schools isn't the answer since private schools are just as behind the times. We need total educational reform and overhaul."

"Does your view have enough support that its followers might resort to radical measures to achieve their goal?" Richard asked as he glanced at Denise's expert pencil sketches.

"Of course, any group might have fanatics among its membership. I would hope that this one would not, but I cannot be sure of that," Senator Salermo replied with a tone of sad realism in his voice.

"As a longtime participant in the life of the Hill, how do you suppose the murderer managed to poison the senators? I realize that we are well past the old days of employing tasters for Caesar, but in these politically charged times is there no way to protect senators, assuming that the food was the source of the poison?" Denise asked as she continued to hunt for causes of the murders and ways to prevent more. Her sketchbook already contained more than enough drawings of the mercurial politician.

Looking depressed as the light from the window cast a golden glow over his features, Senator Salermo replied, "Detective Dory, we are elected representatives of the people and, as such, we are subject to whatever comes our way. We are very visible at political events, fund-raisers, public outings. There's no real way to protect us. Anyone could have slipped the poison into a hurriedly eaten sandwich, a cup of corner-store coffee, or a bagel on the run. I suppose that I'm more surprised that it hasn't happened sooner."

Closing her notebook, she said, "Thank you, Senator, for your time and your hospitality. I hope we will shortly know the identity of the murderer. However, until we do, I would like to request that you and the other senators take some precautions to protect yourselves from harm. You never know when the killer or a copycat will strike again. With that in mind, I would suggest that you not eat or drink anything brought to you by a stranger. Ask your physician to prescribe medications that are prepackaged at the factory. You might also wish to restrict your movement as much as possible. It might be safer to travel in groups rather than solo."

Rising, Senator Salermo replied, "I won't make any promises, but I will consider doing as you say and will suggest to my colleagues that they do likewise. I refuse, however, to curtail all of my activities out of fear for my life."

Silently, Denise watched him leave the room. Senator Salermo's shoulders had slumped and his veneer of confidence had cracked a bit, but he still walked with dignity and regal bearing. After speaking with him, she could understand his meteoric rise to power and authority within the structure of the U.S. Capitol. He exuded an aura of strength and permanence that would cause his colleagues to follow his guidance. Denise was aware that his highly visible position made Senator Salermo vulnerable to attack. She felt strangely relieved to see that he was aware of his nakedness also.

The officers reconvened in the conference room in which Denise listened as the others relayed the information they had gathered. All of them had managed to convince the senators to exercise more caution in their dealings with strangers. Deep in her heart, Denise had a nagging suspicion that the murderer was not a stranger, which made him or her even more dangerous.

In the silence that followed the last presentation, Denise rose and walked to the refreshment table. Mindful of the precautions she had advised the senators to take, she bypassed the aromatic coffee and selected a can of soda. It would be a while before she trusted open packages again.

Turning to the others, Denise said, "For what it's worth, I think we're dealing with more than a simple murder case. I don't think that these deaths were simply random acts of violence. It seems to me that we're facing a killer with a cause. I believe that the killer struck down these senators because of their political leanings. If that's the case, he will continue to attack until his cause is safely in the hands of a man whose philosophy he prefers. The murderer could represent any number of factions, all of which have daily access to the senators. From our investigations, we know that the senators do not speak with one voice on many of these pressing issues. If you will bear with me for a minute, I'll present a visual of our findings."

Approaching the overhead projector, Denise quickly listed the names of the most vocal senators and the two murdered ones down the left column. Across the top, she wrote the most controversial issues facing the Senate. Pointing from one to the other, she placed an X to show which men leaned toward which cause. The others in the room sat in amazed silence as she worked on the chart that illustrated the magnitude of the undeniable details shown on the wall behind her.

Stepping aside, Denise said, "As you can see, four senators show sympathy toward radical changes to Social Security. Senators Morgan and Blackstone favor ending Affirmative Action, and Senator Frank and the deceased California senator backed bills to restrict the use of handguns. Senator Frederick is on the side of the abortion supporters; whereas, Senators Dey and Salermo are moderates who wish to maintain the status quo. For the time being, let us hypothesize that this chart correctly identifies the special-interest groups and the senators as they relate to these topics. If this is true and if the killings were not random acts of violence, then we can say that the two murdered senators were not killed either by the group that wants to modify the Social Security regulations or the antigun folks. These assumptions would place members of the remaining groups high on their suspect list.

"Now, let us graph a chart to show the health of each man. By using systemic poison, it would appear that the murderer wanted the deaths to seem to have occurred from natural causes. Four senators including one of the deceased senators have a history of heart problems. One has respiratory trouble, and one has diabetes. Two have been treated for cancer, and one died of kidney failure, while three of them report no health problems.

"If we compare these two charts, we can say that Morgan, Frank, and Dey are the least likely candidates to be murdered since they are in good health. I'll add Frederick, the diabetic and Social Security and abortion reformer, to that list also for the time being although I realize that someone could easily tamper with his serum. However, he said that the U.S. Capitol physician administers the dosage himself.

"Although we do not know the identity of the specific poison, we do know that the compound was introduced into the bodies of the two deceased senators by means other than force. At the moment, we think that they consumed it in their food. Until we hear otherwise from the lab, we should probably continue to assume that they ingested the poison."

Raising her hand, Greta asked, "If we assume that the senators revealed their true selves during their discussions, we should suggest that the U.S. Capitol police increase its watch over the senators."

"I think we're all in agreement on that point," Richard commented. "I just wish they could identify either the type of poison or the method of application. It's very difficult to protect against something you can't see, hear, smell, or taste."

"If you'll bear with me for just a few more minutes, I think I can shed additional light on our chart. I think that our killer is planning systematically to eliminate every senator who is in opposition to his cause. To that end, anyone in favor of either Affirmative Action or abortion reform will not become a victim," Denise offered as she studied the group.

"According to what you're saying, Frank, Dey, Frederick, and Salermo should watch their backs with Dey and Salermo being in the greatest danger," Richard concluded from his spot at the back of the room.

"Exactly," Denise responded as the others nodded in agreement.

Raul Munoz stated, "We must advise the Capitol police at once. It would be most embarrassing for us and for them if something should happen to another senator while we are here for the purpose of solving the murders."

"Let's summon Senator Salermo and share our findings with him. He appears to be not only the spokesman for the senators and the liaison between us and the U.S. Capitol police but the man with the most authority here," Eugene Chu advised, stretching his long legs encased in a fine pair of cowboy boots.

Everyone nodded in agreement. While Eugene gave instructions to the officer at the door, Denise said, "I think we should acknowledge that we are also in danger. If the killer is working for a cause, he will not allow us to get in his way. We must be careful about what we eat and drink, also."

"But we don't have any control over our food. They serve us," Greta commented with alarm in her voice. Quickly she tossed the soft, chewy chocolate chip cookie into the trash can.

"Maybe we should request sealed packages of luncheon meats and breads rather than meals prepared in the kitchen. We can make our own sandwiches and serve ourselves from canned juices and bottled milk. We could eat unpeeled fruit instead of salads and whole cheeses rather than artfully prepared trays. Boxed cereals are preferable to oatmeal and scrambled eggs. The limited menu will become boring but perhaps that will help keep us alive," Richard offered as he returned his untouched coffee cup to the table.

"Suddenly this trip seems very tiresome. I don't know if I will survive without my coffee," Alexander Hopkins, the detective from Washington State, groaned. His tie lay haphazardly over his shoulder.

"You might not survive if you drink it," Denise retorted with a wry chuckle. "However, all of these precautions presume that the murderer administered the toxin through the senators' food. The toxicology report will give us conclusive information, but until then I don't think it hurts to take precautions."

"To live on packaged foods in D.C. is almost a sin," Greta complained as she eyed the cookies hungrily, "but I'd rather do that than return home in a pine box."

They sat in silence as they digested the information they had uncovered. Like the others, Denise fought off the urge for one more cup of tea and a slice of the chocolate cake. However, until she knew the method by which the murderer administered the poison, she would not take any chances. She had to return to her precinct as soon as possible. She could only imagine the mess Tom was making of her cases.

Senator Salermo joined them a short while later with news that immediately caused the detectives to refill their cups. Smiling, he announced, "I have just heard from the coroner. He has received the results of the tests on the stomach contents. The lab reports did not find any poison in the food ingested by them."

"Well, at least our food source is untainted," Alexander stated as he poured a cup of steaming coffee.

"Did either the report or the coroner suggest in what way the poison might have entered their systems?" Denise asked, hoping to hear more details but suspecting that the senator had shared all that he knew.

"No, the coroner said that all he knows with certainty is that the bodies did not bear any needle marks to suggest that the deceased might have injected toxin. Now they know that it was not ingested either. Regardless of these results, I'll do as you suggest and request additional protection. We don't want any more scandal at this election time," Senator Salermo agreed reluctantly.

"Senator, isn't tomorrow the first day of the Social Security debates?" Denise inquired as she marveled at the calm demeanor of the senator.

Turning toward her, Senator Salermo replied with effort, "Yes, it is. We're hopeful that we'll finish this time without anyone dying."

"Then, we'd better hurry. All of you are in very grave danger," Denise stated carefully but emphatically.

That night Denise paced the floor of her room. She could not sleep; the pieces of the puzzle kept swirling through her mind. A wisp of a thought that would not come to the surface kept reappearing, only to flutter away again. Her intuition worked overtime to sort through the thoughts and make the relevant connections. The group of detectives did not have time to wander down incorrect paths or follow erroneous leads. The lives of the men on the short list were in their hands.

Denise longed for Tom. If only he were with her, she could spread out the pieces and discuss each one with him. She had tried phoning him, but he did not answer. Knowing his habit of working late, she had tried that number, too, only for the line to ring endlessly. She would try again in the morning. For now, all she could do was try to sleep.

FIVE

Pulling on a pair of jeans, a T-shirt, and tennis shoes, Denise hummed softly as she dressed for a walk in the deserted streets of Washington. She had abandoned the idea of sleep and decided that she needed the smell of the city to help her pull together the pieces of the elusive puzzle. When she peeked out of her door, she did not see the usually attentive guard. Delighted to find that she was alone and that no one sat at attention outside her door under the pretext of being her ready assistant, she felt suddenly light-headed at the new freedom.

Rushing into the warm night air of the Pine Cone courtyard, Denise felt liberated. She had not realized that she had missed the fragrance of the outdoors until she breathed its freshness. She had arrived in D.C. only the day before, but she already missed the freedom of leaving the office and trudging through the streets of a big, noisy metropolitan area.

As she strolled among the shrubs, Denise looked up at the starry sky. This was the kind of night that always helped her to clear her mind. With Tom trudging glumly beside her, they would solve their most troubling cases. Tonight as the residents of Capitol Hill slept, Denise walked alone.

She had just found a sheltered bench among the roses when she sensed that she was not alone. Turning quickly and instinctively reaching for the weapon under her arm, she stared into the darkness as a figure stepped from behind the bushes into her path. Although the crime rate had dropped recently in D.C., she was prepared for anything that the night might offer.

"Who is it?" Denise called loudly.

"What are you doing out here? Don't you know that you shouldn't be out here wandering alone?" Richard replied as he stepped out of his hiding place in the shadows.

"The same thing you are, I guess. I couldn't sleep. Being inside all day gives me the willies. I needed to escape for a while," Denise replied softly with a chuckle as she slipped her revolver into the shoulder holster she wore close to her skin.

"Me, too, and I needed a smoke. Ahh, that's much better. My wife told me to leave my pipe at home, but I knew that these long sessions would make me want a good smoke. I'll stay upwind so the smoke won't bother you. Are you married, Denise?" Richard said as he lit the carefully packed tobacco in the bowl of his intricately carved pipe. Standing with his right elbow resting on his left hand, he resembled Sir Arthur Conan Doyle's famous detective. All he needed was the cap to complete the look.

"No, I haven't had the time. I have a high-maintenance partner, so I guess that's about the same thing. That's enough for now," Denise replied with a smile. "I enjoy the aroma of good pipe tobacco. You certainly do look like Sherlock Holmes."

Richard commented from his end of the bench, "I consider myself fortunate in that I mostly work alone. I enjoy the freedom of movement without having to tell someone where I'm going. One partner in life is enough for me. But the job has its exciting moments. I've had my share of close calls. I didn't get this head full of gray hairs from feeding the pigeons in Times Square."

"It's never dull in my office either. There's always something happening, especially in the neighborhoods close to the boundary with Washington D.C. It can get a bit dicey in some of them," Denise commented as she gazed at the night stars.

"Is D.C. really as bad as they say?"

"Sometimes. Is London as calm as it appears?"

"What do you make of this case, Denise?" Richard asked as he puffed on his pipe.

"I think they're in for some serious trouble. The senators are in denial about their vulnerability, which makes them sitting ducks. They haven't a clue to the murderer's identity. The possibilities are endless as to the the nature of the poison. The group responsible for the murder hasn't surfaced to claim a place in the headlines. This is going to get very messy and very complicated before it ends," Denise replied as she worked the tension from her shoulders.

"How difficult do you think it will be to convince the senators to comply with our wishes regarding their safety?" Richard asked as the sweet tobacco cloud circled around his head. "Senator Salermo seemed fairly adamant about retaining his freedom although he doesn't mind limiting ours."

"I think they're up against a centuries-old feeling of invincibility that will be incredibly difficult to penetrate. Even with members of the Senate dying because of someone's maniacal devotion to a cause, these politicians will not admit that they need to take steps to protect themselves. They believe that their positions will protect them and that they should remain passively engaged in their own lives. That attitude alone makes it easy for someone with an ax to grind to get close to them," Denise replied as she studied the stars from which she expected an answer but received none.

"Well, if your hunch is right, someone will soon cause

quite a stir here. Let's hope they're ready for it. I suppose we might as well go back inside," Richard said as he knocked out the remains of his tobacco and buried the ashes in the flower bed. "They'll find out we're missing soon and send out the guards."

"They already have. Look," Denise exclaimed softly as she pointed to the two members of the Capitol police coming in their direction.

"Detectives Dory and Evans, we searched all over for you when we found the lights on in your rooms. Please, allow us to escort you back. It is risky to wander through the streets of D.C. at night," Officer Bartholomew stated as he motioned toward the building.

"Thank you for your concern. We were just about to return when you came out. The night air has done me considerable good. Why don't you lead the way," Denise replied with a forced smile.

"Officer Bartholomew will show you the quickest way," Officer Mathews directed with a brief nod of his head.

At her door, Denise turned to bid her escort good night and saw the officers engaged in grave, whispered conversation. From the animated gesturing, she could tell that Officer Bartholomew was in serious trouble for allowing his charges to wander around unattended. With a faint smile, Denise closed the door knowing that she would have to find a way to divert the officer's attention if she were to have another late night walk around Capitol Hill. The quiet of the dormitory on the Capitol grounds was almost welcome.

While buttering her toast the next morning Denise asked Richard, "How did Officer Mathews say he knew we weren't in our rooms?"

"I think he said something about seeing our lights.

He must have thought that they meant something. Why?" Richard said as he spread jelly on his croissant.

"I didn't leave my light on when I left the room. I dressed and slipped out in darkness so that no one would see the light under my door. I needn't have bothered since no one was in the hall anyway," Denise replied as she sipped her juice.

"Come to think of it, I didn't leave mine on either. My wife has conditioned me to turn out the lights every time I leave a room. I tiptoed out in my stocking feet and didn't even put on my shoes until I reached the door. All of the lights were off when I returned to the room, too. What do you make of it, Denise?"

"I wouldn't be at all surprised if someone has bugged our rooms. They probably heard the door open and sent someone to look for us."

"Why would they want to do that? The senators invited us to help them solve this case," Richard commented between bites.

"I don't know who is monitoring our actions, but I have my suspicions. The senators invited us, but I would doubt that the decision had unanimous appeal. My guess is that someone wants to know if we're coming close to discovering the murderer's identity as a means of protecting his own turf. He might even have convinced the others that he needed to keep us under observation for the good of the U.S. Capitol's worldwide reputation. We should do a check of the rooms today," Denise suggested, reaching for another delicious hard roll.

"It sounds to me as if you're hinting that the U.S. Capitol police and Senator Salermo are behind the surveillance. I'm sure the others will be as concerned as I am about this breech of privacy. It doesn't strike me as being exactly ethical to invite a group of detectives to help solve a murder and then eavesdrop on their conversations," Richard concluded as he abandoned his breakfast. Denise had ruined his appetite.

"I could be wrong, but I'd rather find out for sure than to assume that we're alone and unmonitored. This is the first day of the new debates on Social Security. While everyone is occupied with that, let's take care of our own housekeeping chores. It's possible that Senator Salermo could be completely ignorant of the bugging, but someone in his office might know or someone on the police force," Denise stated as she finished the last of her coffee.

"Maybe Senator Price is the one who ordered it. We need to know who's watching us," Richard replied as they spread the word to the others about a possible bugging and arranged to meet immediately after breakfast.

As Denise predicted, the halls were abuzz with activity relating to the first day's events. No one appeared to notice Richard and her as they moved from one bedroom to the other checking for listening devices. In one room, they found a tape recorder and microphone. In another, they discovered a telephone listening device.

"I don't think that this is the full extent of the surveillance effort. These devices were far too primitive. My guess is that they are decoys to throw us off the scent of the more elaborate monitoring equipment," Denise quipped as she studied the rather aged equipment.

"Denise, come over here for a minute," Richard said as he opened the closet in his room.

In the back of the closet, Denise found a panel of wires and blinking lights concealed behind a fake back wall. Nodding in agreement, they backed out of the semidarkness. Dropping to their knees, Richard and Denise searched the baseboards at the carpet line for wires. Finding none, she used a penknife to pry the molding away from the wall.

Pointing, Denise mouthed, "Look."

Someone had carefully hidden the monitoring wires behind the baseboard and threaded them through a tiny hole into her room and then back into Richard's room again. Following them first in Richard's room, they found a small listening device taped to the back of the desk. Searching for more, they found another behind the mirror in the bathroom. Checking her room, they uncovered similar devices concealed behind the painting over the desk and inside the bathroom linen closet. At the top of both doors, they discovered tiny state-of-the-art motion detectors.

After meeting up with the other detectives and motioning for them to follow, Richard and Denise slipped into the busy street. Finding a small deserted park, they sat among the flowers. From a distance, they looked like a well-dressed group of tourists rather than a gathering of top detectives.

Speaking in low tones, Denise advised, "We must all be careful about what we say. Someone is watching us to learn our thoughts and our whereabouts. I doubt that we have located all of the devices. The conference room is probably very well wired. Use extreme caution not to give away information that would jeopardize our search for the truth in this case. We wouldn't want to give the murderer an even greater advantage."

Greta commented, "I'd say that we've stepped unwittingly into more of a mess than we originally anticipated. This doesn't sound like a simple murder case anymore."

"Considering the importance of Social Security to baby boomers, I don't think we should underestimate the political climate," Eugene added with a knowing shake of his head.

"Let's keep our eyes open. We have to protect each other now more than ever. Not only do we have to uncover the murderer's identity and keep another senator from falling victim, we have to stay out of harm's way ourselves," Raul interjected.

"I know I sound like a cynic in saying this, but I suspect that the U.S. Capitol's own police department is behind the bugging of our rooms," Denise stated bluntly. "Think of the embarrassment the chief must have felt when the senators invited the national law enforcement communities to send representatives to help solve the case. Under the same circumstances, I think I'd monitor the competition, too, and maybe even beat them to the punch if I could get any leads from what I heard. I'd certainly take any tidbit I could get and use it to my advantage. I can't imagine that the chief is any different. We might want to consider asking them to help us as soon as we know the identity of the toxin. They certainly know the U.S. Capitol employees and volunteers better than we do. When we really start our investigation, their knowledge might prove invaluable. However, we'll have to remember to control the flow of information to them since we don't know who on their force might be involved in the murder."

Greta commented as she brushed the grass clippings from her skirt, "Good thinking. That would certainly explain the U.S. Capitol's desire to bring in outsiders. Not only is the U.S. Capitol protecting its face to the world, it's also making sure that no one is overlooked as a suspect."

Returning to the building, they mingled in the hall with throngs of visitors, whose happy faces showed that they were not in the least concerned about the murders that had plagued their elected representatives. Their eyes flicked from one sculpture or painting to another as they tried to catch a glimpse of a famous senator.

As Senator Salermo approached, he smiled wanly and said, "I have arranged for Officer Mathews to drive you to the senators' homes. Take as long as you like in your investigation. He is at your disposal all day. Unfortunately, I will be in meetings all afternoon. Officer Mathews will be able to contact me if necessary. Should you need more than he can provide, my assistant, Michael Pace, will be able to help you."

"Thank you, Senator. By the way, do you think the members of your committee will come to any agreements this afternoon? I'm concerned for the safety of all of you until we solve this case," Denise asked before Senator Salermo could hurry away.

"We'll test the waters today. My straw vote at ten o'clock showed that they have much work to do. They have scheduled the second one for two o'clock. You'll know something as soon as we do. In the meantime, we'll be very careful," Senator Salermo replied as he eased into the steady stream of people that filled the halls and vanished around the corner.

"He's worried," Denise commented to Richard as they walked through the halls to the exit and the waiting car.

"I would be, too, if I knew that my position on Social Security, gun control, or any number of other issues might make me a target for assassination. He's looking down the barrel of a loaded gun," Richard replied as he stepped aside for her to exit.

The drive through the city reminded Denise once again of her need to talk with Tom. The streets, although teeming with people, appeared empty since she could not share this adventure with him. Her assumptions seemed only hunches without having his quick mind to refute or validate them. She missed her partner and wondered why she could not reach him on any of his telephone numbers or his pager. With a sigh, Denise leaned back in the van's seat and tried to push Tom from her mind as she allowed Richard's excited chattering to replace her longing for Tom.

Leaving Officer Mathews at the front door of the first senator's house, they searched for listening and monitoring devices inside. Finding none but remaining cautious, they examined every book, picture, and cranny for anything that would give them a clue about the poison. Although they felt confident that no one was watching them, they worked stealthily so that they might keep any discovery to themselves for a while until they could arrange for impartial testing of the toxin.

Pausing for a moment, Denise suggested in a whisper to her assembled colleagues, "Let's think about this for a minute. We know that the senators did not ingest the poison. Nothing in the contents of their stomachs has indicated that their food or drink was contaminated. We know that neither of them had been drugged. I think we need to look for something unusual, something that the police could easily overlook under normal circumstances."

Greta commented as they searched the bedroom, "I don't see anything that suggests forced entry or foul play. Nothing seems out of place or in any way disturbed. I don't think we'll find anything here. Whoever poisoned the senator was careful not to leave any traces."

"Do you think that someone could have introduced a toxic chemical through the air vents?" Richard asked as he stood on the seat of the closest chair and peered into the duct.

"From here, we can't tell. We should probably ask for a blueprint of the house to see if that's possible. The other possibility is to interview the building's engineers.

But then, wouldn't the senator's wife have been murdered also?" Eugene replied.

"The report said that she was out of town at the time. The same is true of the other senator. In both cases, the spouses were not at home and were, therefore, spared," Richard commented as he peered into the attic through the pop-up entrance in the closet ceiling.

Raul suggested, "Perhaps someone on the laundry staff washed the bed and bath linen in a toxic substance."

"Unfortunately, the housekeeper has cleaned the room since the senator's demise, so we won't be able to have a lab analyze the sheets. We'll have to ask his widow for the name of the laundry service," Denise agreed as she added them to the list of people, both private and public, that they needed to question.

"Let's check the senator's study. His office diary showed that the senator had received several foreign ambassadors only a few hours before he died. Perhaps he came into contact with the poison in that meeting," Eugene offered.

"You could be right although none of the guests reported feeling ill. However, I do think we should become familiar with the layout of each room. You never know when that knowledge will come in handy," Denise replied as they moved through the double doors leading from the living room into the senator's private study.

Entering the majestic book-lined room, they looked for signs of disarray among its masculine décor. As with the bedroom, they saw nothing unusual. The study was in pristine condition. Although easily accessible from the hall and the living room, the study did not look as if anyone had used it recently. Not a single book or chair was out of place.

Surveying the room with a sigh, Denise said, "Whatever evidence we might have found in this room is gone now. Most hospitals aren't this clean. There aren't any footprints on the oriental carpets that didn't come from us. There's no dust anywhere."

"The housekeeper is certainly efficient," Richard added as he carefully searched among the books for hidden cameras and microphones.

"They're too efficient if we're to track down the killer. I bet they even remove the flowers before they start to wilt, and polish all the brass every day to remove fingerprints. It's a shame that the Capitol Hill and D.C. police didn't leave a few clues for us," Denise lamented as she shook her head and checked under the sofas for listening devices and among the books and porcelain figurines for chemical residue.

While Denise crawled around the perimeter of the oriental carpets, Richard worked like a hunter in search of his prey. Unfortunately, he unearthed nothing. Holding up his empty hands, he announced, "There isn't a scrap of wire, telltale sawdust pile, or powder residue of any kind to hint that anyone has entered this room for illicit purposes."

Dusting carpet fibers from the knees of her slacks, Denise replied, "Let's go. We won't find anything here. Maybe the next house will reveal something."

"I doubt it," Richard grumbled as he passed Officer Mathews and his wide smirk.

Richard had been right. They made the return trip to Capitol Hill in silence. Having found nothing to explain the senators' deaths at either house, Denise sat sullenly ruminating over the unprofitable afternoon.

A crowd had assembled on the Capitol steps to hear the results of the morning's meetings. Standing in the midst of the assembled crowd, Denise could feel the excitement and the anxiety of the people as they awaited the news. Their voices were subdued while their bodies radiated their sense of anticipation. Every eye anxiously watched the empty podium.

"Maybe they've made the decision that the murderer wanted. Maybe there won't be another killing," Richard suggested, shouting above the roar of the crowd that greeted Senator Salermo's appearance.

"Or there could be one as early as tonight," Denise commented and turned away.

As the senator cleared his throat and waited for the noise and flashing of cameras to stop, Denise knew that the news would not be good. From the fatigue lines on his face, she could tell that the various committees had not reached their decisions.

Senator Salermo's words only confirmed her thoughts as he announced, "Ladies and gentlemen, you might as well go home. We still have much to discuss on these issues and will not have any news to share with you for quite some time. Thank you for your support."

As the crowd reluctantly dispersed, Denise and Richard entered the cool of the Capitol. Turning her attention toward the corridor that led to the gallery, she felt as if someone were watching her. Shaking off the feeling, she continued to enjoy her stroll through the impressive structure. Putting the day's frustrations and disappointments behind her, Denise decided to spend a few minutes playing tourist.

Denise was so engrossed in her study of the ceiling that she almost bumped into a woman carrying an enormous pot of flowers. "Excuse me," she muttered. Nodding her acceptance of the apology, the woman continued her work. Denise watched as the woman carefully placed the array among the others that brightened the base of a marble statue.

Suddenly, Denise turned to Richard and said, "I think we have our work cut out for us. What we have

here is frightened senators who knew that, by support-
ing the somewhat radical issues of gun control, abortion
rights, and changes in Social Security, they would be in
danger of angering their constituency. They did not,
however, realize that their lives would be in jeopardy.
Now, by dragging their feet on the issues, they think
they'll buy some time and save their lives. My gut reaction is that they haven't fooled anyone."

Scratching his chin, Richard replied, "Then we must
do everything we can to protect all of them."

Leading the way into the conference room, Denise
replied, "That's what makes their job so difficult. They
don't know which pot the media is stirring and which is
about to boil over on its own. In this case, that lack of
knowledge has already resulted in the deaths of two
men and could possibly lead to more."

As the others returned, they took up their former
positions around the tables. They had learned nothing
new and had uncovered no leads. Whoever had been
behind the murder of the two senators was still beyond
their grasp.

SIX

Assembled in the conference room around cluttered tables, they mapped out a strategy that they hoped would save the life of a senator. As they worked, they could hear snippets of conversation in the hall as politicians made plans for their summer trips home.

"It would certainly be embarrassing if someone killed another senator with all of us here. After all, the press has proclaimed us to be the most outstanding law enforcement team in the world," Greta commented with raised eyebrows.

Chuckling, Richard added, "We wouldn't be able to get jobs as dogcatchers if something were to happen while we're practically living under the U.S. Capitol's roof."

"Agreed, but where do we begin?" Eugene groaned. "All we know so far is that the poison was neither injected nor ingested and that the senators were not supportive of the same activist groups. That's not the basis for a case. We don't have any witnesses or clues. We have no suspects. Our hands are tied. The best we can do at this moment is encourage the U.S. Capitol police to provide more security for the senators, but we can't even suggest what or who they should be on guard against."

"That's true, which is why they have to make some assumptions and try to get ahead of the murderer. Let's start by considering the health of each senator on our short list," Denise suggested as she turned on the overhead projector and slipped on the diagram containing the names of the senators.

"The senators have the usual illnesses of people who eat and drink too much and exercise too little," Richard replied as he flipped through the health information in front of him.

"And their stated radical leanings?" Greta asked as she leaned over to adjust the bracelet on her ankle.

"All of them favored at least one slightly radical program, but I don't see anything that should lead to their death," Richard responded as he pushed the book toward the center of the table.

Everyone's eyes followed Richard as he stopped speaking and stared at the scribble that projected onto the screen. "Denise, what is that?" he asked.

"What? Oh, I was just thinking on paper. Sorry, I hope I didn't disturb anyone," Denise replied when she realized that everyone could see her thoughts.

"Your chart looks interesting. Why don't you explain it to us?" Greta suggested as she studied the interconnecting circles.

"It's nothing really . . . just a little exercise my partner, Tom, and I do when we're stumped on a case. He's the one who decided to try diagramming the information we had to locate the weak spots. Sometimes it works, and others it doesn't," Denise began. "I simply constructed another chart that shows the population within the country that supports the status quo, increased gun laws, and the change in the Social Security program. I based my observations on data that Senator Salermo provided us. Each circle stands for the prevailing views held by the majority of outspoken U.S. citizens. The overlapped areas show the numbers of people who favor two or more of the issues."

"Okay, what exactly does this show us? I've never been much on reading diagrams. I prefer text," Raul asked as he squinted at the screen.

"If I've interpreted the figures correctly, I would say that we're dealing with two distinct groups. The first group is composed of the followers of the status quo. According to my analysis of Senator Salermo's figures, these people want the government to stay as it is and do not find either of the day's pressing issues sufficient enough to justify the uproar and certainly not murder," Denise replied, pointing from one group on the diagram to the other.

"That makes Senator Clement a sitting duck," Raul added as he paced the room to organize his thoughts.

Turning reluctantly from the window, Greta asked, "Shouldn't the murderer be content with Clement as the chair of the subcommittee? Looks as if we can go home. I doubt that the suspect will show himself again."

"Hey, wait. Not so fast. I still think we're a long way from solving this murder," Denise said with a wave of her hands.

"Why don't you explain what you mean, Denise?" Richard suggested, sitting up straight in his chair and giving her his full attention.

"The way I see it, there are two possible scenarios. If we're right and a compromise chairman is now in power, then we could go home. The murderer will indeed go under cover and the U.S. Capitol will be safe again. However, if the killer is still discontent and strikes again, we need to ask ourselves if a supporter of stronger gun control would be the best candidate for ending what is unfortunately becoming a serial killing. The murderer might not rest until the gun control issue is secure. Ironic, isn't it? Someone in favor of gun control might be resorting to violence to prove his point," Denise explained.

Rising to his feet, Richard concluded, "Sadly, the only way we'll have an answer to this question is by waiting to see if the murderer strikes again. If he does, then we will be able to eliminate many activist groups."

Denise added, "It seems to me as if two more senators have to die before we have a firm handle on the motive. Our only hope is to catch the murderer in the act, but we still don't have a clue how he administers the toxin or the identity of the poison. We need that lab report."

"Don't forget the issue of the senators' health. Didn't you already show us a chart about that? If I remember correctly, two senators have heart and respiratory problems, which make them likely victims if the murderer wants to continue to make it look like accidental death until he reaches his goal, if there is one," Greta interjected.

"As Richard said, the only thing we can do is wait. We must stress to Senator Salermo that they're still in danger," Eugene commented, drinking deeply from his can of soda.

"Well, maybe we won't be able to go home yet after all," Greta sighed. "We'll still have to stick around and see what happens to validate our suppositions. As I said at the beginning of this discussion, the only thing we know with any certainty is that we don't know who is behind these murders or why. We must wait and see."

They all nodded in agreement as the discreet knock on the door signaled that the van that would take them on a tour of the city and then to dinner had arrived. Joining the others in the hall, Denise mused to Richard, "I just wonder how the murderer did it. If the poison was not injected or ingested, how did the senators come in contact with it?"

"I don't know, Denise," Richard replied. "Unfortunately, that's one of those pieces that will fall into place when he strikes again. I'm just relieved that it wasn't in the food. I don't think I'd last long on fruit." Laughing, they went with the others down the hall.

In silence, they boarded a U.S. Capitol van for a night-time tour of the city before dinner. Denise walked to the back of the vehicle with Richard beside her. Stretching his long legs into the aisle, Richard watched as she pulled out her sketchbook.

"Tell me about yourself, Denise. I don't mean the résumé details we exchanged earlier, but the real inside scoop. You must give your partner a run for his money," Richard commented as he watched her sketch a montage of the faces she saw along the street. So far Denise had captured a fruit vendor with a scar running across his cheek, a haggard sales clerk with wisps of hair falling over her forehead, and a young boy with a dirt smudge on his nose as they stood under the streetlights.

"There's not much that I haven't already told you. I'm the elder of two daughters. My parents still live in the family home in which I grew up. I'm too busy with my work to become emotionally involved with a man other than my very demanding partner. And I'm very happy with the way my life is right now. I don't feel that I'm missing anything," Denise replied without taking her eyes from the street.

"Tell me about your partner. You said once that he's high maintenance."

Shaking her head and chuckling, Denise began, "Tom is one of those cops who has experienced and internalized too much. He tries to be hard and gruff, but he's really a softy when you get to know him. When I first met him, his loud voice, his muscular bulk, and his wiseass attitude intimidated me. I was new to the department, and he was without a partner. His old one had demanded that the captain reassign him. He said that he had spent enough time listening to Tom complain about life, the world, his job, and the idiocy of people. Plus, he was tired of breathing secondhand cigarette smoke. He said that if Tom's attitude didn't kill him, the tobacco would.

"Being one of the youngest detectives in the department, I decided to give Tom a try although everyone said that he would run me away just as he did everyone else. I needed an experienced partner and someone I could respect. Despite his reputation, Tom looked like the perfect match. Besides, I'm a sucker for a hopeless cause.

"We've been together for five years now, and I wouldn't switch for anything. I've found out that he's warm, sensitive, and very vulnerable. I don't care how gruff he is. I know he's behind me and covering my back. I trust him with my life every time we go out on a case. I miss him and can't wait to go home to see him again."

"If I had a partner who felt that way about me, I wouldn't be working alone now. Maybe you should call him," Richard replied with a gentle smile.

"I will when I think he misses me as much as I miss him. I don't want him to think that I'm a softy. Now it's your turn. What's not on your résumé?" Denise asked as she studied Richard's face.

"There's not much of a story here. I've been married to the same sainted woman for fifteen years. She has nursed me through a broken leg and two serious wounds. When she asked me to request reassignment to a desk job, I thought I owed it to her. I had no idea that I'd have to take this detour first. Anyway, as much as I'm enjoying your company, I can't wait to go home. This rich food has activated my gout. I need some of my wife's TLC," Richard replied as a shadow of sadness flickered across his face.

Finishing her sketch, Denise remarked, "I'd say that we're both lucky in having someone who's a perfect match."

"That certainly is a handsome guy. If that's me, I never looked so good," Richard commented as he peeked at the sketchbook in which Denise had recorded the love that shone on his face as he spoke of his wife.

"It sure is. Here, you can have it. I have plenty of others."

"You do? You could have found a better subject."

"Send it to your wife with my compliments."

"Thanks, Denise. I'm sure she'll get a kick out of seeing it. Why do you sketch? Your hands are always busy doing something," Richard said as he carefully eased the rolled paper into his jacket pocket.

"I like to draw pictures of my observations, including people and scenes. They come in handy during trials. Some people dictate into a tape recorder, but I sketch," Denise replied as she began a quick drawing of one of the columns of the Lincoln Memorial.

"You're pretty good at it, too. It's time for my nap. Wake me when you spot something we didn't see on our walk," Richard requested, folding his arms over his chest.

They rode in silence as the wonders of D.C. slipped past the windows. The driver occasionally pointed out the less well known sights, but mostly they gazed speechless into the illuminated majesty of federal Washington. D.C. at night was a marvel that defied words.

With a sigh, Denise returned to her sketches. She missed Tom and wished that he were napping beside her. As much as she enjoyed Richard's company, he simply was not Tom.

Picking up speed, the van rolled into the countryside, heading to a converted monastery nestled in the hillside of the town of Fredericksburg, Virginia. An entrepreneur had converted the structure into a center for entertainment that served fine cuisine and did quality stage productions. The restaurant occupied the old refectory and the theatre kept the converted chapel busy with top-quality performances.

Walking to their seats, Denise absorbed the details of the monastery in which portraits of formidable-looking monks and ancient popes lined the thick stone walls. Iron chandeliers swung from the sturdy beams of the ceiling and cast shadows in the darkened corners as the many candles sputtered over their heads. Heavy crosses hung over every door, reminiscent of the time when monks in long, drab olive brown would glide soundlessly over the highly polished wooden floors. Stairs and hallways that the monks once climbed to their chambers and to the chapel for prayer now led to the offices, dressing rooms, and storage areas. The monks would have sat on hard benches or stood for prayers. The audience sat upon thickly cushioned seats pitched at just the right angle for perfect enjoyment of the play. The delicious aroma of dinner wafted up to them.

Scanning the playbill, Richard whispered, "Wake me if I snore. I don't think I'll be able to stay awake for Shakespeare on a full stomach. It's hard enough when I'm hungry."

"Tom falls asleep during performances, too. I've perfected the placement of an elbow to the ribs. It was nice of Senator Salermo to arrange this evening for us. We should make the best of it. Who knows when we'll have free time if the murderer strikes again?" Denise replied, trying to lessen his anxiety.

"Whatever you say, Denise. This food looks great," Richard responded as he dug into the plate piled high with roast beef, roast chicken, mashed potatoes with gravy, greens, and a roll dripping with butter.

True to his word, Richard fell asleep as soon as the

lights dimmed. The weight of the meal and the words of Shakespeare's *Julius Caesar* quickly had him snoring. Even Denise's well-placed jabs could do no more than muffle the sounds. Richard awoke at intermission and again at the end when the applause jarred him from his sleep.

Shaking her head at him, Denise said, "As soon as we return to the Capitol, I'm going to sketch the monastery and scenes from the play. I'll show them to you so that you can say you were here. You certainly missed a treat. The sight of the lights playing off the old stone walls was wonderful. At times, they looked as if someone were slipping in and out of the shadows."

"I'll take your word for it. My wife always tells me what I've missed when we take in a play. I'm sorry that I'm such a poor partner, but I can't help it. As soon as the lights go down, my eyelids drop," Richard replied as he stretched and joined her for the walk to the van.

Denise commented mostly to herself without expecting the sleepy Richard to notice, "Virginians certainly love their cut flowers. Even in a place like this where you'd expect the traditional monastic austerity, vases of them sit everywhere."

"It's just like in the Capitol. Everywhere I look, I find a flower. It's enough to trigger an allergic reaction," Richard griped as he helped her into the van.

"Why, Richard, I had no idea that you were such a romantic," she quipped with a chuckle.

"Right. I'm not that kind of guy. I wouldn't remember our anniversary or my wife's birthday if she didn't put notes in my jacket pocket. Wake me when we arrive at the Capitol, will you? I'm overdue for a nap," Richard replied as he snuggled into his seat.

Chuckling, Denise gazed out the window as the countryside vanished and the grandeur of D.C. came into view. Each neighborhood consisted of at least one church and a multitude of restaurants. Lights from the closed boutiques, both plain and fancy, illuminated the evening as diners strolled home after a sumptuous meal at a neighborhood bistro. Children, too tired to walk, rode in strollers or their parents' arms. Patrons of the symphony descended the stairs of the Kennedy Center.

As the van pulled into the Capitol grounds past the waiting police, Denise gave Richard's shoulder a nudge. "Another minute, please, Helen," he muttered.

"Richard, wake up. I'm not Helen and you're not at home. At least I hope that's your wife's name. We're back at the Capitol," Denise replied, giving him a stronger shove this time.

"I should have known you weren't my wife," Richard retorted sharply, suddenly awake and grumpy. "She never shoves me. Instead, she whispers in my ear until I wake up. No wonder you're not married. That partner of yours would have proposed by now if you weren't so bossy."

Rolling her eyes at him, Denise commented as the color in her cheeks rose, "Hey, who said I'd marry him if he did propose? Don't make something out of a strictly professional relationship. Just for that, I won't share my ideas with you. It's a shame, too, because I wanted to try out a theory I've just formulated. You'll just have to wait until I work through it without you."

"What theory have you developed while I've been sleeping on the job?"

"Well," Denise asked without requiring any further encouragement, "who is it that we've been suspecting of murdering the senators?"

"We've focused on outside factions with the ability to penetrate the fortress of the Capitol or someone who might have unscrupulous connections inside the Hill. Why?" Richard replied, blinking away the last signs of sleepiness.

"What if the murders were an inside job?"

"You can't mean what you're saying, Denise. Do you really think that one of the senators killed a colleague?" Richard stated incredulously as he stared at her face as if she were a total stranger.

"Why should we stop with a senator? Isn't it possible that one of the young assistants or interns might commit the crime?" Denise postulated.

"What would they stand to gain?"

"A young senator might be able to ingratiate himself with the people by championing their causes. He could make a name for himself faster than the usual snail's pace of moving up the ladder," Denise suggested.

"You're discounting the possibility that he's an elderly senator?"

"Not really. He might want to make a last stab at placing his favorite cause in the public's eye by forcing the selection of someone for chairman who believes as he does. He might even have his sights on the job himself, sort of a final page to his memoirs," Denise continued with enthusiasm for the stream of ideas that flowed freely through her head.

Scratching his head, Richard asked with continued skepticism, "What would an ambitious assistant have to gain?"

"He might think that he would become the assistant to a powerful senator rather than a second-string assistant. He might decide to run for office in the boss's place. He might be tired of basking in someone's reflected glory," Denise replied as she mentally noted the many possible candidates for the suspect list if they enlarged the scope of their search.

"And the female intern on the list? She seems quite content in her subordinate role."

"I'm sure she loves being the fetch-it girl rather than the senator," Denise replied with sarcasm.

"Okay, I see your point. In other words, we can't afford to disregard anyone based on age, gender, or race," Richard said, fully awake now.

"That's right. Just think of the ego trip the wrong person could get from working here. Someone who would allow his or her own aspirations to get in the way of serving all the people could create all kinds of havoc. From encouraging the appointment of the wrong person to the Supreme Court to passing self-serving rules, an egotist or zealot could make a mockery of our democratic process," Denise replied as they followed the others into the Capitol Page quarters.

As they left the warmth of the Washington summer evening and entered the building, Richard agreed, "You're right about the power that the murderer would control. The power the senators possess is enough to make a man's head spin. You might just be on to something, Denise."

"I'll speak with the others tomorrow morning. We have to act fast. The murderer could be in the building right now. We'll have to get a list of the people who have access to the senators from the cleaning people to their assistants. I certainly hope that having this newly named senator as the chairman has bought us some time. Even if he is not in danger, we still owe it to the murdered senators to find their killer," Denise concluded as she stopped outside her bedroom door.

"Well, Denise, I'll see you in the morning," Richard said as he opened his door. "Regardless of how this turns out, we certainly have our work cut out for us. The number of people on the staff of the various senators is huge. I just hope we don't have to investigate the House of Representatives, too. I'll never get home again if we do."

Closing her door, Denise noticed Officer Mathews settled into his chair in the hall outside their rooms.

Once inside, she dialed Tom's number again. However, he did not answer. Only the lonely ringing greeted her ear.

Pulling on her nightshirt, Denise walked to the simple student desk in her room and quickly drew out a piece of notebook paper from the drawer. Using the black standard-issue government pen, she scribbled down a list of advisers, assistants, and other secretaries they would have to interview over the next few days. The task looked daunting, but she knew that a senator's life depended on the thoroughness of their investigation. They had to narrow the scope of their investigation and find the killer before he struck again. At the top of the list, Denise wrote Tom's name. Before she did anything else, she had to find out where he had been the last day.

Satisfied that she had done all she could for the night, Denise once again tried to sleep. This time the gentle whisper of the air conditioner enfolded her, and she drifted far away from the murders of the senators and the suspicions that plagued her mind. Her last thought was not of the senators or the case but of Tom. She missed him and would do everything she could to bring him to her.

SEVEN

Denise rose early the next morning with the intent of driving to her precinct in the Washington suburbs to find Tom before he started work. Pushing the curtains away from the windows, she saw that the sun had not yet risen. A few people dragged themselves through the still-dark street.

Hearing the sound of footsteps in the uncarpeted hall, Denise dropped her hairbrush and eased to the door. Years of training had taught her to be wary of people moving about before dawn. Pressing her ear against the heavy wooden door, she listened but heard nothing.

Strapping on her weapon and slipping into the light-weight linen jacket that completed the suit, Denise glanced quickly at her reflection in the small mirror. The peach silk blouse complemented her complexion perfectly and the suit fitted her figure beautifully. She hoped that Tom would be impressed when he saw her at the office.

Throwing her purse over her shoulder, Denise switched out the light and opened the door. To her surprise, she came face-to-face with a tall handsome man who was searching for room numbers in the semi-darkness. Involuntarily, her face lit up when she recognized his scowl.

"Tom," Denise whispered. "What are you doing here?"

"Trying to find you, but the lights are so low that I couldn't read the numbers," Tom growled as his face split into a grin from ear to ear.

"You could have knocked rather than standing out here frowning at that paper," Denise chuckled softly as her heart fluttered from the nearness of her partner.

"I don't think so! I don't want every cop in this place to take a bead on me. Are you going to invite me in or are we going to stand here all morning?" Tom grumbled as he walked past Denise into her small room.

Tom's presence filled the room as Denise closed the door behind them. His broad shoulders in one of his favorite slightly baggy suits seemed to reach from one wall to the other. When he turned to look at her, the glint in his eyes lit up the drab, gray dormitory room.

"Now that you've found me, would you please tell me why you're here?" Denise asked again as she perched on the end of her twin bed.

"I heard the news on the radio this morning and thought you might need an extra pair of hands, so I put in a leave slip," Tom said as he looked around the small room containing a tiny dresser, night table, desk, chair, and the solitary twin bed.

"What news?" Denise asked as she watched his reaction to her humble room.

"There's been another murder. The newscaster didn't give any details . . . just said that another senator had died," Tom rumbled as he sat on the chair that looked even more fragile under his massive frame.

"Another one? I hadn't heard," Denise said in a stunned voice.

"Yeah, another one. I didn't eat any breakfast this morning. Let's get some coffee. By the way, why are you up so early? I didn't think your sessions got started until eight," Tom commented as he counted the change in his pocket.

"I was on my way to the precinct to find you. You haven't returned any of my calls. I thought something had happened to you," Denise replied in a voice that contained emotion that she struggled to hide now that she and Tom were together again.

Studying her face for a long minute, Tom finally said, gruffly and with difficulty as he struggled with his own emotions, "You left me with enough cases for five men. I've been busy. Anyway, I'm here now. Let's get some coffee before my sweet disposition turns sour."

Taking her arm, Tom propelled Denise toward the door. Without giving her time to object, he turned off the light, closed the door, and led her toward the exit sign. She felt strangely content with his big hand on her arm. Suddenly, all the worries about the case seemed manageable now that Tom's quick mind and strong body were at her side. Over coffee, she would decide the way that she would introduce Tom to the other members of the task force.

An eerie silence surrounded them as the police detectives assembled for breakfast that morning. Denise quickly introduced Tom as her partner on leave from their precinct for a few days. Her new colleagues welcomed him eagerly, stating that they were eager for fresh ideas that might lead to solving the case. They, too, had heard the news and were awaiting the official announcement from Senator Salermo.

The waiters walked slowly and quietly among the tables as they served them. Instead of lingering with them, they saw to their needs and promptly left the room. For once, they did not stand along the walls and eavesdrop. Even Senator Salermo, whose smile brought the sun-

shine when he entered a room, appeared that morning
with heavy feet. He cleared his throat and announced,
"I regret having to be the bearer of such dreadful news,
but Senator Clement died in his sleep last night. The
doctor says that he will perform an autopsy to identify
the exact cause; however, he suspects from the sudden-
ness of his demise that the senator died of cardiac arrest."

"The murderer didn't waste any time, did he?"
Denise muttered a bit too loudly.

Turning his penetrating blue eyes on her, Senator
Salermo replied, "Detective Dory, we are hoping that
our colleague died of natural causes. We will reserve the
right to make a decision until after we read the autopsy
report. Although I will not be with you, I have arranged
for a group of you to join the coroner at ten o'clock.
Good day."

For a moment after the senator's departure, they sat
in silence as the weight of his words penetrated their
morning-fogged brains. Suddenly, everyone started talking at once with Eugene stating their thoughts when he
said, "At least they didn't forget to include us in the
investigation."

"This is embarrassing. The press corps must be having a field day with this news. I hope you don't think
we're totally incompetent, Tom," Richard added with a
shake of his head.

"Not at all. This case is a tough one to crack if the
newspaper accounts have been accurate," Tom replied
as he finished his coffee.

Denise commented as she pushed aside her plate, "If
we're right, this certainly makes us look like a joke. Here
we sit, the brightest and best cops in the country, and a
senator gets killed right under our noses. I certainly
would have included us, too, if I had been in Senator
Salermo's position. I would want to shift the attention

away from the vulnerability of the U.S. Capitol and onto the task force of detectives who could not solve the case. This way, we'll have to answer to the press and the people who want to know why we couldn't keep the senator alive."

"Let's not forget that the Capitol wants the press to believe that the senator died of natural causes until we have the autopsy reports. If the press tries to interview us, we need to give the same answer . . . we're waiting for more details. You picked a good time to join us, Tom. We need all the hands we can get," Richard said.

"I'd be more than happy to help, but don't forget that I'm not really here. If anyone asks, I'm simply a visitor. My captain thinks I'm on leave for a few days," Tom replied with a dry chuckle.

"I'm glad to have you here, regardless of your status," Denise added with a smile larger than Richard had yet seen illuminate her face.

"I think I'll stay here and do some snooping around while you're at the coroner's office. I'm not too fond of looking at dead men," Greta commented as she chewed vigorously on another pastry.

"If no one has any objections," Richard interjected, "I'd like to suggest that Eugene, Denise, Tom, and I represent us with the coroner. We'll return with detailed notes."

"Fine with us," Greta chirped. "There's more than enough to keep us busy here."

The chiming of the massive clock interrupted their conversation. They joined Michael Pace, Senator Salermo's right-hand man, for the short drive to the coroner's office in central D.C. Denise gazed out the window at the signs of mourning outside the U.S. Capitol entrance. The friends of the senator had placed flowers and photographs against the steps. Many prayed silently or slowed to show respect before hurrying to

their jobs. News cameras captured the emotional outpouring as people came to show their last respects to the
senator who had worked so tirelessly and for so long.

The coroner's office was large, brightly lit, and bus-
tling with activity. As expected, reporters from every major newspaper and television station waited in the smoky
lobby for information. Averting her eyes, Denise hurried past the familiar faces and did not stop as a voice
called out, "Detective Dory, a moment of your time,
please."

"That was a close one. That reporter almost charged
the police line to get to you," Richard commented as
the elevator doors closed and they began their descent
to the morgue.

"She's one of the best from the *Washington Post.*
Jeanne Jones has covered every major case Denise has
solved. I could almost read her banner headline . . .
'Detectives Clueless in Latest Capitol Murder.' I don't
think this investigation needs that kind of attention at
the moment," Tom replied with his usual mixture of
honesty and sarcasm.

The coroner, Dr. Grant Leahy, welcomed the detectives warmly as he led the way to the central autopsy suite.
The senator's body lay under a sheet on a stainless-steel
table. The subcommittee of detectives took out their
notebooks or tape recorders as Dr. Leahy shuffled his
notes and prepared to address them.

As the detectives drew closer to study the corpse,
Denise asked, "Could the senator actually have died
from natural causes? We know he suffered from a preex-
isting heart condition."

Turning toward her, the doctor replied, "No, it is not
possible although the condition of the body would
make us think it on first examination. Although he suffered from cardiac arrest, his heart was not damaged
from a fatal heart attack and showed no sign of enlarge-

ment. I have also ruled out violence since the senator's body is without blemish. I have already had my laboratory perform the initial tests on the senator's blood. The reports indicate that a toxin similar in composition to the one that killed the two previous senators was also the cause of his death. As with the other bodies, there are no signs of puncture wounds from hypodermic needles, and the contents of the stomach do not indicate that the poison was ingested."

Tom asked, "What poison could have worked so quickly and provided so few clues?"

With a shrug the physician replied, "That is indeed our dilemma. Without further laboratory tests, we cannot even determine how soon the senators died after coming in contact with the poison and, therefore, can do nothing to safeguard any others who might be a target of the same killer. Whoever poisoned the senators is extremely dangerous and ingenious."

"Would it be necessary for our murderer to have a medical or pharmaceutical background?" Eugene queried as he turned away from the corpse.

"No, not at all. The person could be a botanist, an avid gardener, or even a student of herbal medicine. The possibilities are limitless. I do not envy you in your investigation. Until we can isolate the origin of the poison, we will not be able to pinpoint its source. If we discover that the chemical was man-made, the information will assist you greatly in limiting your search. If it is common in nature, I am afraid that all the modern crime-fighting tools will have to give way to the old methods of relying on judgment, hunches, and informants. I regret that I could not be more helpful, Detectives," Dr. Leahy replied as he made a sweeping gesture of futility.

"Tell me, Doctor, is that bluish tinge to the lips normal in poisoning victims?" Denise asked as she leaned over the body for a closer look. "The nostrils appear quite pinched also and rimmed with white. There's a dustiness to his hair also."

Stepping forward, the coroner responded, "The coloring to which you refer is quite normal in cyanide poisoning victims. However, I would not limit my search to that compound exclusively. The color of the nostrils could indicate that the compound was inhaled. Unfortunately, there is no residue on the skin and no evidence of burning along the lining of the nostrils. I have seen the same discoloration in nasal spray addicts. Perhaps the senator suffered from allergies. I have included hair and skin samples in the material that I sent to the lab."

"Did the other senators have the same markings?" Tom inquired as he continued the line of questioning Denise had started.

"I will have to check my notes to be absolutely certain. I'm sure that I noted the discoloration of the lips; however, I am not as confident about seeing the whitening of the nostrils. I will do a little research and contact you immediately," the coroner replied as he jotted down the number of the telephone in the conference room.

Denise and Tom exchanged quick glances. Their expressions said that they thought the good doctor might be covering up or at least being selective in the information he would share. From the expression on Richard's and Eugene's faces, they felt the same way.

As they walked toward the waiting car, Tom stated, "It looks as if I joined you at just the right time. Sounds to me as if the senators are not only running scared but arranging cover-ups."

"I had the same thought," Denise agreed. "Let's stop at a library on the way back. I want to conduct a little forensic investigation of my own."

"The Library of Congress is almost next door. We'll

stop there," Tom concluded as he stepped aside for Richard to enter the car.

Turning to Richard, Denise said, "I don't want to return to the Capitol just yet. I'm heading for D.C.'s main library. You can come along if you'd like. Despite the heat, I think I'll walk. I'd like to see a bit of the city."

"I think I'll leave that to you and Tom. I'll return with Eugene to share our report with the others," Richard replied as the car pulled away.

Tom removed his jacket a block from the coroner's office. The day was hot and typically humid for summer in Washington. Keeping up with Denise's stride, Tom wiped perspiration from his dripping forehead.

"Are we in a race?" Tom panted as he sprinted across yet another street.

"We are if we want to prevent more murders. What's wrong, old man? Can't keep up?" Denise chirped happily as she looked over her shoulder at her growling partner.

"Keep up this pace, Dory, and you'll be minus one partner," Tom grunted as he removed his tie and unbuttoned his shirt.

Denise laughed as they climbed the steps to the Martin Luther King Memorial Library. Pulling open the heavy door, they left the noise of D.C. behind them. The familiar sights and dusty smells of the library were familiar and pleasing to Denise as she and Tom walked across the wide expanse of lobby.

Approaching the librarian, Denise asked, "I'd like information on plants, but, unfortunately, I can't be more specific than that."

"We have many volumes on flowers. How may I direct your search?" the librarian with the large blue eyes and gold-rimmed glasses replied tolerantly.

Smiling with relief at the librarian's kindness, Denise

continued, "I need information on poisonous plants and perhaps herbs."

"You'll find the information you need in the reference section. It's through there. You might want to browse on-line services as well," the librarian replied, pointing toward the far left room.

"Thanks." Denise turned to Tom and said, "You should stay close to me so that you won't get lost. When was the last time you were inside a library?"

"Back when they were still using rolls of papyrus," Tom snarled as he followed Denise toward the back of the library.

Stepping into the horticulture section, Denise was overwhelmed by the vast selection of books. Turning to Tom, she said, "Maybe we should search the on-line services first. There's so much here that I can't imagine where to start."

"Despite my lack of familiarity with a library, I spotted the computer research room as we whizzed past," Tom replied as he pointed to the sign that indicated the computer room.

Laughing quietly, Denise took a seat at one of the computers, logged on to the Internet, and began to search for information on poisons. Pages of data on the source, administration, and control of deadly poisons appeared. Together she and Tom scanned each one until they found an overview written for the uninformed.

"Dory, this is a bigger job than I thought it would be," Tom lamented from his computer. "I thought we'd only get a few references; instead we get thousands."

"I know, but we can't stop now. We already know that the easiest way to administer a toxin is through the victim's food or beverage Since we know the murderer didn't take that route, I can't think of any other method with any certainty. It's clear to me that we need the lab reports and the help of an expert," Denise concluded as she skimmed yet another page of information.

"I wonder if the senators could have inhaled the poison. You did see that white substance around the nose," Tom mused as he scanned more Web pages.

"I thought about that and, frankly, I still don't think it's possible that they inhaled a substance. I can't imagine them voluntarily sniffing enough of any substance to cause their deaths," Denise replied as she closed the file.

Placing both hands on his knees, Tom stated, "Unless they were cocaine users. Anyway, where do we go from here, Dory?"

"To the nearest coffee shop."

"Wouldn't you rather have an ice cream or iced tea?"

"No. I just need a place to think."

"You can't think in a cool library? You want to drag me into the sweltering heat once again?" Tom groaned as he dragged himself toward the exit.

"Complain, complain. I saw a shop at the corner," Denise offered as she led him into the late afternoon sunshine. Blending into the foot traffic, she could hardly believe that they had spent so much time in the library. It was almost five o'clock, and people jammed the sidewalks and cafés for drinks before dinner.

Taking their iced frappaccinos to the nearest table, Denise said, "This won't take long, Tom. Since you're not officially assigned to this case, I'd like you to do me a favor and get the specifics on the poisons that killed the three senators. It'll take us forever to get the information through these carefully controlled channels. You might be able to use some of your contacts and get the information for us a lot faster. Will you do that for me, Tom?" Denise queried as she sipped her refreshing drink.

"Sure. It'll take me a little while, but I should be able

to find someone who knows. Actually, there's a guy at the CDC who might be willing to snoop a bit," Tom replied with confidence.

"You're a lifesaver. By the way, did you present our evidence at the Harrison hearing?"

"Yeah, but he got off. Don't worry, Dory, we'll catch him again. Next time the videotape will be clearer," Tom replied as he drained his cup.

"That's a tough break," Denise commented with a sad shake of her head. "We thought we had him. How did the captain take the news?"

"No problem. He understood. Well, I guess this means that I'm not going to see you for a day or two. I'll be back as soon as I have the information," Tom commented with a trace of sorrow in his voice.

"If I didn't know you better I'd say that you either missed me or that you're making polite conversation. Either way, I'll milk it for all I can get," Denise replied, smiling sweetly into Tom's gloomy face.

"Whatever," Tom muttered, ashamed that she had read his emotions so easily.

"If it means anything, I've missed you. There's something about starting the day with an old grouch that warms my heart and gets my engine all revved up," Denise teased as she laid her hand on his.

"Okay, Dory, cut the mushy stuff. Yeah, I missed you. You're the best partner I ever had. Okay? . . ," Tom replied with distress at having to admit his feelings, however briefly.

Tossing her cup into the trash and heading out the door, Denise said, "If that's the best you can do, I'll let you off the hook this time. You're a good man. If there's a way to get the test results, you'll do it. I'll see you in a few days. I'm going back to the Capitol. I need the addresses of any groups that might have made previous threats against members of the Senate. I'm sure the police will have the information."

"I'll get in touch as soon as I know something," Tom said.

"I'll be waiting," Denise replied, watching him turn the corner and vanish out of sight.

Already Washington seemed dull without him. Shrugging her shoulders, Denise prepared for another evening without Tom. With luck, the investigation would keep her too busy to miss him. She only hoped that he would return quickly.

Denise was right about the Capitol police knowing the identity of agitators. Captain Carter with the help of the FBI maintained a file cabinet with information on hundreds of known pranksters, letter writers, and potentially dangerous types. However, he was reluctant to share the information. His hesitation confirmed her belief that, because of either suspicion or jealousy, he had been the one to place the monitoring equipment in their rooms.

Speaking slowly and carefully to keep her impatience in check, Denise explained, "We need to interview members of these groups to find out if they have any idea who might have murdered the senators. Unless we do, we'll have to consider that all of the members of the Senate are in danger and take steps to protect all of them."

"I share your concern for the welfare of the senators, Detective Dory, but I do not know if the powers-that-be have given you and the other detectives the necessary clearance to enable me to turn over these files to you. I will need to check with Senator Salermo. However, at the moment, he and the other senators are in a very

important meeting," Captain Carter replied with his
hands folded resolutely over his chubby stomach.

Feeling her frustration peak, Denise replied, "I think
for this you can interrupt them. It won't take but a minute for Senator Salermo to give his consent."

"I am sorry, Detective, but he left strict instructions
that he did not wish to be interrupted for any reason. I
will have the information for you by noon tomorrow. It
is too late tonight for you to do anything now anyway,"
the captain replied with a smile that Denise could tell he
normally reserved for irritating children.

"But I need the information tonight so that I can get
an early start in the morning," Denise protested as he
took her by the elbow and led her to the door.

"Tomorrow," Captain Carter repeated as he closed
the door behind her after giving the front of her white
blouse a lingering gaze.

Denise heard the click of the lock as she stood in the
humid evening air. Almost everyone had gone home for
the day. The usually congested streets appeared strangely
still.

Muttering to herself, Denise decided, "I'll try my old
contact at the FBI. They probably have the same information."

Deciding not to go alone, Denise stopped by the conference room long enough to phone her contact and
drag Richard into the streets of Washington. Although
reluctant to locate information at this hour, he agreed
to accompany her. He had spent a rather uneventful
afternoon briefing the others in their party and interviewing uncooperative senators.

"What makes you think that the FBI will give us any
more information?" Richard asked as he hailed the cab
that would take them across downtown Washington.
"They've already provided us with some pretty good

preliminary information. They might be as close-mouthed as the Capitol police for any detail."

"Maybe, but my friend loves to unlock puzzles. He might uncover more," Denise replied as the cab flew through the streets with the speed of a New York cabbie.

Flinging the door open after they had stopped, Richard commented, "This might be a wild-goose chase."

"Maybe, but it's worth the effort," Denise called over her shoulder.

Running up the steps beside her, Richard puffed, "Are you sure we need this information tonight? We'll have to verify it anyway. Couldn't we have waited until tomorrow morning?"

"You're sounding like Captain Carter," Denise stated with a chuckle as she pushed open the door.

"Do you run Tom around town like this?"

"Sure, only worse. He's used to it by now." Denise laughed, thinking of the expression that always played across Tom's face whenever she suggested one of these late night treks.

A man in shirtsleeves walked across the ornate marble foyer to greet them. Shaking their hands, he asked, "What can I do for you at this late hour, Denise? It's been a while since you've asked me for information. I was beginning to think that you'd found another source."

"I'd never forget you, George," Denise replied with a mischievous grin. "I've been able to solve a few easy cases without your expert help. However, I'm on a particularly tough one now. Do you think you can get me the names and addresses of the leaders of the major political factions operating in D.C.? By my count, four are especially active. Two are currently working toward the repeal of abortion and stronger gun control laws. The third group wants a change in Social Security. The last one advocates no change despite stock market fluctuations."

"Denise, contrary to what you think, I don't keep that kind of information sitting in a file cabinet. It'll take me several hours to pull it together for you. It's not that I can't get it, it's just that it's late and my sources have gone home for the evening. I'm only here because you asked me to stay. Unfortunately, the best I can do on such short notice will be ten o'clock tomorrow. If you return at that time, I'll have everything you want," George Christian replied with confidence in his staff.

"But you don't understand, George. If I don't have that information tonight, I will lose considerable investigative time in the morning. Are you sure there's nothing you can do for me this evening? I'd be more than happy to help run the program," Denise begged, trying to play on their long years of friendship.

"I'm sorry, Denise, but it's just not possible. I'd do it for you tonight if I could, but I just can't access the information at this hour. Security would arrest all of us before you could leave the building. My hands are tied," George replied as he walked with Denise and Richard to the door.

With a deep sigh, Denise replied as they left the cool of the building, "If I have no other choice, I'll just have to live with it. I'll see you tomorrow morning."

Climbing into the taxi for the ride to the Capitol, Denise reluctantly conceded defeat. "Well, if I can't work on this project, I'll go out after dinner to find a florist shop or a pharmacy open somewhere in this busy city. Maybe someone can give me some suggestions about the poisons. I think my first stop will be the Botanical Gardens."

"Would you mind terribly if I didn't go with you? I have painful corns on my feet and need to soak them,"

Richard said as they approached the Capitol with the Botanical Gardens only a few blocks in the distance.

"No problem, I'm fine alone. I'll let you know what I discover." Denise smiled into Richard's relieved face. "However, Tom would have been able to stick with me."

Chuckling as he waved goodbye, Richard said, "He's a better man than I am. I'm way past my sitting-down time. See you later, Denise."

As Denise passed the gate, she watched as a flower truck pulled into the drive. The officer returned her greeting without taking his eyes from the identity papers of the deliveryman who brought the latest shipment. Denise noted the name and address of the nursery in her sketchbook.

As soon as the officer was free, Denise stepped forward and asked, "Good evening, Sergeant Johnson, I was wondering if you could tell me the location of the nursery that just delivered the flowers. Is it far from here?"

Sergeant Johnson replied, "That's an easy one. Although the truck says Morgan's florist, the flowers come from the Botanical Gardens. A new exhibit opens tomorrow. We always get the excess flowers. Not a bad deal. If you hurry, you might be able to see the display before it opens. It's pretty good for flowers. I took the wife to see it last year. She liked it; I prefer car shows."

"Thank you, Sergeant. I'll take a look," Denise said as she hurried toward the big glass greenhouse that contained some of the most fabulous permanent floral displays in the country.

The sweet perfume of flowers in full bloom greeted Denise as she entered the Botanical Gardens. The display of colors and textures was as overwhelming as the mixture of fragrances. Despite Denise's love of flowers and the abundance of orchids and African violets that bloomed in her home, she was in awe of the skill and patience exhibited by the botanists whose flowers augmented the skillfully created displays of the Botanical Gardens. Armed with the name of the curator, she eased toward his office, deep in the splendor of the blooms.

"Doctor Piper, I am Detective Dory on special assignment to the Capitol investigating the murders of the senators. I'd like a few minutes of your time. I'm sure you're busy with an exhibit scheduled to open tomorrow, but I need your help," Denise explained as she showed him her Montgomery County Police Department badge and her Capitol identity card.

Dr. Piper replied with a quizzical smile, "I'd be more than happy to do anything I can. And as for disturbing me, this is probably the best possible time. Everything is go for tomorrow, and I can actually breathe easy for the first time in weeks. What can I do for you?"

"I need a crash course in plant toxins. I know that there are many that are indigenous to this area. Could almost anyone have access to them? Are there people in the D.C. area who grow them as a hobby?" Denise asked as she studied the gentleman whose desk was cluttered with photos, reference books, and rooting plants.

"You're asking for specifics that are over my head. You see, I specialize in plant ecology. All I can tell you is that many flowers can be poisonous in the hands of the right person. The rose, apple, and peach contain poisonous seeds. The onion, garlic, amaryllis, and tulip can produce convulsions, dizziness, and cardiac arrest if ingested in large doses. The great Greek philosopher drank a brew of hemlock, a deadly poisonous herb of the carrot, parsley, and parsnip family," Dr. Piper replied patiently.

"I had no idea that so many ordinarily benign plants and flowers could be poisonous. I suppose I thought mostly of the hallucinogenic effects of eating certain mushrooms," Denise replied as she realized the far-reaching extent of her search.

"Yes, I suppose most people have read *Alice in Wonderland* and know the power of the magic mushroom. I assume that there are people who practice herbal medicine or have read Shakespeare's plays. If I'm not mistaken, he mentions mandrake roots in *Romeo and Juliet*. Even the friar was an apothecary who grew his own medicinal herbs," Dr. Piper commented as he studied her closely.

"I had forgotten about that. I certainly hope that fewer people are engaged in growing medicinal herbs today than in the sixteenth century. The success of my investigation depends on having to question a relatively small number of people," Denise replied as she returned his honest, friendly gaze.

"For your sake, I hope that the number is small. However, a botanist with a specialty in either morphology or pathology would be able to provide you with more information and perhaps even the names of practicing herbalists. I will give you the name of an associate of mine. Just one minute, please," Dr. Piper offered as he vanished into an office hidden behind an incredibly tall and robust parrot plant.

In his absence, Denise took a minute to look around his immense office. Every imaginable flower bloomed in lovely vases, filled glass-front refrigerators, and clustered at the tops of thriving potted plants. Each flower was more beautiful than the last. The fragrance clung to her skin and lined her nose like the dust that lingered on the corpse of the deceased senator.

"I hope I haven't kept you waiting too long. Here's my colleague's name and address. Just show him my card, and he will assist you in any way he can. He maintains an extensive laboratory adjacent to his home in addition to his duties at Maryland University. I phoned him to say that he should expect you soon, tomorrow if you're free," Dr. Piper stated as he handed her Dr. John Nester's name and address neatly printed on the back of his card.

"I appreciate your kindness, Doctor Piper. I will definitely keep that appointment. Before I leave, I was wondering if you know the driver who delivered flowers to the U.S. Capitol this evening," Denise inquired as she walked toward the door.

"The U.S. Capitol is one of our largest customers. We regularly transport flowers to the offices, delivering as many as three trucks of flowers at a time if a special event is about to take place. The drivers place the boxes of flower spikes in a special refrigerator. By morning, the buds will be of a perfect size to decorate the offices and special tables. Tonight, we transported all of the unused plants and flowers from this exhibit to the Capitol. The exhibitors had brought more than they needed," Dr. Piper replied as he lightly took her elbow and escorted her onto the sidewalk.

"Are you a hobbyist?" Denise asked curiously.

"In my own way, I do what I can. However, my time is limited by the demands of running the gardens. If you have time, you should visit the local nurseries that are scattered all over the D.C. area. You'll find the Fleet Nursery a font of botanical knowledge. They're one of the biggest flower suppliers in the area . . . specializing in large quantities for churches," Dr. Piper responded as he smiled tiredly.

"Would it be possible for anyone to tamper with the flowers or to mix a poisonous one among the perfect blooms?" Denise asked as they lingered in the evening air.

Tapping his fingers together, Dr. Piper replied without hesitation, "It's possible, but it would have to have been done by someone with access to the flowers after the nurserymen deliver them. You see, the Fleet Nursery is a family business. They're all very proud of their reputation as the best nursery in the D.C. area and would do nothing to risk it. Mr. Fleet's sons and nephews maintain the warehouse and drive the delivery trucks. What they don't grow themselves, they order from reputable suppliers who deliver directly to them. They inspect every delivery personally to insure that only the best buds arrive. I have seen them turn away entire cargoes of damaged flowers. No, if someone were to tamper with the flowers, the incident would have to take place once the flowers arrive in the Capitol."

"You've been most helpful, Doctor Piper. I'd better let you lock up. Good luck with the exhibition tomorrow," Denise said as she shook his hand.

"Come back anytime," Dr. Piper replied as he stifled a yawn. "I'll be more than happy to help you in any way. Don't forget your appointment tomorrow."

"Don't worry. I'll be there. Good night." Denise waved as she walked the short distance to the Capitol grounds.

While she was out, someone had taken a phone message and slipped it under the door to her room. Smiling, Denise walked to the telephone and dialed the familiar number. She had planned to phone him as soon as she returned. She had much to share with her old partner.

"Tom, it's Denise. Any news?" she asked, slipping off her shoes and stretching full length on her little bed.

"Not yet, but I should know something tomorrow. My contact at the CDC needs until the morning to gather the information. Anything new on your end?" Tom replied with his usual mixture of interest and boredom.

"I just left the curator of the Botanical Gardens," Denise answered. "He wasn't too much help, but he has made a good contact for me. Any chance you can join me in the morning?"

"Sure. I'm still on leave," Tom agreed. "Call forwarding will take care of the message from my CDC contact. What's up? Why not take old Richard, your new partner?"

Chuckling at Tom's attempt to hide his jealousy at being replaced by another man, Denise replied, "It's plain and simple; I need you. Besides, Richard's feet give out too fast. He complains all the time about his arches and corns."

"All right. What'll we do?" Tom said as he tried to disguise his happiness at working with Denise again.

Their separation had not been long, but Tom's time away from Denise had seemed like an eternity. He would never admit it, but she had been on his mind constantly. He had missed the daily annoying pranks she played on him. Tom had eaten his lunch at his desk rather than at their regular restaurant because he could not stand the idea of sitting across the table from an empty chair. He had gone to bed early to escape the loneliness of not having their nightly phone conversation.

Enjoying the affection in Tom's voice, Denise said, "I want to examine the refrigeration in which they store the flowers that the florist delivered tonight. The others checked out the main kitchen but found nothing. Perhaps we should broaden the scope of our investigation to include outsiders. I thought we might visit the Fleet Nursery although I'm sure the Capitol Hill police have investigated the company thoroughly."

Offering another angle, Tom suggested, "It might be a good idea to check every corner of the Capitol itself and meet the people who work there. I think you're right in assuming that someone on the staff committed the murders. If the others wouldn't mind, I'd like to interview as many of them as possible myself."

"I'm sure they won't mind," Denise stated with confidence. "We have so many angles to investigate and not enough hands to do it. Even if every state had responded to the call for help, I don't think we'd have enough people. The murderer might not even live in this area. He might travel from, say, Wisconsin to do the deed and then leave. This case has the potential to become a nationwide manhunt."

"Let's hope it doesn't extend that far," Tom commented sleepily. "You'd have to call in the FBI if it does. Anyway, the captain wouldn't let you stay away from the office indefinitely."

"What about you?" Denise asked softly. "Would you miss me if I didn't return for a few months? Let's just say we called in the FBI, and they wanted some of us to stay on the case. Would you miss me?"

Snorting softly, Tom answered, "Yeah, I'd miss you. I'd probably have to break in a new partner if you were gone that long. Maybe even find a new home for this cat of yours."

Laughing gently, Denise replied, "You know as well as I do that no one would have you or that cat as a partner. I'm the only soft touch in the world. We're destined to be together forever."

"Forever? That's a long time, but I guess I could handle that," Tom commented softly in the voice that Denise recognized as the closest thing to an expression of affection that he could muster.

"I guess it's not such a bad idea," Denise almost whispered. "We're already used to each other . . . know each other's quirks. It's not such a bad way to spend eternity."

Clearing his throat, Tom responded, "I'll see you tomorrow. Let's meet at the restaurant on First Street at nine. Sleep well, Denise."

"Good night, my dear friend," Denise replied as she hung up the phone.

Sliding between the covers, Denise reflected on the success of her evening. For the first time since arriving at the Capitol, she felt as if she was truly making progress and doing investigative work. Denise enjoyed the thrill of discovery and sensed that she was moving in the right direction in her pursuit of information. She was ready for the challenge of new avenues to explore. Having Tom by her side would make the job even better. They had come so close to admitting the feelings that they would not share. Perhaps the change of scenery would help their personal life, too.

EIGHT

Following breakfast, Denise and Tom visited the flower-arranging room that housed the special refrigerator in which the Fleet driver had deposited the order of flowers. Already workers toiled at arranging the blossoms in vases to decorate the nooks and tables. The workers quickly pulled out the wilting flowers and replaced them with fresh blossoms that would open in the warmth of the Capitol.

Mr. Philips greeted them enthusiastically and graciously assumed the responsibility of answering their questions. Leading the way, he showed Denise and Tom the refrigerator in which the flowers passed the night. Cool air washed over them as soon as he opened the door. Buckets and vases of cut flowers, pots of growing plants in bloom, and boxes of greenery covered tables and lined the walls. The fragrance was almost overwhelming as the roses competed with the orchids and the jasmines tried to outdo the lilies.

Walking among the flower arrangers, Denise inquired, "Is your staff composed entirely of volunteers?"

"Mostly, although for special occasions we use paid help. The people you see here have specialized skills that they need for these particular arrangements," Mr. Philips answered with a proud smile.

"Why do they wear gloves?" Tom asked as he quietly blew his nose.

Mr. Philips replied, "Some of them have allergies to the plants, others want to keep from getting green stains on their hands, but most of them wear them to protect the plants and flowers from the salt and oils in the skin in the hopes of making them last longer."

"Do they work at this pace every day?" Denise inquired as they surveyed the vast array of blossoms that the people had already turned into gorgeous sprays and noted the amount that still lay ahead of them.

"When we need to decorate for a special occasion they do. We're getting ready for the senators' wake," Mr. Philips responded with awe in his voice for the workers who skillfully arranged the flowers that added their beauty to the Capitol.

Pulling his jacket closer, Tom commented, motioning to the storage refrigerator, "It's rather brisk in there. I know the flowers need it that way to stay fresh, but how do the people stand it?"

"I suppose they have become acclimated to the temperature change. It's really not that cool. It just feels that way since you were recently outside. The other thought is that they're wearing long underwear that they peel off before going home." Mr. Philips chuckled gaily.

"How many people are assigned to this job? Can twenty people handle all of the work?" Denise inquired as she quickly sketched the workers. Their heads bobbed over the tight blossoms as if they were one with the flowers. No one had looked up since she and Tom entered the room.

"This is our usual complement of volunteers for a special event. We need fewer people on a regular day. However, others of us are trained to do the work and substitute in case of illness when we're preparing for an event. Fortunately, that rarely happens. They are a very hearty group of people. Of course, they can always go to their list of part-time help if necessary. You should have seen the troupe of people in here while we were decorating for the last inaugural luncheon," Mr. Philips replied.

For a few minutes Denise and Tom watched in silence as the flowers and ferns changed from a mass of blooms into breathtaking arrangements. As they watched, an elderly woman with a cart returned for more pots of forsythias. She fleetingly looked up at them and gave a brief smile before turning her attention to gathering another load. When she had finished, she left as silently as she had arrived.

"I think I've seen her arranging flowers in the Capitol," Denise commented as Mr. Philips led them along the hallway.

"You probably did. She's Mrs. Benedict and is our oldest volunteer at eighty-five years of age. She has been in this job for five years. She can hardly see over her ever-present cart, she's so shrunken with age, but she's here every day. Her husband passed away, leaving her without anything to do. She decided to volunteer here," Mr. Philips responded with pride for Mrs. Benedict's dedication to her work.

"Do you think you could arrange for me to interview her?" Denise requested. "She might have seen something during her rounds of the Capitol."

"I can arrange it, but Mrs. Benedict's a very private person. She probably didn't see anything. Mrs. Benedict comes here and works without wasting any time. It is not likely that she noticed anything not directly related to her task."

"Just the same, she might have seen something that jarred her sensibilities," Denise stated with appreciation for his devotion to his employees. She watched as Mrs. Benedict quickly replaced the wilted flowers with fresh ones.

"Okay. I'll arrange an interview tomorrow, if possible. If you don't need me any longer, I'll leave you to explore on your own." Mr. Philips reluctantly waved as he walked down the hall.

The light streamed through the windows, illuminating the ceiling of the Capitol. Already at just a little past nine-thirty people were waiting patiently to enter the Capitol. The police checked bags and turned away anyone who looked suspicious.

The heat beat down on Denise and Tom as they walked toward the office of the U.S. Capitol police. As promised, Captain Carter handed her an envelope containing the identities and the addresses for each of the activist groups. As she and Tom left to pick up information from their FBI colleague before their interview with the Social Security reformists, the other detectives went on their rounds of questioning. They had plans to question members of the U.S. Capitol police itself and the laundry staffs, the senators' staffers, and anyone else who might have had access to the senators. Richard was happy to lead the inside group and leave the legwork to Denise and Tom.

"Let's catch a cab," Tom stated as the sweat poured down his forehead and into his eyes.

"No way," Denise replied without breaking her pace. "We're almost there. It's only another three blocks. You're not getting soft, are you, Tom? I don't want another Richard on my hands."

"That's what you said twenty minutes ago, Dory. I made the mistake of believing you then, but I won't this time," Tom griped as he opened the neck of his shirt.

"This time it's the truth," Denise chuckled. "See? There it is."

The imposing redbrick structure rose up and filled

the block. FBI employees scurried from one office to another. After obtaining their pass from the guards, Denise and Tom were free to wander as they chose.

As they entered George Christian's office, he smiled and said, "Nice to see you, folks. I have the information you wanted right here. If this isn't exactly what you want, come back and I'll try again."

"Thanks, George. I hope I can return the favor one day," Denise replied as she scanned the sheets of paper. "I would say that you've been most thorough, as always."

Leaving the FBI office, they entered the nearest coffee shop and ordered iced drinks. Spreading the papers on the table in front of them, they studied the addresses and plotted them on the map George Christian had given them. Most locations were close to the Capitol and would have been an easy walk on a cool day.

Comparing the information from the FBI with that of the U.S. Capitol police, Denise said, "Do you think there's any significance in the proximity of the headquarters of these groups to the U.S. Capitol?"

"I thought about that myself, Denise, but I think it is probably coincidence that the Social Security activists have an office within the shortest walk of the Capitol," Tom replied as they studied the more distant locations of the other three groups.

"Let's start with them. Maybe we'll see something that will give us a clue to the murderer," Denise suggested as they finished their drinks and gathered their information.

Quickly retracing their steps, they arrived at First Street that ran perpendicular to the Capitol. From the corner, Denise could see Union Station only a few blocks away. Tom, however, was more interested in the pub on the corner.

Climbing the dark stairway that led up a steep flight

of stairs, Denise and Tom came to the suite of offices occupied by the Social Security reformists. Entering, they were immediately welcomed by a robust gentleman in navy-blue slacks and white shirt rolled up at the cuffs and unbuttoned at the collar. He smiled as he called from his desk, "Good morning! Hot enough for you?"

"Good morning," Denise replied to the usual Washington D.C. summertime greeting.

"Ah, Americans! Welcome, come in. My name is Forest Houseman. How may I help you?" he said as he rounded the corner with outstretched hands.

"We're Detectives Phyfer and Dory. We're part of the team that's investigating the deaths of the senators. We'd appreciate a little of your time if that's possible."

"Of course, I'll make time for you. Their deaths sounded suspicious to me. What can I do to help?" Mr. Houseman replied as he motioned toward the sitting area in the bright, spacious office.

"I'm a bit confused," Tom said as he scanned the room for any signs of printing materials. "I thought you published a newsletter here. I don't see any equipment. Have I been misled?"

Speaking proudly, Mr. Houseman responded, "We are very high tech on a modest budget and produce the *Social Security Tribune* on computer disk with all of our work originating from this office. A local printer runs off the copies for us. I have the latest edition right here. I can give you a copy, if you'd like."

"Thank you. It'll be very informative. We're following up possible leads and would like to understand the purpose of your group and its association with the Capitol more fully. Could you explain, please, exactly what it is that your organization does?" Denise asked as she pulled out her sketchbook and pencil.

"I'd be very happy to help any way I can," Mr. Houseman replied. "I am the president and founder of an organization that lobbies on the Hill for Social Security reform. We recently conducted a letter-writing campaign that covered every state and gathered over forty thousand signatures from people in favor of reform. This outpouring is in addition to the more than four million letters or one hundred thousand per month that the Capitol has received over the last few years. Our hope is that our effort will convince the Hill that Social Security needs an overhaul."

"If your campaign is successful, doesn't it mean that the retirement pension of millions of people will change and maybe not for the better?" Denise queried as she quickly sketched Mr. Houseman's expressive face.

"You have asked a very important question. Let me answer as fully as I can. First, people are desperately afraid that Social Security will cease to exist. Second, today's workforce is larger than ever and will work longer than anyone anticipated. Third, workers will pay more into the system than previous generations and have the most to lose by allowing it to remain unchanged. It's time for a change," Mr. Houseman explained clearly as if he had recited the information many times.

"What impact will this have on retirees who rely on Social Security as their main source of income?" Denise asked as she flipped the sheet and began a new sketch.

"They'll have to trust their government to take care of them. The changes we've proposed won't be so sweeping that people will immediately starve to death. Those on Social Security will experience little if any impact on their lives. The next generation to retire would likely feel only the slightest change," Mr. Houseman replied with candor.

"How can you guarantee that people will not go hungry?" Tom queried carefully. "The young workers have more than enough time to begin saving, but the fifty-year-olds have counted on Social Security to make up for the money that's not part of their pension pack-ages."

Shaking his head slowly, Mr. Houseman replied, "We have conducted extensive studies that show the lack of impact on people's bottom line. We've already begun to educate the young that they shouldn't count on Social Security for retirement. Many companies offer plans that actually downplay the effect of Social Security on retirement planning. I don't foresee any problems."

As Denise sketched, Tom again asked a question, "Many have proposed allowing people to withdraw their Social Security benefits or at least manage the invest-ment of them. What's your group's opinion?"

"We're in favor of allowing people limited access to their funds," Mr. Houseman replied. "We'd like to see a smorgasbord of investment opportunities from which people might select. We don't favor total access to the funds, but we do want people to be able to move the money to other investment opportunities on the preap-proved list."

Casting a quick glance at Denise, Tom asked, "Do you think that it would be possible for any of the reformists in your group to go so far as to murder senators to insure the passing of these changes?"

With a deep sigh, Mr. Houseman replied, "As with any movement, there are those who have become impa-tient and might decide to take matters into their own hands. I prefer to believe that no one in our fellowship would commit such heinous crimes. However, anything is possible. Any number of individuals might prefer to take action than to sit back and wait for Social Security to die a slow death."

Rising, Denise gathered her things and handed him the card bearing the telephone number to the confer-ence room. Picking up the last of her pencils, she said,

"I'd like to thank you for your help. If you think of anything that we should know, I would appreciate a call at this number,"

"I hope I've been of some help to you. If I hear anything that might lead you to find the murderer, I'll give you a call," Mr. Houseman replied as he held the door.

The sun shone brightly as they stepped from the stairway into the light. Turning to Denise, Tom stated, "I could easily see that someone from his organization might commit murder to advance the cause of reform. He was certainly caught up in his work. Imagine devoting your time to a cause with this much potential for affecting so many people's lives."

"That's probably what our colleagues will discover during their interviews, too. I have a feeling that we'll become very knowledgeable in the reformist groups active on the Hill but come no closer to finding the killer even after all this work," Denise commented as they strolled away.

"Where are we going? The Capitol's behind us. It's lunchtime. Aren't you hungry?" Tom asked as he pointed in the opposite direction to which they were walking.

"We're going to see a botanist whose laboratory is only a few blocks from here . . . near the Folger Shakespeare Library. He's an expert on plant toxins. I'll treat you to an ice cream when we finish," Denise answered with a chuckle.

"I'll need more than an ice cream after all this walking. I can feel my stomach hitting my backbone already," Tom complained as he trudged beside her.

Unlike the clean, bright office of the Social Security reformists, the botanist lab was dark with only pockets of sunshine that tried to shed light on the gloom. Mustysmelling mushrooms grew in flats on tall shelves. Their bright colors and the pure white of the young growths belied the poison in their nature. In an adjacent room, flowering plants raised their heads to the sunshine that penetrated the strategically positioned skylights. Their sweet fragrances made a heady combination with the mist and humidity.

A loud bell rang as they entered. A voice from the back of the lab called, "Yes?" Dr. John Nester immediately appeared with a plant in each hand. From the dirt on his lab coat and the smudge on his forehead, it did not look as if he was expecting company.

"Doctor Nester, I am Detective Dory and this is Detective Phyfer. I called earlier to confirm an appointment to see you," Denise said loudly into the light-speckled darkness.

"Ah, yes, the detectives working on the unfortunate murders of the senators. Come in," Dr. Nester replied with a bright smile on his dirty face. "Excuse me for not shaking your hand but, under the circumstances, I think you'll understand. Please, follow me to my office. I'm in the process of repotting these, and their roots are very fragile."

Stepping carefully over the wet boards that served as a pathway, Denise and Tom followed Dr. Nester to his office where the clutter of plants almost obscured the top of his desk and littered the two rickety chairs. Dirt, leaves, blooms, and notebooks covered every surface.

Turning with a helpless shrug, Dr. Nester said, "As you can see, I do not have many visitors."

"No problem, sir. We'll stand," Tom replied as a large worm crawled across the toe of his shoe.

"How may I help you? I hope you don't mind if we talk while I work. These species are at their prime and my data depends on exact timing," Dr. Nester said as he busied himself in making slides from carefully scraped segments of root and leaves.

"As I explained over the telephone, we hope that

you'll be able to shed some light on our investigations by helping us understand the nature of toxins. We know that the senators all died from some kind of poisoning. I was hoping that you might be able to help us understand some of the other ways in which someone might succumb to poison," Denise restated as she sketched the botanist in the setting of his laboratory.

"Very good likeness," Dr. Nester replied as he peered over the top of her notebook. "First, let me tell you that there are many kinds of poison, natural and synthetic. I am a specialist in the ones that come from nature. Every plant in this laboratory can be lethal. Some require that the victim ingest a large quantity of the substance. Others are potent in incredibly small amounts that break down in the stomach very quickly when thrown into contact with the appropriate enzymes. Still another group is so toxic that I do not handle them or come near them without wearing a mask, gloves, and disposable jacket."

"Would it be possible for you to give us a brief course on these plants?" Tom asked.

"Of course, but it will indeed be brief. It would take me years to tell you all the complexities of and interactions among these poisons. It is sufficient, I think, that you understand that they are highly lethal and widely available. Everything you see growing in this lab, you can grow in your kitchen with the correct light and moisture. That is what makes these plants and their poisons so deadly. Anyone can misuse them. People think that they are experts on herbal medicines and overdose on these plants all the time. I am called to the hospitals almost daily to help them with an antidote. Unfortunately, I am usually too late," Dr. Nester explained over his glasses. He was a relatively young man but stooped from years of bending his tall frame over the slides he so lovingly prepared.

"These mushrooms look like the ones I ate on my salad last night," Tom interjected with a quick shiver.

"I assure you, Detective, that you would not be standing here now if you had ingested a quantity of the assortment on that tray. That one is the *Amanita virosa* and is so deadly that I would not think of touching it with my bare hands. That is why it is under the glass dome. I am conditioned not to touch anything I cover without taking the necessary precautions first," Dr. Nester explained without looking up from his microscope for more than a second.

"Explain the symptoms of poisoning by this one, please, Doctor," Denise asked as she sketched the fungus.

"What you see there is the *Amanitas* in its button stage, which is why it looks so much like the common salad mushroom. However, let me assure you that it is definitely uncommon in its lethal effects, which is why they call it the 'destroying angel.' As little as thirty grams or half a mushroom cap is fatal to a healthy person. According to the papers, several of the senators were elderly and in poor health; therefore, a smaller amount could have killed them. The onset of illness usually takes about ten hours and the patient often lingers for as long as ten days. Again in the case of the senators, the duration of their illness would have been much shorter but no less severe. The toxin produces abdominal pain as well as liver, kidney, and circulatory system failure. The poison is fatal with no known antidote. It is a dreadful death with much suffering. When I arrive at a hospital and discover that the patient has consumed these mushrooms, I immediately call a priest," Dr. Nester replied sadly.

"Must the victim ingest the mushroom?" Tom asked as he put more space between himself and the mushroom regardless of the protective dome.

"That's the usual method because of people's tendency to harvest them accidentally along with the harmless varieties. However, considering its potency and the fact that touching it can also lead to death, I usually advise people to avoid any contact with these particularly lethal fungi. As you can see, in their button stage it is difficult to differentiate them from salad mushrooms, a fact undoubtedly known by those who use them for their poisonous quality," Dr. Nester responded as he continued to study his slides.

"Are any of the other plants or fungi in this collection as deadly?" Denise asked, looking through the dirty office window at the myriad species that grew in abundance in the dank lab.

"Hemlock was the poison of choice of the ancient Greeks and is still very effective. Socrates chose it as what he called a 'humane' form of execution. Its leaves look much like parsley, carrots, or parsnips, and the tiny white flowers have attractive purple spots. It causes a severe depression of the nervous system, paralysis, and death. However, it does give off a very strong almond smell that the murderer would have to camouflage. It's possible that someone would use it to poison the senators, but I doubt it. The lady's slipper orchid has a nasty little kick to it, if you'll excuse my tasteless pun. No, I think that mushrooms or perhaps plants containing alkaloids such as mandrake would be my guess," Dr. Nester replied as he scribbled notes in a diary and selected another slide for examination.

"Doctor Piper, the florist who referred us to you, mentioned mandrake also. Tell me about it, please," Denise requested as she watched his long, thin fingers carefully snip and scrape a section of leaf.

"It's growing over there in the purple pot." Dr. Nester indicated by gesturing with his pen at a cluster of feathery leaves that grew in a pot outside the office door. "Its foliage is similar to that of carrot or hemlock, but its curvaceous root suggesting a woman's figure is what lent it wide appeal in literature. Many believed that it was an aphrodisiac or love potion although its medicinal and poisonous properties have been known for centuries. We believe that the early Egyptians used the plant as a sedative. Its scientific name is *Solanaceae*. The poisonous plant belladonna has possibilities. Surprisingly, the simple potato, eggplant, and tomato belong to the same family, which might account for allergic reactions to these foods. Do you know with any certainty that the senators died as the result of poisoning from natural compounds? Could the poison have been synthetic?"

"We don't have the lab report yet, unfortunately. All we know with any certainty is that they were poisoned with a substance that they neither ingested nor injected," Tom replied as he wrapped his arms more closely around his body as if to keep the plants from reaching out to touch him.

Straightening, Dr. Nester commented, "I would be very careful if I were you. You are obviously dealing with someone who knows quite a lot about the effects of poisons and the way to conceal their identity. If he used a natural poison, he either has a lethal garden at his disposal or knows how to identify and find these plants in the wild. He would have to know how to administer it so that its presence could neither be traced nor counteracted by antidote in the case of the lesser toxins. If he had used the *Amanita* mushroom, he is a very dangerous person indeed and capable of a very cold-blooded act. I wish you luck in finding him before someone else dies."

Closing her notebook, Denise said, "Thank you, Doctor Nester. You've provided us with much valuable information. I can tell that we'll have our work cut out for us. We'll let ourselves out. We've already taken enough of your time."

"I'm always happy to have visitors. Few people come to see me here. I think they're afraid of my plants, and perhaps they should be. Carelessness around any of these plants could lead to death. Well, goodbye. Please come to see me again," Dr. Nester called from his office door.

Breathing deeply for the first time in over an hour, Denise looked up at the birds fluttering overhead, the traffic passing noisily on the street, and the people walking blindly past on the sidewalk. Denise felt relieved to be free of the cloying smell of decay. The lab had been too much for them.

Spying an ice cream vendor on the corner, Denise turned to Tom and asked, "Are you ready for that ice cream now?"

"I'm game for anything that doesn't contain fungi or plants. That was certainly an eye-opener. I'll look at the humble mushroom with more respect from now on. It's hard to believe that something that small could be so lethal," Tom replied as they headed for the vendor.

Denise ordered and paid for their treats. "After we finish these, let's go to the nursery that Doctor Piper mentioned. Now that we've talked with Doctor Nester, I'd like to take a look around the place. Maybe we'll find something interesting among the roses," she said as she licked the rapidly melting raspberry sherbet from her fingers.

"How far out of town is it?" Tom asked, enjoying his ice cream.

"It's in Sunshine, so we'll rent a car. I remember passing it many times," Denise replied.

The drive into the lush countryside as they traveled north from D.C. offered a pleasant change from the bustle of the city. The farther they traveled into the familiar territory of Montgomery County, the more rural the setting. Fields of corn and other vegetables lined the road on either side. Pastures and farmhouses dotted the horizon. Although the traffic moved briskly along the main road, they could still enjoy the beauty of the surroundings.

They left the press of traffic behind as they turned onto a side road that led to the nursery. Periodically amid the acres of flowers they saw rows of grapevines and sprawling greenhouses. The sign on the gate read FLEET BROTHERS NURSERY. Denise pointed to the parking lot as Tom negotiated the turns that brought them to the front of the massive warehouse and greenhouse complex. Parking just beyond the first building that served as the office, they entered the humidity of the structure.

"What's that smell?" Tom asked as he covered his nose to block out the scent.

"I think it's manure or very rich commercial fertilizer," Denise replied as she sniffed the air. "I've smelled something similar to it in the Pennsylvania farmlands, especially around the Amish farms where they use natural fertilizers. It has a strange kind of sweetness to it when mixed with compost and the fragrance of flowers."

"It's disgusting," Tom remarked without the slightest indication of appreciation in his voice.

"You'll get used to it. Think of the beauty it produces rather than the smell," Denise advised as she watched Tom wipe his eyes and blow his nose.

"Let's wrap this up as soon as we can. I'll stroll the outside and leave the buildings for you. This stench is terrible," Tom said as his allergies kicked in in full force.

Before Denise could answer, a gentleman wearing boots, a soiled leather apron, and jeans emerged from the office. He had rolled up the sleeves of his red-striped shirt. On his hands he wore thick leather gloves.

He smiled and said, "Good morning. What can I do for you? I'm Robert Fleet, one of the owners."

"Good day, Mr. Fleet. We're part of the special team from the U.S. Capitol investigating the deaths of the senators. I'm Detective Dory and this is Detective Phyfer," Denise replied, giving the man's hand a hearty shake.

"You can count on me to do anything I can to help you find the killer," Robert Fleet replied sternly.

"If possible, we would appreciate a tour of your nursery, especially the area from which you regularly cut flowers for the U.S. Capitol," Denise requested as she scanned the sea of flowers that spread through the building.

"Certainly, but I can't think of anyone associated with the nursery who would do this. I have twenty-five employees and can vouch for all of them. All but three are family, and I am godfather to the children of those three," Robert Fleet stated with confidence.

"Unfortunately, we must investigate all leads that might steer us to the murderer," Tom responded as he wiped his nose vigorously.

"Very well, I'll take you on a tour of the greenhouses and the warehouse first and then we can walk through the fields. I will explain our operation as we go. I'm sure you'll see that we take too many precautions with the production of our flowers for anyone to have infiltrated our nursery," Robert Fleet offered.

"If you wouldn't mind, Mr. Fleet, I would prefer to see the fields while you and Detective Dory view the buildings. My allergies are killing me," Tom said.

"I don't blame you one bit," Robert Fleet quickly agreed. "In addition to the flowers, we use manure, compost, and chemical fertilizers. A certain amount of mold is inevitable in a place with humidity such as this. I will ask my brother to escort you on a tour of the fields. Wait a minute while I page him."

As soon as they were alone, Denise turned to Tom and said teasingly, "Poor baby! He can't stand a few little flowers. His nose is all stuffed."

Looking at her with disgust, Tom replied through the stuffiness of his nose, "Dory, one of these days you'll get yoursth. You're not very nithce."

Holding her sides against gales of laughter, Denise left Tom in the capable hands of Peter Fleet while they toured the greenhouses and warehouses. As expected the humidity was almost stifling as they walked through the rows of thriving plants. Every imaginable variety grew in abundance in the sunlight that shone through the glass ceilings. Birds, too, seemed to flourish in the warm air as they swooped and fluttered in the eaves.

"Do you grow mushrooms here, also?" Denise asked as she shaded her eyes from the bright rays.

"Oh no, Detective. We're not set up for them. Everything we cultivate here needs lots of sun to grow. Mushrooms wouldn't thrive here; they prefer shady areas."

"Would it be possible for someone to raise nightshade or hemlock among your exquisite plants either in the greenhouses or the fields?" Denise asked as she sniffed a fragrant blossom.

Clearing his throat for emphasis, Robert Fleet replied, "Anything is possible, Detective, but it's not probable. We work these rooms and the fields constantly. A weed or the seed from a wildflower could ruin our business. We're very careful here. As you can see, the rows are very neat and tidy. We use a heavy layer of compost to eliminate as many intruders as possible and to reduce the backbreaking labor of pulling weeds."

"Could anyone plant a poisonous variety in your gar-

dens without someone on your staff recognizing it?"
Denise persisted as they continued the tour.

"Again, it is possible but highly unlikely. We're intimately familiar with all the varieties of our flowers and can recognize them on sight. We should be able to identify an impostor and root him out," Robert Fleet replied with a smile at his own pun.

They walked in silence for a while as Denise took in the glory of the flowers and tried to think of anything she might have missed. Stopping to sketch the most beautiful cattleya orchid she had ever seen, Denise almost forgot that Robert Fleet stood at her side. She looked from her sketchbook to find him smiling appreciatively at her paper.

As they continued down the narrow aisle, Denise asked, "I was just wondering if someone might have gained access to the van you use to transport the flowers to the Capitol and the Botanical Gardens. Perhaps someone could have contaminated your delivery with a malicious plant of his own."

"Not possible, Detective," Robert Fleet replied emphatically. "My sons and nephews are the only drivers, and they never leave the flowers unattended. They personally load the flowers onto five carts and personally supervise their delivery to the arranging room where they store them in the refrigerators. We are very careful to insure that only the best flowers leave here and that they arrive in perfect condition.

"I'd suggest, Detective, that you not look for your killer at a large nursery," Robert Fleet said. "He would most likely be someone who cultivates his own lethal herbs. I will ask my family to meet with you individually if you wish, but I do not think that any of them could tell you anything that I haven't already."

Making the last sketches, Denise replied, "That will

not be necessary, Mr. Fleet. You have been most helpful. Thank you.''

Returning to their car, Denise and Tom waved to the brothers as they drove away. Tom looked greatly relieved to be on the open road as Denise drove on the return trip to D.C. His nose was still stuffy, but his spirits had improved greatly and he looked a little better than the last time Denise had seen him, since his eyes no longer streamed tears.

"Did you learn anything?" Denise asked as she negotiated the lanes of traffic and headed toward the Capitol.

"Nothing other than they're a very proud family with complete control over their business. From planting to distribution, the brothers and their children manage every aspect and do not delegate authority to anyone," Tom replied.

"I didn't either except that Mr. Philips helps to unload the truck every night. I'll check with him again to see if he's seen anything suspicious. I think we have time to do one more interview before dinner. What'll it be . . . the group that is involved with gun control, women's rights, or the status quo bunch?"

"If you don't mind, Dory, I'll go back to the Capitol. My sinuses are killing me. I'll find Mr. Philips and speak with him." Tom sniffed noisily.

"Okay. I'll go to see the gun-control group. Their offices are in Northern Virginia. I'll visit them and then return the car. We'll meet and exchange notes later. Use my room and take a nap if you'd like."

"I'll see Mr. Philips first and then nap. See ya. Just what I need; another building full of flowers." Tom coughed as he walked from the car.

Leaving Tom at one of the many entrances, Denise traveled through town and across the Key Bridge. She was almost glad for Tom to leave her. His sniffling and

blowing had started to get on her nerves. He always
needed extra attention when he was not feeling well,
and today, with three dead senators and the possibility
of more, she did not have the time to spend on holding
his hand. As she pulled into the group's parking lot,
Denise made a note to buy Tom a pint of chocolate ice
cream on her way back to the Page School. She hoped
that the cold sweetness would make him feel better.

NINE

The converted house stood on a quiet side street. Its walls were a dull gray stone with little in the way of ornamentation. A sturdy locked iron gate, beyond which Denise could see a lovely fountain and red begonias, separated the courtyard from the residents of the neighborhood. She pushed the button that activated a distant bell and a woman in a business suit and sensible flat heels with a thick gold cross on her lapel appeared.

Smiling, she asked, "May I help you?"

"Good afternoon. I'm Detective Dory from the U.S. Capitol's special investigative branch. I understand that your organization espouses stricter gun-control laws. I was wondering if I might have a few minutes in which to interview the organization's president."

"You're speaking to her. I'm Helen Cage. Please come in. The murders at the Capitol were very upsetting. I hope you don't think that anyone in our organization might be connected with them. I assure you that no one among us would commit such dreadful deeds. We're advocates for stricter gun control in order to improve safety, not jeopardize it."

"Ms. Cage, we have no clues as to the identity of the murderer. Since no one has come forward to claim responsibility, we must investigate everyone who might have even the slightest motive for wanting these particular senators out of the way. Unfortunately, that leads us to every outspoken special-interest group that lobbies on the Hill."

"Very well, what would you like to know about the organization?" Ms. Cage asked as she motioned to a seat facing the elegant fountain.

"I know that the membership is nationwide," Denise replied as she sketched the fountain and the flowers around it. "I'm aware that you lobby for tighter gun control regulation. What I need to find out from you is the personality makeup of your group. Are there radical members? Is the membership dissatisfied with its progress? Has there been any recent discord among the members?"

"If you're asking me if I think that anyone in the organization would murder the senators, I cannot think of anyone who would take such drastic steps to advance our cause. We've always been very peaceful in our dealings with the members of the Senate and House of Representatives. Our most aggressive act has been the mailing of thousands of petitions to our membership. In my memory, no one has voiced discontent with the leadership. Of course, in any organization there are those who want progress faster than we can make it happen, but they wouldn't do anything to ruin our chances of reform," Ms. Cage responded quickly.

"What do you mean?" Denise asked as she studied the other woman's face. Ms. Cage was thin with short dark hair and strikingly black eyes. Her face, although not beautiful, showed that in her youth she might have been stunning; whereas, now she could have been best described as handsome.

"We think that our cause will gain support from even larger numbers of people as school violence increases. As people look for a scapegoat and someone to blame other than the decline of the family, more will push for stronger gun control," Ms. Cage explained earnestly.

"Do you really think that will happen?"

Shaking her head, Ms. Cage replied, "The reasoning behind not wanting stricter gun control is that tighter controls would infringe the rights of the individual, but violence of all kinds has already done that. All we need to do is to force people to face the issues and the dreadful numbers."

"How does your organization plan to accomplish that?"

"Advertising is the key," Ms. Cage stated with assurance. "The more print and TV ads we endorse, the more people we involve in the issue. For a while there, we were preaching to the chorus, as it were. Our membership knew that this country needed to do something and soon, but we couldn't get the word out to the nonbelievers. I think our approach was too heavy-handed. We were too much like our competitor organization. We've softened our approach."

"You seem very comfortable with my questions, Ms. Cage. As the head of the association, you must be accustomed to giving interviews," Denise commented as she quickly sketched her tranquil face.

"Definitely, but they've never been in association with a murder. Although our organization often feels that we're moving very slowly, we would never condone the use of force to accomplish our goals. We have always advocated peaceful change and interaction with often stubborn bureaucrats on the Hill. With everything moving along so favorably for us now, I would hope that no one would jeopardize the success of our work."

Sitting quietly for a moment, Denise studied the fountain and the begonias before she asked, "Ms. Cage, do you grow any flowers here other than these?"

"Oh no, we're too busy for that. The wife of one of our volunteers planted them for us. I wouldn't say that she has a green thumb, but she has done well with these few plants. Fortunately, the rain and sunshine help out when she forgets to water or fertilize them," Ms. Cage replied with a little chuckle.

"Thank you, Ms. Cage, for speaking with me. I appreciate the time you've taken from your day," Denise said as she rose and closed her sketchbook.

"Any time, Detective. I hope you'll find the person responsible for the murders," Ms. Cage commented as she locked the gate behind her.

Denise returned the car and then retraced her steps until she came to the ice cream shop around the corner from the Page School. After ordering a double hand-packed rocky road for Tom and a single chocolate raspberry for herself, Denise hurried through the hot evening back to her room. She wanted to share the contents of her conversation with him. By now, he might even have news for her from the CDC.

Sadly Tom did not turn out to be the fountain of information that she had hoped. "Well, hello, Dory," he sniffed as he ate his ice cream. "I don't have much to tell you. I hope you were more successful than I was."

"I didn't turn up much either," Denise admitted, digging into her cup. "Ms. Cage doesn't think that any of her membership would resort to violence."

Reluctantly putting his ice cream down for a few minutes, Tom reported as he flipped through his notes, "My contact at the Poison Control Center division of the CDC has isolated the substance as a natural poison, meaning that it was produced from plant matter. But the botanist with the task of identifying it has not yet finalized his analysis of the blood samples that the Capitol police sent him. He refused to guess the possible identity since there are so many plants that could be poisonous without being ingested."

"When you call him back, would you ask him to search for the *Amanita* mushroom, the lady's slipper orchid, and hemlock?" Denise asked as she licked her spoon. "I have a hunch that it will turn out to be one of those or perhaps the three combined."

"Sure, but what's so special about those flowers? My mom used to grow lady's slippers in the garden and thought nothing of it," Tom asked as he scraped the bottom of the cup.

"According to the botanist, people who practice herbal medicine often use the rhizome of the lady's slipper as a tranquilizer. Some people think that the oil can paralyze the brain. As for the mushroom, well, you remember the way you felt just being in the same room with it. It's so lethal that half a cap is fatal as is any contact with the skin. And everyone knows about hemlock, although I think that it's the least likely on my list. The bitter taste and smell of almond would warn the victim before he drank it," Denise explained with a shiver at the memory of the toxin.

"I guess it would unless he liked amaretto," Tom replied.

"I'd forgotten about that drink. You're right. Well, find out what you can, please. For some reason, the Capitol did not send samples to the local botanist, who is also an expert on poison. He might have been able to solve this mystery immediately if the Capitol police had included him in the loop," Denise continued.

"I'll do what I can, you know that, Dory," Tom said with a slight chuckle. "I'd better get going. I forgot to tell you that the captain found another sucker to work with me."

"A new partner?" Denise asked quickly.

"Yeah, and her legs are even better than yours," Tom teased as he walked toward the door.

Feeling a tinge of jealousy she could not deny, Denise asked, "Does she bake brownies for you, too?"

"No, but she's hell in a game of Frisbee."

"What? What kind of cop do you know who has time to play games? Are you pulling my leg?"

Laughing his deep-in-the gut laugh that she found so infectious, Tom replied, "My new partner is a canine officer. The captain has been waiting for the opportunity to try teaming detectives with canine cops for a long time, and your absence gave him the opportunity he needed. So far, it's working out just fine."

"What kind of dog is she? Is she better housebroken than you are?" Denise asked, relieved to hear that her replacement was a four-legged female.

"She's a four-year-old-chocolate Lab and completely trained for obedience. Actually, she's much more agreeable than you are. When I say I'm ready to go, she follows. Maybe I'll keep her after the trial is over," Tom teased with a chuckle.

"Yeah, right! Just wait until her fleas get on you. You'll trade her in for your old, faithful partner in no time flat," Denise responded with a laugh.

"Why should I want to return to the old ways? This partner doesn't argue with me, and she's obedient. I couldn't ask for more." Tom continued to pick at her.

"I don't need this kind of harassment, especially after I buy you an ice cream," Denise joked. "Will I see you tomorrow?"

"I'll be here," Tom said with a smile in his usually stoic face as he left her sitting cross-legged on her bed.

Tom liked being needed by Denise. She was so self-sufficient that he often felt as if he were a third wheel. He had never been in a good work relationship before they teamed up. He enjoyed their bantering as much as she did.

Locking her room, Denise joined the others in their debriefing session. She forced her mind away from Tom and onto the material at hand. At least she would not have to wait long until his return.

Eugene and Greta began the discussion with information on the U.S. Capitol's laundry facility. Eugene stated, "Although the demand isn't really too great with only the Page School making consistent demands on their time, the laundry staff is still pretty busy. According to the supervisor of the laundry, their workload is manageable until they have to handle the table linens from a special event. During especially busy times, they operate round the clock."

"The idea that anyone could poison the laundry of one person is out of the question," Greta interjected. "They wash all the garments together. I can't envision any possible way that anyone could single out one person's clothing from another. The laundry does not appear to be the source of the poison."

Richard said, "Housekeeping spends most of its time cleaning behind the pages. They do the usual vacuuming in the offices, but that's about it. I suppose that it's possible for someone on that staff to have found a way to poison the senators, considering that they're in and out of the offices without anyone questioning them."

Interrupting him, Greta disagreed. "We examined the daily log and saw that each one of the employees had to account for every activity without exception. I don't think that it would be possible for any one of them to have the extra time it would take to introduce poison into the room. I think we should look elsewhere for the killer."

Richard rebutted, saying, "I think the staff could have found a way to deposit the poison if any of them were of the mind-set to do it. Let's look at our possibilities. Isn't it possible that while in the process of cleaning the bathroom they might rub a poisonous substance onto a lightbulb or incorporate it into the soap? I followed one of the women during her activities and discovered that she worked very quickly even with someone watching her. She knew what she had to do, and she went about the task without letting me distract her. I would think that a quick swipe with a poison-saturated cloth, a random dusting of poisonous powder, or the addition of a tasteless substance into the water pitcher would be all it would take to kill a senator."

"If such a tasteless, odorless powder exists, I might agree with you," Greta replied, "but at this point we don't know that it does."

"Neither do we know that it doesn't," Denise interjected argumentatively. "Until we do, we might want to consider all possibilities open to further investigation regardless of how remote they appear."

With a stubborn shrug, Greta commented, "If you wish to devote time to useless investigation, by all means proceed. I, however, intend to look elsewhere. Unless someone objects, I'll interrogate the Capitol police tomorrow. Perhaps one of them might remember seeing someone suspicious."

Distributing her handouts, Denise drew the attention of the others. As always, they were impressed by the charts that showed the results of the investigation of the nursery and the office of the Social Security group and her conversation with Ms. Cage. They listened attentively as she shared her findings.

As they scanned the sheets, Denise said, "In terms of ranking the suspects, I'd place the association for the repeal of women's rights behind the Social Security reformists and an amateur botanist with skill in cultivating poisonous plants who believes that he is the champion of a cause. As you can see from the chart, there are many natural substances readily available in the woods of D.C. that could kill a man. The killer could obtain anything that isn't indigenous to the area quite easily over the Internet or from friends in neighboring states and grow the crop in his basement, closet, or backyard garden."

Richard added, "We are dealing with someone who is either very skilled via education in the powers of poisons or through dedication to a hobby. If the person is a scientist who has concocted a chemical compound, we will be able to isolate the components more easily than if the person is a botanist who relies on natural organisms to assemble his poison."

Denise added with a gesture of futility, "Unfortunately, in dealing with the elderly senators, no one thought that their complaints of stomachache were serious ailments and, therefore, no one suspected poison. If the physicians had consulted with a botanist, he would have been able to identify the substance in the senators' blood although it is unlikely that an antidote would have been of any use by the time he arrived, according to Doctor Nester."

"Doctor Nester told us that there isn't an antidote for the *Amanita* mushrooms," Richard interjected. "The person who comes in contact with that destroying angel is lost, if that's what the murderer used."

"Destroying angel? That's some name for a poisonous mushroom. Seems like an oxymoron, doesn't it? And to think I just ate a plate of them sautéed in butter and garlic," Greta commented with a shudder.

"Now you see how easy it would be to poison someone. The mushrooms you ate were harmless, but we didn't question that they wouldn't be. The senators wouldn't have either. To make things worse, the symptoms could take as long as ten hours to appear and then they imitate the flu," Denise said as they sipped piping-hot coffee.

Richard concluded with obvious pleasure with his new knowledge, "What makes me especially fearful of natural poisons is that some of them can work without being ingested. The *Amanita* mushroom is just one of them. Dozens of plants can cause deadly reactions simply by coming in contact with the skin. A flower as beautiful and seemingly benign as the lady's slipper orchid can be poisonous to someone of ill health who touches the rhizomes according to our sources at the nursery and Doctor Nester."

"Well, what do we do next? I don't want to sit around until the killer strikes again. We need to find the murderer now," Greta said.

"I don't know about you, but I'm ready for a long soak and a pipe," Richard replied, rising from his chair. It's been a long, hot day. We have more than enough to digest, and I could use a little solo thinking time. I'm going to my room."

"That's a good idea," Denise agreed. "Let's call it quits until tomorrow. As soon as Tom arrives, I'm heading to Nester's lab. Let's meet again to share our information. By then, we'll know something about the other groups."

The phone rang as soon as Denise entered her room. Dashing around the bed, she announced, "Dory here."

"You can relax a little, you know. You're not on duty now," Tom scolded as his new partner barked in the background.

"Old habits die hard," Denise replied with a laugh. "I didn't expect to hear from you tonight."

"I guess I'm getting soft or it's the antihistamine that I'm taking for my sinuses," Tom grumbled.

"Don't you ever feed that dog?"

"She eats better than I do."

"Then why's she barking?"

"Jealous, I guess. She knows I'm on the phone with you."

Laughing, Denise asked, "Does this conversation have a purpose?"

"I guess. I called to tell you good night," Tom admitted with difficulty.

"That's nice of you."

"Think nothing of it."

"Okay, I won't. Good night and good-bye."

"Dory, one more thing."

"Yes?"

"Take care of yourself," Tom advised. "You might be closer to the killer than you think. He knows that you're looking for him."

"I will," Denise replied, her voice soft with unspoken warmth at his concern. "I'm already planning my next office prank. I don't want that dog to be your permanent partner."

"I'll see you early tomorrow. Good night, Dory." Tom yawned.

Denise held the receiver to her chest as the sound of Tom's voice lingered in her ear. She already missed him tremendously. Despite the affection in his voice, Denise wondered if he would ever be able to say the words she needed to hear. Until he did, she was afraid to open her heart to him. Denise knew he cared, but she did not want to scare him away with words of love. For the time being, she would have to be content with dreaming of the day that he would open himself to her.

TEN

True to his word, Tom arrived early the next morning before Denise could even have a cup of coffee with the other detectives. Although he did not have any information to share with her, he was eager to see for himself that she was still safe. If Tom had only voiced the concern that played across his face, Denise would have been a very happy woman.

"I'd like to stop by John Nester's laboratory again. You don't have to go with me if you'd rather not. The flowers attacked your allergies when we visited the nursery," Denise suggested as she led the way to the lab.

"The mushrooms give me the willies, but it's the blooming plants that played havoc with my allergies. I'm game for another session with the good doctor," Tom replied as he matched his stride to hers.

Rounding the corner that led to the lab, Denise noticed that the garage door stood ajar. She would not have thought anything of it if Dr. Nester had not mentioned that any draft could kill his precious specimens. Still, it was a warm day and the breeze that found its way into that humid environment would mix with the smell of mold, fungus, and plant greenery without causing any damage. Denise pushed the fleeting worry from her mind and did not mention it to Tom.

They rang the buzzer, but Dr. Nester did not answer. Denise was not surprised, considering he took a long time to respond when he expected guests. She remembered that Dr. Nestor had commented that few people visited him. He probably did not respond to the sound of the buzzer unless he had an appointment.

Trying the knob, Denise and Tom let themselves into the lab. Again, she was struck by the stuffiness and odor of peat moss and humus. The gloom of the semidarkness was almost overpowering.

Leading the way, Denise proceeded cautiously along the moist, slippery floorboards to Dr. Nester's office. At the back of the room, she could see the last rays of the afternoon sun through the open side door that led to the garage. The humidity in this section of the lab was much lower than it had been on their first visit because of the breeze that swept through the facility.

Unlike the rest of the lab, the office lights were on and that door was closed. Humidity had fogged up the windows so that she could not see if the scientist was inside. Denise knocked, but he did not answer. Pushing open the badly warped door, she backed up involuntarily as the steam and smell of plant decay rushed out to greet them.

"Doctor Nester, are you in there?" Tom called into the steam.

When he did not answer, Denise turned to Tom and commented, "How could anyone work in these conditions? This humidity is stifling, and it must be almost a hundred and fifty degrees in here."

As the mist cleared, Denise carefully entered the room. Remembering that the desk and worktable sat at the far side, she picked her way through the pots and soil that littered the floor. The smell of peat moss clung to their clothes.

Stopping short, Denise said, "Doctor Nester. It's Detectives Dory and Phyfer."

Dr. Nester did not answer. He sat slumped in his chair

with the slides, stain, and microscope spread in an orderly pattern around him. He looked as if he were only taking a nap. Taking his hand, Denise searched but could not find a pulse. When she pressed her ear to his nose, she heard no breath sounds. Even the glass she held under his nose revealed nothing. Dr. Nester was dead.

Denise dialed the D.C. police and spoke to the police officer who answered her call. He promised immediate response from the officers on the beat. Slipping on a pair of Lycra gloves she kept in her purse, Denise carefully examined the table and the body. The table contained the usual scientific tools of notebooks, slides, tweezers, and scalpel. However, the body told a different story.

Tilting Dr. Nester's head backward so that his jaw dropped slightly, Denise found what she had suspected. To the unskilled observer, Dr. Nestor only appeared asleep. However, to Denise's trained eye and inquisitive mind, the body told a different story.

"Tom, look at this," Denise called as she pointed into the darkness of the scientist's throat.

Stepping closer, Tom saw it, too. Someone had wedged the cap from one of Dr. Nester's *Amanita* mushrooms down his throat. Its size had undoubtedly cut off Dr. Nester's breath.

Pulling the little camera from her purse, Denise photographed the body. Despite the position of the mushroom cap, she was not convinced that it had been the sole cause of death. The corpse was too much at rest. Someone choking on food would have struggled, kicked over furniture, and made a mess in an effort to breathe. Nothing had been upset in the office.

"Someone must have seen us pay him a visit. Pity, too, he had been most helpful. Whoever it was used one of his own plants to kill him. Whoever did this certainly knows his way about this lab," Tom commented as he studied Dr. Nester's face and hands for signs of trauma.

"I don't think the mushroom was the only weapon," Denise observed. "My guess is that we'll discover that the killer used the mushroom cap to block Nestor's windpipe and cause suffocation. He wanted to make it look like an accidental death. I bet he first gave Doctor Nester something to suppress his bodily functions. Otherwise, he would have struggled."

"I don't know, Dory," Tom replied with a shake of his head. "There's nothing here except the half-eaten salad and the covered mushrooms on the doctor's desk."

As the sound of the sirens echoed down the street, Denise turned to Tom and said, "We'll have to wait for the autopsy results. However, I think someone used either an extract from the lady's slipper orchid or a dose of hemlock to tranquilize Doctor Nester and make him less prone to struggle. After his bodily functions slowed, the killer finished him off with a mushroom shoved down his throat to imitate suffocation."

"Dory, what have we stumbled into?" Tom exclaimed. "No murder case is ever simple, but this one has branched out past the Capitol itself. If Doctor Nester was murdered because he talked with the police or because the killer realized that Nester was the only expert who could point to him with any reliability, then the murderer is becoming quite desperate and even more dangerous."

"After we finish here with the police, we should call everyone together sooner than we'd planned. I have a feeling that we've uncovered a hornet's nest. We've made him angry and now we're going to feel the sting," Denise said as she walked toward the door to usher in the police officers.

The D.C. police were thorough in their investigation. When they discovered that Denise and Tom were not simply vacationing detectives, they were more than delighted to include them in everything they did. Denise and Tom were able to recreate the scene as they encountered it upon their arrival at Dr. Nester's laboratory. Both sides exchanged copious notes that would help them in their investigations. As they photographed the scene, Denise made multiple sketches of the body, the mushroom in the throat of the corpse, and the office. She knew that this was only the beginning of their troubles.

The Capitol had asked for their help in dealing with the murder of two senators. Now that a private citizen had died from what looked like the result of their investigation into those deaths and the most recent one, the crime had taken on a wider scope. Suddenly, they were in the middle of something much larger than politics. The killer not only wanted to control legislation, but he wanted to stop anyone who stood in his way. They had to stop him before someone else died.

They met after dinner to discuss the latest developments in what had become a case with far-reaching ramifications. They had all watched the evening news with the details of Dr. Nester's murder. Fortunately, the press had not mentioned the possible connection with the murder of the senators or the fact that two detective-guests of the U.S. Capitol had found the body.

The evening was warm as they sat on benches or the grass with the Capitol building behind them. Although the Capitol police did not pay any attention to them now, the wires still remained in their rooms and the conference and dining rooms. Until they had a better handle on the events that had brought them to the U.S. Capitol, they wanted to keep their thoughts and information to themselves and considered the courtyard the only safe place.

"All right, everyone," Denise began as soon as they

were comfortably seated under the warm summer sky, "I think we have to step up our efforts. Our killer is either feeling panic or arrogance in reaching beyond the Capitol into the city to kill Doctor Nester, a renowned botanist who specialized in identifying poisonous plants and developing antidotes. The murderer knew of his expertise and his reputation in the field. Further, he surmised that we would soon know of Doctor Nester if we did not already. If he did not know that we had visited Doctor Nester, the murderer killed him to prevent him from sharing his knowledge with us. If he knew about our meeting with the botanist, then the murderer punished him for helping us. Either way, the murderer sent a message to anyone who might be inclined toward working with us in our investigations."

Packing his pipe, Richard commented, "I think the murderer knew about your meeting and wanted to silence Doctor Nester to keep him from helping us any further. If the murderer is someone who works in the Capitol, he would know that we're at our wits' end and virtually without clues. I think the murderer targeted Doctor Nester to guarantee that we wouldn't learn anything more."

"I agree," Greta said, joining the conversation. "But didn't the murderer's actions tell us that we're on the right track in thinking that the poison had been natural and not chemical?"

"That's true," Denise agreed, "although the murderer had no way of knowing that Tom would come through with that information. Since he's not officially on the team, the murderer might have underestimated him. Besides, I hadn't had the opportunity to share the information with you. I think he was worried that Doctor Nester would give us a solid lead."

"And didn't he?" asked Eugene.

"Doctor Nester certainly did and Greta's right that

his death confirmed it," Denise responded. "Even without Tom's report, we know that the senators were killed using plant toxins. According to Doctor Nester's information, the *Amanita* mushroom called the destroying angel is the likely suspect. Its ability to go undetected for up to ten hours would have given the killer enough time to poison the senator and remove himself from suspicion long before the toxin took effect. The victims would not have been suspicious of mild stomach discomfort. By the time the pain became intolerable, it was too late. The patient was beyond the help of medical science."

"It looks as if Doctor Nester's death simplified things for us. Not to reduce the task, but it looks to me as if we are on the right track and simply have to reel in the murderer," Richard interjected.

They sat for a few minutes thinking about the extent of their knowledge. Although they did not feel secure in the small amount that they possessed, they felt that the pieces of the puzzle were fitting together nicely. If the information continued to fall into line, they would have solid leads very soon.

Denise broke the silence and summarized their discussion, saying, "Although we do not have enough information to narrow the suspect list, we at least have caused the murderer to come out into the open. We know that he has killed three senators with unrelated political views and a botanist whose only connection to the case was his knowledge of plant toxins. The killer has become sufficiently comfortable in his ability to work with the poisons that he has become bold. My thinking is that unless the senators start thinking along his lines, he will strike again. He has nothing to lose now that the only person who could possibly lead us to him is dead."

"Then, we must work quickly because Senator

Salermo told me that the senators are hoping to wrap up all loose ends quickly so that they might begin their summer campaigns at home," Greta remarked as she waved at a pesky fly.

Nodding in acknowledgement, Denise said, "We need to involve the Capitol police in this investigation. They turned it over to us thinking that once we solved it, we would fade from the picture and they would take the credit. Now it's time to bring them into the action. I suggest that we ask them to interview every single employee between now and Friday . . . from staffer to mailroom assistant. They should also speak with every person who had access to the senators during the ten hours before their deaths.

"Next, we must provide security for Salermo, Dey, and Frederick even though I don't think that Frederick is truly at risk. His health is so poor that I doubt that the senators would select him to head any committees. However, he works tirelessly on issues of Social Security and abortion. The senators will object, especially Salermo, but they must have armed guards around the clock. Let's contact the Capitol police tonight so that they can post the guard and plan the interviews for tomorrow."

"I'll do that right now," Richard commented as he tapped the ashes from his pipe and packed his smoking supplies.

Denise urged, "I think we should also warn Doctor Piper, the florist who satisfies the Capitol's flower order, and Mr. Fleet, the nurseryman who grows the flowers. They might be in danger, also. Although they are not botanists, they are specialists in their fields. The murderer might not know that they were unable to isolate the toxin for us and target them for attack."

"Just give me their numbers, and I'll take care of the calls right now," Eugene said as he stretched out his hand. Denise quickly copied them onto a sheet in her sketchbook and passed it to Eugene.

While they waited for Richard and Eugene to return, Denise sketched the faces of her colleagues. The struggle of each one to sift through the information to assess what they knew and what they still needed to discover played across their faces. Several of them chewed on their nails or their lips. Still others plucked at blades of grass, stripping them into thin slivers or chewing on them absentmindedly. A few took refuge in their study of the stars that shone over the Capitol. Denise buried her concerns in her sketchbook.

Tom was the only one who looked at ease. As always, his calm demeanor hid the churning of his mind as he sorted and categorized the information they had gained. The others did not know him well enough to see the lines of concentration that knotted between his brows. At the moment, Denise could tell that Tom was deep in thought.

As Denise had always done since she was a child, she drew pictures instead of keeping a diary. Sometimes the sketches were of only facial features, but most of the time she tried to capture a mood or a feeling of the people and surroundings. Often, her drawings reflected her reactions to a situation. She found her drawings to be very helpful in her investigations.

Before Denise decided on criminology as a major in college, she thought about becoming an artist or a graphic designer. However, for some reason, the excitement of solving crimes suited her better than the design studio or the solitary life in a sunlit loft. Denise had never regretted the choice because she had met wonderful people in this line of work. She never would have met Tom with his multifaceted personality and bravado or Richard with his cool demeanor or Greta with her sharp edge if she had chosen another profession. She would not have filled her sketchbook with visions of D.C. and Boston and San Francisco and all the other exciting places her work had taken her.

By the time Richard and Eugene returned, Denise had finished her sketches. Richard announced as he again packed a pipe with fragrant cherry tobacco, "Captain Carter has agreed to assist in the questioning of everyone who has had access to the senators. He will also assign officers to guard the ones we've designated. Salermo was not at all happy about it. He reluctantly agreed, saying that it was a gross intrusion into his personal and professional privacy."

Eugene, however, had only enjoyed partial success. Shaking his head, he offered, "I contacted Fleet at his nursery. He had heard of Doctor Nester's death. He had not, however, made the connection with our investigation of the death of the senators. As soon as I explained as much of our theory as appeared prudent, he quickly agreed to provide his family with additional security. He'll instruct his son in particular to be cautious. Although he occasionally accompanies the young man on his trips to the Capitol, Fleet said that he would warn the boy against being approached by strangers. Unfortunately, I couldn't contact Piper. I left a message on the answering machine and asked him to contact us here."

"He is probably out for the evening. Well, I suggest that we get some rest because we have much to do tomorrow," Denise said as she collected her things and tried to rise from her spot on the grass.

"A little stiff, Dory?" Tom teased as he pulled her to her feet.

"Just a bit," Denise replied, stretching. "I can still run circles around you, old man. I think I'll take a walk before going to bed."

"I had the same thought. We can see Doctor Piper at the Botanical Gardens. You can treat me to an ice cream on the way," Tom said as they walked under the city lights.

"If you're not careful, you won't be able to fit into that new suit you just bought," Denise reminded him.

"You sound like a wife, Dory," Tom chuckled between licks.

"That wouldn't be so bad. Almost all my friends are married," Denise replied with a glance at her partner.

"Yeah, so are mine. Everyone had to call it a day eventually," Tom commented as he chomped noisily on the cone.

"You make marriage sound like a death sentence," Denise retorted. "My friends are very happy. Marriage was a logical next step in loving relationships."

"Not for everyone," Tom stated under his breath.

"Whatever," Denise replied, not wanting to engage in a big argument.

Feeling the full impact of Denise's glare, Tom said, "Look, the lights are on at Doctor Piper's shop. I guess he didn't hear the telephone ring."

Pushing open the door, Denise and Tom entered the brightly lit shop. It was eleven o'clock at night, but, with the clutter on the desk and the bright lights, it looked like midday. The first time Denise had visited, the office in the Botanical Gardens had been reasonably neat considering the preparations for a major show. This time, papers were strewn over everything as if someone had been hunting for a misplaced order.

"Doctor Piper, it's Detective Dory and Phyfer, we'd like a word with you if you please," Denise called as they entered his work area.

When no one answered, they stepped around the toppled piles of newspapers and display posters and walked to the storage room. All the while, Denise called for Dr. Piper. The usually tidy garden was in a shambles everywhere she looked.

"What a mess! I wonder who knocked down all of these things and left them on the floor? It's hard to believe that this is the same office," Denise commented as they entered the equally messy back room in which broken clay pots and overturned plants littered the floor.

"Looks like my workroom at home," Tom commented as he righted the trash can and threw away his napkin and again called for Dr. Piper.

When Dr. Piper did not answer, they walked deeper into the room. More articles, posters, and plants lay strewn along the floor.

"This doesn't look right to me," Denise commented as they stepped over even more clutter. "It's almost artificially messy. It almost looks as if someone planned this for our benefit."

Denise and Tom stopped as they reached a darkened remote corner of the storeroom. Feeling around for a switch, Tom found a cord hanging from the ceiling. A florescent light flickered on as he pulled it. As the light spread through the room, it revealed a most unfortunate sight. Dr. Piper sat slumped on the floor amid the sphagnum moss and ferns with soil covering his clothing and his hair. His lips were a slightly bluish color and his eyelids a deathly white. Dr. Piper would never again arrange shows at the Botanical Gardens.

Tom made a routine but unnecessary check for vital signs while Denise returned to the showroom and telephoned the police. This was becoming an embarrassing habit. Everywhere they went, they discovered corpses.

Joining Denise at the desk, Tom said, "Because I'm suspicious by nature, I'd say that someone wants us to think that Doctor Piper stumbled his way from the showroom to the back desk, pulling down things along the way. From the looks of this room and the next, I think that someone decided to make it appear as if Doctor Piper had suffered a heart attack or taken ill while walking from here to the workroom with his arms full of supplies. Someone made it look as if he grabbed for things to keep himself from falling only to land in a heap in the back corner. At least, that's what someone wants us to think, Dory."

"You're right; it is too staged," Denise agreed. "The rubble is so carefully placed that it looks as if someone deposited him in the back and then backtracked to leave the trail leading to the body. How do you think he died?"

"I didn't see any signs of struggle or trauma," Tom replied as he removed a string from his shoe. "However, unlike Doctor Nester, Piper didn't suffocate on a piece of salad mushroom. His air passages are clear."

"Someone certainly wants to slow down our investigation. We must be closer than we think. I'm beginning to feel very unwanted," Denise replied as they waited for the police.

"Dory, refresh me on the connection between Piper and Doctor Nester," Tom requested as he looked for a place to sit but settled for leaning against the wall.

"Piper sent me to see Nester because of his reputation in the field of botany and in organic poisons in particular. I don't remember him saying that they were anything other than professional associates. Piper referred us to Fleet also. Now that the murderer has gotten to Piper, I certainly hope Fleet takes the precautions he said he would. I'll call him as soon as we return to the Capitol," Denise replied as the first of the police detectives entered the room.

"Good evening, Detective Dory," Detective Swan said as he entered. A charming smiled played across his handsome face.

"Detective Swan," Denise replied as they shook hands. "We called Doctor Piper to tell him about our concerns for his safety following Doctor Nester's death, but he didn't answer. Thinking that he wasn't in his office this evening, we decided to stroll over to leave a note for him to call us as soon as he returned. This is what we found when we arrived. His body is in the workroom."

"Did you see anyone when you arrived?" Detective Swan asked as he followed Tom and Denise to the back room.

"No, as a matter of fact, it looks as if Doctor Piper might have had a heart attack and staggered into the workroom," Tom commented. "At least, I think someone wants us to believe that's what happened."

"You're correct in your assessment . . . no trauma, no violence. Looks like natural causes. Only, it's too perfect, don't you think?" Detective Swan suggested as he surveyed the mess.

"Just what we said," Tom commented as he helped the detective's men lay the body on the floor and examine it for evidence.

Denise added as she and Tom moved toward the exit, "There's a slightly bluish tinge to his lips, which would be present on a coronary arrest victim. I'd appreciate it if you'd give us the results of the autopsy as soon as you have them."

"Do you have any suspects in mind?" Detective Swan asked as he joined them in the main garden.

"Yes, the same man who killed the senators," Denise replied. "Unfortunately, we don't have more than a supposition. That's why we need the autopsy results. I think you'll find that in both cases, the gentlemen died as the result of coming into contact with a poison that inhibited their vital functions. When we discover its identity and where it grows, we'll have their killer."

Escorting them to the door, Detective Swan said, "I'll call you in a day or two as soon as I have the results. Let me know if there's anything else I can do. Now that the Capitol murders have spilled into the city, we need to coordinate our efforts."

Denise and Tom rushed back to the Capitol to alert the others of the latest murder and to make the call to Mr. Fleet. He assured them that he and his family were taking every possible precaution to insure that he would not be next on the list. Unfortunately, he had not been able to reach his middle son. The young man was dating a woman who lived a few miles from the nursery and had not yet returned from their evening together. Mr. Fleet assured Denise that he would caution his son as soon as he returned home.

Leaving the others, Tom stated, "I'm tired, Dory. I'll see you early in the morning. Call me if anything breaks tonight."

"Why don't you stay the night?" Denise asked without considering the implications of her suggestion.

"Are you making a pass at me, Dory?" Tom quipped quickly, not allowing the moment to slip past him.

Blushing, Denise replied, "No! I meant in one of the empty rooms. I'm sure Captain Carter would unlock one for you."

"In that case, I'll go home. I have to feed that darn cat of yours and walk my dog anyway. I'll wait for a proper invitation and a larger bed. See you in the morning," Tom chuckled with a touch of disappointment in his voice.

Watching him walk away, Denise almost wished that she had made the offer. She wondered if Tom would have stayed. In another time and place, she would try him and see.

Retiring to her room, Denise tried to sleep, but she could not rest well that night knowing that the murderer was so close and still beyond their grasp. She had an uneasy feeling that he would strike again soon. Their presence had not deterred his most recent actions. Denise did not believe that he would stop until he had reached his goal. He was dedicated to his cause and would not allow a flock of detectives to push him off course.

The jingling of the telephone startled her briefly. Turning on the light, she reached for the phone in the silence of the night. Although it was late, the familiar voice helped to soothe her nerves.

"Under different circumstances, I would have been tempted to accept your offer, Dory," Tom stated as soon as he heard her voice.

"What offer?" Denise joked.

"Ask me again once you're off this case and back home," Tom replied in a husky whisper.

"Tom, are you actually saying that you have feelings for me? I'm more than simply your partner?" Denise teased, trying to lighten the serious tone that lay between them. When they finally spoke of their feelings, she wanted to see his eyes. She knew that Tom's voice could play tricks, but his eyes were always honest.

"Damn it, woman. You're frustrating. Go to sleep, Dory. I'll see you tomorrow," Tom growled as he hung up the phone.

Snuggling into the pillow, Denise took one last look at the photograph of Tom beside the bed. He was bright, strong, handsome, and honest . . . everything a woman could want in a man. With luck, she would crack two hard cases.

ELEVEN

The next day, the news media repeated the stories of the murder of Dr. Nester, linked it with that of Dr. Piper and the senators, and gave the details of the deaths, including reference to natural poisoning. With the D.C. police actively involved in both cases, it was not possible to keep inquisitive reporters from making the connection. With so many detectives on the case, no one, not even the senators, was exempt from scrutiny.

And still no one had found any new evidence that would point to the identity of the murderer. Denise interviewed over fifty people who had been in the buildings on the days of the murders and turned up nothing that would qualify as a lead. No one had seen or heard anything unusual, and everyone had proof of their whereabouts at all times.

After an afternoon of double-checking their interviews for clues, Denise had become frustrated and ready to call it quits and head back to her room when she received a call from Mr. Fleet. His son, Paul, had not returned to the nursery after an evening with his girlfriend. They had looked everywhere and could not find the twenty-year-old who had left with the family's car almost twenty-four hours ago.

Leaving Richard to finish their portion of the interviews, Denise and Tom drove out to the nursery in his car. Despite the chaos and worry within the family, the business operated at the same pace with trucks pulling out carrying deliveries, customers entering the grounds to make purchases, and gardeners tending the plants according to their prescribed routine. Only Mr. Fleet and his wife appeared distressed.

It was late when they reached the nursery. Neither of them had mentioned the conversation of the previous night. The sun had already set and thundershowers had cleaned the air. Denise and Tom sat at the Fleets' dining room table as they shared their concerns and a bottle of wine with them.

After listening carefully, Denise asked, "What is the possibility that Paul decided that he and his girlfriend needed some time alone or maybe that they eloped?"

"Oh no, I'm sure that they did not elope although he and Maryanne are very happy together. They know that they are too young now to marry. Besides, when the time is right, they will have our blessing. Maryanne and Paul never argue. I'm so worried. This is not like Paul," his mother began tearfully.

Mr. Fleet continued, "The poor girl calls here every hour looking for him. Her mother says that the child cannot eat and that she cries constantly. No, their relationship is wonderful. Paul did not need time away from her. Someone has hurt my boy. I know it in my heart. Someone has done something to him."

Tom asked gently, "Is his relationship with the young woman in good shape? Have they been arguing? Perhaps he needed time out and isn't really missing."

Dabbing the tears that ran down her face, Mrs. Fleet added, "Paul is very responsible. He would not take off without telling us. Besides, he has all the freedom he could possibly want right here. We never hound him to do anything. He knows what he must do for the efficient operation of the nursery, and he does it. I never have to ask him to do anything. No, my husband is right, something has happened to him. Between Maryanne's house and here the night Doctor Piper died, something happened to our boy."

"What did the police say when they were here?" Denise asked as she finished the last of the delicious wine.

"They have no clues," Mrs. Fleet replied angrily. "They suggested that Paul was young and that he had perhaps gone off to visit another girl. They do not know him as we do. Our son would never do anything like that. That is why we called you. You told us that we should be careful and that someone might try to hurt us, too. I think someone has kidnapped Paul."

Believing the mother's instinct, Denise made a simple request. "If you could provide me with a map of Paul's usual route to his girlfriend's house, I'll check the woods for signs of his car. I'm sure the police have already done this, but it never hurts to have a second look."

"I'll go with you myself," Mr. Fleet offered as he followed them to the car.

Driving slowly through some of the most beautiful, lush farmland Denise had ever seen, they retraced Paul's path. Fortunately, Maryanne lived on the main road, which meant that this was the only route to her home from the nursery. Any other road would have taken Paul a considerable distance out of the way before bringing him back to his destination.

Mr. Fleet pointed out the lovers' alcoves along the route, saying, "The young people know that they are safe here, so they park their cars and walk deep into the woods. We tell them that it's not safe, but they still do it."

Chuckling along with him, Denise commented, "You would be amazed by how much children hear. I remember very clearly the lessons my parents taught me, but I chose to apply them for later in life."

"That's Maryanne's house. As you can see, she lives only five or six miles from us," Mr. Fleet said as he pointed to the white house in the clearing.

After driving past the girl's house a short distance, they turned around for the return trip. They had seen nothing along the way to indicate that anyone had pulled off the road, swerved into a ditch, or hit a tree. Still, Tom and Denise wanted to explore some of the little side roads that Mr. Fleet said that the young people used as make-out havens.

Stopping the car at the entrance to the second wooded area, Denise, Tom, and Mr. Fleet walked through the muddy footpath to the place where the trees formed a natural screen that blocked out view from the flow of traffic on the road. The evening rains had given the area a clean smell and blurred the footprints. No one had left any personal articles lying around to indicate that this was anything other than a serene woodland setting.

"Are you certain that this is one of the love nests?" Tom asked. "I don't see any signs of car tracks, not even police vehicles."

"Oh yes, the young people frequent this place almost nightly," Mr. Fleet insisted. "Sometimes we drive by here to see three or four cars parked near these alcoves. It's only the rain that keeps them away tonight."

Scanning the deepening darkness, Denise said, "Let's check another one."

"Follow me. I'll take you to the next one," Mr. Fleet replied as he steered her toward the road.

They returned to the car and drove the half mile to the next alcove where they found tracks in the muddy soil. Someone wearing heavily etched soles had made these footprints, which now held a slurry of mud and rain. The rain had almost completely erased the faint ones. However, they did not see Paul or the family car.

They returned to the car for the short drive to another spot within a mile of the nursery. Parking on the graveled shoulder of the road, they left the car and walked into the thickly wooded alcove although the path showed signs of much vehicular traffic. Mr. Fleet feared that Tom's car might get stuck in the sucking mud if they tried to drive any farther. Wet leaves brushed against Denise's face and moist vines grabbed at her ankles as they intruded into the primeval setting. It was darker now and, with only a single flashlight to light the way, they made slow progress as they picked their way toward the lane that led to the most secluded part of the lovers' retreat.

Cautiously, Denise, Tom, and Mr. Fleet followed the path through the woods until they reached the alcove. Shining into the opening, the beam reflected off the bumper of a black sedan. Denise heard Mr. Fleet gasp in the darkness as he froze in his tracks. The light wavered as the impact of the sight hit him.

Touching his arm, Denise offered without waiting for a response, "We'll check the car while you hold the flashlight." Mr. Fleet only nodded in response.

Walking forward, Denise and Tom followed the beam that led to the dark car. Following the line of the car around the side, they peered into the semidarkness as they tried to make out the shadow in the front seat. The shaky beam of light followed her from a distance. Slowly, Tom opened the door and looked inside at the face of a handsome, dark-haired young man. Peering over his shoulder, Denise could see a slight movement of his chest although his lips were tinged with blue and his breathing was frighteningly shallow.

"Someone has killed my boy!" Mr. Fleet moaned in a plaintive mixture of paternal anguish and fury.

"No, he's still alive," Denise replied. "You stay with him until the police arrive while I search the car."

"I'll wait for the police on the road," Tom volunteered as he quickly used his cell phone to call the police.

In her gut, Denise knew that whoever it was that had murdered Dr. Nester and Dr. Piper had attacked Paul. The murderer wanted to remove the last person who could possibly identify him. Paul Fleet, as the driver of the delivery van, had inadvertently become the target. She hoped fervently that the murderer had not used the *Amanita* mushroom this time.

While Mr. Fleet lovingly held the hand of his son, Denise searched the car for evidence and found a discarded bag of popcorn, a can of soda, and a candy wrapper. Neither looked life threatening. However, knowing the nature of the poisons that Paul's attacker might have administered, Denise took samples for the FBI and the Center for Disease Control. Opening a little medicine bottle she always carried in her purse, Denise filled it half full with the flat soda. Then she dumped a few kernels of the popcorn into a plastic sandwich bag along with a portion of the candy wrapper.

Soon Tom returned from his vigil with the sound of sirens from the local police department resounding through the woods. As the police rushed into the clearing followed by the medics and Tom, Denise stashed the evidence in the bottom of her shoulder bag. Mr. Fleet had not released his son's hand.

The police and medics worked quickly and efficiently to remove Paul from the car and transfer him to the ambulance with Mr. Fleet beside him. Denise and Tom returned to their car for the drive back to town. Rather than going straight to the Capitol, they stopped first at the FBI after phoning Tom's contact to ask him to meet them.

Leaving Tom to watch the double-parked car, Denise bounded up the stairs and hurried inside where George Christian waited in his office for them. He looked tired and worn from his long day, but he graciously welcomed her as he opened the door and stepped aside. The coolness of his office felt refreshing after the dampness of the woods.

"Good evening, Mr. Christian," Denise began as soon as he closed the door. "I'm so very sorry to trouble you at this late hour, but I need to ask you to analyze some samples for us,"

"I'm always happy to help you," George Christian replied as he eased the samples into bags marked TOP SECRET and placed them with the others in his "out" box.

Settling in the first chair, Denise immediately restated her request. "I took these from the car of a very sick young man whose family owns the nursery that supplies the flowers to the Capitol. He is in very grave condition from what I suspect is the same poison that the murderer used on the senators and perhaps on Doctor Nester and Doctor Piper. Would it be possible for your people to analyze these for plant toxins? I need the information as soon as possible. I realize that this is a rush, but the man's life depends on it. I've provided the hospital with a list of the suspected toxins, but I don't want to leave any stone unturned in the event that they can't isolate it."

George Christian smiled broadly and said, "I'll call the pathologist immediately. He can be here in a matter of minutes. I'm sure that under the circumstances he'll be more than willing to do what he can. You say you have a list of toxins? I'm sure he would appreciate having something to use as a starting point."

"I'll write it out for him immediately," Denise replied as she quickly ripped a page from her sketchbook and scribbled the names of the plants that should be at the top of the pathologist's list. While she worked, George Christian eased from the room. When he returned, he reported that the pathologist was on his way.

Thanking Mr. Christian for his efforts, she left the office as quickly as she had arrived. They needed to get to the U.S. Capitol and share the information with their colleagues before they retired for the night. Denise had a feeling that they were getting close to making contact with the murderer. Either they would catch him or he would come after one of them. Either way, they needed to be even more careful.

The others listened thoughtfully as Denise and Tom spoke of the sad discovery in the woods. The hospital officials had not phoned with any news, good or bad. Everyone in the room knew that they would all spend a long, sleepless night. If Denise and Tom were correct, the murderer was much too close and brave for comfort.

"I'd say we'd all better be careful," Richard advised after listening to Denise and Tom. "We're all sitting ducks here."

"Can't you just read the headlines?" Greta added. " 'Detectives bite mushroom while trying to save senators.' "

"Scary thought, isn't it?" Eugene commented. "We come here to help the Capitol police solve a case, and we become potential victims."

Turning to Tom, Richard said, "Look, I know you have Denise's cat and your canine partner to tend, but you really should stay here tonight. There's an extra bed in my room. You can stay with me."

Winking at Denise, Tom agreed, saying, "Sounds like the second best offer I've received in as many days."

Shaking her head, Denise walked toward the door. Turning, she called, "I'll see you tomorrow morning. I think we should be very careful from now on. Make sure that everything's in order before you go to sleep tonight."

Following her to the Page School, Tom and Richard continued to compare notes. Neither had any new insights, but they could not put the details of the case from their minds. Richard did not suspect that Tom was also trying to squelch his disappointment at sleeping in the wrong room.

Tom walked Denise to her door. Unlocking it, he searched her room until he was satisfied that she was safe. Observing him, Denise once again realized that he was a wonderful partner to have watching her back.

"I can do that myself," Denise stated as Tom checked the bedding.

"I know, but I wouldn't be able to sleep unless I did this myself," Tom replied as he continued his search in the bathroom.

"You won't find anything here. I don't think the murderer will come after us so soon," Denise commented as he checked the unopened box of toothpaste and her soap supply.

"Use a new bar of soap and the new toothpaste tonight, Denise," Tom instructed. "You can't be too careful. You're probably right, but take the precaution anyway. I'll see you in the morning."

"Good night, Tom. Have I told you that I'm glad you joined me on this case?" Denise asked as he lingered at the open door.

"No, but I'll let you pay me back for the leave time I'm using, if it'll make you feel better," Tom joked, touching her gently on the nose. The warmth of his finger eased through her body.

"I'll do that," Denise whispered through dry lips.

A thick silence rested between them as they stood together in the doorway. Neither wanted the night to end, and neither could take the next step. Two respected detectives were stuck and unable to move their interests further.

Without taking his eyes from her face, Tom leaned closer to Denise. She smiled gently as his breath tickled her cheeks. He slipped his arm around her waist and pulled her toward him. His lips lightly touched hers in a whisper of promises to keep.

As their bodies pressed together and the room faded, Richard's voice burst into the silence. "Tom, it's time to turn in. We need to get up early tomorrow," he called from the hall.

Tom snapped back and released Denise. Quickly, they stepped apart. Wonderment illuminated their faces as they realized that they would never again simply be partners. The moment ended as Tom sighed and turned away.

"What timing! Good night, Dory," Tom said as he looked over his shoulder at Richard's retreating back.

"Another night, perhaps," Denise suggested.

"You can count on it," Tom promised as he closed Denise's door and walked up the hall. One day, no one would stop him from showing Denise all of the feelings he had kept to himself for so long.

After a fitful night's sleep, Denise and Tom drove to the local hospital with the pathology results from their friend at the FBI. Denise had been unable to contact the Fleet family to find out about Paul's condition. She hoped that they would not arrive to find that the poison had claimed another victim.

Neither spoke of the missed opportunity of the previous night. They smiled often at each other and joked more freely, but they did not touch. Despite the unspoken words waiting to be heard, they had a case to solve. Love would have to wait.

Paul's father and mother greeted them with tired faces when Denise and Tom reached his room. Taking their hands in hers, Paul's mother said, "You saved my son. The doctors told us that if you had not found him when you did, the poison would have killed him. He is still a very sick boy, but he will live. Thank you and God bless you." The tears flowed down her lined cheeks.

Mr. Fleet echoed her sentiments, saying, "The doctors used your list of possible poisons to isolate the one that the man used on my boy. They were able to administer an antidote in time to save him. I don't know how I'll ever be able to thank you enough."

Even in his weakened condition, Paul Fleet was an extremely handsome man. His thick black hair shone with blue highlights. His puffy eyes were raven-black. His sensuous full lips, although still pale, had lost the bluish tinge.

"Paul, how are you feeling?" Denise asked as she reached for his outstretched hand.

Looking from Tom to Denise, Paul replied, "Alive, thanks to you."

Smiling in acknowledgment, Denise asked, "Do you have any idea who poisoned you? Did you eat anything you shouldn't have? Did any strangers approach you?"

"I've been lying here reconstructing the evening. We ate popcorn, soda, and some candy at the movie after dinner at Maryanne's house. I didn't go anywhere out of the ordinary either. I delivered flowers to my regular customers during the day. Before going to Maryanne's, I made the usual delivery to the Capitol," Paul replied with a scowl on his forehead.

"Did you feel ill before going to the movie?" Tom asked.

"No, I felt fine. I didn't start to feel sick until after I

left Maryanne at her house. I remember feeling very light-headed and didn't think I could make it home. The road was coming up at me in waves, and I was having trouble focusing my eyes. I don't remember anything else until I woke up in here," Paul replied weakly.

"Did you handle anything out of the ordinary at the U.S. Capitol?" Denise inquired.

"Nothing unusual. I helped Mr. Philips unload the hand truck, picked up a few pots to return to the nursery, and left. I'm very tired now. Would you mind if I took a little nap?" Paul asked as he fought to stay awake.

"I think you've told me all I need to know. Thanks, Paul," Denise replied as Dr. Milton motioned her to come to him.

Dr. Milton greeted them, saying, "Thanks to you, Paul pulled through. We never would have thought to check for organic toxins. Our first thought would have been food related and then chemicals. We isolated it on the second try. Paul had been exposed to the poison of the mandrake root, a close relative of the deadly nightshade. We've analyzed the contents of his stomach and found that he did not ingest it; at least, it was not in the meal he consumed."

"Our murderer is very careful to make every attempt appear accidental," Denise said. "He probably envisioned that Paul would run his car into the woods while driving home. He didn't anticipate that the young man would pull off the road for a nap. I'm just grateful that it wasn't *Amanita* mushroom poisoning. You wouldn't have been able to save Paul if the murderer had used that poison. Thank you, Doctor Milton, for your help."

Turning to Mr. Fleet, Denise said, "I'd like to see the van if I could. Is it at the nursery?"

Mr. Fleet replied, "Yes, we used it to make deliveries. I'll go with you."

As Denise and Tom followed Mr. Fleet, Tom whispered, "What are you planning, Dory? I can hear those wheels turning. You think someone put some nightshade dust on the pots, don't you? Even if that happened, the pots wouldn't be in the van now."

"That's what worries me," Denise whispered back. "I'm afraid that someone else might have come in contact with the same poison-covered pot."

Shaking his head, Tom said, "If that's the case, then everyone in that nursery could be in danger."

"That's why we have to act fast," Denise muttered.

Denise and Tom drove in silence as they followed Mr. Fleet to the nursery. The long line of vans filled the lot. Workers moved from the buildings to the parked vans with carts of flowers.

Following Mr. Fleet, they found the empty van. Turning to him, Denise asked, "Who emptied this van last night?"

"My son, Anthony, did. Why? Is he in danger, too?" Mr. Fleet asked as the emotions played across his face.

"Yes, I'm afraid he might be," Denise replied carefully, not wanting to upset the father more. "You'll want to clean the van thoroughly to remove any residual traces of the dust. This toxin is, as you know, capable of causing great illness. Is it possible for me to speak with Anthony?"

Without a moment's hesitation, Mr. Fleet called through the nursery's intercom for Anthony to meet them in the office. Everything was in order as it had been on their previous visit. When he arrived, Denise explained about the poison and the pots.

Visibly shaken, Anthony replied, "I used gloves as I always do when I work with the plants. I'm allergic to several of them, so I always pull on protection before I start work. They're in my locker. I haven't used them since last night. I've been in the office all day balancing the accounts. I'll put them into a plastic bag and bring them to you."

"Has anyone driven the van today?" Tom asked before Anthony could hurry away.

"No. It's still where I parked it last night. I have the only key in my pocket," Anthony replied as he pointed toward the sagging pocket of his jeans.

"You get the gloves for the detectives, Anthony, and I'll block off the van. I don't want anyone touching it until we have thoroughly washed it, inside and out," Mr. Fleet added as he rushed off to cordon off the van.

"The police might want to search the van before you clean it. Call them first before you do anything," Tom advised. Mr. Fleet nodded and hurried away.

As they waited, Denise commented, "I'll never be able to look at flowers the same way again. Until this happened, I thought they were so beautiful, and now, after only a few days in D.C., they look totally different to me. Their beauty conceals so much potential for evil. I guess that's what the alchemists of the old days knew."

Tom replied as he blew his nose and coughed, "A little of the poisonous dust certainly goes a long way. The FBI information showed that nightshade, lady's slipper orchids, hemlock, and numerous other plants have very lethal properties. I didn't know that so many people practiced the ancient art of alchemy anymore. No wonder I'm allergic to flowers, Dory, they're killers."

"If they get into the wrong hands, they are," Denise replied with a shake of her head. "Friar Lawrence in *Romeo and Juliet* used plant toxins to help Juliet feign death and Romeo used them to kill himself. Someone with misdirected devotion to a cause has used a toxin to kill three senators and the people who could identify the substance and perhaps lead us to the murderer. Not to wax philosophical, but man's inhumanity to his fellow man is shocking."

Mr. Fleet returned at that moment with his son at his side. Anthony carried a trash bag containing the gloves. In the distance, Denise and Tom could see the van surrounded by bright yellow tape.

"The pots are no longer in the car," Anthony explained as he handed her the bag. "I remember now that Paul moved them to the shed for soaking last night before he went on his date. I've already changed the water two or three times. The runoff would have been absorbed into the lawn by now. I doubt that there's any trace of the poison left on them. I'm sorry, but at least I have the gloves."

"Good, thanks for the help." Denise smiled at both men. "I'll give these to the lab for analysis. If you can think of anything that might seem unusual in your dealings with the Capitol, please give me a call."

Denise and Tom stopped at the police station on the way back to the Capitol so that they could share the evidence with them. The same smell of burning coffee greeted them as they entered the squad room. The customary cloud of smoke lingered near the ceiling. Detectives cradled telephones against their shoulders while they typed their journals and filled out paperwork.

"Looks like home, doesn't it?" Denise asked Tom over her shoulder as they followed the pointing finger to Inspector Cast's desk.

"It makes me homesick, Dory. What I wouldn't give for a cup of that thick, nasty coffee," Tom replied with a laugh.

Inspector Cast recognized Denise and Tom from newspaper articles as they approached, and he came around his desk to greet them. As if sensing Tom's thirst, he immediately led them to the table where the brew blackened. Sipping deeply, Tom exclaimed, "Now, this is coffee—nice and thick with an undertaste of burned beans. Delicious!"

Denise was less than impressed by the brew. However, it did remind her of their office. Returning to the inspector's desk, Denise handed him the bag containing one of the gloves; the other one she planned to deliver to the FBI for testing.

"I understand from the police in Amelia that Paul Fleet is a very lucky man. Our lab will run a test for the mandrake poison and any other possibilities and give you a call in about two days when the results come back," Inspector Cast commented as he instructed a messenger to deliver the bag to pathology without touching the contents. He attached a big HAZARDOUS MATERIALS sticker to the outside as a safeguard against curiosity.

"Thanks," Denise replied as she put down her barely touched cup of devil's brew. She knew there was no point in asking if the lab could work faster, having already tried that approach and hitting a brick wall. Anyway, she planned to use Tom's FBI contact for speedier results.

"Do you really think this is the same poison that killed the senators and Nester and Piper?" Inspector Cast asked as he accompanied them to the door.

"I think the possibility exists that the murderer used it to make them drowsy, lethargic, and vulnerable to attack. However, I think the toxicology reports will show that he used something much more lethal than that to kill the senators. He wanted them to look as if they died of natural causes from the stress of work, maybe even a heart attack. My theory is that with Paul, the murderer decided to help him have a car accident. No one would have any difficulty believing that a young man had crashed his car on the way home while driving on a slippery road. However, they would become suspicious of a heart attack in someone so young and in such excellent physical condition."

"Do you have any clues as to the murderer's identity? We've come up empty-handed. You would share with us if you had anything, wouldn't you?" the inspector asked with a sly but steady gaze.

"Of course we'd do anything we could to help you with your investigations, Inspector, just as I'm sure you would help us," Tom replied. "The faster we can find this person, the sooner we can stop these serial killings. Unfortunately, we have nothing of substance at this point."

"We'll know in a few days if your theories are correct about young Fleet," Inspector Cast replied as he stood on the precinct's stoop. "Let's hope the murderer doesn't panic and strike again before we can identify and apprehend him."

Denise replied as Tom eased the car into gear, "I'd like to think he has already panicked. He has taken his fear of discovery into the streets of D.C. and into the suburbs. By exposing himself, he has in many ways made it easier for us. With more of us on the case, we'll find him sooner or later."

Denise and Tom stopped at the FBI long enough to leave the other glove with George Christian, who promised a quick turnaround. So far, they had a growing list of toxins but no firm list of suspects. Despite Denise's outward optimism, she did not feel confident that they were close to apprehending the murderer.

The Capitol buzzed with unusual activity as Denise and Tom returned to the grounds. Television and newspaper reporters filled the walks and tourists milled around everywhere. An eerie tension filled the air.

"Boy, am I glad to see you," Eugene called as he greeted them at the gate.

"What's happening? Why are all these people here?" Denise asked as she surveyed the area.

Shaking his head in dismay, Eugene replied, "They're

here because Senator Salermo found Senator Tobias dead in his room after lunch today. He wasn't even on our list. That makes four senators. The press has been crawling around here for the past hour. I don't know how they found out, but they're waiting for a statement from Senator Salermo. I don't know how he's holding up. Someone is systematically murdering all of his closest friends."

Pushing their way through the crowd, Denise and Tom followed Eugene into the heart of the Capitol where close to one hundred reporters had set up their lights and cameras. They could have bypassed all of the chaos by entering through the Page door, but Denise wanted to eavesdrop on the reporters to see if she could find out who had leaked the story.

Denise was curious about the reactions of the people to the latest murder. She had learned early in her career that casual comments often lead to revelations, and, since the investigation was stuck, she needed all the help she could get. During the time Denise had been in D.C., four people had died. It appeared as if the same murderer was responsible for all four deaths.

Wandering casually from one group of reporters to another, Denise listened carefully to their speculations but heard nothing noteworthy. She lingered for several minutes at the group from the *Washington Post* and heard a gentleman of the press say, "I think it's an inside job. How else can you explain it? There's nothing random in these murders. It's obvious to me that someone wants this job in the worst way and is trying to make it look as if a faction were behind the murders. Let's look at the facts. Someone killed each of the senators before he could make any changes. It's clear to me that he'll keep killing people until the one he supports has the majority seat. I'll bet that when he reaches the top, this killing will stop."

"Naw, you're wrong, man. One of the senators wouldn't do this thing to his friends," rebutted a young man who still wanted to believe in the existence of good in the world.

The older man responded, "You're young yet. If you stay in this business long enough you'll see that man will do some pretty dreadful things to his fellow man for less than this."

"Maybe you're right, Bill, but I still hope it's an outsider," the young man replied as he patted his buddy on the shoulder.

Joining Tom on the steps, Denise said, "We need a serious lead. We don't have the time to go on a wild-goose chase. Lives are at stake."

"I agree, Dory. The clues must be right under our noses, but we're so busy looking that we don't see them," Tom commented dolefully.

Eugene added hopefully as he joined them, "Maybe Senator Salermo will have something to add to the investigation. Perhaps he has had a chance to think about the possible motive in these killings. We should speak with him."

"I'm already on his calendar for today, but, after this latest death, I'm not sure that he'll have time for me. I'll check back later. I need to get away for a while," Denise said as she motioned to Tom to follow her.

Stopping at the nearest pay phone, Tom dialed his FBI contact. Denise waited impatiently as the traffic whizzed past. The noise kept her from being able to eavesdrop on his conversation.

After a long conversation Tom turned to Denise and said, "The lab tests show that the murderer used three different poisons on the victims. The killer used *Amanita* mushrooms just as you thought as well as belladonna and cyanide overdose, which would account for the appearance of heart attack and suffocation."

"Well, at least we know now why the botanist became a target," Denise responded with a deep sigh. "He would have been able to lead us to the source of the poison. Even if the others overlooked it, he would have known what tests to suggest, and he would have shared his suspicions about possible suspects with us. He probably would have known who in the vicinity of D.C. was an avid gardener of the destroying angel mushroom. Now if we could only figure out the murderer's connection to the florist and the nurseryman, we'd have the case solved."

"I know you like an old shoe, Dory. You're working on a theory. Share it with me. It might help you to talk it out," Tom suggested as he flicked the cigarette lighter that he no longer used since Denise made him stop smoking.

"I don't have all the pieces of the puzzle yet," Denise commented. "I want to find out the cause of death of Senator Tobias first. We'd better hurry back. By the way, have I told you that I'm really glad you're here? I wouldn't be able to do this without you."

Smiling contentedly, Tom replied, "That's what partners are for."

Touching him lightly on the arm, Denise said, "About last night . . ."

"Don't worry, Dory," Tom replied as he gently kissed her fingers. "That'll keep. The way I feel about you won't change overnight. We'll have time for ourselves as soon as we solve this case."

Nodding in agreement, Denise and Tom continued on their return to the Capitol. They stopped only long enough to buy Tom an ice cream against the blistering hot sun. Washington in the summertime sweltered and steamed, adding to the urgency for solving the case quickly.

TWELVE

The crowd was so massive in front of the Capitol that Denise and Tom decided to enter by the Page School door. Slipping inside, they avoided the crush of tourists and reporters and went straight to the pressroom where Senator Salermo would speak in a few minutes. The room was packed with congressional representatives, staffers, and the press.

Richard had saved them a seat on the aisle beside him. Leaning over, he asked Denise, "How was your phone call home? Any news?"

"I suggest that you not eat any mushrooms," Denise responded cryptically, not knowing who sat near them and might overhear.

"Really? Sounds like we're on the right track," Richard replied softly.

"In more ways than one. If we could just figure out the connections, we'd be able to go home," Denise commented and was about to say more when Senator Salermo entered and the hushed conversation stopped.

Senator Salermo looked drained of all energy. He seemed to have aged twenty years since she last spoke with him. More than anyone in the room, he appeared genuinely touched by the death of the members of the Hill community.

Stepping toward the microphone, Senator Salermo spoke slowly as emotion caught in his throat. "Ladies and gentlemen, this morning our colleague Victor Frederick passed away. The coroner has ordered an autopsy although it would appear that he died from heart failure. However, we cannot ignore the possibility that Victor was the victim of violence. I, for one, am tired of living under these conditions. If Senator Frederick was murdered, I pledge to do all in my power to apprehend the suspect. We must stop these assaults on representatives of the people."

Leaving the senator to field questions from the press, Denise, Tom, and the others gathered on the Capitol grounds. They took turns sharing thoughts about the direction in which their investigation should proceed. They had tried so many different paths but had still come up empty-handed. The murderer had eluded them at every turn.

"I was afraid it would be the mushrooms," Greta stammered. "We eat them on our salads every day. The murderer is very smart. By using something that is so much a part of our lives, he thinks that we'll overlook it."

"Let's not forget about the other natural toxins at the murderer's disposal," Denise reminded them. "The doctor said that Paul was also poisoned. I suspect that the lab reports will confirm that the murderer used nightshade dust on him. He probably sprinkled it on the pots that Paul returned to the nursery."

"If that's the case, we have to look for someone who has the ability to grow and harvest mushrooms and other toxic plants without causing suspicion. Maybe someone who is an amateur botanist," Eugene offered.

"Or someone with a very green thumb," Greta suggested.

"All right, Denise, what about Doctor Nester and Doctor Piper?" Richard asked. "How did they die? From what you and Tom described, their deaths were too staged and too neat to have happened as the murderer wanted us to think they did."

Looking around at the others, Denise replied, "We haven't seen the autopsy results yet, but our source at the FBI said that preliminary lab reports confirm our suspicion that the killer probably used a solution of belladonna and cyanide. We'll know for certain tomorrow when we get the results."

"Why do you think the killer went after Senator Frederick? He was in poor health and suffered from diabetes," Eugene inquired as he waved a friendly bee away from his soda.

"Despite his health and age, he was on our short list, if I remember correctly," Greta replied as she plucked the petals from a pale mauve rose.

Richard suggested, as he pushed his hair from his furrowed brow, "We need the autopsy results on Senator Frederick as soon as we can get them. If he died from mushroom poisoning, we'll know that we're dealing with the same killer. If not, it could be a copycat murder and not related to the others at all. The other possibility is that he died of natural causes."

"I'll call the D.C. medical examiner and share our suspicions with him," Denise said as she finished her most recent sketch of her colleagues. "Maybe by mentioning Paul's case, we'll give him a lead. Tom'll contact our man at the FBI to find out if the lab has finished the tests on the gardening gloves. If nightshade poisoning traces are on the gloves, then I think it's safe to conclude that the same perpetrator murdered the senators, Nester, and Piper and tried to kill Paul. From that we'd be able to say with certainty that we're on the right track and that it's simply a matter of time before we catch the murderer."

"I'm concerned about the easy access to their food.

Shouldn't someone monitor it to be sure that it isn't poisoned?" Eugene suggested.

Stretching the stiffness of sitting on the ground from his back, Tom replied, "I think we'd call even more attention to them if we tried to arrange for special food. Besides, a truly determined murderer would find a way to infiltrate the local deli if he really wanted to get to the senators."

"Then we can't protect them. Senators Salermo and Dey are sitting ducks," Greta summarized.

"That's right, they are. And don't forget we are, too. The murderer has already killed a botanist who would have been able to give us a good lead to his identity. The florist, whose knowledge of the employees and volunteers of the U.S. Capitol might have been able to narrow our search, also fell victim to him. The murderer might tire of our interference in his mission and try to remove us, too," Denise reminded them as she mentioned the intricate connections between people in this case.

"I certainly hope Paul Fleet recovers completely," Richard added. "The young man could be an invaluable source of information. Once we have all the pieces together, he might be able to make them fit. He's the one who has contact with the killer when he delivers the flowers."

Rising from the hard ground, Denise added, "True, but don't forget that the murderer has skillfully disguised himself from all of us while working under our noses. Paul might not recognize him either. We should ask the police to double their security efforts around him. There's not much they can do to protect him, but maybe the presence of officers at his door would frighten the murderer away. I think the gloves will prove to be significant clues."

Stretching his long legs, Tom commented, "Let's conduct our investigation as if we're only looking for the finishing touches to the case. If we're very self-confident, the killer might begin to worry about us and panic into doing something that will allow us to catch him. The more he slips, the better off we are."

"When should we meet again?" Greta asked as they prepared to continue their interviews.

"Tonight after dinner would be good," Denise replied as she watched Tom walk away without her. "By then we should have the results of the toxicology reports on the garden gloves. We're going to the FBI now."

Rushing to catch up with her partner, Denise chuckled at the familiarity of the scene. Not once in their entire partnership had Tom waited for her. He simply made up his mind to leave, stretched his long legs, and moved out. He always left her to carry the cases and trot after him.

"Okay, Denise, I can tell from the set of your mouth that you have a hunch. Tell me. Who do you think is behind these murders?" Tom demanded as soon as they were a good distance from the others.

"You're right, I do have a hunch, but I'm going to keep it to myself until we get the autopsy results on Senator Frederick. I might be wrong. The last thing we can afford to do is wander down the garden path to nowhere. Too much is at stake for that," Denise replied as she took a detour to the FBI contact's secluded little office.

"Why are we stopping here?" Tom demanded as Denise led him into the Capitol. "George is probably waiting for us."

"Let's see if anyone is in the flower-arranging room. I'd like to speak with Mr. Philips and take another look around the place. Whoever poisoned Paul either works there or has access to the flowers and the van. I need a list of all the people who were in the room between

Paul's last delivery and the time he picked up the pots,"
Denise replied as she steered a path around the sight-
seers and reporters.

"I hope you know, Dory, that it could be almost anyone. It might even be someone who volunteered to help
out when he saw Paul unloading the van. The possibilities are endless. George Christian is our best bet," Tom
commented as he walked beside her.

"I know, but we have to explore every possibility. At
this point, the flower room and its volunteers appear to
be the source of at least one poisoning attempt," Denise
replied as she led him toward the closed door.

In her haste, Denise barely noticed the now familiar
older woman who pushed the heavy flower cart. Mrs.
Benedict was one of the regular fixtures. She delivered
pots of flowers and removed the wilted ones. Her green
thumb and loving care of the flowers showed in every
lush bloom. Mrs. Benedict smiled sweetly as they rushed
past, no doubt thinking that she preferred her tranquil
days to their frenetic pace. She waved but did not stop
to chat this time.

The flower room was just as they had last seen it. Cut
flowers overflowed buckets of water, and pots of growing
plants sat on another cart waiting. Workers wearing
aprons and gloves snipped the ends of stems and then
added them to the carefully arranged vases. Volunteers
loaded them onto carts or hand-carried them to the
offices. The orderly process reminded Denise of an as-
sembly line with the difference being that most of the
men and women in the flower room worked in silence
and gave Tom and Denise only the slightest notice as
they wandered through the fragrant room.

Mr. Philips joined them almost immediately. Smiling,
he asked, "What can I do for you today, Detectives?"

Returning his hearty handshake, Denise replied, "If
possible, we'd like to have a list of the people who

worked here on the day Paul Fleet made his last delivery. I'm sure you know that he became ill after leaving here that night. We know that he came in contact with a very potent poison, which I believe that someone had sprinkled on the pots he loaded onto his truck. Whoever did it knew when Paul would return. I have a strong suspicion that the person might also be the murderer of the senators."

Wringing his hands, Mr. Philips replied, "I'd do anything I could to help you, Detective Dory, but my list of volunteers is incomplete. Follow me and I'll give you what I have. Perhaps one of the workers would be more helpful."

As Denise and Tom followed Mr. Philips to his office, they passed Mrs. Benedict again. Her eyes twinkled merrily and a little smile played at the corners of her mouth. Although she never struck up a conversation with them, Mrs. Benedict appeared very approachable and friendly. Denise decided to ask her what she knew about Paul's pots.

Rummaging through his cluttered desk, Mr. Philips managed with some difficulty to locate the list of volunteers who regularly worked in the flower room. Quickly scanning it, he found and photocopied the page that bore the twenty names of the regular volunteers. He seemed very happy to have been able to help in the investigation and to remove Denise and Tom from the quiet of his domain.

Smiling with relief, Mr. Philips said, "I hope this will help you. However, as I said, the workers themselves will be able to add names to the list."

Glancing over the list, Denise found a familiar name and asked, "Do you think we might be able to speak with Mrs. Benedict? She is always here and might have seen something suspicious."

"I'm sure she'd be happy to help you," Mr. Philips

replied with a nod of relief at being temporarily out of the loop.

Thanking him, Denise and Tom returned to the room in which Mrs. Benedict was busily arranging pots on her cart. Her thin fingers gently picked off the spent blossoms and misted the leaves to remove the dust before polishing the larger ones to a bright shine. Denise watched her smile sweetly as she caressed each of her charges.

"Mrs. Benedict," Denise began as she approached her cart, "May we have a few minutes of your time?"

Bowing her head slightly, Mrs. Benedict replied, "I'd be happy to speak with you, Detective Dory. Let's sit over there so that we can be alone."

A sweet smile illuminated Mrs. Benedict's soft brown eyes and pretty face. Her fingers bore faint green and brown stains from working with her flowers. Her soft voice seemed to enfold and caress the two detectives with the same warmth she showed the plants.

"Mrs. Benedict, we were wondering if you saw anyone unusual around the flowers or Paul Fleet's truck. We think someone poisoned him by contaminating his flowerpots with a toxic substance," Denise inquired as she studied the woman's face.

"I'm sorry, Detective, but I didn't see anyone. The same people work here all the time. Cannot the doctors find out what made poor Paul sick?" Mrs. Benedict replied with great concern in her voice.

"The doctors know that he had plant toxin in his system. What we don't know is how it got there," Denise replied as she made a quick sketch of Mrs. Benedict's face.

"But surely the police can test the pots and Paul's truck," Mrs. Benedict suggested.

"Unfortunately, Paul put the pots to soak as soon as he returned with the van that night. The poison washed off the pots in the soaking process. The soil samples they took from the drainage area did not contain any conclusive evidence," Denise replied as she added the finishing touches to her drawing. Although she had captured the classic lines and details of Mrs. Benedict's face, she had been unable to sketch the serenity that illuminated her alabaster skin.

"Will Paul get well? He is such a lovely young man. I hope that the person who tried to harm him will not strike again," Mrs. Benedict said as she struggled to find the right words.

"He's still very gravely ill, but the doctors think that he'll make a complete recovery. Don't worry about Paul's safety. The police have posted guards at his hospital room. No one can get through without permission," Denise replied as she showed Mrs. Benedict the sketch.

"Oh, it's lovely. Your work shows great feeling," Mrs. Benedict said as she blushed.

"Mrs. Benedict, where do you store the pots that you want Paul to return to the nursery?" Tom asked as he looked around the room for signs of anything suspicious. "We think that someone gained access to the pots prior to the time that Paul loaded them into the van."

Pointing across the room to a small door, Mrs. Benedict explained, "We put everything for Paul in that closet. That way when he delivers flowers at night he'll be able to find the things he needs for the return trip to the nursery."

"Speaking of volunteers, are there any names missing from this list that Mr. Philips gave us? I'd like to speak with as many of them as possible," Denise said as she collected her things.

"It looks very complete to me. Perhaps one or two are missing, but they're not regular volunteers. They only

work here when the others are on vacation," Mrs.
Benedict replied after giving the list a quick perusal.

Walking across the room, Denise opened the closet
door to find a small storage room full of clay and plastic
pots, glass vases, and sturdy boxes with remnants of
ferns still sticking to them. The room smelled of peat
moss and greenery. Aside from the gardening tools and
containers, nothing else was in the room. There were no
containers of pesticides or fertilizers on the empty
shelves to contaminate the blooms. The room was very
clean and orderly considering the number of people
who had access to it and the nature of their work.
Hardly any dirt littered the floor, and she saw only one
bloom abandoned in a corner.

Feeling someone standing beside her, Denise turned
to find Mrs. Benedict looking over her shoulder. She
appeared pleased that Denise had found the room in
almost pristine order. It reflected the neatness of her
little flower cart.

"You don't lock this door?" Tom asked as he noticed
the empty keyhole.

"Oh no, Detective. Too many people need to use it.
I'd spend my day locking and unlocking it or giving
people the key. We don't keep anything of significant
value in there, so there's no real reason to secure it. No
one would want to steal empty flowerpots," Mrs.
Benedict replied with a soft chuckle.

Thanking Mrs. Benedict for her time, Denise and
Tom left her as she returned to her work. They walked
in silence until they reached the main door; then
Denise suggested, "Let's ask the Capitol police to run a
quick check on the names of these people and all the
others who work in the Capitol. Maybe they'll learn
something about people's political interests."

"I'm with you, Dory," Tom replied. "If we don't find
something conclusive soon, we might be too late to stop

the next murder. For all the help I'm being here, I should go back to the office. If I can't help save lives, I might as well work on our cases."

"Don't get discouraged yet. This is a tough case, but we'll solve it. I know we will," Denise responded.

"Let's just hope we find the murderer before he comes after one of us," Tom snorted as he followed her to the Capital Hill police office. Waiting outside, he listened to the casual conversation of staffers as they passed.

As Denise entered the Capitol Hill police office, Captain Carter looked relieved to see her. Rising, he immediately clasped her hand in a hearty handshake. The stress of the unsolved murders showed in the lines around his mouth.

Looking from one to the other, Captain Carter asked, "What information have you come to share with me? I'm at a total loss to explain the murders and now the attack on Paul. It's unthinkable that someone within these walls could be so vicious."

"Captain," Denise began, "I have nothing new. Actually, I came to see you to request a favor rather than to share information. I'd like to request a brief background check on these volunteers. Each of these people had access to the storage room from which Paul removed the pots that we think someone dusted with poison."

The captain quickly scanned the list and replied, "I can personally vouch for all but three of these people. They have been either volunteers or on the staff here for well over ten years. The only relatively new people are Mr. Thirston, Mrs. Nelson, and Mr. Baptist. All of the others are old friends. You won't find anything in their records, I assure you."

"Very well, then would your people be able to provide the information I need on the remaining three by tomorrow morning? If the murderer hasn't advanced his cause to his satisfaction, he might strike again," Denise said with genuine concern in her voice.

"Detective Dory, it would be my pleasure to do anything I can to help you crack this case. My people are busy interviewing the staff, so I'll do this for you myself. I'll have brief biographies on each of these people by breakfast time tomorrow," Captain Carter replied with a broad smile

Denise thanked the captain, aware that the gleam in his eyes said that he expected friendly compensation from her. His eyes had barely left her lips and cleavage. With a sigh of frustration, she met Tom where he had waited for her in the hall. He preferred the hot sunlight to the cramped police office.

"You look upset. Did he leer at you again?" Tom asked with a chuckle.

"Again? I hadn't noticed it until now, but today I felt like a melting ice cream cone under his gaze," Denise replied with irritation as they walked into the city streets.

"Shall we walk so that you can burn off some steam or catch a cab?" Tom asked as they started off at a brisk clip in the sweltering heat.

Chuckling, Denise conceded, "Let's ride. I'm not that angry. Besides, the traffic is dreadful."

With perspiration dripping from his forehead, Tom hailed the first taxi he spotted. By the time they arrived at the small FBI office, Denise had briefed him on everything the captain had said about the people on the list. Since they knew that Carter would not be impartial, they needed the help of George Christian even more.

Handing her the envelope with the results of the analysis of the substance on Paul's glove, George Christian accepted the list with pleasure. Scanning it, he said with barely disguised glee, "To think that our little resources were largely untapped before you arrived on the scene, Detective. We were simply a support group for internal investigations. Now we're embroiled in the investigation of several murders. It's all very exciting."

"I certainly hope we're not overworking your staff. Captain Carter of the Capitol police is too familiar with those people on the list to provide reliable information," Denise replied with gratitude.

"No problem. As always, I enjoy the challenge of the cases you bring me," George Christian chuckled. "My life would be so dull without you and Tom. I'd only have FBI work to do rather than Maryland and now D.C."

As the taxi took them back to the U.S. Capitol, Denise squinted into the darkness at the toxicology report until Tom pulled a penlight from his pocket. "I can see that you were never a Girl Scout, Dory. Don't you have a regulation flashlight?"

"Yes, but I dropped it the night we found Paul in the woods. It fell from my pocket as I helped move him from the car. I haven't taken the time to buy another one," Denise replied with a grin at the good-natured ribbing.

"Keep this one. I have a spare in my car. What does the report say?"

"It states conclusively that Paul's work gloves were covered in belladonna dust. Now we need the results of the autopsy on Senator Frederick. Maybe we'll find out that the person who tried to kill Paul murdered the senator with the same substance," Denise commented as she leaned heavily against the seat. The combination of the heat and the weight of the unsolved murders rested heavily on her shoulders.

"Dory, the murderer is very clever. He knows that any investigation of this magnitude will be slow and tedious. Added to the equation is the fact that the poison is very difficult to trace, the killer is using a variety of them. All of this makes the case almost impossible to crack. I think the most we can hope is that the killer will stop now that he has exposed himself to discovery by attacking several people from the outside. However, if he's really dedicated to his cause, he'll strike again and ignore the fact that we're on his back."

"But we're not close enough. I just can't shake the feeling that the murderer is right under my nose. I feel his eyes on me all the time. I just wish I could prove my suspicions," Denise replied as she breathed deeply of the smell of D.C. in summer.

"You're just paranoid after your encounter with the lustful Captain Carter." Tom chuckled.

"I am not," Denise rebutted with a sneer. "I've felt this way long before Captain Carter drooled on me. I feel so certain that I'm on the right track."

Dragging her tired body and mind from the cab, Denise accompanied Tom as they strolled through the grounds to the area in which the others were already waiting. Flopping down on the cool grass, Denise asked, "Any news? Did you find out anything?"

"Not a thing," Greta replied with a shrug. "Everyone has alibis that check out. They were sleeping, watching television, attending a play, or preparing a late snack. It seems that no one was alone that evening. They all had at least one other person with them."

Denise commented with an expansive wave, "Well, going on the assumption that we have a complete list of all the people who worked here that day, I guess that means that the person who tried to kill Paul with the toxin had access to the pots earlier in the day. Mrs. Benedict told us that the storage closet is never locked. Someone could have dusted the pots without anyone noticing. It would have been easy enough to do while adding another pot to the pile."

"Where does that leave this investigation?" Eugene asked as he plucked the petals from a lovely yellow daisy.

Greta quipped, "Stuck in the mud with a handful of decaying mushrooms and other plants, that's where. We still don't know who killed the senators or why."

"Yes, but at least we know the nature of one of the poisons. Tom and I took the liberty of asking the lab to check the stomach, blood, and tissue samples of the dead senators against the *Amanita* mushroom toxin and the ones used on Nester, Piper, and Paul. I'll call our contact tomorrow. Let's keep our fingers crossed that he'll have something conclusive to add to our investigation," Denise advised as she lay on her back on the thick grass. The coolness of the grass and the brightness of the stars immediately made her feel better. She did not care if she got grass stains on the back of her white blouse. The serenity of the moment was well worth the cost of the cotton blouse.

"Let's hope we get the autopsy results on Senator Frederick soon," Greta commented as she blew on a dandelion and sent the white seedpods flying in the hot evening air.

"I just hope we can stop the murderer before he strikes again," Denise replied as she picked tiny blades of grass from her skirt.

The other detectives said good night and wandered off to their rooms. Denise and Tom stayed behind, Denise on the lawn, Tom sitting on a bench.

Turning to Tom with a slow half smile, all that she could manage in her present mood, Denise said, "You don't have to wait up with me. I know you're tired, so go to bed. I'll be perfectly safe here."

"Don't worry, Dory. I'll go to bed when I get tired. The stars are too bright for me to go inside. I remember nights like this when I was a kid growing up in Baltimore. The sky would look so far away as I sat on our front porch in the summertime. My family didn't have any money, but, at night with the stars sparkling overhead, I always felt rich. I used to imagine that the stars were diamonds, and that all I had to do was to reach out and scoop up a handful and all of my parents' money problems would melt away. It's amazing what the imagination of a child can produce."

Stretching, Denise asked, "Do you think that if we could reach those stars we could stop the murders? I've searched many an empty alley for clues and interrogated many suspects who proved to be innocent, but I've never lived among the potential victims and watched the fear in their eyes mix with the pain of losing a dear friend. Watching the strained faces of the senators as they try to put on a brave front is so difficult and heartbreaking. I sketched a few of their faces and found that I just couldn't bear to capture the agony. I feel so helpless, and I don't like it."

"You're a cop with a heart, Dory, and it makes you human. I guess that's why I, well, like having you as a partner. I've seen many cops become hard and calloused by what they've experienced in this job. You've been on the force for ten years, and you're still untouched. Stay that way, Dory, it's what makes you a good cop. You care and you try to do your best to end the suffering. You're good people. Don't let this get you down too much. I know we'll solve this case soon. He has already panicked once when he went after Paul. He'll slip again, and when he does, we'll catch him," Tom counseled as he looked deeply into her eyes.

The moonlight cast shadows on his face and highlighted the hollows and crags and made his eyes shine warmly. A few stray strands of mixed gray hair played in his temples as he hoisted his frame from the bench and extended his hands for her to grasp. With one quick motion, he pulled her to her feet and into his arms.

"You'd better not hold me so close," Denise whispered as she melted into the warmth of his arms. "People will think we're in love."

Smiling into her upturned face, Tom replied, "We are."

Gently, Tom pressed his lips against hers. As Denise yielded to the tenderness of his kiss, she realized that she had been waiting for that moment for years. Being in his arms felt so natural that she sighed and buried her head in his shoulder.

"Are you okay with this, Dory?" Tom asked softly as he cradled her against his wide chest.

"Completely," Denise sighed as she snuggled even closer.

"I've been waiting a long time to do this," Tom confessed as he smelled her hair and gently kissed her neck.

Looking into this warm eyes, Denise asked, "Why didn't you do it sooner?"

"I guess the time was never right," Tom said as he pressed her head against his shoulder again.

"We're always together. You could have done this anytime," Denise whispered.

"No. The time had to be just right. The moonlight on your skin and your vulnerability convinced me that this was the moment," Tom replied.

"Don't wait so long before doing it again," Denise commented with a chuckle.

"Not to worry. I intend to hold you in my arms every chance I get," Tom replied as he kissed the tip of her nose.

Taking her hand firmly in his, Tom led the way to the Page School. Turning down the hall that led to their rooms, Denise again studied the tapestry and paintings along the walls and saw that even they looked somber in their deep bloodreds, blues, and browns. Although she had originally been impressed by the colors, Denise was now dazzled by them. Everything seemed more intense and important now.

Stopping in front of her door, Tom smiled and kissed her good night. His hands lingered lovingly on her shoulders and back. Lightly stroking her cheek, he stepped away and motioned her inside.

"Let's solve this case and get out of here. I don't know how long I'll be able to stay on my side of that thin dormitory wall," Tom commented as he wistfully looked inside.

"I guess we'll have to wait a little longer. I don't especially want the others to suspect anything between us. They might think that we're distracted from our work," Denise said, giving them an excuse for not entering her room together.

"Denise, they're not very good detectives if they didn't figure me out when I first arrived here. No man uses leave to be with his partner unless he has feelings for her," Tom replied, smiling warmly in a way that illuminated and softened his gruff face.

"Denise? I don't think I've heard you call me that more than once or twice. I guess that does mean that you have feelings for me," Denise teased lightly as she slipped into his arms again.

Before Tom could respond, they heard Richard fumbling with the lock of the door that Tom shared with him. Stepping apart, they watched as Richard appeared, rubbing his eyes and peering into the hall. Seeing Tom and Denise engaged in deep conversation, he cleared his throat noisily before greeting them.

"Well, I see you've finally come in," Richard commented without appearing to notice the blush on Denise's cheeks. "Good timing. I was about ready to turn in. I'll leave the door open. Good night, Denise."

Richard had gone back inside the room before she could answer. Turning her attention to Tom, Denise looked at him and said, "I guess that's the end of our romantic interlude. See you in the morning, partner."

"Good night, Dory. This is only the first of many nights between us," Tom replied as he walked toward his door.

Taking off her clothes and turning off the light, Denise hoped that there would indeed be many more nights like this between them. As she knew she would, Denise liked being in Tom's arms. She loved the feel of his strength against her body. She loved the smell of the closeness of him. She could hardly wait until they explored the full extent of their feelings. Crawling under the covers while the air conditioner blew cool air into the room, Denise knew that they had to solve this case soon so that she could continue to live her life.

THIRTEEN

Unable to break the old habit, Denise and Tom arrived at the Capitol in the morning to listen to the press conference. The somber faces of the senators spoke the words that their lips could not as they met in the halls and on the grounds. Even the newest members had assumed the same gloomy expression.

Denise and Tom left the others to pay a visit to Captain Carter, who had promised to have the results of his investigation early in the morning. "Let me talk to him," Tom said as Denise prepared to leave him on the steps. "He'll give me the information and won't stare at my chest."

Laughing, Denise touched Tom's cheek gently and asked, "Are you jealous? That's so sweet, Tom. Thanks, but I can handle Captain Carter."

"As long as you're the one doing the handling, we're okay." Tom sulked as he sat on the nearest chair.

Chuckling, Denise vanished into the stuffy office. True to his word, the leering captain had an envelope waiting for her. As he stared at her cleavage, she read the information about the three newest members of the Capitol's large volunteer staff. As Denise had expected, his resources had uncovered nothing that would make her suspicious of the private lives of any of the employees.

"You see, Detective Dory," Captain Carter commented as he stepped a little closer, "we're a close-knit family here. It's not possible that anyone here could have killed the senators."

Stepping back to reclaim her comfort zone, Denise replied, "Captain, if that is true, then you have a serious breech in security here and someone is entering the premises despite the best efforts of your people. However, I don't believe that is possible. From what I've seen, your men are very thorough. I have accompanied them and have been most impressed by their efficiency as they search and seal every office and storage area. I can't imagine that anyone from the outside could possibly penetrate this level of security. If the murderer is from the outside, then I can only assume that he is working with someone who has access to the building."

"I would hate to think that someone on the staff is helping an outsider commit these murders," Captain Carter replied, more interested in her than in the discussion. "Who do you suspect? We have interrogated everyone and have found nothing. Despite all of our efforts, the murders continue."

As Denise replied, Captain Carter looked over his shoulder at Tom, who stood like her guardian angel at the door. "Who on the staff might grow poisonous plants? Who has unquestioned access to the senators? Who has reason to want to kill them? All of these are questions that we haven't yet answered."

Throwing up his hands in exasperation, Captain Carter responded, "People have all kinds of hobbies and undisclosed interests. The woods are filled with poisonous plants. I don't think we'll find the killer until we catch him red-handed."

Denise stated firmly, "Then, Captain, I'd suggest that you post your men at the office door of Senators Salermo and Dey. I realize that this puts a tremendous strain on your police force, but those two senators are the most likely candidates to be murdered. Their offices and their homes will have to be protected twenty-four hours a day. I'm sure the D.C. police will be willing to help."

Captain Carter said as he tried to look charming, "I have faith that our combined forces will find him. He cannot hide from us forever. I'll implement your suggestion on one condition."

"And what's that?" Denise asked, dreading the possibilities.

"Shall we make a little wager on the identity of the murderer?" Captain Carter asked as he invaded her comfort zone again.

"Captain, I don't usually bet on a man's life," Denise retorted as she folded her arms across her body.

"Let's say that we're wagering on the success of our investigative instincts. I propose that if I'm correct that the murderer is from the outside, I'll take you out to dinner," Captain Carter commented with a droopy-lid expression on his face that he imagined to be sexy. His round belly fairly quivered with lust.

Denise found everything about the lecherous police captain to be repulsive, but she did not wish to alienate him. She managed to ask with a smile, "And if I'm right and the murderer is an insider, what'll be the prize?"

Beaming brightly, he announced, "The same thing, only you get to name the restaurant."

With a chuckle, Denise replied, "I accept your wager."

Captain Carter looked toward the door where Tom lounged scowling against the frame. With a self-confident grin on his bloated face, Carter replied, "Wonderful. I'll post my men and search for our intruder. I hope you're hungry since you've forgotten that all regular employees and volunteers wear identity badges. I have only to search for people who are not wearing them. I can hardly wait for our evening alone."

"Don't count me out yet. I might still win that wager. You forget that it's easy to forge almost anything from birth certificates to identification badges these days," Denise replied as she left the office. She could barely contain the laughter that had threatened to bubble over at the sight of the offensive man's preposterous amorous behavior.

Tom immediately followed her. With a frown on his forehead he asked, "What was that all about, Dory? I heard parts of the conversation through the door. Are you really going to dinner alone with him?"

"I'll have to go if I'm wrong, but I don't think that I am. I wanted to insure that Senators Salermo and Dey would be safe, and I knew that Captain Carter would never agree to post a guard on their office door without seeing something in it for him. I asked him before and he refused. This time he accepted the suggestion as the way to win our wager."

"I don't like this one bit, Dory," Tom growled as they strolled toward the satellite FBI office. The morning was too fresh and the city too beautiful to spend the time in a cab.

"Don't worry, Tom. You're the only man for me," Denise flirted with a laugh at Tom's discomfort. "Look at all this information he gave us. It's just as I thought; these three people checked out clean. I'm sure that George Christian's investigation will show the same thing, but I'm hoping for a little more information than Captain Carter's brief bios."

Scanning the sheets, Tom commented as he pointed toward the gentleman walking down the brick stairs, "Let's hope for more. Here comes George."

George Christian greeted them enthusiastically,

"Hey, guys, you saved me the walk. Here's the information you wanted. I'm off to the back."

Slipping into a booth at the nearest restaurant, Denise and Tom read through the lengthy dossier on each of the members of the Capitol office and police staffs. George Christian had compiled data that incorporated Carter's and more. Dividing the stack in half, they quickly sorted out those people whose backgrounds were so clean that they squeaked from those whose lives contained questionable elements. By the time they finished, they had a stack of ten three-page dossiers.

"What about this guy?" Tom asked as he shared a paper with her. "His name's Peter Dominic and he's a proclaimed gun-reform supporter."

"What are his hobbies?" Denise asked as she continued to scan the reports on the table.

Flipping the papers, Tom responded, "This says riding and hunting, which makes him an outdoorsman with access to the woods. Let's see, he works in the kitchen full-time. Depending on the cause of death of Senator Frederick, this guy might be our man."

Picking up another dossier, Denise asked, "All right. And this one? No, his hobby is antique furniture restoration, but he's ultraconservative and thinks that government is becoming too liberal. No, I don't think he'd do anything like this."

"But this one might," Tom suggested. "Listen, Dory, he's a former priest who left for marriage. When the relationship soured, he turned his energies to the anti-abortion efforts. George Arman's hobby is gardening. He works in the laundry and tutors in the evening."

"Look, I think we have one. He's Anthony Guido and a former member of the park police. He's currently on the Capitol police force. No wonder the captain wanted to keep the investigation to himself," Denise recited quickly as her heart pounded with the excitement of discovery.

"Here's the last one. The name is Joseph Martin, and he's a florist who is adamantly opposed to any further change to Social Security. Well, I'd say that list gives us four very likely candidates, wouldn't you, Dory?" Tom commented as he smiled broadly.

"I have a strange feeling about this. I can't explain it, but I don't think the murderer's name is on our list. We might have found his accomplice, but not the master-mind himself," Denise replied as she tried to reign in her skepticism and share his enthusiasm for pending victory.

"Dory, don't you want to solve this case and go home? I've had enough of this town. Besides, as long as we're here, we won't have time for us," Tom complained as he gathered the files and paid their bill.

As they walked into the bright sunlight, Denise answered sweetly as she slipped her arm through his, "I want to go home as much as you do. I just know that we've isolated the killer. We'll be home soon and will have plenty of time for ourselves."

"With my luck, our caseload at home will keep us too busy for any alone time," Tom sulked.

"We'll make time for us, steal it if we have to, don't worry," Denise replied as she pressed closer to him as they stood at the crosswalk.

"Whatever," Tom growled. He did not receive too much comfort from the idea that they would have to steal time to be together.

Leading a sullen Tom in the direction of the FBI office, Denise smiled at the beautiful day. She would remember her work on this case for the rest of her life. If it had not been for this assignment to D.C., she might never have learned that Tom loved her.

George Christian smiled broadly as they entered his

office. Shaking their hands, he said, "I just got the report. It says that all three senators died from *Amanita* mushroom poisoning. You were right in asking the coroner to run another test. He said that he never would have found the existence of the toxin if you hadn't tipped him off. It's not something he encounters every day."

"That's great news. All we need now is the autopsy results on Senator Frederick," Denise replied as the feeling of relief and accomplishment surged through her body. Now they had a list of possible suspects and the method the murderer had used. With luck and a little more time, she knew that they would catch the killer.

"Does that move the florist, Joseph Martin, up on the list?" Tom asked as he hastily thanked George Christian and followed Denise into the sunshine.

"It certainly does. Let's see if we can interview him as soon as we return to the Capitol," Denise replied as they hailed a cab at the corner.

The ride in lunchtime traffic took even longer than usual, but Denise doubted if they could have made any better time on foot. Tourists, shoppers, children, and vendors clogged the sidewalks, making foot traffic barely crawl along. The comfortable temperature caused the restaurants to set up their tables and umbrellas in a mad profusion of color. People jostled each other for space on the narrow sidewalks as they veered around the feet and packages of the dining crowd. They darted between parked cars and blocked the flow of traffic as they crossed the street in search of more shopping or a less crowded place to eat.

Denise and Tom managed to navigate their way through the crowd to the police station. As usual, Tom waited outside while Denise briefly spoke with Captain Carter, who rubbed his meaty hands together with glee at the toxicology results. The sight of the almost drooling little man made Tom's stomach sick.

As Denise left the room Captain Carter called after her saying, "This information will make it even easier for me to win our wager, Detective. I hope you're ready for a hearty meal."

"If I were you, I wouldn't make a reservation for two just yet," Denise replied with a quick teasing smile.

Waving good-bye, Denise rejoined Tom for the walk to the side entrance. "How did it go with the captain?" he asked as they entered the building.

"Let's just say that I'm still the blue plate special," Denise replied as she led the way to the flower-arranging room. Along the way, she waved to Mrs. Benedict, who was busily at work setting out fresh pots of plants near Senator Salermo's office. She smiled and nodded in response.

Joseph Martin was bent over a huge basket of mauve carnations when they entered the room and did not see them until they stood beside him. Straightening, he asked, "Detectives, what brings you to the arranging room today?"

"We'd like to speak with you for a few minutes if you can spare the time. We have a few questions we'd like to ask you about your political leanings," Denise replied as she watched his face register the significance of their visit.

"I see," Joseph Martin replied as he removed his work gloves, "You've discovered my connection to the Brotherhood for Reform. Let's talk in my office. It's small but very private."

The room was little more than a closet with a tiny desk and chair in the center, an old wooden file cabinet in one corner, two wooden folding chairs stacked in another, and an assortment of plant catalogues piled in every available space. It looked as if all the chaos of the Capitol had found a way to that one room.

"Tell us about the Brotherhood. What exactly does it espouse?" Denise asked as soon as she and Tom made themselves as comfortable as possible in the messy little room.

Looking first at his hands and then unwaveringly at the two detectives, Joseph Martin replied, "The Brotherhood advocates the removal of all handguns from homes. We work for the repeal of the Second Amendment."

Leaning forward, Tom asked, "Exactly how does the Brotherhood advocate making this change? As its vice president you probably have a leadership role."

"We are a group of men who think that gun violence has grown to outrageous proportions," Joseph Martin replied without hesitation. "We've sent tremendous volumes of mail to the Capitol asking the Hill to rethink its direction. We've identified and met with the senators who support our cause. Despite the recent events, we'll continue to push."

"How does the Brotherhood feel about murder as a means to an end?" Denise asked as she sketched his very expressive face.

"We abhor it. We're appalled that someone has taken the life of the senators as a way of making a political statement," Joseph Martin replied with flashes of anger darting from his eyes.

Taking an even more direct approach, Tom inquired, "Why did you hide your association with the Brotherhood from the detectives who interviewed you? You must have known that they would find out eventually."

Without moving his eyes from Tom's face, Joseph Martin responded, "I'm a coward. Out of fear for myself, I hid my connection with them. I was afraid that I would become a suspect in the murders. I would never harm the senators, and, as far as I can tell, none of my colleagues would do such a dreadful thing either. They are people of passionate words, not angry deeds."

"Can you think of anyone in your organization who might be antagonized by the slow approach and feel that more direct action would work better?" Denise demanded as she adjusted her body on the hard seat.

Joseph Martin was either well rehearsed, extremely cold-blooded, or innocent, because he showed no sign of stress at meeting with Tom and Denise. Again he calmly replied, "None of us would jeopardize the Brotherhood's successful completion of goals by striking out independently. We're not that kind of organization."

Closing her sketchbook, Denise said, "Just one more question, Mr. Martin, and we'll leave you to your work. Our investigation showed that you became the vice president upon the death of Edward Barr. Could you tell us the cause of his death, please?"

With a downturn of his mouth, Joseph replied, "Edward was a very elderly man. He died of congestive heart failure in his sleep one night. His wife said that he never uttered a sound but simply stopped breathing. He was my father-in-law, and I miss him very much."

As if on cue the three of them rose and left the little room. Watching him return to his flowers, Denise was satisfied that Joseph Martin had told them the truth about the Brotherhood and himself. At least, the information matched what the FBI had provided. The Brotherhood was a benign organization that used words and not violence to bring about change. Denise and Tom were relieved to see that Joseph Martin advocated the organization's tenets.

Their next stop was the laundry complex in which orderliness was the mode of operation. Soiled linens filled hampers along one wall and waited to be sorted onto the conveyor belt that would take them to the appropriate machines. The hum of washers and dryers and the hiss of steam reminded Denise of the activity of a beehive.

The supervisor greeted them and pointed toward the man operating one of the pressing machines. As they approached, George Arman looked up from the stack of sheets and tablecloths over which he had been working. Perspiration dotted his forehead and upper lip and his thick black hair hung limply over his forehead, but his smile was bright as he extended his hand and motioned toward the lounge. They followed him to a sun-filled room that was amazingly silent after the noise of the main laundry and sank into a firm leather sofa while George sat in a chair facing them.

Leaning back in his chair and crossing one leg over the other at the ankle, George Arman stated with a sly smile, "I was wondering how long it would take you to find out about me. What can I do for you today?"

"Tell us about your hobbies, George," Tom demanded as he studied the man whose demeanor spelled cool confidence.

George said with a chuckle, "Oh, so you know about my gardening interest. It's harmless. I only grow flowers and an occasional marijuana plant. Nothing stronger than that. Why?"

Knowing that the newspapers would have carried the story, in their morning editions, of the toxin the murderer had used to kill the senators, Denise replied, "We think the killer is someone who either grows or harvests *Amanita* mushrooms. I was just wondering how your garden grows."

"I wouldn't touch that stuff. You can't afford to be careless around that mushroom, and I'm a dig-in-the-dirt kind of guy. A little bit of that toxin goes a long way," George replied, waving his hands as if brushing away the poisonous fungus.

"How do you know so much about the mushroom?" Tom asked as he continued to study the man's face. "I'd never heard about it until this investigation."

George offered without hesitation, "I majored in botany in college and taught science in high school for a while. You couldn't tell by looking at me now, but I have a doctorate in plant reproduction. The *Amanita* mushroom and other poisonous plants always interested me. I worked with Doctor Nester for a while when I first moved here. He wanted to hire me as his full-time assistant. He said we'd author studies together, but I wasn't ready to settle down. I guess I still hadn't found myself. Maybe I still haven't. Anyway, we parted on good terms. It saddened me to hear of his death."

"What do you think killed him?" Denise asked quickly.

"I only know what I read in the paper," George offered. "As a former colleague of his, I don't think he choked to death on a salad mushroom. He might have come in contact with the rhizomes of the lady's slipper orchid or a little nightshade. He grew both of them in the lab."

Stretching, Tom commented, "I thought that both of those had to be ingested to take effect."

George seemed to have warmed to them and was sprawled in the chair, obviously enjoying the conversation. He replied confidently, "They do. A little bit of the powder in his food would be enough to cause slight paralysis and maybe suffocation and choking if he were still chewing on the salad at the time."

"He grew the *Amanita* mushroom in his lab, too," Denise commented casually.

George responded with a wave of his large, square, immaculately clean hands, "That's true, but he really respected the potential for harm of that fungus. He was a funny kind of guy. Instead of planting the angel in a separate section of the lab, he marked its flats with red banners. Whenever he worked with a specimen in the lab, he covered it with a domed lid to prevent accidental contact. There's no way he willingly touched that one."

"Did you have a key to his lab?" Tom asked.

"Sure, but I gave it back when I stopped working for him. Why?" George demanded as he suddenly sat erect. Veils settled over his eyes and showed the increased caution he felt.

"The person who killed Doctor Nester let himself in. There was no sign of forced entry," Tom responded in a nonchalant manner.

"I'm sure I wasn't the only assistant Doctor Nester had over the last few years. You might want to check his file cabinet for the list of the others," George suggested warily.

"I'm sure the D.C. police have done that already, but I'll suggest it if they haven't. Well, thanks for the talk, George," Denise said as she gathered her stuff.

"I'm a suspect, aren't I? It's because of my hobbies. Well, I didn't grow the mushrooms that killed the senators. That stuff is too dangerous," George stated as he followed them into the steamy laundry.

"You say you didn't grow the mushroom, but did you help the person who did?" Denise asked, staring into his now closed face.

"No, I didn't, and I haven't a clue as to the identity of the murderer either," George responded with his hands shoved deeply into his pants pockets.

Turning to him, Tom stated, "If I were you, I wouldn't change my address without notifying Captain Carter of the U.S. Capitol police force."

"I'll keep that in mind, and don't worry, I'm not going anywhere. I'm here to stay. I'll see you both again soon, I hope. Let me know if you need any help in identifying vegetable substances," George said with a wave and a very long face.

As soon as they stood in the sunshine again, Denise said, "He's on the top of your list, isn't he?"

"Give me one good reason why he shouldn't be, Dory," Tom replied confidently. "He's knowledgeable about plants, especially mushrooms. He admits to having worked with Doctor Nester."

"I don't think he did it. Besides, he doesn't have access to the senators," Denise replied as she studied the sketches she had made of George's face. To her mind, it was not the face of a murderer.

"No, but he might be the person who grows the fungi. Someone else might have actually slipped the senators the poison. I'm keeping him on my list till we find someone else who fits the profile. This time, I'm going to see Captain Carter to tell him to be on the lookout for suspicious behavior," Tom stated as he started walking toward the police station.

"Okay. Meet me in the kitchen. I can't stand the thought of his leering at me twice in one day," Denise replied as she slipped away. She knew she was right about George. He had not participated in the senators' murders, but she still did not know who had. Besides, it would not hurt for the suspect to see an increased police presence. If Captain Carter's men started watching George, the real murderer might feel that he was off the hook and make a false move.

As Denise hurried through the Capitol halls on the way to the kitchen, she passed Mrs. Benedict in the hall. This was the first time that Denise had seen her away from the arranging room. Although Denise was surprised to see Mrs. Benedict, the older woman did not appear startled by her presence as she whizzed past Denise. She looked up from the arrangement of flowers she was repairing and smiled. Before Denise could speak, Mrs. Benedict had collected the dead stems, gardening scissors, and the cart and had started toward the next arrangement. The fragrance of the fresh flowers mixed with the clean smell of cold marble and the dust of old books.

FOURTEEN

As Denise entered the kitchen, she spotted Tom standing openmouthed in the doorway. Quickly, she became equally as impressed as she watched the kitchen buzz with activity. The chefs and their crew prepared the afternoon tea and began the first preparations for the evening festivities. Bushel baskets of potatoes and crates of lettuce sat beside equal amounts of fresh green beans, beets, and ears of corn. A cloud of fine white dust surrounded the pastry chef as he rolled piecrusts for tarts and dough for scones for tea. His assistants worked feverishly on the cakes and pies for the evening's dessert.

The head chef pointed out Peter Dominic in the corner with the other assistants. He stood surrounded by potatoes that he had to peel and slice for the creamed potatoes that they would consume later that night. His face was a study in concentration as he guided the sharp blade in one continuous movement around the tubers. The peels fell into a pail that someone would add to the compost bin.

"Mr. Dominic, I'm Detective Dory and this is Detective Phyfer. May we have a few minutes of your time, please?" she asked somewhat reluctantly. The man was so obviously engaged in his work that she hated to interrupt him.

Nodding, he replied in a pleasant baritone, "Of

course, Detectives, I remember you from your first visit to the kitchen. Let's step into the herb garden. We can talk there."

The herb garden was almost the size of the living room in Denise's apartment. Every imaginable herb grew in abundance in the sunny court off the kitchen. The three of them found a bench beside the largest rosemary bush she had ever seen and made themselves comfortable while the bees buzzed around them.

Taking out her sketchbook, Denise explained, "Mr. Dominic, we've come to ask your help in the investigation of the senators' murders. We've learned that you are an avid huntsman and woodsman. Perhaps you can tell us something about the fungus that the killer used in the crimes. It's the *Amanita* mushroom."

Peter Dominic shifted uneasily on the hard bench before responding as he searched for the words to express his thoughts. Haltingly he replied, "I know nothing about the mushroom other than what I've read. It's true that I hunt, but I've never seen one of those plants in the woods. If I had, I would have stayed far away from it. I understand that it is highly toxic."

"Yes, it is. A very small amount can kill a man or his mount. Have you seen any other poisonous plants in the woods around here?" Denise asked as she drew.

Peter Dominic's long tired face looked as if he carried the weight of the world on his bent back. Denise wondered what could make this full-time kitchen employee look so uncomfortable. Certainly, it was more than the bags of potatoes that waited for him.

"Sometimes I see a little mandrake root or maybe a lady's slipper," Mr. Dominic replied with a shrug and a quick glance at the east door that led to the hall.

Following his gaze, Tom asked, "Are you expecting someone?"

Becoming even more agitated, Dominic replied, "No, I have much work to do, that's all."

"We won't keep you much longer, Mr. Dominic. I know about the poisonous lady's slipper, but what makes mandrake toxic?" Denise inquired as she watched a long shadow move across the panes of the door.

"It's a form of nightshade plant, so I've heard, and works in much the same way to cause paralysis. If you don't have any more questions, may I go now? I have so many potatoes to peel," Mr. Dominic begged as his eyes darted once again to the door.

"Yes, of course, but you will contact us if you think of anything we should know?" Tom stated as he studied the man's nervous movements.

"Yes, yes, but I don't know anything more to tell you. I come here, I peel my potatoes, and I go home. I don't mix in politics," Mr. Dominic replied as he rose and prepared to run away.

"But the dossier we have on you says that you're an activist. I'd say that you're quite political, Mr. Dominic," Denise rebutted in a casual voice.

He stopped in midstep and swirled around to face her. Speaking angrily, he demanded, "Who told you that? The police, I suppose, but it doesn't matter. You would have found out anyway. Yes, I'm politically active, but that doesn't make me a murderer. I would not kill a man for any cause."

"No, perhaps not alone, but if you've helped someone else poison the senators, you're equally responsible. If you saw the person do it and did not tell the police, you would still be an accomplice," Denise advised, watching his posture revert to his customary slouch from the erect carriage of the past minute.

"I would never help anyone who wanted to kill the senators. If I had definite knowledge of the person who did this terrible thing, I would share it with the police, but I know nothing. No cause, no matter its importance, is worth murder. If I had any suspicions, I'd keep them to myself. It's not wise to accuse a man falsely. Excuse me, but I have to go now," Mr. Dominic said as he vanished through the doors.

"Mr. Dominic," Tom called, following him into the kitchen, "we can protect you if you know something that will help us solve the murders and prevent more. We can keep you safe."

"I don't believe that, Detective Phyfer. With all respect, three elected politicians have died since you arrived. You could not protect them. What can you possibly do for a humble kitchen worker?" Peter Dominic replied with a shrug of his shoulders as he hurried away.

Denise stood in the doorway for a few minutes collecting her thoughts about what had just happened. Peter Dominic had seen someone's shadow at the door and become frightened enough to want to flee from their company. He knew something and was terrified of the knowledge he thought he had. Perhaps he was right in doubting their ability to protect him if he disclosed his information. Their presence had not saved the others. Short of jailing their informant, Denise did not believe that she could really protect anyone who worked in the Capitol from the killer.

"Let's go," Tom suggested. "He won't talk anymore. Something scared him badly."

"Maybe he'll be more cooperative tomorrow," Denise stated as she allowed Tom to lead her from the kitchen.

Tom and Denise saw Mr. Dominic busily at work when they left the kitchen. He did not acknowledge them as they walked past and only worked harder to avoid looking up. Something in his silence told Denise that he would not speak with them again.

"I could almost smell his fear when the shadow appeared. I wonder if he'll report to work tomorrow," Denise commented as she caught up with Tom, who had, as always, outpaced her.

"We need to interview Anthony Guido," Tom commented as he slipped off his shoes and massaged his tired feet.

"I hope he's more talkative than Mr. Dominic. That poor man was scared out of his wits. I doubt that he's much older than fifty, but the weight of what he's carrying around has made him look older," Denise replied as she glanced at her watch. The day had passed quickly; it was almost five o'clock. She needed a bath and a change of clothes before dinner.

They sat in silence for a minute until Tom complained, "Denise, my feet are killing me. I'll never complain about our workload at home after this."

Laughing at his discomfort, Denise replied, "Quit your bellyaching. We're almost done here. If I'm right, we'll know the identity of the murderer in the next couple of days."

"What makes you so sure? The group can't even agree on the same suspect," Tom retorted, squeezing his swollen feet back into his oxfords.

"We're getting too close for comfort. Already the killer has slipped and tried to murder Paul Fleet, but fortunately he failed. We've been able to identify the poisons he used, and Mr. Dominic is afraid of being seen with us. Let me help you up, old man. I need a nap and a shower before dinner, and you need some salts for your feet," Denise said as she took Tom by the hands and pulled him to his feet.

Slipping his arms around her slim body and pulling her tight, Tom said, "I bet I can still keep up with you in everything that matters."

"Let me go! We still have work to do." Denise replied as she tried without success to pull away.

"Even you can take a short break," Tom replied as he buried his lips in her neck.

With a sigh, Denise relaxed and allowed the pleasurable feelings to run the length of her body. Tom's arms felt so strong and his lips so tender that she could have remained wrapped in his body. Reluctantly, she pushed back and broke his grip.

"That's enough of that. For a man with aching feet, you certainly are frisky," Denise laughed as she extricated herself from his grip.

Chuckling deeply, Tom replied, "My feet aren't the only things aching."

Looking gently into his eyes, Denise promised, "We'll find a cure for that later."

Leading him down the hall, Tom muttered, "Promises, promises."

Leaving Tom at his door, Denise called Mr. Fleet to inquire about Paul's recovery before stepping into the shower. The conversation helped to perk up her mood after her afternoon with Peter Dominic. She could hear the smile in his voice as he said, "Detective Dory, it is so good of you to call. Paul is feeling much better, and the doctors say that he won't suffer any lasting effects from the toxin. He's a strong boy and should be back home in a few days."

"That's wonderful news, Mr. Fleet. You will keep a guard on hand at all times even when he comes home, won't you?" Denise advised cautiously. "Until we apprehend the murderer, Paul is not out of danger."

"Do not worry about that, Detective. We have family members that sleep in his room in addition to the police that never leave the door. When we get him home, he'll be even safer. I'll have taken care of that. Believe me when I say that no one will be able to come close to my son again," Mr. Fleet replied with confidence that completely alleviated her fears.

The shower was more comforting than Denise had expected. Not only did it wash away the grime and sweat, but it relaxed the tension from her shoulders and helped to erase the turmoil of her thoughts. She slipped under the crisp, clean covers and immediately fell into a sound sleep.

Denise awoke from her nap with a splitting headache, which she immediately attributed to a day in the sun. Popping two aspirins, she dressed slowly. With every step, her head felt as if it would separate from her body and roll across the floor. When she joined Tom and the others in the dining room, they were already in animated conversation and only briefly acknowledged her presence as she eased into one of the groups. The cool iced tea felt comforting as it slipped down her parched throat. Denise rubbed the frosty glass on her temples to relieve the fever that burned brightly on her face.

Dinner would have been delicious if her stomach had not rebelled so fiercely at the sight of the food. The Cornish hen was grilled to perfection; the potatoes had been cooked with chicken broth and whipped with sweet cream; the green beans were garden-fresh and incredibly tasty; and the ice cream with strawberries was homemade. She would have enjoyed every bite ordinarily, but she felt too sick.

"You look a little green, Dory. What's wrong?" Tom whispered when he saw that she had pushed aside her untouched plate.

"I think I have a touch of sun poisoning. Look, I don't want to spoil everyone's meal, so I'm going to interview Anthony Guido and then I'll turn in for the night. Why don't you meet me in the police office when you've finished?" Denise replied as she scooted back her chair. The aspirin had not even made a dent in the pounding inside her head.

"I'll go with you," Tom offered as he turned away the plate of shimmering ice cream.

Denise knew that he was worried about her when he left it untouched and joined her.

They slowly and painfully made their way to the office. The effects of his aching feet and her overall flushed, slumped condition made them an odd couple. For the first time since arriving at the Capitol, Denise did not notice her surroundings. She simply wanted to conduct the interview and go to bed.

Anthony Guido had just reported for duty when Denise and Tom arrived. Denise did not know if it was the sight of them or his usual inclination, but he smiled warmly and immediately pulled two chairs over to the desk he occupied in the corner of the office. They eased their aching bodies gratefully into them and began their conversation.

"Officer Guido, we'd like to ask you a few questions, if you don't mind, about your political affiliations, especially those concerning Social Security, gun control, and women's rights," Denise stated as she made a few half-hearted attempts at sketching his face. Her drawings looked as feeble and disoriented as her thoughts.

"I'll help any way I can. However, I'm not what most people would call a zealot," Anthony Guido responded calmly.

"How does your group plan to change the senators' opinions on strengthening women's rights?" Tom asked in his usual laid-back way.

"We've met with every senator. Unfortunately, we've found resistance from most of them except Senator Dey, who alone supports our cause. At this moment, we are lobbying for his selection as the head of a few important subcommittees. Our voice is loud and our insistence great. However, our patience is running thin. We demand to be heard this time. Senator Dey is our best hope for change," Guido barked fiercely. His determination was unmistakable. Anthony Guido was a dangerous man.

"Do you think that anyone in your organization would commit murder to advance your cause?" Denise asked casually as she watched his expression soften from anger to concern.

"Never," Guido replied without hesitation. "We are soldiers with words, not with violence. We intend to make a change and to be heard, but we don't advocate violence to accomplish the end. It is only a matter of time before the senators agree with us. Dey would make a strong chairman who would be able to sway the opinions of many others. They will heed our voices this time, I'm sure."

"What if they won't select him? I'm sure you know that many senators are equally as well respected," Denise stated with caution.

"We know of the popularity of Senator Salermo, but we're confident that the senators will select Dey this time. He has their full backing. If he is not selected, we'll continue to encourage him to be the spokesman for the cause. Our time has come, and we will not be denied," Guido replied adamantly.

The determination shone on his face and glowed from his eyes. This man was a true politician whose force of conviction was enough to convince people to take up the fight and follow him. In her weakened state, Denise had found his passion difficult to resist.

Hoping to catch him off guard, Denise asked, without even trying to make a graceful transition, "By the way, what do you know about gardening?"

With a chuckle, Anthony Guido replied, "My sister is the one with the green thumb. Our mother had a small garden behind our house when we were children. My sister continued the family tradition. I can do nothing for you along those lines."

Tom asked carefully, "Have you seen any suspicious-looking people hanging around the grounds lately? I understand from Captain Carter that you change shifts with your fellow police officers often. You would have the most opportunity to see many people since you are on the job at all hours."

"No, I can't say that I've seen anyone unusual," Guido replied as he reflected on life within the Capitol walls. "For the most part, the same people come here every day. There are always foreign dignitaries paying visits to the senators, but they do not usually stay long. They conduct their business and then they leave. Paul Fleet or his brothers and cousins deliver the flowers from his family's nursery every evening at the same time. Stephen Grant arrives with the mail truck every day at ten o'clock. If he's late, we know that the traffic was a mess. Toni Danza pulls into the gate at seven every morning with newspapers from around the world. We live by routine here. We have to or else this place would become too chaotic with all the tourists flocking through here. We need order for survival."

Denise would have nodded in agreement, but her head hurt too badly for her to move. Instead, she smiled as she closed her sketchbook and left the goodbyes to Tom. She could tell that they had uncovered all that Anthony Guido would share with them in one evening. Although she had an uneasy feeling about him, Denise did not think that he would run away. Unlike Peter Dominic, who was afraid of shadows, Anthony Guido feared nothing.

Outside, she breathed deeply of the fresh summer

evening and watched the last tourists stroll the grounds. From the unaccustomed silence, Denise imagined that she would hear an echo if she shouted her name among the marble columns. If her head had not pounded dully at the thought, she might have given it a try.

Feeling guilty for taking Tom away from his dessert, she offered to buy him an ice cream at the corner stand. Of course, he accepted and immediately propelled her onto the main thoroughfare. Denise had a raspberry cone that tasted sweeter than usual and reminded her that she had not eaten since lunch. The effects of that last meal had finally started to wear off, and she was feeling as if she wanted to be among the living again.

After consuming their treats, Denise and Tom joined the others for their usual debriefing session in the garden. Now that her headache was only a dull memory, she was far more talkative. Since his feet were still painful and were making him rather grumpy, Tom sat and smoked on the outskirts of their group as Denise brought them up to speed on the results of their investigation.

When she finished, Eugene summed up, saying, "It looks to me as if we should be watchful of Guido and Dominic. I've been wondering about our own safety, too. What's to say that we won't become targets? We're getting close, and the killer has already slipped up once and botched a murder attempt."

"I was thinking the same thing," Greta commented, "but how can we protect ourselves from a substance that we can't detect? In its powdered form, the toxin from the *Amanita* mushroom should look like any other dust. As for the other toxins, unless they give off a strange taste or odor, we'd never know that we'd come in contact with them."

Eugene interjected, "If a botanist with a specialty in plant toxins fell victim to the murderer, how can we protect ourselves when we don't even know what to look for?''

With a sigh Denise reminded them about the nature of Dr. Nester's death, saying, "Nester died as the result of consuming the toxin from a lady's slipper orchid that subsequently caused him to suffocate on a mushroom bit that the murderer pushed into his windpipe to re-semble choking. My theory is that the killer sprinkled it on his salad while they were engaged in casual conver-sation. Remember that Nester knew his assailant. There was no sign of forced entry and the doors were un-locked. The lady's slipper toxin caused paralysis, which inhibited swallowing. The killer probably watched him die of asphyxiation and then left the lab through the garage when he heard us enter from the unlocked front door. From what we saw at the scene and from the D.C. police reports, Nester did not struggle with the killer. If he realized what was happening, he probably didn't know until it was too late. The toxin had already started to work, and he couldn't breathe.''

"What a way to die! I think I'd rather have the *Amanita* mushroom take me out," Eugene exclaimed, shak-ing his head.

"I don't know if I'd prefer that way or not. It makes the victim very sick—headache, nausea, and body aches like the flu—and then the stomach cramps take over. It can take the victim as long as ten days to die from liver, kidney, and circulatory system failure," Denise replied with a shiver as she remembered her own discomfort from simple sun poisoning.

"Where do they grow around here?" Greta asked.

"They grow freely in the forests, but someone would have to cultivate them here since digging them is very time consuming. My bet is that the killer has a green-house where he grows lady's slippers, mandrakes, and the destroying angel mushroom, and probably more,"

Denise replied, thinking about what Nester had told her about the growing conditions for those species.

With a dry chuckle, Greta added, "That certainly gives a different meaning to 'brown thumb.' This guy doesn't kill plants; instead, he uses them to kill people."

"And don't forget that it's not ordinary people who are his targets, it's senators who don't further his cause. This guy is a real zealot," Tom piped in from his seat on the outside of the circle.

"Okay, so what's our next move?" Eugene asked. "It's obvious we can't just sit here and wait for him to strike again."

"Tom and I are going to ask Captain Carter and the D.C. police to begin surveillance of the suspects and maybe even get search warrants for their homes," Denise replied as the others nodded in agreement. "Unfortunately, until we have hard evidence, we can't make any arrests. Right now all we have is circumstantial bits and pieces. We know that the suspects maintain at least part-time jobs at the Capitol for maximum exposure to the senators so that they can lobby them with ease. We have to wait for him to strike again and catch him in the act."

"With the exception of the one slip in going after Paul Fleet, the murderer has been very deliberate and patient. I hope the surveillance will turn up something," Denise told the others the next morning at breakfast.

Pouring another cup of strong coffee, Tom offered, "I suggest that we make our presence even more obvious than we already have. Whenever Peter Dominic sees shadows, he cringes. Let's make sure that we step out of them so that he knows we're watching him. Anthony Guido likes to change shifts, so we should be visible whenever he's on duty. George Arman works in the laundry and should feel more than steam breathing down his neck, although, in my mind, he's the least likely suspect. And Joseph Martin should see our faces over every vase of flowers he arranges."

Breaking the silence as they nodded in agreement, Eugene said, "I forgot to give you this envelope from Senator Salermo. It completely slipped my mind. Here. What does he have to say?"

Denise carefully opened the sealed, heavy vellum that bore Salermo's elaborate signature. The others listened attentively as she read, "Detective Dory, I have just received word from the coroner that Senator Frederick died of natural causes. The heart of our dear friend simply gave out from the stress of his chronic illness."

"What does this do to our investigation and the list of suspects?" Greta asked as she watched Denise refold the thick paper.

"It changes some things and clarifies others. Senator Frederick was the only known Social Security reformist on the short list. His murder would have meant that the killer wanted either a senator who would return to the old ways or one who advocated improvements to women's rights. Now that we know the cause of his death, we have to broaden the scope of our investigation to include all possible factions. That would make a traditionalist a likely target for murder," Denise replied as she explained her suspicions.

"But, Denise, we don't have any other candidates who profess to belong to splinter groups," Richard commented as he drank the last of his coffee. "What would the murderer achieve by killing more senators? He would never be able to find one to champion the cause."

"Profess is the operative word," Denise replied, pushing aside her empty plate. "What if Senator Salermo withheld information from us and is really in favor of stricter gun laws or the repeal of the abortion laws? If he

isn't a traditionalist as he claims, then he could be a
likely target. I think we need to question him again."

"If the Capitol grapevine is correct, we'll have to
work fast," Eugene commented.

"What do you mean?" Denise queried.

"Everyone expects them to select the new majority
leader tomorrow. They've even leaked the word to the
media."

Ruefully, Tom commented, "I guess there's no time
for another doughnut."

Denise and Tom rushed to the conference room in
which the senators were in session. Ripping a sheet from
her sketchbook, Denise scribbled a quick note to Senator Salermo and asked the aide at the door to slip it to
him as soon as possible. Looking her over with a skepti-
cal expression, he nodded and entered the room as the
door closed silently behind him.

They watched as the man returned to his desk and
resumed the correspondence that Denise had interrupted. Touching him lightly on the shoulder, she
asked, "Did Senator Salermo make any reply?"

Looking less than pleased that she insisted on disturbing him, the man sighed and folded his hands over
his stationery. In slow, carefully chosen language, he
replied, "The senator is a very busy man. I placed your
note before him. He nodded to acknowledge it and
waved me away. You will have to trust him to come to it
in his own time."

"But he must read it immediately. It's very important," Denise urged as she motioned toward the closed
door in an effort to get him to press her concern with
Senator Salermo.

"Senator Salermo read the word 'urgent' in bold letters on the front of the envelope and knows what it
means. However, he currently presides over a meeting
to select the new majority head, a rather important mat-

ter in itself. You must be patient," the aide replied with
a brush of his hand that signaled the end of their conversation.

"Maybe I could crash the meeting," Denise commented as she considered the serious expression on the
aide's face.

"Give up, Dory," Tom advised as he took her arm and
pulled her away. "There's nothing more that you can
do. It's up to Senator Salermo now"

Every reporter in D.C. must have heard the news. So
many people packed the Capitol grounds that Denise
could hardly move among them. A podium and microphones sat in the middle of the portico.

Suddenly, Tom pressed closer and whispered in her
ear, "This is it, Dory. You'll see if Senator Salermo
heeded your warning."

Denise's throat was so constricted that she could not
answer. Her heart pounded in her ears as she strained
to listen. Senator Salermo's aide read the terse statement.

As the disappointment filled the members of the
news media, Denise felt like jumping for joy. She and
Tom hugged each other gleefully and pushed their way
into the Capitol's rotunda. As always, she saw Mrs.
Benedict hovering with her flower cart. She smiled wearily and waved.

"It looks as if we're the only ones who wanted the
election postponed," Denise commented as they followed their usual route to the conference room.

When they reached the senator's conference room,
Senator Salermo immediately joined them. With his
arms folded over his chest he demanded angrily, "What
is the meaning of this delay, Detective Dory? I have done
what you wanted although we could have selected the

majority leader today. You're interfering in government business."

Quietly Denise replied, "I want to save your life."

For a moment, Salermo only stared at her with his mouth clamped shut in anger. Then, slowly the reality of her words registered and his body began to crumble. Sinking into the closest chair, he muttered, "This is all too unbelievable. It is unthinkable. Who would ever think senators would have to hide from their constituents? It is almost too much to bear."

Speaking the few words of comfort that popped to her mind, Denise said, "Senator, we are confident that we are within a day or two of apprehending the murderer. We ask your indulgence only a little while longer."

Raising his head slowly, Senator Salermo replied as he struggled to his feet, "I'm very sorry for being short-tempered with you, Detective. You're only doing your job."

Seeing that he no longer appeared resistant to their presence, Denise stated, "We would like a moment alone with you, if you wouldn't mind."

Leading the way down the hall with leaden feet, Senator Salermo replied, "Follow me to my office. I have some time now."

Senator Salermo's office was not what Denise had expected. Fabulous works of art decorated the walls and thick oriental carpets lay on the shiny dark oak floors. A massive carved desk sat in the center of the room, and comfortable overstuffed leather chairs gathered in conversational groupings.

"Please, make yourselves comfortable. Would you care for some coffee or tea? My secretary usually brings me a cup around this time. He would be happy to provide some for you as well," Senator Salermo offered as he eased into the sofa across from the inviting leather chairs.

"Tea would be perfect," Denise replied as she glanced at Tom, who nodded in assent. Denise knew that she needed something comforting to settle her nerves although the summer weather was almost intolerably hot and humid.

"Do you have any suspects?" Senator Salermo asked with interest.

Feeling encouraged, Denise said, "We've interviewed everyone who works at the Capitol in any capacity, from volunteers to the staffers. From that, we've prepared a short list of suspects, which I'd prefer not to share with you at this time. However, we must catch the assailant in the act in order to have enough evidence to make an arrest."

"And you think it will be fairly simple now to trap him while in the past he has escaped your efforts?" Senator Salermo commented with a touch of skepticism in his voice.

Trying to remove his concern, Tom replied, "Earlier in our investigation, we didn't know that the killer had used natural poisons. Now that we're aware of its identity and know that the killer must gain close access to the victim as opposed to lacing food or drink with it, we're confident that the arrest will come very shortly."

"Very well, I'll allow you to assign whatever guards you consider appropriate. I'm too tired of all this to try to stop you. I only hope you're correct. I'm ready for life to return to normal. Nothing will stop us this time tomorrow when we cast our votes for the majority leader," Senator Salermo replied with a finality that told them that the interview was over.

"Thank you for your time, Senator Salermo. We understand your position completely," Denise remarked as she stood to leave. The exhausted senator only nodded his farewell.

Rushing to Senator Dey's office, Denise and Tom passed a group of younger senators huddled in conference under a massive reproduction of the Constitution. Denise and Tom did not stop to speak, and neither did the senators look eager to stop them although they nodded in recognition. They seemed to have other business on their minds.

Sitting across the desk from Senator Dey as he listened attentively, Denise explained the nature of their visit. His thick black brows knitted frequently, and his fists tightened in irritation as he gave ear to the plan. When she had finished, he sat back and said with indignation, "Am I to understand that I'm to be virtually under arrest and that a police officer will watch everything I do?"

"Senator," Tom replied, "I'd prefer that you look at this as protection, not incarceration. We want to do this to protect you from a most unpleasant outside element that wishes to do you harm."

Senator Dey paced his well-appointed office, which looked much like Senator Salermo's, only a bit smaller, yet still illustrious of the wealth that surrounded some of the senators. Stopping, he replied, "I'm quite capable of taking care of myself. Unlike several of the others, I've maintained my health and weight by regular workouts and vigorous tennis."

"Although I'm confident that you could defend yourself from an attacker you could see, I'm not so certain that you could do anything against a powerful toxin like the *Amanita* mushroom," Denise responded as she watched his opposition begin to soften. "A murderer using the destroying angel would have an unfair advantage over you. Guards protecting your person as well as your home would help to even the odds."

"Reluctantly, I'll allow you to have someone tail me for a few nights. However, I will not live with this restriction for long. After that, I insist on returning to my normal way of life," Senator Dey commented as he picked up his pen and opened a folder on his desk. His body language said that he had dismissed them.

Tom and Denise glanced quickly at each other as she gathered her things. She hoped that Senator Dey's abundant self-confidence and disdain for police protection would not lead to trouble. He seemed to her to be the kind of man who thought very highly of himself. He might be the type whose arrogance would thrust him into difficult situations with no visible means of escape.

FIFTEEN

With Captain Carter's help, the detectives posted guards at the office door of all the senators with an extra man in the corridor that housed Senators Salermo and Dey. All of the detectives took turns wandering the halls, checking doors, and investigating shadows in the hopes of apprehending the murderer. Having the senators sleeping on cots in their offices limited their actions and the involvement of the D.C. police department. For once, Denise and Tom were happy to see that the wheels of democracy turned slowly. The task of protecting the senators would have been daunting if they had been able to return to their homes.

Captain Carter joined them to insure that he would win the wager and would be the first to identify the murderer. Since one of his men, Anthony Guido, was a prime suspect, Captain Carter graciously agreed to monitor his actions and those of his other officers. He still did not believe that Guido was involved in the murder of the senators.

The night seemed longer than usual as Denise and Tom prowled the silent halls on what they hoped would be a fruitful ten hours that would not end until seven o'clock the next morning. Shadows played in corners, behind statues, and lingered around doors, causing them to investigate everything with equal vigor. They were afraid to give anything short shrift for fear that they would miss an important piece of evidence that would identify their elusive murderer.

Denise and Tom passed often in the corridors to compare notes although neither had seen or heard anything unusual. The Capitol grew eerily still at night with almost no one on the move. Only the presence of the small army of detectives differentiated this night from all the others.

"Here, Dory, I thought you might need a little fortification," Tom said as he offered her a steaming cup of coffee.

"Where'd you get this? Everything was supposed to be locked up tight," Denise replied as she gratefully wrapped her hands around the hot cup. Although the day had been warm, the night felt cold with tension.

"You can always count on a police station to have hot refreshments. Besides, I would have walked to our office in the suburbs for a cup tonight. Too bad I couldn't find a little bourbon to give it a little kick," Tom replied with a chuckle.

"You look really tired. It's almost midnight. I'm fine by myself for a while. The others have already broken the night down into shifts. Why don't you get some rest and spell me around three?" Denise commented as she studied his lined face. Dark circles had formed under his eyes and long lines outlined his mouth.

"I don't want to leave you, Dory. What if something goes down? You won't have any backup. It's not like me to be so sleepy," Tom objected through a yawn.

"Don't worry about me. Go, I'll wake you at three. In the meantime, I'm going to the basement with my two-way radio for company," Denise insisted as she gave Tom a little push.

"Well, if you're certain that you don't need me, I could use the rest. I'll set my alarm for three, but you should come for me just in case I oversleep. I'll put the

radio on my pillow should you need to call for help,"
Tom replied as he staggered off.

Alone again, Denise decided to check the kitchen
and laundry rooms in the bowels of the Capitol. Although Captain Carter had assured her that both had
been locked, she wanted to see for herself. Taking the
only working elevator to the basement, she wandered
through the dimly lit halls, shining the flashlight Tom
had given her into the corners and doorways as she
walked. Denise checked each door along the way and
found all of them secured. As promised, the kitchen
entrance to the loading ramp was locked and bolted
with only the hum of the massive refrigerators giving off
any sign of life in the vast area.

However, when Denise jiggled the knob of the laundry room door, it opened. Holding the flashlight in her
left hand and her service revolver in her right, she carefully entered the room. She activated the switch on her
radio, pressed the silent signal, and called for backup.

Knowing that one of Captain Carter's men would arrive shortly, Denise squinted into the massive room illuminated only by the glow of the exit lights. She could
not wait until he arrived. She had to take the chance
that she might catch the prowler in the act of trespass-
ing. With luck, he might turn out to be the murderer.

The laundry room was impeccably neat. No dirty
laundry littered the sparkling clean white tile floor although baskets of soiled linen lined the left wall just as
they had when she visited George Arman earlier in the
day. If Denise had not found the door unlocked, she
would not have thought that anything was amiss. However, knowing that the day shift would not arrive until
four in the company of the kitchen staff, she had to
continue to investigate in the semidarkness.

As Denise turned the corner and headed to the pressing tables, her flashlight cut through the darkness as the

alarm bell in her head started to clang. She tried to silence it with the thought that she was merely reacting to the deafening silence of the room, but it would not cease its clamoring. Worse than the silence was the feeling that she was not alone.

Casting her flashlight in a broad arc, Denise shined the light into every corner, around the tables, and under the baskets of laundry waiting to be ironed. Finding nothing, she continued toward the supply closet in which they stored the brooms, dustpans, starches, small ironing boards, and hand irons. The door squealed as she opened it, causing her to jump back into a stack of neatly folded napkins that tumbled onto the floor. Denise pushed them aside impatiently with her foot. Her eyes followed the light as it illuminated the contents of the closet in which she saw carefully labeled canisters and boxes of starch, detergents, and bleaches.

Quickly picking up the napkins and stacking them as best she could while holding her revolver, Denise retraced her steps. Just as she was about to chalk up her alarm bell to caffeine jitters from too many cups of strong coffee, Denise saw a pile of sheets on the floor. She would not have been intrigued by dirty bed linen in a laundry if the room had not been so immaculately clean and orderly.

Stepping forward slowly, Denise approached the oddly shaped heap of sheets. She took another look around the room before reaching down to lift a corner. Carefully peeking inside, Denise shone her flashlight into the darkness. The lifeless body under the sheets confirmed her suspicions that something was dreadfully amiss in the laundry room.

At that moment, Denise heard the soft squishing sound of shoes on highly waxed tile. Darting behind a large hamper, she doused her light and crouched down as the sound came closer. Peering cautiously into the shadowy light, Denise saw the figure of a man approaching her, silhouetted against the moonlight that filtered through the shutters. He walked slowly without the assistance of a flashlight as if he knew where he was going even in the semidarkness.

Denise held her breath and watched quietly as the man walked past her row of hampers toward the pile of sheets on the floor. He bent down and with difficulty lifted the bundle. Carrying it toward the end hamper, he lowered it inside and closed the lid. Then he quickly began to push it toward the service entrance that led to the delivery bay. Denise knew that the corpse would soon be off the grounds if she did not stop him.

The squeak of the hamper's wheels masked her movements as she carefully followed the man into the main section of the laundry room in which the only light shined in the ceiling and cast a ghastly blue glow over everything. As he approached the door, she found and quickly flipped the light switch. The florescent lights flickered and then glared brightly.

"I strongly suggest that you stop what you're doing and empty the contents of your pockets onto the floor," Denise ordered as her eyes adjusted to the light.

Freezing in his tracks, the man replied, "Gladly, Detective Dory."

"Please do as I asked. Empty your things onto the floor," Denise repeated in an even firmer tone.

"And if I don't, what can a lone woman do to me? I'm stronger and more powerful," the man replied as he turned to glare at her. His hands stayed away from his pockets and the weapon strapped to his waist.

"Officer Guido, I suggest that you not test me. I've encountered some rough men in my career on the force, and I've held my own against all of them. I won't lose now," Denise promised through clinched teeth.

"You female cops are all the same. You're so confident. You think you own the world. Well, you don't. What makes you think that I'm going to do what a black woman orders me to do? I'm leaving with my basket, and there's nothing you can do to stop me. You're just a woman. At least you've found your place in the laundry room," Officer Guido replied as he started to push the squeaky basket toward the doors.

"Stop, or I'll shoot! Try me and see if I don't blow a big hole in your arrogant, racist hide," Denise shouted over the noise of the wheels.

"No, you won't shoot. You don't have the guts to do it," Guido sneered with a snide chuckle at his own pathetic attempt at humor.

"I wouldn't push her to the wall if I were you, Guido," came a voice from the door.

Surrounded, Officer Guido stopped.

"Empty your pockets and throw down your revolver," Denise repeated. This time, he obeyed.

Stepping forward, Tom picked up Officer Guido's weapon and keys and then patted him down. Using the officer's own handcuffs, he pulled Guido's arms behind him and pushed him into a nearby chair while Denise held her revolver poised to fire.

Using the two-way radio, Denise contacted Captain Carter and said, "We have Anthony Guido in custody. Come to the laundry room as soon as you can. We caught him trying to remove a body from the crime scene." Then she turned her attention to Guido and asked, "What's in the basket?"

"Laundry."

"Mighty heavy laundry," Denise replied as she lifted the layer of sheets. Looking at Tom, she commented, "It's George Arman. I guess he found out about you, so you had to kill him, too."

Looking smug, Officer Guido replied, "I didn't kill

anyone. He died of natural causes. There are no bullet holes or bruises on him. You can't prove a thing."

"An autopsy can prove plenty especially if the natural causes came by way of an *Amanita* mushroom or any other assortment of plant toxins. Those are the murder weapons of choice, aren't they? Did you kill the senators, too?" Denise asked.

"Humph!" Guido snorted as he turned to stare stubbornly away from her.

"Maybe while you're sitting behind bars, you'll have time to reconsider your opinion of black women," Denise commented with a slight smile. Officer Guido said nothing more as they waited for Captain Carter to arrive.

The captain appeared quickly, accompanied by two officers and a great deal of noise. In his excitement, he had forgotten to remove the napkin that covered his ample belly and protected his uniform. His fingers still carried the stains of chocolate.

Bursting into the room, he glared at Guido and sputtered, "You're a disgrace to the uniform and our office."

"I didn't do anything. You fat fool, you couldn't solve a case if your life depended on it. Just look at you. Even now, you're covered in chocolate," Guido sputtered, in rage at being handcuffed.

Pulling off the napkin, Captain Carter retorted, "Throw him into a detaining cell until the D.C. police cart him away."

"Don't think for a minute that I'll tell you or them anything. You're all incompetent clowns," Guido spat as they pulled him to his feet.

As the officers escorted Guido from the room, Captain Carter remarked with a forlorn expression on his heavy jowls, "You were right about him. I should have seen it myself, but I was blind."

"Don't blame yourself. You had no way of knowing the evil that lived in his heart," Denise replied as she watched Captain Carter wipe his sticky fingers on a clean towel and toss it into a corner.

"Ah, there are always signs of discontent among the ranks, Detective. I should have guessed that he would become involved in something like this. Officer Guido has always been a hothead. I've known him since he was a young troublemaker. I've seen his temper flare at a moment's notice. I should've suspected him from the beginning. Officer Guido has always championed one cause or another. By the way, who's in the basket?" Captain Carter asked as he uncovered the body.

"It's George Arman, but I don't think Officer Guido actually killed him. He's only the cleanup man," Denise replied.

"If Guido is nothing more than an accomplice, who is the actual murderer?" Captain Carter queried as he replaced the sheet.

"That is what we still need to uncover. The only thing we know for certain is that the murderer moves among us with ease. We should return to the offices. Do you think you could stay with the body?" Denise asked as she moved away from the basket.

"That's the least I can do," replied Captain Carter as he sank into the chair vacated by Guido.

As Denise and Tom rode up to the third floor on the service elevator, she said, "Thanks for coming to my rescue. I thought I'd have to shoot it out with him. I guess the alarm worked."

"What alarm? I never heard anything," Tom responded with a quizzical expression playing across his forehead as the doors opened.

"I pushed the silent alarm to call for backup," Denise responded. "Captain Carter assured us that all units would receive the call and come immediately. I thought you had responded to it."

"Dory, I didn't hear a thing. I just had a feeling that I should check on you," Tom replied with his usual cavalier shrug when caught in a kindness.

"I'm glad you did, but I thought you were sleeping. Why did you follow me?" Denise asked with gratitude for having a reliable partner at her back.

"Call it a sixth sense, but I knew you'd find trouble in the basement. I couldn't sleep with you wandering around down there. I'm glad I followed my hunch. It's not every day that a man finds the perfect woman. I didn't want to take the chance of losing you," Tom whispered as they wandered through the empty hall.

"Don't go getting all mushy on me, Tom. There's plenty of time for that later. Now, if your sixth sense would only tell us who Officer Guido is protecting, we'd be in business." Denise laughed softly.

Although Denise tried to send Tom away, he remained at her side until the first rays of sunshine broke over the Capitol. They were only halfway through breakfast when the message arrived that the senators were convening in their conference room. Pushing aside her barely touched plate of scrambled eggs and pancakes, Denise joined the others as they almost sprinted down the stairs and around the corner. Although they were all tired from their night of watching, they knew that they had to be present at the press briefing.

Standing at her side, Tom whispered, "Can we stall them another day?"

"I doubt it. You know how angry Senator Salermo was yesterday. He won't postpone again today. We'll just have to redouble our efforts," Denise replied as they jockeyed for space in the crowded hall.

"That's easier said than done when you're bone tired," Tom grunted.

Before she could respond, the long line of senators rounded the corner led by Senator Salermo, whose face showed the determination to get on with the selection process. Denise could tell that it would be useless for her to approach him with any suggestion of postponement.

Stopping at the door, Senator Salermo surveyed the assembled senators as if silently taking attendance. Speaking to an aide who stood directly behind him, he muttered something that Tom and Denise could not hear. Turning to the others, Senator Salermo spoke a few words and then beckoned them to follow him into the conference room.

"What's happening?" Denise asked Captain Carter.

"It seems that Senator Dey is late. Salermo refuses to start without him and has sent a messenger to fetch him immediately," the chubby captain replied.

Denise looked at Tom and the others quizzically and waited while the senators chatted softly among themselves. In only a few minutes, the aide returned. His face was pinched, and he wrung his hands in distress as he approached Senator Salermo, who sat at the head of the long conference table.

Motioning for all of them to enter the dark-paneled room, Senator Salermo spoke softly as he said, "Once again, I must share bad news. According to his aide, the senator complained of fatigue and slumped onto his desk. He's in Georgetown University Hospital."

Immediately, the senators began to twitter. Turning from one to another, they shared their sorrow, shock, and disbelief. Senator Salermo waited until their conversation subsided before he said, "I have decided to postpone our meeting until later this afternoon. We'll reconvene at two o'clock this afternoon."

As he walked through the door, Senator Salermo

turned momentarily and beckoned for Denise and Tom to follow him. Motioning to Richard and the others, they accompanied him down the hall. When the senator did not stop at Dey's office door, Denise began to wonder about the purpose of this session with him.

"Senator Salermo, isn't this Senator Dey's office?" Denise asked softly, thinking that Salermo was so deep in thought that he had forgotten his destination.

"Yes, it is, but we changed rooms last night in the hopes of confusing the murderer," Senator Salermo replied with grief etched across his face.

"But, you didn't tell us. Do you know what that means?" Denise sputtered awkwardly.

"Yes, Detective, it means that someone tried to kill me and instead has succeeded in injuring one of my dearest friends," Senator Salermo replied in a voice so utterly devoid of emotion that it sent chills down her spine.

Walking past the guard that Captain Carter had posted, they entered Senator Salermo's office. With the exception of the remains of medical supplies left behind by the Capitol's physician, nothing looked out of place. As Denise searched the chamber, she found no signs of forced entry and no syringes or weapons. Not even a tray of leftover midnight snack or breakfast food gave a clue as to the cause of Senator Dey's sudden and mysterious illness. All they knew for sure was that the doctor did not believe that the illness was the result of a chronic digestive condition although the senator had complained about an upset stomach and cramping. Finding him in good health otherwise, the doctor had prescribed an antacid and thought nothing of it until this morning when Senator Dey had slumped in his chair.

"When Senator Dey suggested the ruse, I initially objected," Senator Salermo lamented woefully. "Then he convinced me that we might be able to confuse the attacker and throw him off guard. I guess we wanted to do a little police work ourselves. We thought he'd enter, see the wrong man sleeping on a cot, and leave. Knowing that Captain Carter had stationed officers in the hall, we thought they'd catch him. We had no idea that one of us would come to harm."

Carefully lifting a corner of the sheet on the little cot, Denise said, "I know that this isn't a comforting thought, but I don't think the murderer entered the room during the night. We had guards posted outside your door and his all night, plus another in the hall. In addition, we patrolled looking for anyone who might have been roaming the halls. With the exception of the incident in the laundry room, none of us saw anyone."

"Then what do you think made Senator Dey sick?" Senator Salermo inquired, wringing his hands.

"Someone knew that you'd sleep in your office last night. You were the intended victim, not Dey. The change you made only put the wrong person in the wrong place at the wrong time," Denise replied, studying the bed linen on the simple military-issue cot.

"You think he will try?" Senator Salermo asked.

"I think he is becoming desperate," Denise replied. "Last night's murder of George Arman in the laundry room shows his level of fear. He knew that Arman could identify him. Now that he knows that we have his accomplice in custody, I think he'll strike again because he has nothing to lose. If Guido discloses his identity, we'll arrest him. If we catch the murderer in the act, we'll arrest him. He might as well try to finish what he has started because he has come to the end of his rope in any case."

"But what does he want?" Senator Salermo asked, looking far less confident than when she first met him.

Denise explained, "I think the murderer is intent upon removing anyone from the candidacy for the majority leader who doesn't support his cause. Guido is a follower of that movement, not a leader. I don't think that he is only the accomplice in this case. If I'm correct, the murderer is also an advocate of that cause."

For a while, no one spoke as they combed the room for evidence. Senator Salermo was badly shaken and in need of privacy to collect his thoughts, but Denise was afraid to leave him alone. If the murderer knew that he had been in error in his attack on Senator Dey, he might not wait until night to strike again in his desperation.

When Captain Carter joined them, he managed to convince Senator Salermo that he should have someone with him at all times. He suggested that the senator would not even be safe at home. Reluctantly, Salermo agreed to stay in his office that night under the protection of Captain Carter's men.

As they left the room, Captain Carter's cell phone rang, shattering the stillness in the tomb-silent hall. Answering it, he listened carefully and nodded. When the call ended, he softly relayed the news, saying, "That was the chief of the D.C. police department. The medical examiner found that George Arman died as a result of a massive dose of hemlock poisoning."

"Has Guido disclosed the identity of the murderer or the source of the hemlock?" Tom asked.

"No, he has refused to tell the D.C. police anything other than his name and address. Even under direct questioning, he has remained silent. I'm sure he'll break eventually," Captain Carter replied.

Turning to Captain Carter, Denise requested, "Call the hospital, please. The doctors should have some information on Senator Dey's condition by now. If my hunch is correct, he's suffering from *Amanita* poisoning."

They waited as Captain Carter dialed the number and spoke with the officer who had accompanied Senator

Dey to the hospital. With an expression of admiration on his chubby face, he said, "You're right, Detective Dory. The destroying angel has struck again."

"He's dead?" Tom asked in dismay for their failed attempts to keep the senators safe.

"Yes, about five minutes ago. The levels of the toxin were too high in his blood for his body to fight them. He went into respiratory arrest followed by a coma and never awakened," Captain Carter explained with sadness.

"Of course, there were no signs of struggle or trauma on his person," Denise commented as fatigue threatened to overtake her.

"You're right, Detective," Captain Carter replied.

"Then the poison is still in the room and they must find it," Denise replied as she led them back into the senator's suite.

"But where should they look?" Greta asked as she glanced about the pristine room. "Nothing is out of place here. There isn't even a glass to suggest that Senator Dey drank the poison."

"Did the physician say how Senator Dey was poisoned?" Denise asked Captain Carter.

"He only said that there were no needle marks, no signs of struggle, and nothing in the contents of the senator's stomach to suggest that he ingested it," Captain Carter replied.

"Let's think about what we know so far in this case," Denise suggested. "We have a natural toxin that does not require ingestion or injection and a dead laundry worker who knew too much. Therefore, I think it's in the linen. Captain, I think you should ask the lab to analyze the fibers of the sheets and towels to see if they contain traces of the *Amanita* toxin. Remember that it only takes a little of it to be fatal."

"Don't forget that we're pretty certain that Guido

acted as an accomplice. Perhaps he sneaked into the laundry and dumped some of it into the dryer. That way the sheets would be impregnated with it," Tom offered.

"That's possible, but if he had done that, everyone who touched the sheets would have been exposed to it and would have suffered symptoms from poisoning," Denise countered. "Did either the laundry or house-keeping staffs report an increase in absenteeism today?"

"No," Eugene replied, leafing through his notebook. "I looked through their figures and didn't see anything unusual. I thought that maybe the murderer took the day off following a night of violence, but I didn't find that to be true. If he is part of either of these staffs, he reported to work as usual. He is certainly confident that no one would be able to connect him to the murders."

"Yet, Peter Dominic in the kitchen is afraid of shad-ows because of something he knows or has seen. We'll have to speak with him again now that Guido is in cus-tody. Maybe he'll be more open with us this time," Tom added as he checked the desk for signs of tampering.

"If the linens didn't arrive here containing the poi-son, then someone must have entered the room with a key and added the toxin. Captain, who else other than housekeeping has a key to the senators' suites?" Denise asked as she tried to make the connections work in her mind.

"They're the only ones. Of course, I have the master keys in a safe in my office for which only I have the combination," Captain Carter replied with confidence in the security of his arrangements.

Looking around the room, Tom asked, "Does house-keeping supply all the flowers, too?"

"Oh no, the florist and his staff are responsible for doing that. But they don't have keys. We accompany housekeeping on the days that they have to change the arrangements in each office, which is usually every three days," Captain Carter commented with a scowl.

"Then it looks to me as if we have to speak with Joseph Martin, the florist, as well as Peter Dominic," Denise instructed. "Let's get these sheets and towels to a lab immediately and post extra watch around Senator Salermo. The murderer is close at hand, and he is someone who has access to the senators' offices on a daily basis. I'm confident that he'll strike again."

Commenting carefully, Tom added, "We should all be very careful. Remember the day Denise had that horrible headache and sick stomach? I bet that was a warning from our murderer. We've come too close for the murderer's comfort. Who knows what would have happened if she had slept longer or if he had used the *Amanita* mushroom toxin?"

As they left the room in the captain's charge, Denise heard him assign his officers to the required tasks and instruct them to don gloves and masks. While they searched for clues, Denise and Tom would visit the kitchen and the flower-arranging room. The other detectives would make themselves visible throughout the building as deterrents to further action.

Alone at last, Tom pulled Denise into his arms. The hallway was delightfully quiet as everyone scurried to their positions in the Capitol. Looking into her face, Tom stated, "Be careful, Dory. You've exposed yourself to the murderer. I don't want anything happening to you. Keep your guard up."

Leaning into his chest, Denise sighed. Tom had always been a conscientious partner. Now he was a loving one. Under other circumstances, she would have been extremely happy.

"Don't worry, Tom. I don't intend to give you the chance of getting another partner. I'm jealous enough as it is about the dog." Denise chuckled tiredly. The nearness of Tom's sturdy body and the lack of sleep almost made her fall asleep in his arms.

"I'm not kidding, Dory," Tom scolded softly. "I don't know what I'd do without you. Take care of yourself. I'll watch your back, but even I can't be there all the time."

Denise and Tom cherished the moment of peace as they held each other close. In their line of work, they never knew when they would have another one.

SIXTEEN

Everyone who worked on the Hill appeared to be in shock over the murder of Senator Dey. Even the usually lively and noisy kitchen staff went about its business with downcast faces and slow steps. No one laughed as they peeled potatoes or complained as they sliced onions for the luncheon soup.

Denise and Tom found Peter Dominic sitting alone in a deserted corner cleaning a mountain of brass pots and pans. Despair drew heavy lines around his mouth and tears etched traces down his face. His shoulders slumped and his hands trembled as he rubbed the pink solution onto the bottom of the pots with a blackened cloth. He looked up as the two detectives approached and immediately turned away as soon as he recognized them.

Pulling two chairs into his lonely corner, Denise and Tom sat down to talk with him. Immediately Peter Dominic waved them away, saying, "Leave me in peace. I'm so ashamed."

"We didn't come here to add to your misery, Mr. Dominic. We need help with this investigation, and we think that you might have some of the answers. Please, won't you help us catch Senator Dey's murderer before he strikes again?" Denise pleaded as she watched a fresh stream of tears cascade down his cheeks.

Tom added, "You're the only one who has any clues as to the identity of the murderer. We need your help."

"I'm such a coward. If I'd been honest with you yesterday, Senator Dey would still be alive. Instead, I let my fear of shadows silence me. What do you want to know? I'll help you in any way I can," Peter Dominic replied between sobs.

"Who is it that frightens you? If it's Anthony Guido, you don't need to worry about him. The D.C. police have him in custody for the murder of George Arman," Denise stated as she opened her sketchbook. With considerable difficulty she drew the stricken face of the man who only yesterday had been too frightened of shadows to speak.

"No, he's a mean, cruel man, but I'm no longer afraid of him. He can't hurt me now. My conscience and cowardice have done more than he ever could. He haunted me because he thought that I had seen his partner's face. He wanted to guarantee my silence," Peter Dominic answered as he loudly blew his nose.

"Have you?" Tom asked pointedly.

"No, I only saw him conversing with someone in a very low voice. They were standing in the hallway between the kitchen and the laundry room. Guido's back was turned to me. His body blocked my view of the person. I couldn't even hear the voice because they stood too far down the hall," Dominic replied as fresh tears of contrition sprang into his eyes.

"Can you tell us anything at all about the other person?" Tom asked with impatience in his voice for the man's sniveling.

"No, I only saw the shadow on the floor." Dominic sniffed. "The person looked to be a short, plump man with long clothes. Anthony thought that I'd seen more. He threatened to kill me if I said anything to anyone about the conversation. He hounded me day and night

with reminders to keep silent. Sometimes he called me
in the middle of the night to whisper threats and warn-
ings. At first, I thought that maybe I had caught him
talking with his girlfriend, and he did not want me to
tell his wife. But, after he became so vicious, I decided
that it must have been more serious than that. I tried to
tell him that I hadn't seen anything, but he wouldn't
believe me. He even left things in my locker.''

"What kinds of things?" Denise demanded.

Peter Dominic replied slowly as he looked around the
kitchen to be sure that no one was watching him,
"Newspaper clippings about people who spoke out
against organized crime bosses and the horrible things
that had happened to them. Then, when that famous
botanist died, he put that article in my box, too. Only
this time, he added a little note in the margin. It said
that Doctor Nester had spoken with the wrong people
and had paid the price. He said that if I did the same
thing, I'd be next. He asked me what kind of dressing I
liked on my salad, making reference to the fact that
Doctor Nester had died while eating his lunch. The article said that the police found him with a mushroom
stuck in his windpipe.''

Following his gaze to the east door, Denise asked,
"Did he send you any other clippings? Maybe one about
the death of a local florist?''

"Yes, as a matter of fact, he did. The day after the
police discovered Doctor Piper dead, Anthony put that
clipping in my box with the sentence underlined that
said the florist provided many of the U.S. Capitol's flowers. He really was serious about killing me if I talked with
anyone. I wonder if I'd have been next," Peter Dominic
commented but this time he did not cry. The reality of
his close brush with death had dried up his tears.

Rising, Denise said, "Thank you, Mr. Dominic, you've
been most helpful. Your information has connected

many loose ends for us. If you think of anything else we should know, do not hesitate to contact us."

"I feel so much better for having told you everything that I know. Are you sure that I will be safe from Anthony?" Dominic inquired as he pressed himself into his corner again. All the confidence he had gained while speaking with them had suddenly faded away.

"You don't have to worry about him. Your testimony will keep him in jail for a long time. I'm sure the D.C. police will be grateful for your help. We'll want to see the articles if you still have them," Denise said as she closed her sketchbook with a gentle whisper of pages.

"I keep the originals with me all the time and copies in my safe deposit box. If Anthony had carried out his threat, I wanted the police to know where to start their investigation. I'll entrust them to you now," Dominic responded as he pulled the clippings from his tattered leather wallet and handed them to her.

Denise slowly opened the carefully clipped articles containing photographs of crime bosses. Folded inside them were the reports of the deaths associated with the U.S. Capitol. She had no doubt that Anthony Guido meant them to silence Peter Dominic until he could do it himself.

Looking over her shoulder, Tom commented, "Guido certainly guaranteed your silence with these. I can understand why you were so hesitant to speak with us. This information will keep him behind bars until they can prove his connection to the murdered senators. Thanks."

Looking more relaxed than they had ever seen him, Peter Dominic replied, "My regret is that I wasn't strong enough to help out sooner. Senator Dey might still be alive."

Leaving the kitchen and Peter, Denise and Tom walked down the halls to the flower room. The feeling of greatness that filled the Capital had kept Denise in awe when she first arrived on the Hill, but now she hardly noticed it. She had become one of the many workers who moved through those wide corridors. She did not like the transformation.

Tourists and the press filled the building as usual. Perhaps it was her imagination, but their voices appeared more subdued than in the past. Their flashbulbs illuminated every nook. They were all part of the fabric of the city as was Mrs. Benedict who dutifully replaced the potted plants in the senators' offices.

Mr. Philips joined them as soon as Denise and Tom entered the flower-arranging room. Wringing his hands, he led them to his office where they perched among the brochures and plant supplies. He looked weary and tearful like all the others who were associated with the Capitol and its inhabitants. By now, everyone knew about the murders of Senator Dey and George Arman and the arrest of Anthony Guido.

"What dreadful news! How could this happen again? Do you think that Anthony Guido is the murderer?" Mr. Philips asked as soon as they drew up their chairs.

"We don't believe that Guido acted alone," Tom replied as he looked through the open office doors at the workers for possible clues to the identity of the murderer.

Leaning forward, Denise added, "He may have been the muscle behind the murders, but he has a partner who knows a considerable amount about plant toxins and has access to the offices. We were hoping that you would be able to provide us with information about the people who either work or volunteer their time here. Have you seen anyone behaving suspiciously? Has anyone suddenly shown an interest in growing mushrooms?"

"I'm sorry, Detective Dory, but I don't know any

more than I've already told you," Mr. Philips replied as he wrung his hands even more vigorously. "We're responsible for maintaining the flowers in the public rooms and offices. I've never had any reason to question the truthfulness of my coworkers and have never seen any unusual behavior. I'm very distressed to think that one of my associates might have been involved in committing murder."

Out of respect for the man's obvious distress, Tom requested in a gentler voice than usual, "Can we interview a few of them today? Perhaps they might have seen someone while on their rounds. We'd like to begin with Joseph Martin if we could."

"I'm afraid that he hasn't arrived yet. As a matter of fact, I haven't heard from him, which is most unusual. I was planning to phone his home when you entered. Joseph is usually here when I arrive in the morning," Mr. Philips replied. Suddenly his eyes widened, and he sputtered, "You don't think something happened to him, do you?"

Without hesitation, Denise replied, "I think you should not waste any time. Please, call his home, Mr. Philips."

Dialing the number with fingers that shook so badly that he had trouble punching only one button at a time, Mr. Philips waited while the telephone rang unanswered in his ear. Looking at her with eyes filled with fear, he said, "This is very strange. If Joseph is not here or at home, then where is he? He is not the kind to have stayed out all night and have to sleep off the effects of too much alcohol at this hour of the day."

Tom asked cautiously, "Is it possible that he's here, but you haven't seen him?"

"I suppose that anything is possible, but it's not probable," Mr. Philips replied, looking very worried. "Everyone, paid staff and volunteer, has to punch in every morning and punch out when they go home. That way we can account for their time and budget for personnel increases as they arise. For instance, we need more staff at Inauguration and holidays than we do at other times. The system lets us know the number of additional employees to assign to the duties of caring for the plants and flowers. Joseph is the one who designed and implemented the system, so I know he would never forget to use it. As you can see from his card, Joseph clocked out at midnight after receiving the latest delivery of flowers."

Sensing that Mr. Philips's frazzled nerves could not handle too much more, Denise said quietly, "Mr. Philips, as you probably know we found the body of George Arman lying in a laundry basket under a pile of soiled linens. Would it be possible for someone to conceal a body any place within these rooms?"

Walking unsteadily into the arranging room, Mr. Philips surveyed the workers standing in the spacious sparsely furnished area filled with pots and buckets of flowers. Motioning for them to join him, he replied, "I can't imagine where anyone would hide a flower seed, let alone a body. You see that everything here is open. We have only the barest accessories so that nothing can get in the way of our creative efforts. Every square inch has a purpose."

Standing beside the storage closet, Denise could not resist the urge to open the door although it would have been unlikely that someone would hide a body in the flower room closet. However, Anthony Guido had hidden a victim in a laundry basket. She decided that he enjoyed playing with their minds by doing the obvious, knowing that they would ignore their instincts to search under their noses.

Turning the knob, Denise found that the door was

locked. "Do you have the key? I'd like to take a look inside."

"Certainly. I'm surprised that it's locked. There's nothing of value in there—only Paul Fleet's flower-pots," Mr. Philips replied without hesitation. Swinging the heavy wooden door open wide, he jumped back in horror.

Denise frowned at Tom briefly before stepping past the horrified man. The lifeless body of Joseph Martin lay on the floor in the spot formerly inhabited by the discarded flowerpots that Paul Fleet retrieved when he unloaded the new plants. Although it would take a medical examiner's skill to determine the exact time of death, Denise could tell that he had been lying there for many hours from the stiffness of his limbs and the set-tling of blood at the back of his arms and neck.

"What do you think, Dory? Did Anthony Guido kill him before or after George Arman?" Tom asked as he looked at the body.

"I'd guess that he probably helped with the flower delivery and then killed Mr. Martin as soon as he had logged out for the evening," Denise speculated. "An-thony Guido might have suggested that they leave the room together since it was so late. He could have men-tioned the increased security and hinted that Mr. Martin would be free from suspicion if they left together. It would have been easy for Guido then to strike him over the head or apply a toxin-saturated cloth to Martin's nose and mouth."

Slipping on a pair of rubber gloves that by habit he kept in his jacket pocket, Tom carefully examined the body. Turning to her, he said, "There are no visible wounds on Mr. Martin although his nails do show traces of something that might be skin."

"What's that cloth in the corner?" Denise asked as she peered into the closet.

Carefully Tom stepped forward and retrieved a plain very generic-looking white cloth. "I don't see anything distinctive about it. It's probably just a cleaning rag."

"No, Detective, that's not true. We don't put anything other than plants and plant-related material in that room. I'm sure it wasn't there last night when I left at ten. I would have removed it if I'd seen it. We can't afford for bacteria to grow and infest the potting medium. What does it mean?" Mr. Philips said with his hands thrust deeply in his pockets.

"I think it means that we've just found the murder weapon," Denise replied as Tom carefully placed the cloth inside a plastic bag and sealed it tightly. "It's probably saturated with plant toxin. Perhaps an extract from the lily of the valley or autumn crocus that would cause cardiac arrest."

"Why would anyone kill Joseph?" Mr. Philips moaned as he sank into the nearest chair. "He was totally harmless and a hard worker. He served on countless committees and gave generously of his time to many causes."

Denise replied as Tom phoned Captain Carter, "I can only assume that Anthony Guido thought that Joseph knew the identity of the murderer and wanted to make sure that he never used that information. He was a victim of being in the right place at the wrong time."

Turning his attention to Mr. Philips, who sat slumped in his chair, Tom said, "Captain Carter's men'll be here soon. In the meantime, you should lock the door. I don't want anyone interfering with the investigation or disturbing the body."

Lifting his sorrowful eyes, Mr. Philips groaned, "Whatever you say, Detective Phyfer. This is dreadful. Something must be done to stop this madness."

Denise and Tom waited until Mr. Philips had secured the door before they left to meet Captain Carter. As they hurried down the empty corridor, Denise said, "It's clear to me that we will not catch this murderer unless we set a trap of some kind. He's too familiar with the day-to-day operation of the Hill for our efforts to have any success without setting up a surveillance operation."

"A sting operation?" Tom queried with interest as they stepped into the hot, sunny afternoon.

Denise replied with a slight smile at his enthusiasm, "We already know that the Capitol police are capable of installing recording devices. If we can convince Captain Carter to do the same thing in Senator Salermo's rooms, I believe we'll finally have an advantage over this killer."

"It sounds like a good idea to me, Dory, but we certainly don't have much time. The senators should cast their ballots at two o'clock this afternoon. Senator Salermo has already told you that this time they'll elect a new Senate leader. If Captain Carter is to install devices in Senator Salermo's rooms, he has to get started immediately. I'm not convinced that he'll go along with the idea. He might be a hard sell," Tom suggested.

"Don't worry. He'll agree to it. He wants to win our little wager. I'll put it to him so that he'll see that this is the best opportunity he'll have for success," Denise replied as she straightened her shoulders against the necessity of cajoling Captain Carter into agreeing to the surveillance.

Opening the door to Captain Carter's office, Tom whispered, "If anyone can do it, you can. Go get him, Dory! I'll accompany his men to see Mr. Philips."

Nodding, Denise entered the office in which Captain Carter sat poring over a set of floor plans while munching on a doughnut. Between bites, he stopped to lick his fingers clean so that he would not get chocolate on the papers. He looked up and smiled a sugary grin at her as she approached his desk.

Rising, Captain Carter said, "Detective Dory, you are a treat for my eyes even on such a day as this when they're tired and faced with yet another murder. I've sent my men to begin the terrible investigation. If you and Phyfer are correct, we're dealing with a madman of extreme proportions. None of us will feel safe until he's behind bars."

Taking the offered seat, Denise replied, "Captain Carter, that is exactly why I've come to see you. We must take drastic measures to ensure the safety of Senator Salermo, who, as you know, is on the short list."

"So true, but what can we do?" Captain Carter moaned as he stuffed the last bite of the pastry into his mouth. "The murderer has outfoxed us at every turn. Even while we stay awake patrolling the halls, he strikes again and kills two more people. He is always one step ahead of us. That is why I've been studying these plans. I'd hoped to discover a tunnel or a passageway through which our murderer manages to escape. Unfortunately, I've found nothing."

Denise replied as she studied his worried, chocolate-smeared face, "I don't think the killer troubles himself with escape routes. He's too confident to resort to hiding in shadows. At least now with Anthony Guido behind bars, we might have a chance of keeping our activities private. He was the muscle behind the operation with a direct connection to our investigation. This time, we're looking for the brains, and I'm afraid that his partner will be more difficult to uncover. That is why I'd like to suggest that we use surveillance cameras and listening devices to catch him."

"Detective Dory, we could never install monitoring equipment on the Hill. That would be unthinkable," Captain Carter objected as he rose to his full height to stand behind his desk.

"Really? You've bugged our rooms. I don't see why

you couldn't do the same to Senator Salermo's suite," Denise remarked in an offhand manner accompanied by a radiant and winning smile.

With a wave of his hand, Captain Carter eased his plump frame into his seat and replied, "I ordered the surveillance of your rooms before any of you arrived. We needed to know that you would share your information openly with us. It was my intent to remove everything once we learned to trust you, which we have, thanks to your thorough reports. Unfortunately, we have been too busy with the murders to remove the devices. We were simply protecting our turf, as it were."

"You had no reason to doubt that we would share everything we learned. After all, we are here at your invitation as your consultants. But let's not quibble about that now. The important thing is that it is imperative that we provide protection to Senator Salermo immediately. I believe that cameras in his rooms would enable us to see the murderer in action."

"Why can't we simply move Salermo to another room?" Carter inquired with a leer.

"We could for tonight since he's only sleeping on a cot. However, we can't move him around indefinitely since he stays here so often. That is no way to live, and it would be most disruptive to his work," Denise protested softly but firmly.

"Very well, we'll install the cameras in his office, but I don't think that we can do it before he goes to bed tonight. The room is still under scrutiny by the D.C. police and has not been properly cleaned since Senator Dey's death. We'll have to ask him to give us more time," Captain Carter replied with resignation in his voice.

"Just think of the headlines when the news media discovers that your police force caught the murderer.

You'll be a national," Denise replied with enthusiasm, pulling out all the punches.

Adjusting his snug uniform jacket, Captain Carter grinned and replied, "That would look good on my résumé, wouldn't it? I'll post guards outside while we're working so that no one will figure out what we're doing."

"That would certainly send the murderer a message, but not necessarily the one you want to convey. I'd think that you'd want to be less overt so as not to tip off the murderer that something is different in the office. I think you really wanted to say that you'd use subterfuge while wiring the room," Denise commented as she tried to steer him from his disastrous course.

"You're so right," Captain Carter commented as he feigned absentmindedness. "I'll dress my men as plumbers and have them inspect a few of the rooms. They could pretend to repair sinks or toilets to fool the murderer into thinking that nothing out of the ordinary was happening. While in the senator's office, they would install the monitoring devices in very concealed locations. If I remember correctly, the rooms contain not only portraits and sculptures but heavy drapes, all of which might come in handy for hiding equipment."

"Sounds like an excellent plan to me," Denise agreed.

Taking the bait, Captain Carter gloated as he replied, "Detective Dory, I hope you have a hearty appetite because this plan will mean that I'll win our wager. A murderer is like a moth drawn to a flame; he cannot resist the feeling of power he gets from the deed."

Smiling as she rose from her seat, Denise replied, "You're absolutely correct, Captain. However, the success of your plan depends on the ability of your men to work in complete secrecy and to wire the offices as quickly as possible. I'm confident that the murderer will continue to strike until he has his way. We must stop him tonight before someone else dies. Can your men have the equipment in place before dinnertime?''

Taking her hands in his, Captain Carter looked deeply into her eyes and said, ''Trust me, my officers will do as I say. I'll make them understand that this is important to me personally. They will want their captain to be victorious and to claim his prize.''

As Denise watched the chubby captain gaze longingly at her, she suggested, ''This is too easy for you, Captain. Shall we add to our wager?''

''Whatever you'd like, my dear,'' Captain Carter replied, practically salivating at the suggestion.

''I propose that we each write the name of the person we suspect as the murderer on a piece of paper and seal it in an envelope. If my answer is correct, I'll bring another detective to dinner with us. If you are the winner, you'll have me all to yourself for the evening,'' Denise replied with a smile.

''Denise, you're on,'' Captain Carter eagerly agreed as he extracted two index cards and envelopes from the drawer.

Walking away from his desk, Denise quickly jotted down the name of the person she had long suspected of being the murderer and closed the envelope. For extra security, she wrote her name across the seal before she placed it in his outstretched palm. Immediately, he did the same and tossed both of them into the open safe.

Giving the combination a twirl, Captain Carter grasped her hands again and said, ''Your ballot is safe with me, just as you will be when we enjoy our evening alone together.''

''Captain, I hope you are not being premature in your reactions. Your men must work quickly. They must catch the murderer before we can give ourselves our just rewards," Denise replied as she slipped away from his sweaty grasp.

"In that case, the night is ours," Captain Carter crooned and began to follow her.

Suddenly the little office was unbearably close as the hot air eased in through the open windows and door to mix with the lecherous heat that Captain Carter exuded from every pore. Turning at the door, Denise replied, "I wish you much success, Captain."

Rushing across the grounds filled with tourists and media, Denise shook off the effects of the meeting with Captain Carter. He would not have been so reprehensible if he had not oozed such questionable charm. He was not an unattractive man, but his lascivious ways did not ingratiate him to her. Although she wanted to apprehend the murderer, Denise dreaded the thought of having dinner alone with him. She would have to convince Tom to interrupt them at the restaurant to foil Captain Carter's plans for an evening alone if she lost the wager.

"Dory, over here!" Denise heard a voice calling through the crowd. Shading her eyes from the afternoon sun, she saw Tom standing among their colleagues at the center of the grounds. He waved until he was sure that he had gotten her attention. From the size of the assembled throng, Denise could tell that everyone had read the paper and made the same assumption that Senator Salermo would announce the new majority leader today.

Pressing through the packed bodies, Denise joined her colleagues and stated, "I convinced Captain Carter that his men should install monitoring equipment in the senator's quarters. He said that they would have everything in place by dinnertime tonight."

With a scowl on his face, Tom commented, "I hope the price for this installation wasn't too steep."

Smiling, Denise replied, "No, it just means that I might lose the wager and have to go to dinner with him. But I've already figured out a way to get around being alone with him. I've developed a plan that will work if you'll help me."

"Sure, Dory, I'd love to burst the bubble of that aging Romeo," Tom replied with a laugh.

"You can count me in, too, if it means a free meal," Greta added, with Richard nodding.

Before Denise could share the plan with him, the masses of people became silent. All eyes turned to the front steps of the Capitol as a spokesman stepped forward. As expected he announced that they had finally made the selection.

"Senator Salermo said they couldn't wait any longer," Richard commented as he stated the obvious. "Well, that gives us less than ten hours to get some rest, assign shifts in the monitor room, and prepare for the vigil."

"No, it gives us only until housekeeping comes to make up the room after the plumbers leave," Denise retorted with a quick glance at her watch. "If our murderer strikes, he'll do it tonight."

"Denise, I hope Captain Carter's men are up to it," Richard replied skeptically.

"Don't worry about them. He has assured me that they'll do everything they can to help him win his bet. In the meantime, let's meet somewhere quiet to finalize our plans," Denise said as she led the group away from the Capitol grounds.

Settling into the soft grass, Eugene mused as they gathered on the Folger grounds, "Who do you think they selected?"

"Senator Salermo," Denise replied without a moment's hesitation.

"I know he's at the top of the list, but he's in favor of

retaining the status quo, which seems rather conservative in today's climate. I'd think they'd elect someone with a more liberal view," Richard rebutted as he stretched his long legs.

"I wouldn't be surprised if Senator Salermo doesn't reveal that there's more to him than his previously stated political views," Denise commented as she picked the petals from a lonely dandelion.

"Do you think he has been hiding something from us?" Tom asked. "Everything I've read about him says that he is very conservative."

"I could be wrong, but I picked up something in a conversation with him that told me that he isn't really what he presents himself to be," Denise replied. "I don't think Senator Salermo is lying, but I do think that he's being strategic in his disclosures."

Tom commented, "That would make sense in light of Senator Salermo's reputation."

"Unless I've missed the mark, there's more to his story than he's telling us," Denise suggested as Mrs. Benedict waved to them from the bus stop. Her face looked tired and drawn as if she had spent a restless night.

"I wonder what's keeping her here so late," Tom remarked, leaning close enough to Denise to smell her spicy warmth. His shoulder pressed lightly against hers.

"No idea. Maybe she needed to place flower orders for Salermo's luncheon," Denise commented as she leaned into his shoulder.

For a few moments, among their colleagues, Denise and Tom exchanged glances. The noise of D.C. seemed to fade away as they looked into each other's eyes. Until they solved the case, they would have to be content with the stolen moments and the furtive touches that meant so much.

SEVENTEEN

Denise should not have worried about Captain Carter's men. When she and Tom arrived at Senator Salermo's suite, they found plumbing tools everywhere and men dressed in grimy overalls crawling under the sinks, tightening gaskets in the toilets, and tapping away at the shower stall fixtures. If she had not known that they were police officers, Denise would have thought that the distinctive smell of pipe dope and sewage gases was legitimate. As it was, she wrinkled her nose as soon as the stench assaulted her.

Denise looked around the room for any signs of surveillance equipment. Except for some wires that appeared to have been connected to the plumbers' power tools, she saw nothing. Glancing at Tom, she could tell that he had also visually searched the senator's private study and was equally pleased that no one could tell that anything other than plumbing work was under way.

Seeing Senator Salermo walking toward his office, Denise motioned to Tom that she would follow him as he hastily vanished around the corner.

"Senator Salermo, I'd like a word with you if I might," Denise called as he placed his hand on his office doorknob.

"Now, Detective Dory? I'm very tired and would like to take a brief rest. This entire situation has been very taxing. I'm not as young as I used to be," Senator

Salermo replied as he pushed open the door and entered his study.

Trying to assure him, Denise said, "Yes, if you would be kind enough to spare me a few minutes, Senator, I'd greatly appreciate it. I promise that I won't take much of your time."

"It is not that you ever overstay your welcome, Detective. It's that you cause my mind to whirl with tormenting questions after you leave. I can't believe that this afternoon will be any different," Senator Salermo replied as he motioned to a chair near the sofa on which he deposited his weary body.

"You're a very astute judge of people's minds, Senator," Denise replied as she studied his tired face. "The selection of Senator Pars has raised many questions. Can you explain the shift in loyalties from you to him? I was so certain that you'd be the one they'd select."

Tapping the tips of his fingers silently together, Senator Salermo replied, "That's easy to explain, Detective. You see, we decided that we couldn't afford more murders on the Hill and decided to elect a man with an open stance on all issues. He's neither strongly for nor against any of the issues, whereas I'm a stated conservative and believe in maintaining the old traditions. We believe that he'll satisfy everyone while upsetting no one. Besides, he wasn't on the short list. No one saw him coming."

"And what about you? Don't you feel left out?" Denise inquired as she studied him.

"You know my position on maintaining the status quo, Detective Dory. I've been very outspoken in that regard, a tendency that cost my dear friend his life," Senator Salermo replied as he walked toward his window and looked into the Capitol grounds where Denise and the other detectives usually gathered.

"And you think that Pars can make things better?" Denise asked.

Senator Salermo replied, fighting the fatigue that threatened to overwhelm him, "No. As long as political factions exist, we're too busy arguing with one another to hear the voice of the messenger. We need a cooling-off period that I don't believe Senator Pars will provide. We now have a leader without internal direction. I'd prefer one of conviction who would help us make good decisions."

Looking into his eyes, Denise instinctively knew that this man would one day be the majority leader. His patience would do much to heal the wounds of division and produce a unified government. Denise hoped that they would be able to apprehend the murderer before senator Salermo, too, fell prey to the destroying angel.

"Senator Salermo, once again I have to warn you against moving too freely around the Capitol. Please do not assume that Pars's selection has removed the danger to your life. Until we have the murderer behind bars, you must continue to take precautions," Denise urged with fear that he might become careless.

"I'll be careful, Detective," Senator Salermo assured her as they walked toward the door. "I've never believed in putting myself at risk. Causes need living advocates, not martyrs. Good-bye."

As Denise hurried to meet the others, she passed Mrs. Benedict in the hallway. She had stopped to replace the wilted flowers outside the conference room with fresh ones. Mrs. Benedict nodded and smiled as she approached.

"Good afternoon, Mrs. Benedict. It's nice to see the selection process finally complete," Denise said as she approached.

"Yes, if Pars can end the troubles on the Hill," Mrs. Benedict answered as she pulled the wilting arrange-

ment of orchids, roses, and baby's breath from the vase
and replaced it with delicate pale-yellow roses.

"Don't you believe he can?" Denise probed, unclear
as to her meaning.

"I'm not a politician, Detective Dory. I spend my time
growing and arranging flowers. However, I hear things
as I walk through these halls, and I know that there are
many here who do not think that Pars is the man for the
job. I've already heard mutterings. I suppose that only
time will tell," Mrs. Benedict replied with a shrug.

Curious about something she said, Denise asked,
"What have you heard and from whom?"

"I passed several men in the hall and heard a group
of them say that they think the murderer will not be
content with Pars either," Mrs. Benedict responded absently as she moved to another arrangement.

"Can you identify these people?"

"No, they could have been tourists or journalists for
all I know, Detective. Hardly anyone of significance,"
Mrs. Benedict replied, tossing the wilted flowers into the
tub on the bottom of the cart.

Momentarily distracted, Denise asked, "What do you
do with all those discarded flowers?"

Smiling, Mrs. Benedict said, "I take them home and
mulch them into a fine dust. It's a great addition to the
compost pile."

Following Mrs. Benedict along the hallway, Denise
stopped with her outside Senator Pars's office. Denise
could hear the sound of drills and hammers inside. Anyone would think that the most industrious carpenters
and electricians were on the job. Denise, however, knew
that Senator Pars's office would soon be wired for surveillance also.

As Mrs. Benedict refilled the vase with a mixture of
pink carnations, pale lavender gladiolus, and white hol-

lyhocks, she commented, "I hope those plumbers finish their work before it is time for me to leave."

"They've been at work for quite some time now. I doubt that they'll take much longer," Denise commented without giving much thought to Mrs. Benedict's worries. "Well, I'll leave you now, Mrs. Benedict. I'm already late for a meeting with my friends."

"Good-bye, Detective Dory," Mrs. Benedict replied with an inclination of her head.

Leaving Mrs. Benedict, Denise hurried to join her colleagues. They had been waiting for her for almost an hour while she met with Senator Salermo and chatted with Mrs. Benedict. She was surprised that she felt light-hearted when she should have been worried about protecting Senator Pars. Denise could not shake the overwhelming confidence that they were finally on the verge of an arrest.

They were not alone in the court as tourists wearing special passes attached to their shirts strolled through the grounds. From her seat on the grass near the familiar bench, Denise looked up at the office windows. Senator Salermo's was on the left. He had drawn the blinds, probably for the nap he wanted to take before dinner at eight. The office of the majority leader was around the corner and to the right. There, too, the windows were shrouded but to prevent the curious from watching Captain Carter's men.

Turning toward her colleagues, Denise stated, "Senator Salermo told me that he has observed our nightly meetings. Mrs. Benedict has seen us, too. We must be the topic of discussion at the coffee bar around here."

"As long as no one has overheard us, I don't care who sees us," Eugene replied as he looked disagreeably at the tourist invaders.

"I agree," Greta interjected. "I've found our sessions very helpful. As a matter of fact, I've drawn up tonight's surveillance schedule. I've paired everyone in two-hour shifts with Denise and Tom on roaming duty and the monitor room from ten until midnight. Captain Carter graciously provided us with more radios so that we can keep in touch at all times. His men will be out of the room by five o'clock, at which time housekeeping will have access to the office. We won't have much time to test the cameras, but Captain Carter says that there's no reason to think that they won't work. He has used the equipment before without any difficulty."

With a chuckle, Tom quipped, "I can imagine where he used it recently. He has a thing for our friend Dory."

The others turned toward her with amusement written on their faces. Embarrassed, Denise countered, "He's just a bit friendly, that's all."

"That's one way of putting it, Denise." Tom chuckled dryly.

"Okay, enough of this fun at my expense. Since I have a feeling that I'll miss dinner tonight, I'm going to find something to eat," Denise stated as she brushed the grass from her black skirt. Tom followed with a less than pleased expression on his face. As usual, they took off at a brisk pace despite the warmth of the evening.

"Wait. I'll join you," Greta replied as she matched her stride with theirs.

"Good," Denise replied, unable to think of a way to deter Greta from making it a threesome.

Panting as she trotted beside them, Greta asked, "What makes you think you'll miss dinner?"

"I just have a hunch that the murderer will strike between five and eight," Denise responded as they entered the little café immediately outside the Capitol gates. It was mostly a tourist hangout, but it served decent pizza and cold sodas.

Unable to restrain himself, Tom interjected, "Dory has a bet with Captain Carter about the identity of the murderer. If she wins, he has to take us to dinner. If she loses, she has to go alone with him. That was the only way she could convince him to hurry the wiring job."

The three of them found a table and ordered a pizza. A little while later, as they were eating, Greta leaned forward and asked in a conspiratorial whisper, "Who do you think did it?"

"You'll have to wait until I open the envelope in the captain's safe," Denise replied with a wicked smile.

"That's not fair, Denise. We promised that we'd share all information. You must have seen or heard something that led you to your conclusion, so give it up," Greta demanded firmly.

Shaking her head, Denise responded, "I don't want to throw anyone off the scent if I'm wrong, which is a very real possibility. And, besides, I've already shared everything I know. I think the murderer has been in our midst all the time."

Sulking, Greta mumbled as she bit into the thick cheese topping, "I still think you should tell me."

"You know everything that I do. I don't want to lead you on a wild-goose chase," Denise replied, finding herself relieved that Greta had decided to pout through most of the dinner. The silence was wonderful. It gave her a chance to share meaningful glances with Tom but no personal conversation.

Tom sulked silently also. They had little time together and now Greta had stolen the few precious minutes they had. He kept sending darts her way, hoping that the tagalong would get the idea and leave them. Unfortunately, she never did.

By the time their dessert arrived, Greta had made some assumptions of her own and offered them with the dessert. Smugly she said, "Unlike you, I'll share my thoughts. I think that Senator Salermo is the murderer. He has the motive and the opportunity. True, he does not have access to a garden, but someone could provide him with the destroying angel and any other plant toxin he might want. I intend to keep a watchful eye on him tonight."

Smiling at her smug attitude, Denise commented, "Don't forget that the Capitol has lovely gardens right here. He might have a secret plot where he grows everything except the mushroom. After all, nightshade, hemlock, and lady's slipper orchids are not deadly unless used in large quantities. Any one of these could grow on the grounds without anyone noticing. As for the mushrooms, they're amenable to the back of a closet."

"See, then you think he's the murderer, too. I knew I was right," Greta proclaimed with her usual confident, almost pushy air.

"I didn't say that. I'm simply pointing out evidence that supports your hypothesis," Denise replied as Tom paid the bill and they exited the busy restaurant.

"But you didn't say no either," Greta persisted as they walked toward the Page School.

Chuckling for the first time, Tom commented, "Now, ladies, don't bicker. Dory hasn't shared her hunch with me either. We'll just have to wait to see who's right. In the meantime, I agree that the killer will strike tonight."

"Humph," Greta replied as she slipped into her room.

Happily linking arms, Denise and Tom left Greta and hurried to the senators' offices. After making sure that the hall was empty, Denise knocked softly. Captain Carter must have been standing at the door, because he opened it immediately and ushered them inside. Shaking his head, he informed her, "Detective, my men didn't have enough time to wire all of Senator Salermo's rooms. They ran into some difficulty and could not finish as planned."

"This isn't good news, Captain," Denise sighed.

"They've had almost four hours. That's usually enough for any surveillance team. What haven't they done?"

"There are still no monitoring devices in Senator Salermo's private office and bath. The other rooms have camera surveillance," Captain Carter replied dejectedly.

"Captain, I'm not too concerned about the bathroom, but the unmonitored private office could cause us considerable trouble. Is there nothing you can do?"

"I'm sorry, Detective Dory. I'd do anything in my power to be of assistance to you, but my hands are tied by the housekeeping department," Captain Carter responded as he returned to his men. The expression on his face said that he could see their dinner date slipping through his fingers.

Surveying the bedroom, Denise stated with resignation, "We'll have to make the cot and dust in here ourselves. I don't want to take any chances that someone will saturate the bed linens with mushroom dust. I still believe that the murderer was trying to give me a warning when I developed that migraine and sick stomach."

"I'll bring you the vacuum and a dust cloth myself," Captain Carter replied as he helped pick up discarded tools, his face growing red with the effort.

Tom and Denise made light work of removing the old police tape and returning the furniture to its customary position in the rooms. By the time Captain Carter returned, all signs of the police investigation had vanished. Quickly, they made the cot and dusted while Captain Carter put fresh towels in the bathroom and ran the vacuum over the thick carpets. Although their efforts were not professional, the office was quite presentable by the time they had completed their task. Unfortunately, Denise could do nothing to fill the emptiness of the flower vases. It was already too late to ask Mrs. Benedict to provide them. When they finished,

Captain Carter posted a guard in the hall with explicit instructions that no one other than the senator should enter the rooms.

Although they had secured the suite, Denise worried about their ability to protect Salermo. Without a monitoring device in the bedroom, they would lose valuable coverage and give the murderer ample hiding places. Denise had hoped that the guard would be enough for tonight. In the morning, Captain Carter's men would return to finish their work.

Senator Salermo accompanied by his secretary returned to his office promptly at ten o'clock. Denise and Tom were waiting outside his room along with a small band of loyal observers to see him safely inside. Before they left for the monitor room, Denise spoke with the guard on duty. He assured her that no one had entered the room during his watch.

Stepping into the hall, Denise whispered, "I'm getting tired of this. All the uncertainty and the waiting is getting to me."

"To me, too, but it won't be long now," Tom replied as he gave her shoulder a light tap.

"After all this work and time, we still might come up empty-handed," Denise moaned.

"It's not like you to get down, Dory," Tom stated gently.

"I know, but I've taken you away from our cases long enough. We have nothing to show for it," Denise sighed.

"You will soon. I know your plan will work," Tom commented. "After all, it always does. I don't have a stupid partner."

Chuckling, Denise said, "Thanks for the vote of confidence."

They continued their trip through the empty halls in silence. For once Denise relished the sound of her shoes padding along the marble corridors. Until they caught the murderer, the smaller the number of people on the move at night the better she liked it. If something happened, they would have fewer suspects to question instead of the usual legions of Hill staffers.

Richard looked up from the television screens as they entered the monitor room. "It's about time you two got here. This is boring work without company. Pull up a chair. It's almost like being a paid voyeur."

"If it keeps Senator Salermo alive, I'll do it," Denise replied as she lifted the paper cup of steaming coffee Richard handed her.

The monitors in both senators' private offices showed that no one was in the rooms. By changing the direction of the hidden cameras, they could view every corner, watch the doors and windows, and see anyone who might enter.

Happy to have company, Richard chatted nonstop. Denise and Tom would have preferred silence, but there was no way of stopping him. Finally, when he had exhausted every imaginable topic, his shift ended. Richard bade them good night, saying that he needed to phone home.

Despite being alone, Denise and Tom refrained from thinking thoughts of love. Their work would have to come first. The first hour of their watch passed without incident. Near the end of the second hour, Denise was just beginning to become drowsy when she saw someone enter the darkened study of Senator Pars's office. Nudging Tom she said, "Look at this. Two men have arrived. Do you recognize them?"

Scanning the screen, Tom replied, "The shorter one looks like the senator's secretary, but I don't recognize the second one. They look as if they've come for a purpose, but maybe you should check them out."

Before Denise could rise from her chair, the two-way

radio in her pocket started to chatter and an unfamiliar voice called, "Detective Dory, this is Sergeant Risso on duty outside Senator Pars's office. You should come immediately. The senator is ill and has called his personal physician and his secretary. I've just admitted him and the secretary."

Pressing the response button as she sprinted out of the room with Tom behind her, Denise replied, "I'm on my way. How sick is he?"

"He collapsed in his bathroom. I think he's a very sick man," Sergeant Risso responded.

They took the stairs two at a time and ran to the senator's office. Sergeant Risso met them at the door. His face was ashen from the strain and the need to provide security at the same time. He smiled wearily when he saw them.

Directing Denise and Tom into the room, Risso said, "I'll return to the hall now that you're here. No one other than these two men has entered these rooms."

Placing her hand on his arm, Denise replied, "I know that you've done your best to protect Salermo and Pars. If this is a murder attempt, someone administered the poison before the senator returned to his rooms."

Denise and Tom waited impatiently in the outer office usually filled with assistants for news from Senator Pars's physician. A messenger from the hospital's laboratory arrived and carried away a sample of his blood. Thirty minutes later, the telephone rang.

When the minutes continued to tick off without anyone else coming from Senator Pars's office, Denise turned to Tom and said, "I have to know what's going on in there. I'm going to get Senator Salermo. He'll find out for us."

"No, I'll go. You stay here. You know more about the destroying angel than I do. Besides, this waiting is making me jumpy. I need to stretch my legs. I'll come right back with the senator," Tom replied as he eased past Sergeant Risso, who had not moved from his post at the door.

Alone, Denise paced the outer office. Despite their best efforts, Senator Pars had fallen ill. She only hoped that it was not another murder attempt and simply a case of indigestion or a bout of nerves from the exhausting day. Until Senator Salermo appeared, she could only wait and try to hear the conversation from the other room.

Senator Salermo arrived in less than five minutes with Tom on his heels. He nodded to her and immediately disappeared into Senator Pars's office. His shoulders were stooped with worry and his face lined with concern. If only pressing government business had not prevented them from going home, Pars would be alive.

Denise and Tom did not have long to wait before Senator Salermo reappeared. The expression on his face told them that he did not bring good news. Looking at her through immensely sad eyes, he said, "Senator Pars has died. He had all the symptoms of the others . . . severe stomach cramping, bloody bowels, and cardiac arrhythmia. The hospital laboratory has confirmed *Amanita* mushroom poisoning. He died of massive organ failure."

In less than twelve hours after becoming the majority leader, Frank Pars was dead. Someone had killed him.

"What is it? What has happened?" puffed Captain Carter, who had hastily rushed from dinner on his short legs. His chest heaved with the effort of hauling his chubby body up the steps at a fast pace.

"Senator Pars is dead from mushroom poisoning," Denise stated flatly, feeling drained, angry, and frustrated.

"How could this happen? We did everything we

could to protect him," Captain Carter sputtered as he wiped the perspiration from his forehead.

"Obviously we didn't do enough. I want every corner of this office and Senator Salermo's bedroom wired as soon as the coroner removes the body. We can't let this happen again," Denise replied tartly. Her nerves were on edge and she was in no mood to nurse him along.

"Certainly, Detective, my men will be more efficient this time. You have my word on it," Captain Carter replied as he stepped away. He could sense that she was not in a pleasant frame of mind.

Staring at the pattern in the carpet, Denise tried to organize her thoughts. No one had entered the room since she left it. She had made the bed herself, so no one could have impregnated the linens with mushroom toxin. She had even pulled the bed linens and towels randomly from the shelves of many different linen closets. Denise had dusted the room and removed all possible traces of poison residue from the furnishings and floor. If she had inhaled the poison, she would have had some symptoms by now. No, the toxin had not been in the room.

Suddenly, Denise had the answer. The murderer had surprised her by showing great ability to avoid traps, but he had not outsmarted her yet. Turning to Tom, she said, "I want the lab to examine a sample from the senator's clothing. I think the murderer sprinkled the toxin on the garments while they hung in the closet."

"If that happened, then we'll have to destroy all of his clothing. We need to find out where he stored the clothes he kept here," Richard said as he approached Michael Pace in the anteroom.

Pace looked drawn and pale, but he was willing to help in the investigation in any way he could. Listening to her request, he said, "All of the senators keep at least one change of clothes in addition to formal wear in the wardrobe in the laundry. I can get whatever you need."

"Thanks, we appreciate your help. We'll need the suit that the senator wore earlier today if you can get it for me. Make sure you wear gloves and hold your breath while you stuff the clothes into a plastic bag," Denise instructed as he listened carefully.

"I can't imagine who would systematically kill all the majority leaders. This is simply dreadful," Pace commented as he rushed off to do her bidding.

While Denise gazed into the night from the office window, Tom phoned their contact at the FBI, who assured him that his chemist would have the results within the hour. Joining her at the window, Tom also wondered at the beauty of the night that stood in cruel contrast to the ugliness of the murderer's latest victory.

Turning to Tom, Denise said, "I hope this is the last man who has to die before we catch the murderer. I don't know how much more the government can take of this turmoil. If we don't solve this case quickly, they're going to give us a swift boot out of here."

"I don't blame them," Tom commented with a sad shake of his head. "So far, we haven't been much help. We don't know any more than the Capitol or D.C. police. Pathetic."

"As soon as we hear from the FBI, let's have a meeting with the others," Denise replied as they left the office. Already red-eyed staffers were beginning to gather. Slipping silently past them, Denise and Tom left them to their grief.

The first place they stopped was the makeshift monitor room to tell Greta and Eugene about the morning meeting and to leave a note for the next shift. Then they slipped notes under all the bedroom doors of their colleagues with instructions to meet at seven. Tom's cell phone rang as they left the last of their colleagues.

Standing in the hall with their heads together, Denise and Tom listened as George Christian from the FBI provided them with much-needed information. Providing careful details, he said, "Detective Dory, you were correct. Someone brushed the dust of the destroying angel mushroom into the fiber of Senator Pars's suits and the two samples Pace brought from the wardrobe. From the quantity that would have come in contact with his skin and that he would have inhaled, I'd say that he never had a chance to survive the effects of the toxin. A healthy man would have eventually succumbed to the poison. With his medical history, he was doomed from the moment he got dressed yesterday morning."

Answering for both of them, Tom replied, "Thanks, Christian, we owe you one."

"You owe me more than one, but who's counting?" Christian responded with a chuckle as he hung up the phone,

With a sigh, Denise said, "Let's go out to the grounds. I want to follow up on something Mrs. Benedict said today."

"Dory, it's three in the morning. Can't it wait until sunup?" Tom asked in disbelief.

"No, it can't. I have to know now. You know how I am about following a hunch. You still have that flashlight, don't you? Let's go," Denise replied as she grabbed him by the hand and pulled a reluctant Tom behind her.

"Yeah, I know," Tom growled. "You're a real pain when you're on to something. Remind me why I keep you as a partner."

"I'm thorough and dependable," Denise detailed as they walked into the night air. "I make great brownies and don't nag you too much. Besides, you love me. I think that's the best answer of all."

Grumbling under his breath, Tom said, "I almost

wish I hadn't told you that last one. I might be in bed now instead of following you all over the Capitol."

The small garden felt strangely alive as each plant cast a short, fat shadow in the light of the flashlight that Tom swung from one corner of the garden to the other. Denise half-expected the bushes to free themselves from their mounds of mulch and begin to twirl in the spotlight as they disturbed the peace of their community. A carefully choreographed waltz would have fit nicely into the mystic element of the night. The bushes reminded her of what Peter Dominic said about the shadow of the person he had seen with Anthony Guido . . . short and round.

"What are you looking for, Dory?" Tom asked with a yawn as he held the light steady while she crawled around the base of the bushes.

"Come a little closer, and I'll show you," Denise replied as she carefully pushed away the mulch in the far corner of the garden. She had discovered a spot where the rain had left the ground wet and soft. The sun had not been able to shine through the thick leaves of an evergreen.

"Jeez, Dory, if anyone sees us out here, they'll think we're crazy. Don't you ever think about appearances and your reputation? Out here in the middle of the night digging in the dirt like a demented cat. Woman, what *are* you thinking?" Tom griped as he followed the path around to where Denise knelt among the mulch.

"Stop fussing and look at what I've found," Denise instructed as she pointed to the ground under the little tree.

"I don't see anything except some button mushrooms. Let's go, Dory, I need a nap," Tom replied as he impatiently pulled her to her feet.

"I bet they aren't button mushrooms at all. My guess is that they're the murderer's little crop of destroying angels," Denise responded as she brushed the mulch from the front of her navy-blue skirt.

Looking at her as if she suffered from moon fever, Tom rebutted, "The murderer wouldn't grow them out here where anyone could find them. He wouldn't take that chance."

"Why not?" Denise demanded. "You thought they were harmless button mushrooms. Anyone seeing them would believe that the rain had brought them out. No one would imagine that someone would deliberately plant poisonous fungi in the Capitol's little garden. The gardener wouldn't think anything of the find and probably leave them alone. He certainly wouldn't recognize them as poisonous. Mushrooms themselves help the soil retain moisture and are harmless."

"You're a madwoman, Denise, but you're a damn good detective. Once you sink your teeth into a matter, you stick with it. Well, I'll take these little devils to the FBI lab. The chemist should be able to identity them in a matter of minutes," Tom replied as he carefully slipped on two pairs of rubber gloves and opened a plastic bag to hold the specimens.

"Good," Denise said as she watched Tom drop six glistening white mushrooms into the bag. "I'm going to the conference room to wait for Senator Salermo."

"They're pretty, aren't they?" Tom commented as he turned his gloves inside out and closed them inside the bag with the mushrooms. "No wonder people eat them by mistake. Everyone thinks of poisonous mushrooms as ugly with upturned caps and warts. These look as if they're just begging to become part of a salad."

"If I'm right, a salad made with two mushrooms would be enough to wipe out the twenty of us," Denise said as she gazed at the destroying angels that glistened in the light. "I'll be upstairs when you return."

"Right. I'll be with you in a bit," Tom replied as he

trotted off, holding his cell phone in one hand and the bag in the other. Denise could only imagine the delight of the person on the other end of the phone at hearing Tom's voice that late at night.

All the lights were on in the conference room. Word of Senator Pars's death and the committee session had spread through the ranks of the Hill staffers. They had left their comfortable homes to wait bleary-eyed for the results of the unprecedented meeting that would decide the course of action for the next few days. Everyone looked sleepy, but no one wanted to miss receiving the historic news firsthand.

With the exception of Tom, all of the detectives were in attendance also. The last shift had secured the monitor room as soon as they heard about the senator's death. They saw little point in monitoring the office of a dead man.

Approaching Pace, who smiled wearily, Denise asked, "How much longer do you think they will take?"

"Senator Salermo felt confident that the senators would agree with him that the government needed to get on with its business regardless of the threat to yet another senator. If he is correct, they should have an announcement in a matter of minutes," Michael Pace said as he removed his glasses and rubbed his tired eyes.

"Good. I have a feeling that we're on the murderer's coattails at this moment," Denise replied as the door swung open.

Immediately Pace rose to his feet and in one step closed the distance between himself and Senator Salermo. As his secretary, Pace wanted to be at the senator's side when he faced the gathered community. From the way that Senator Salermo leaned on the younger man's arm, Denise could tell that he appreciated the support and attention as he faced the microphone again to announce their decision.

Despite his obvious mental and emotional fatigue, Senator Salermo spoke clearly, saying, "It is with great sadness that I inform you of the death of Senator Pars at the hands of a vicious murderer. I have extended our sympathies to his wife, who will keep us informed of funeral arrangements. So far, all we know is that the coffin will lie in the rotunda. The president also has phoned her with his heartfelt sympathy. However, the work of government must continue. At two o'clock this afternoon, we will meet to select the new majority leader."

With that announcement, Senator Salermo and the other members of the Capitol Hill family left for their homes and offices. As the crowd thinned, Tom jostled his way through the remaining people wearing a particularly incongruous smile considering the darkness of the morning and the somberness of the Capitol.

"You were right again, Dory. They are the destroying angel mushrooms rather than button mushrooms. The chemist confirmed the identification by comparing them to the dust samples you left with him earlier," Tom reported almost gleefully.

"Good, and just in time, too. The senators are determined to select their new majority leader this afternoon. We have to make sure that Captain Carter's men have everything in place this time. Housekeeping should arrive in the early afternoon. We will accept no excuses for failure this time. We'll need to begin our shifts prior to their arrival. I'll brief everyone over lunch. We'll catch our murderer this time," Denise said with renewed confidence.

Denise left Tom with the task of notifying Captain Carter of the lab results and arranging for his men to finish their work during the morning. She was too tired to face his less than subtle leering. Besides, she had to visit Mr. Philips in the flower-arranging room. When the day of the funeral arrived, the rotunda would be appropriately bedecked with carefully selected flowers, some of which could undoubtedly be lethal.

EIGHTEEN

Pandemonium was the only word appropriate to describe the atmosphere of the flower-arranging room as sleepy employees called in early from their beds hurried to arrange vases of flowers. The usual clutter of discarded blossoms and florist wire had grown as the task of providing special floral arrangements to the already full load of regular work fell into the capable lap of Mr. Philips and the rest of the staff. Petals, leaves, and ribbons flew everywhere as the clusters took on the appearance of orderly creations suitable for the funeral of a beloved politician and statesman.

"Detective Dory, I'm sorry, but I don't have time to speak with you this morning," the usually tranquil Mr. Philips lamented, waving hands filled with wire, scissors, and ribbons. "Maybe in a couple of days. By then everything will have settled down, but right now I feel as if the end of the world were coming and I'm the first to go. A great yawning abyss has opened before me and, if I don't get these arrangements made, I'll fall in."

"Don't mind me, Mr. Philips. I only want to observe your operation at work. It isn't often that I get to watch talented floral arrangers create their masterpieces. I'll be as inconspicuous as possible," Denise replied as the poor man smiled bravely and scurried away. His relief at being free to return to his work was almost palpable.

Denise moved to a distant corner from which she

could watch the staff at work without being observed. Standing in the shadows, she sketched their movements as they created the spray that would cover the senator's casket and the arrangements that would sit on the floor next to it. She was amazed at their efficiency despite the unaccustomed early hour as random stems of flowers joined to form stunning displays of color and design. When they finished the immediate tasks, they moved into their normal day's work with the hope of completing it early and returning to their homes for rest.

Mrs. Benedict did not immediately see Denise standing in the corner out of the way when she entered the room. She looked as tired as the rest of the staff as she rolled up her sleeves and started arranging delphiniums and gladiolus in a massive brass urn. Her fingers moved skillfully as she intermingled the main flowers with carnations, roses, and ferns. The end result was a stunning display of colors and textures.

After fashioning three more creations, Mrs. Benedict turned her attention to her usual charges as she collected her cart and the plants for the offices. As she loaded the last pot, she looked into Denise's hiding place and nodded. She did not appear startled to find Denise in the corner, unlike several of the others who had reacted with quick intakes of breath when they saw her. Mrs. Benedict smiled and waved serenely as she approached, pushing the heavy cart.

"Good morning, Mrs. Benedict," Denise said as she stepped from the shadows to walk with her into the rotunda.

"Detective Dory. We're certainly busy around here this morning. It's terrible that yet another senator has died," Mrs. Benedict replied as she allowed Denise to help her push the overloaded cart.

"He didn't die of natural causes, Mrs. Benedict. He was murdered as were the others. Someone is systematically killing the senators using plant toxin—the poisonous *Amanita* mushroom to be exact. I was wondering if you might know of anyone associated with the Capitol who would grow such a crop. As you're a botanist, someone might have sought your assistance in cultivating them," Denise inquired as they entered the quiet rotunda. At this hour of the morning, they had the massive structure to themselves.

Mrs. Benedict carefully repositioned a pot of geraniums before turning to face Denise. Her eyes sparkled with a strange fire although her face remained as impassive as ever. Taking a deep breath, she replied, "I gave up that profession years ago, Detective. Few people know about my former life and, therefore, they wouldn't have asked me."

Denise suggested as she handed Mrs. Benedict another pot, "But you were once a well-respected botanist, and, if I'm not mistaken, you worked beside Doctor Gianni on several important toxicology projects. Surely someone has connected your current interest in flowers with your past work."

"No, until now, no one has. You have gone to great lengths to uncover this information," Mrs. Benedict replied with her usual sweet smile.

Watching her work among the flowers that would soon grace the bier, Denise marveled at the agility of Mrs. Benedict's long, thin fingers as they encouraged each cluster of blooms to stand tall among the others for the benefit of the entire display. She bent close to some and seemed to breathe strength back into them as she carefully wrapped wire around their stems to reinforce them.

Denise asked, studying Mrs. Benedict's tranquil face, "I needed to know everything I could about everyone who had access to the senators. However, my investigation could only provide so much information. Now, Mrs.

Benedict, I need your help. I've read your study of the *Amanita* mushroom, and I know that you are an expert in their biological makeup. I need to know who might have decided to grow them in the Capitol's own garden. If you can remember anyone mentioning an interest in them, I would appreciate your help."

In the rotunda's low light, Denise thought that she might have seen a momentary tightening of Mrs. Benedict's mouth. Turning her full attention to Denise, Mrs. Benedict responded quickly and without hesitation, "Detective, there's nothing I can do for you. I coauthored the study to which you are obviously referring with Doctor Gianni more than ten years ago. Since then I've lived in obscurity and tranquillity. No one has asked me about growing the destroying angel in either a greenhouse or garden setting. Doctor Gianni would have been the best source of information, but, unfortunately, he is dead. If I think of anything that might help you, I'll let you know."

"Do you grow them, Mrs. Benedict?"

"As you stated, Detective Dory, I was a botanist in my former life," Mrs. Benedict responded with a sigh of resignation. "Occasionally, I succumb to pride and cultivate some of the plants that used to populate my world. The *Amanita* mushroom as well as exotic orchids and water plants often find their way into my little garden at the retirement home. Old age has crippled my body but not my brain. However, I always dispose of them so that their toxin will not harm anyone."

"Was that cluster of mushrooms I found in the rose garden yours?" Denise inquired while continuing to study her face for signs that Mrs. Benedict might know more than she was willing to share.

"No, I've never grown any of them here. Not many people know the difference between the *Amanita* and the button mushroom. An unsuspecting garden assistant could come in contact with the toxin. When I give in to my former passion, I grow them in my little apartment," Mrs. Benedict replied as she pushed the now empty cart toward the flower room. Its wheels squeaked softly on the marble floor.

"How do you dispose of them?"

"I mulch them into a fine dust, which I bury in the woods near the retirement community. I'm always careful to use precautions when working with them," Mrs. Benedict responded as she returned to the waiting bank of plants.

Studying her closely, Denise asked, "You don't mix them into the compost heap along with the old flowers from the Capitol?"

"Oh no, I'd never do that. The dust is very toxic. Anyone mulching with it would be in serious danger from the mushroom's poison," Mrs. Benedict answered as she surveyed her choice of flowers.

Most of the activity had quieted by the time they returned to the flower room. The flowers for the funeral had been placed in the refrigerator for use at the funeral. The staff had turned its attention to the usual task of providing flowers for the Capitol offices.

As Mrs. Benedict reloaded her cart, Denise commented, "By the way, Mrs. Benedict, your birth name is very beautiful. It's a shame that you changed it."

"Yes, it was, but I'm no longer Angelica Fiorelli. Even though my husband has been dead these many years, I prefer being called Mrs. Benedict. Excuse me for asking, Detective, but you've been in D.C. for quite some time now. Aren't you becoming homesick? I hate being away from my few little rooms. Surely, you must feel the same way, or does a certain detective keep you from being lonesome?" Mrs. Benedict asked with a curious inclination of her head.

"You don't miss much, do you, Mrs. Benedict?"

Denise chuckled. "Tom's my partner from the Montgomery County Police Department. He's joined our little group. I've enjoyed my stay in D.C., but you're right, I'm ready to go home. I think we'll finish our work here very soon. My partner and I have a lot of work to do at home."

"Then, we'll shortly say goodbye. I'll miss our little conversations. I'll see you later, Detective. I'd better deliver these plants now," Mrs. Benedict replied as she carefully added one last pot to the collection and rolled it toward the offices. Denise could always count on Mrs. Benedict to be calm even as the world crumbled around her. She carried out her responsibilities as if none of the chaos and death had touched her.

Rushing along the mostly deserted halls, Denise found Pace in his small office around the corner from Senator Salermo's suite. He looked up, smiled tiredly, and asked as she entered, "Would you like a cup of tea, Detective Dory? I was just about to pour myself another one."

"I'd love one, thank you, Mr. Pace," Denise replied as she accepted the offered cup laced with a heaping spoonful of honey. "Why aren't you involved in the funeral preparations? I thought that Senator Pars's widow had delegated the responsibility to the Hill staff."

Holding the steaming cup in both hands, Mr. Pace responded, "Someone had to mind the shop. Besides, I've arranged enough funeral masses in the last few months to last a lifetime."

Looking at him over the rim of her cup, Denise commented gratefully, "Delicious tea. Just what I needed after last night. Very soothing."

"I hope it's not too sweet. I should have asked rather than assuming that you would take it the same way I do. Considering you haven't had much sleep in the last two days, I don't think the extra sugar will hurt you," Mr. Pace replied with a gentle smile.

"After tonight, I could use a few calories," Denise replied with a chuckle.

Looking over the rim of his cup, Mr. Pace asked, "Are you so sure that you'll catch the murderer tonight?"

"If we don't, I might as well go home," Denise commented with a sad shake of her head. "I can't stay here much longer without making a contribution to this project. I'm beginning to feel like a moocher as it is, Mr. Pace."

"You shouldn't feel that way. You've done quite a bit to provide security during this time of chaos," Mr. Pace replied soothingly.

Thanking him, Denise said, "I hope you're right. In the meantime, have you removed the suits from the closet? It's imperative that no one come in contact with them again."

"Oh, yes, I found and bagged six of them. They'll be gone by the next trash pickup. I placed them in a hazardous debris bag," Michael Pace replied with confidence.

"Great. I'd better run. Thanks for the tea," Denise replied as she rose to leave.

"Any time, Detective."

Denise rushed to the restaurant where the others waited for her. They had already ordered omelets and were munching fruit as she entered. Sliding into the chair beside Tom and gazing from one tired face to another, she said, "Sorry to be so late. You're certainly a wide-eyed group."

"Hey, what do you expect? We're going on zero sleep," Tom retorted as he passed her the breadbasket.

"Since we're so tired, it's possible that we're not operating at our full potential. Let's review what we know so far to refresh our minds," Denise suggested, taking a thick slice of warm bread.

Greta offered quickly, "We know that the murderer is close and not at all timid. He has unquestioned access to everything in the Capitol, or so it seems from the toxin he placed on the senator's suits."

"He's very dedicated to his cause and will stop at nothing to advance it," Eugene added between chews.

Richard interjected, "He doesn't appear to fear the gaping mouth of hell, or at least he has convinced himself that the result of his efforts justifies the punishment he'll have to face."

"And he has even struck at us to warn us away," Tom offered as he buttered a slice of bread. "I agree with Denise that the migraine she suffered was probably the result of someone sprinkling some kind of plant toxin on her pillow. It's a good thing she only took a nap. If she'd lain down for a night's sleep, she'd have been in even worse shape or dead."

"It gives me the chills to think that he's so bold," Greta commented with a visible shiver.

"It makes me mad," Eugene stated. "He's taunting us, almost daring us to find him. He's so blatant with his actions."

"I've been thinking that the murderer might be Senator Salermo trying to advance his career. He certainly has the most to gain by the deaths of the others. I wouldn't be surprised if he's selected majority leader," Richard suggested.

Shaking her head, Denise commented, "I don't think that would necessarily prove his guilt. According to the list of casualties so far, he should be at risk as an outspoken advocate of maintaining the status quo. However, there's always the possibility that the murderer will simply stop. It's a small chance but it does exist. He might realize that we're close to discovering his identity."

"Denise, I hope Senator Salermo knows that keeping him alive is a tall order," Richard stated, sipping a second cup of strong coffee. The bags under his eyes showed that he needed it badly, as they all did. "He's known as a conservative and, as such, he is a likely target."

"He knows and he's willing to take that chance. It's up to us to catch the murderer, and we will," Denise responded with confidence.

"How can you be so sure?" Greta queried. "He might poison the food this time."

"From the killer's established mode of operation, I'd say that he'll try to plant something in the office. The surveillance cameras will find him if he does," Denise answered.

They paid the bill and left the café. As they strolled toward the Capitol, Eugene suggested, "There's always the possibility that Pace might be the murderer. He certainly has the opportunity."

"He has the most common motive of all. He might hate Senator Salermo, his employer," Greta commented bluntly.

"Who's on your list, Dory?" Richard asked.

"I think it's someone whose presence is so much a part of the fiber of the Capitol that we don't even notice when that person is in our midst," Denise replied slowly.

"Do you have a name?" Eugene asked as he squinted against the brightness of the sun.

"I'd prefer not to say. We should be open to anyone who looks suspicious. This might be our last chance to catch the killer. If it's the person I think it is, we won't see much of our suspect after today. Our murderer will return to anonymity after tonight," Denise replied confidently.

"Then he's even more dangerous," Greta commented as she looked around the grounds, which again were filling with visitors and the press. "The press has already started to arrive."

Gazing at her watch, Denise said, "I think we should stop by the monitor room to make sure everything is ready, and then we should try to get some rest. I strongly suggest that you get fresh linens from the laundry room before you lie down."

"Becoming a bit paranoid, Dory?" Tom queried with raised brows.

"No, only taking very necessary precautions. No one has reached into the Page School, but you never know when someone will," Denise responded as they took the long way through the rotunda on their way to the offices. This time when they passed Mrs. Benedict, she did not look up. She was much too preoccupied with her plants to notice them.

The monitor room showed that all the cameras were working and ready. From the outer office, Denise waved to Greta, who turned the camera hidden in the bookcase in response. Repeating the same process in each room, Denise assured herself that Captain Carter's men had satisfactorily completed the job.

Everything was just as they had left it in the early hours of the morning, including the empty coffee cups and the rumpled bed on which Senator Pars had died. Housekeeping had not yet prepared the rooms, but Denise knew that someone would appear soon to put everything right before the new occupant arrived. The largest office had to be in perfect condition for the new majority leader. Denise certainly hoped that she was right and that the Hill would not have to endure more attacks after tonight.

"Try to get some rest, Dory," Tom instructed as he pulled her into his arms.

"You know I won't until this is over," Denise replied as she momentarily rested against his chest.

Tipping her head up so that he could look into her eyes, Tom said, "I know, but you should. You've been going full out for a long time. You need a break."

"I know, and I'll have one as soon as we solve this case," Denise agreed. "Maybe we can get away somewhere."

"Take a vacation together? That really will be a novelty. Neither of us has taken a vacation in three years. We've always been too busy," Tom joked as he kissed her forehead and the tip of her nose.

Sighing deeply, Denise replied, "Or we haven't wanted to leave each other. Confess it, Tom. We've been fighting the feeling for a long time. A vacation together would be great."

"Yeah, lying on the beach, swimming on the shore. I can hardly wait to rub lotion into your body. Let's do it," Tom smiled warmly.

Pushing him gently away, Denise unlocked her door. Turning to him teasingly, she stated, "I'll be all yours once we solve this case."

Laughing, Tom replied, "Mine and Captain Carter's. See ya later, Dory."

Although Denise was exhausted, she could not force her mind to stop processing the details of the murders. Not even visions of Tom in a swimsuit with water glistening on his skin could stop her from thinking about the case. Lying on top of the new sheets, she tossed and turned but could not sleep.

Feeling even more frustrated, Denise got out of bed and wandered into the rotunda, where the preparations for the funeral appeared complete. Workers had draped black bunting around the pillars and polished the floor until it looked like glass. Chairs filled the room in readiness for the funeral.

To Denise's surprise, Mrs. Benedict stood only three feet away from her. She was not surveying the rotunda but watching Denise. Mrs. Benedict smiled slightly and nodded.

Deciding that returning to her room was futile, Denise wandered from the Capitol into the teaming city. Suddenly having a taste for an ice cream, she stopped at the usual little shop from which she purchased Tom's treats. Stepping inside, Denise found Tom already enjoying a cup of one of his favorite flavors.

Looking up, Tom commented, "I was wondering when you'd join me."

"I almost didn't come, but at the last minute I decided that I'd rather be here indulging my appetite than trying to force myself to sleep. I guess you couldn't rest either," Denise replied as she ordered a triple raspberry without giving much thought to the calories.

"The way I look at it, Dory, if we don't catch the murderer this time, it won't be a total loss. I wouldn't have found out that you loved me if you hadn't been assigned to this case. Something good has come from all these murders," Tom said as he scooped up a big spoonful and conveyed it to his mouth. His lips smacked appreciatively as the cool confection slid down his throat.

Smiling, Denise asked, "Do you agree with the others that Senator Salermo is behind the murders?"

"No, and you don't either," Tom replied as he licked his spoon. "We both know that he's scared that he'll be the next victim. We could read it on his face the last time we spoke with him. I think it's someone else. Whose name did you write on that slip of paper?"

Chuckling sadly, Denise replied, "I don't want to say because I'm hoping that I'm wrong. It would certainly upset my childhood memories if I'm right."

"I don't follow, Dory," Tom responded. "How do your childhood memories fit into this discussion?"

"I once thought of being a science teacher . . . botany," Denise replied. "I changed my mind when I found criminology more interesting than plant dissecting. I don't want to find out that a scientist is behind this."

"It's dangerous to put people on a pedestal. Humans have clay feet," Tom commented as he finished the last of his ice cream. "I hope I never disappoint you, Dory. Let me know if I do and I'll change."

Denise could not respond over the lump in her throat as they left the shop. She knew that she often expected too much of people, but she had never been disappointed. When everyone told her to stay away from Tom, she selected him as her partner and she had never regretted the decision. His strength and vulnerability had endeared him to her. His ability to analyze the trivia of their workload and separate it from the necessary elements had made him an invaluable asset and freed her from the tedium to focus on the investigative work. His detractors said that he was mean and difficult. By expecting the best of him, she had found a perfect partner. He rose to the challenge and exceeded her expectations. She could not imagine that he would ever disappoint her.

By the time they reached the Capitol, Denise whispered, "I prefer to see angel wings and not devil horns. I know that you'll always be here for me. I love you, Tom."

Linking her arm through his, Tom commented hoarsely, "I love you, Denise, and I always will."

Something in the feel of Tom's hand on her arm and the warmth of his body close to hers told Denise that everything would soon be okay again. For the first time in her career, solving a case would not mean the end of an adventure but the beginning of one. Denise could hardly wait.

NINETEEN

Senator Salermo gave them a few minutes as the housekeeping staff prepared his office. On what should have been a joyous occasion, the senator sat dejectedly at the conference table unable to shake the memory of his deceased colleagues. Despite the security precautions, he looked ill at ease.

"Detective, I wanted to thank you personally for all you've done for us. Yes, I know that it looks to you as if you've fallen short of your goal, but I want you to take heart in the understanding that because of your efforts the investigation is on the threshold of success. I'm pleased to hear that Captain Carter's men have finished their work. I confess that I'm not exactly overjoyed at the idea of being a decoy, but I'd rather be that than a victim," Senator Salermo stated as he motioned to chairs on his right.

"I hope you understand that, although necessary, this charade is not without danger. Your life is at risk until we catch the murderer and perhaps even after we're successful. Once someone breeches the perimeter of an institution's security, everything changes. Security will have to increase around you," Denise remarked as she gazed at his tired face.

"I know and I'm prepared to follow your instructions at the same time hoping that this level of security will not be necessary in the future. It's disheartening to think that I must continue to take extreme precautions while serving the people of this country. I prefer to believe in the goodness of mankind. I especially hate having to keep things from Pace. We've worked together a long time, and he knows the workings of my mind completely," Senator Salermo replied with a touch of sadness in his voice.

"Sadly, not everyone is good, Senator, and we must take precautions against those who would hurt us. It's not enough to serve, we must protect as well," Denise advised. "In that respect, we're ahead of the game at the moment, but we can't afford to become complacent and assume that our progress will continue to be this smooth. We still have to make it through the night."

"Excuse me, Senator, but did you say that Pace knows your mind on all things?" Tom asked as he gazed at the unhappy man.

"Don't worry, Detective Phyfer, I keep some things to myself and share others only with my wife. However, we do confer on most important political issues. Take tonight for instance. Pace and I are planning to do something quite different from the ordinary in that we are going out to dinner. When we're busy and can't go home, we usually order sandwiches from the deli. You and Detective Dory are invited to accompany us if you'd like. As a matter of fact, I insist that you come with us. You probably have not had much opportunity to explore the city and to enjoy any of our famous restaurants. Dinner with us would give you a taste of D.C. as well as the ability to protect me," Senator Salermo suggested with the first signs of joy that Denise had seen on his face since her arrival at the Capitol.

Responding for both of them, Denise said, "Thank you, Senator, we'd love to accompany you."

"Wonderful. Meet me at my office at six o'clock. We'll take a leisurely drive through the neighborhood and perhaps even stop at some of the sights along the way. We'll dine at one of our more elaborate establishments," Senator Salermo replied with the glee of a child as Pace joined them, carrying an armload of files for him to read. Immediately, the senator forgot everything and turned his attention to his work.

Slipping into the hall, Denise commented as they walked toward his office, "This might actually work to our advantage. At least we won't have to worry about someone poisoning his food."

"True, unless Pace is the murderer and he picks a restaurant of his accomplices," Tom replied skeptically.

"Then, we should suggest the place. Let's call L'Esquilino's, the restaurant we saw while walking to the FBI office. Let's see if they'll prepare a table toward the rear of the restaurant for us. That way, we'll know that he's safe," Denise suggested as she peered into Salermo's office to see the housekeeping staff in a frenzy of activity vacuuming and dusting, straightening books in the library, and making up the senator's cot in the inner office.

Denise and Tom parted company with her heading to her room in the Page School and him going to the monitoring room to relieve Greta. Along the way Denise passed groups of congressional staffers who looked as tired as she felt. It seemed as if they were all holding their breaths in the hopes that nothing would happen this time.

The Page School was empty except for the guards who regularly patrolled the area. Denise waved to Sergeant Henry as he came toward her with a package in his outstretched hands. "This arrived for you about an hour ago," he said as he handed it to her.

"Who delivered it?" Denise asked, turning the gift-wrapped box over to look for any markings or cards.

"A woman brought it to the main gate. Don't worry

about incendiary devices. Captain Carter already X-rayed it," Sergeant Henry stated as he continued to patrol the hall.

"Thanks, but I wonder if he checked for plant toxins," Denise replied with a nervous giggle as she entered her room.

Denise continued to puzzle over the contents of the package as she peeled off the carefully applied paper and slipped her nail under the tape to break the hold and slowly opened the lid. Inside, she found a sealed envelope on which the presenter had typed her name. On a single sheet of white paper the sender had inscribed a quote from Matthew 12:50 that read: "For whoever does the will of the heavenly Father is brother, and sister, and mother."

Immediately, Denise phoned the monitor room. Tom picked up on the first ring and listened intently as she told him about the message. Slowly he said, "The murderer is trying to justify his next move by quoting Bible text. I think we should get the senator out of there immediately. I don't trust anyone around him without one of us being there."

"I agree. I'll call for relief and meet you in his office," Denise stated as she quickly hung up the phone, grabbed her radio, and dashed from the room.

Almost colliding with Sergeant Henry, Denise rushed to the senator's original office, knowing that his new quarters as majority leader were not ready. Barely waiting for him to respond to her knock, she entered to find him in conversation with Pace in his study. Pace was in the process of serving tea from a lovely floral service. He had already poured one cup when Denise entered.

"Excuse me, Senator, for breaking in on you like this, but I have reason to believe that you're in even more danger than we originally suspected. I've just received a note from the murderer. Might I ask where you obtained the tea?'' Denise demanded without giving thought to etiquette and protocol.

"Pace brought it to me. Surely, you don't think . . . ,'' Senator Salermo responded as he studied her worried face.

Turning her attention abruptly to his longtime secretary, Denise demanded, "Mr. Pace, who prepared the tea for you?''

"I prepared it myself. I always keep tea in my office. Don't you remember, Detective, that I served some to you the other day? Is there a problem?'' Pace replied as he wrinkled his brow in concern.

"I notice that your cup is empty. I'm concerned that someone might have tampered with your supply. You haven't drunk yours, have you?'' Denise asked as she studied their faces.

"No, I was just about to pour mine when you entered. You don't need to worry, Detective. I keep this antique tea service locked in my closet. No one could tamper with it. Now, would you care to join us? It would only take a minute for me to get you a cup,'' Pace said as he reached for the teapot.

"Thank you, no, but don't let me stop you from enjoying yours,'' Denise replied without taking her eyes from his face.

With a smile, Pace poured his tea. As he reached toward the sugar bowl, his fingers stopped in midair. Thinking better of it, he decided against adding the sweetener. He lifted the cup to his lips and drank deeply of the hot brew.

"Michael, you usually use sugar. Why not today? You certainly aren't watching your figure, as thin as you are,'' Senator Salermo joked as he reached for his full cup and dropped in three teaspoons of the white powder.

"That's true, Senator, but I'm careful about my sugar

intake and plan to eat a big dessert tonight," Pace replied a bit hesitantly as he gingerly placed his cup on the table.

Noticing that his hands shook slightly, Denise commented, "I don't think a teaspoon or two would hurt you, Mr. Pace. Here, let me sweeten that for you."

Out of the corner of her eye, Denise watched his face tighten as she added the sugar and stirred the tea for him. Returning the cup, she said, "That should make it taste even better. A good cup of tea needs a touch of sweetener. Isn't that what you told me?"

Shifting his eyes from her face to the senator's and back again, Michael Pace slowly raised the cup to his lips. At the same time, Senator Salermo lifted his own and prepared to take a sip. Breathing heavily, Pace ordered, "No, Senator, don't drink it. It has been poisoned."

Taking the cup from Senator Salermo's hand, Denise watched as Michael Price dissolved into tears. His hands shook so badly that tea spilled onto his shirt. Dropping the cup and covering his face, he sobbed, "Forgive me."

Senator Salermo's face contorted with the pain of recognition. His longtime confidant had intended to murder him. Placing his trembling hand on Michael Pace's head, Salermo asked, "Why, Michael, why would you do this? You have been like a son to me. I even introduced you to my daughter. Why?"

Lifting his tear-filled eyes, Michael Pace replied, "I didn't think that it would get to this point when I first started working for the cause. They wanted to insure that you would select a senator who believed as they do on all issues. However, despite the letters, the audiences, the calls, no one would listen to us. You continued to select senators who refused to recognize our position. You kept pushing Affirmative Action. We became desperate and decided to send a stronger message of our discontent.

"When your colleagues selected you, I begged my partner to abandon this effort, but I knew it was hopeless. She would not listen. She wanted to continue to press onward. The cause has become everything to her."

"Why did you use plant toxins?" Denise demanded as Pace continued to wipe at his streaming eyes.

"Very few people know anything about them. We were safe until Doctor Gianni started snooping around. It was just a matter of time before he discovered the identity of the poisons and us," Pace replied as he wiped his face with one of the linen napkins.

"What kind of poison are you using tonight?" Denise demanded with growing impatience at his sniveling.

"The sugar is laced with *Amanita* mushroom toxin," Pace replied without hesitation as if glad to be rid of the weight.

"So this is the way you repay the senator's years of affection toward you." Denise watched as Pace returned to his chair; then she asked, "Why did you continue to murder one senator after another when they didn't respond to your pressure tactics?"

"We knew that we'd eventually stumble upon a senator that we might be able to influence to see things our way. The next senator on the list is such a man," Pace explained with his hand tightly clasped to control the shaking. His bottom lip continued to quiver with emotion.

"Who is your accomplice, Pace?" Denise demanded from the shrunken man.

"No, I won't divulge my partner's identity. We agreed when we began this mission that we would maintain the strictest silence about each other," Pace responded with determination as he wiped his eyes again.

"Earlier you said that 'she' wanted to continue when you felt that you should stop. Who is she, Pace?" Denise insisted, pressing hard in the hopes that he would break.

Looking at her with renewed determination, Pace replied, "Did I? That must have been a slip of the tongue. You'll have to discover my partner's name yourself. I failed here but I won't betray her, too."

"Was it your idea or Anthony Guido's to bug our rooms?" Denise inquired impatiently, seeing the inflexibility in the set of his jaw.

"It was a joint decision. We needed to know your whereabouts and the extent of your knowledge. You might as well stop questioning me because that's all I'll tell you," Pace replied stubbornly.

A knock at the door broke the silence. Rising, Denise opened the door to find Tom with Captain Carter and one of his men. Looking past her shoulder, Tom asked softly, "Michael Pace is the murderer?"

"He tried to murder Senator Salermo with poisoned tea, but he isn't acting alone. There's still one other," Denise replied as Captain Carter rushed forward to handcuff the submissive staffer and lead him away. Lieutenant Christoff carried off the tray containing the evidence of Pace's crime.

"Did he say who it is?" Tom asked as he stepped aside.

"No, he refused, but don't worry, we'll catch her."

"Her? What makes you think it's a woman? Women don't traditionally commit this kind of crime. They act in passion, not in cold blood, Dory."

"Pace slipped up and used the feminine pronoun. Why is it that men don't think that women are capable of doing something this heinous? You don't ever suspect a woman unless it's a case of domestic violence, and then you're quick to point the finger at her. That's so sexist," Denise said as they closed the door to the bedroom where Senator Salermo sat in quiet contemplation.

"I don't think I'm being deliberately sexist," Tom explained. "It's just that the stats show that men commit the bulk of violent crime. Sorry."

"You're forgiven." Denise chuckled. "Anyway, Pace and his partner aren't your typical cold-blooded murderers. They're acting on behalf of a cause, which in my mind makes them even more dangerous. If I hadn't intruded, we'd have another dead senator on our hands."

"Aren't you hungry?" Tom inquired. "You haven't taken time to eat much in the past few days."

Smiling tiredly, Denise commented, "Starving. Let's see what we can find downstairs."

As they helped themselves to the food laid out on the tables, Denise asked, "By the way, how's everything in the monitor room?"

"The equipment is working just fine. So far, however, we haven't seen anything out of the ordinary," Tom replied as he filled his plate with chicken con pepe and rice.

"Enjoy the silence. I think something's going to happen soon. Pace's partner will have to finish what he started," Denise responded as she bit into a thick burger.

Leaving Greta and Eugene in animated conversation regarding the identity of the murderer, Denise and Tom reported to the monitor room for their shift. The screens showed that the cleaning staff had left the majority leader's offices. All was ready for Senator Salermo's occupancy. All they could do now was wait and watch.

Denise slipped into her chair as fatigue and lack of sleep made watching the monitors difficult. She blinked and shifted repeatedly to focus her eyes on the screens. She found herself nodding as the machinery hummed a monotonous, comforting tone. She relished the diversion when Tom burst into one of his off-key songs.

As Tom reached the refrain, Denise saw the shadow of someone enter the room. The figure appeared to be short and stocky. It could easily have been a person wearing a long apron similar to the ones worn by the flower arrangers and the kitchen staff or a woman in a long dress. It might even have been a cleaning woman with a scarf on her head to protect it from dust. With only the hall light casting a momentary illumination on the figure, Denise could not make a positive identification.

At first, Denise wondered at the person's ability to gain access to the rooms without arousing the suspicion of the guards. Then she saw it. The silhouette carried a steel bucket that glinted in the low light in its right hand. The guard had followed instructions and allowed the visitor's work to continue as usual.

"Tom," Denise called in a subdued voice, "look at this."

"Looks like an intruder," Tom replied as he worked to adjust the screen for a clearer picture.

"I can't make out who it is," Denise commented.

"Me either. Let's watch for a while and then call for backup," Tom suggested.

Denise and Tom sat mesmerized by the form that moved slowly through the semidarkness without turning on any lights. It appeared content with the moonlight that streamed through the windows and the dim glow of the night-lights. The person appeared quite familiar with the surroundings and did not stumble over any of the furnishings on the way to the senator's inner office. The shadowy form did not stop until it reached the little cot that sat ready for the long night.

"Who do you think it is, Dory?" Tom whispered although they were alone in the room and no one could hear them.

"I don't know for sure yet. It could be almost anyone. We'll have to wait and see. Remember, we need to catch the person in the act of doing more than simply snooping around the senator's rooms," Denise replied as Tom returned his attention to the screen.

They watched as the shadow turned back the starkly white sheet on the single cot. Then it fluffed the two pillows and replaced each in its rightful place. The movements were slow and leisurely, without any sign of fear of being apprehended.

"It must be someone from housekeeping," Tom commented as they studied the screen.

"I thought they'd already finished," Denise said. "It's curious that he hasn't turned on any lights."

As Denise watched, the figure stopped its activities and bowed its head over the contents of its bucket. She could tell from the movement of the shadow's arm that the person was searching for something. In a moment, it ceased the routing and returned to the head of the bed with its back to them. It raised its hand in what might have been a sign of greeting.

"Damn, I can't tell what it's doing. Can you?" Denise asked as they squinted at the screens.

"No, its back is blocking my view. Maybe it'll turn around soon," Tom replied as he studied the image.

Slowly, the shadow moved from the bed to the nearby closet in which hung the senator's change of clothes for the early morning session. The shadow raised its arm over the garments before closing the door again. As the figure turned to face the camera, the glow from the night-light glinted off a small box in its hand.

"We have to do something. We can't wait any longer," Tom stated without taking his eyes from the shadow.

"Turn on the lights, Sergeant," Denise ordered through the radio into the ear of the waiting guard as the figure moved toward the door.

Immediately, bright lights flooded the senator's bedroom and momentarily blinded the intruder. The figure stopped and covered its eyes and face with its arm. Slowly, adjusting to the glare, the intruder began to look around the room for an avenue of escape, giving Denise a clear view of the familiar face and form.

Turning to Tom, Denise announced, "I've seen enough. Let's go."

Denise raced to the offices. Captain Carter's men stood waiting for instructions. They quickly stepped aside as Denise and Tom approached, joined by Captain Carter, who had monitored the radio frequency and overheard her call.

"Good evening," Denise said as she opened the door. The intruder sat calmly on the sofa. Denise eased into a chair across from her with Tom standing incredulous at her side.

"Good evening, Detectives," Mrs. Benedict replied serenely as if nothing had happened.

"I'm surprised to see you here tonight, Mrs. Benedict. I thought you said that you had to be home by eight o'clock," Denise said as she studied the woman's composed face.

"I needed do a little extra work in preparation for the senator's meeting tomorrow," Mrs. Benedict replied with a slight smile.

"What's in the bucket?" Denise asked, pointing to the metal bucket at Mrs. Benedict's feet.

"Only a few flowers, Detective," Mrs. Benedict replied softly as she motioned toward the stalks of gladiolus and stems of mums and roses. Unlike Pace's earlier, her gloved hands did not tremble, and tears of remorse did not flicker on her lashes.

"And what's in the box at the bottom of the bucket?" Denise continued.

Without hesitation, Mrs. Benedict replied, "Nothing in particular. Just a little powder for the flowers. It makes their blooms last longer."

"Why did you sprinkle it on the senator's cot and inside his closet if it's intended for the plants?" Denise asked as she continued to study Mrs. Benedict's face. Only now did the woman begin to look in the slightest bit worried.

"How do you know? Were you watching me? Oh, yes, surveillance cameras, I guess I overlooked them. This must be one of those 'sting' operations I read about so often. Have I been stung, Detective?" Mrs. Benedict questioned with a dry chuckle.

"You could say that, Mrs. Benedict. What special plant toxin did you use in this powder? It must be rather potent since I see you're wearing heavy gloves," Denise commented, wishing that she had her sketchbook to record the passivity of the woman's expressions.

Looking her directly in the eyes, Mrs. Benedict responded as she continued the charade, "It's a powder composed of a few of my favorite plants and guaranteed to reduce tension and produce sound sleep. I thought that the senator might need a little help after his grueling day."

"Sleep is something that none of us has enjoyed lately," Tom interjected. "I'd like to see the box, Mrs. Benedict, if you wouldn't mind."

Slowly, Mrs. Benedict removed the flowers, ribbons, and wires that hid the white box from view. With a beatific smile, she replied, looking at Denise, "I'm sure you don't need any assistance sleeping, Detective Dory. You're very active. You're probably so tired when your head hits the pillow that you fall sleep immediately.

Nothing short of a migraine would keep you from getting your rest."

Remembering the foiled nap, headache, and nausea, Denise retorted, "Just the same, I'd like to know the names of the plants involved in this compound of yours, Mrs. Benedict. I might want to have a botanist make up some of the powder for me when I get home if it works so well. I do occasionally have sleepless nights."

"He might have a little difficulty finding the mandrake root, but he shouldn't have any trouble with the other ingredients. Lady's slipper orchids are quite common," Mrs. Benedict replied softly.

"Will he have any trouble acquiring the *Amanita* mushroom for the compound?" Denise asked as she watched Mrs. Benedict cradle the little box protectively on her lap.

"The *Amanita* mushroom is highly toxic, Detective. I wouldn't use it in a harmless mixture. Would you like a sample to take home? You may have whatever remains in this box. It should be enough to do the trick quite handily," Mrs. Benedict responded confidently as she extended the box toward her.

As the little white box crept closer to her, Tom shouted, "Be careful, Dory. Any contact with the toxin could be lethal."

Nodding to him, Denise replied, "Place it on the table, Mrs. Benedict. If this powder matches the substance that killed the senators, you'll have a lot of explaining to do."

"I'll save you the trouble of analyzing. I'm at peace with what I've done regardless of your opinions. I've acted not for myself but for the good of democracy."

"I suppose you wouldn't have stopped this killing spree until you insured the selection of the senator who would champion your cause," Tom conjectured.

Nodding, she replied, "You're correct. Nothing and no one until now has managed to stop me."

"Even the arrest of your brother couldn't stop you," Denise commented.

"Dear Anthony is a good man, but he is not patient. He jumped at shadows rather than waiting to see what would develop. I would have done my work without him if I hadn't needed him for access to police information," Mrs. Benedict replied calmly and without fear.

"He's the person who wired our rooms and the conference room, isn't he, Mrs. Benedict?" Tom asked.

"Yes, he is," Mrs. Benedict remarked. "He convinced Captain Carter that you might withhold information from the Capitol police in order to keep all the publicity and the glory for yourselves. Captain Carter agreed with him because he is a very insecure man. It would have worked if you hadn't become suspicious and started meeting in the open."

Tapping her fingers impatiently, Denise asked, "How did Michael Pace fit into your plans? You know we have him under arrest. Fortunately, his assassination attempt on the senator failed."

Mrs. Benedict replied with a shrug, "Michael tried to convert Senator Salermo to our way of thinking, but he would not abandon his devotion to the old ways. It was Michael's idea to host the afternoon tea with the senator. He was afraid that you were watching me too closely and would prevent me from being able to act. I guess he was right."

Studying Mrs. Benedict's composed face, Denise stated, "One thing that Pace didn't know is that Salermo isn't as traditional as he appears; he also believes in stronger Social Security laws. So you see, you have tried and, fortunately, failed to kill a man who has the power to bring your dream to reality."

For the first time since they turned on the lights, Mrs.

Benedict's face registered surprise and her shoulders dropped. "Then, it's good that you stopped me. I'm ready to go with you now," Mrs. Benedict replied as she looked from Denise to Captain Carter.

Denise watched as Captain Carter clicked on the handcuffs and led away the little woman in the calf-length black and red cotton dress and matching scarf. Her shadow looked exactly like that of the figure Peter Dominic described as standing in the basement hallway with Anthony Guido.

Standing at her side, Tom asked softly, "How long have you known?"

"I think I've suspected her from the first time we met, but I didn't want to believe it. Even when I wrote her name on the index card in Captain Carter's safe, I hoped that I was wrong. As much as I hate to admit it, I'm like you in thinking that women commit mostly crimes of passion," Denise replied as Captain Carter's men left the office with the bed linens safely tucked inside large, black plastic bags.

Slipping his arm around her shoulders, Tom consoled her, saying, "I guess for Mrs. Benedict this was her passion. You'll feel better in the morning after you have a good sleep."

"Maybe, but I'd like to visit the rotunda for a few minutes," Denise replied, following the familiar corridors that led to the rotunda. "Something about the majesty of the structure fills me with such awe for the power of democracy that I forget everything else. You're welcome to come along with me."

Linking his arm through hers, Tom responded, "I was wondering if you'd ask me."

The next morning, D.C. papers carried the news about Mrs. Benedict on the first page, in bold letters

that read, FLOWER ARRANGER ARRESTED FOR MUR-
DER OF SENATORS. All of the television stations echoed
the story. Looking toward D.C., everyone could now
breathe easily knowing that the wheels of democracy
could once again turn smoothly.

The alarm clock woke Denise at 10:15. She had stayed
up late preparing a report that they would file with the
Capitol police. They wanted to provide a complete and
unbiased account of their investigation and the trail
that had led them to Mrs. Benedict, Anthony Guido,
and Michael Pace.

Dressing as fast as she could, Denise decided to pay a
visit to Captain Carter. Since he had said nothing at the
arrest, she wondered if he had forgotten their wager.
Finding him engaged in an animated telephone conversation, Denise decided to see what she could stir up.

"Detective Dory, come in, please. Excuse me for
keeping you waiting. I was on a very important call to
the captain of the D.C. police. It seems that Michael
Pace started to sing like a baby and blamed everything
on his partner," Captain Carter stated as he motioned
toward the familiar uncomfortable chairs that faced his
battered desk.

"Really? A man of true character," Denise exclaimed.

"What can I do for you today? Why aren't you out
enjoying the sights? You've certainly earned the vacation," Captain Carter said as he tapped his fingers over
his bulging stomach.

"We're leaving in a few minutes, but before we go,
I'm curious about our wager," Denise replied, trying
not to stare at the tomato sauce stain on the front of his
shirt.

Tapping his forehead in exasperation, Captain Carter
walked to the safe, deftly spun the dial, and extracted
their sealed envelopes. Turning, he suggested with a
leer, "Much has happened in the short time since we

made our little bet. I wonder if either of us was right. We can abandon it and make other arrangements if you would like."

Smiling at his attempt at seduction, Denise replied, "I think I prefer to see the results of our original wager, if you don't mind."

Dragging his eyes from her cleavage, Captain Carter shrugged and seized a letter opener in his meaty hands. Ripping the paper with great gusto, he extracted both handwritten notes and placed them facedown on the desk. "Would you care to do the honors?" he asked as he stepped back to allow her to join him.

Turning them over simultaneously while the captain breathed lustily on her neck, Denise said with feigned feeling, "It looks as if we were both right. You picked Pace and my choice was Mrs. Benedict. That's such a shame because it negates our wager. It's just as well. You're too busy these days to take time out for dinner with me."

Fairly salivating with the thought of pleasures that danced in his imagination, he followed Denise to the door as she made her escape into the sunshine. "But I'm sure I could find a few minutes for us to be alone. How about this evening?" Captain Carter pleaded.

"I'll be on my way home by then. As a matter of fact, all of my evenings are booked for many nights to come," Denise replied, stepping into the sun with the lusty captain in hot pursuit.

"I'll gladly accept whatever minutes you can spare," Captain Carter begged in the bright sunlight.

"No, Captain, it is not in the stars for us. Goodbye," Denise replied as she waved and vanished into the crowd.

Denise found Tom eating a double ice cream at their usual shop. The other detectives had gathered around the table to share the delicious treat. Now that the assignment was over, they could relax.

"You're late. What took you so long?" Tom demanded between spoonfuls. "We've almost finished. Did you forget that we said we'd meet here?"

"Sorry. I had some business to finalize. Let's just say that the captain took some convincing," Denise replied as she accepted the cup of ice cream he had ordered for her. "That man is certainly tenacious. He tried every angle to convince me to find time for him. Fortunately, a handsome man I know will soon occupy every free minute of my time."

"Who?" Tom asked as he tried to imitate Captain Carter's leer.

"You!" Denise replied as she laid her hand lightly on his.

Beaming, Tom asked, "Was he a sore loser?"

"No, not exactly. Both of us picked the correct suspect. Let's just say he's a firm believer that the darker the berry, the richer the juice, and he regrets not having any. He desperately wanted to prove it to himself," Denise quipped as she ate several appreciative spoonfuls of her ice cream.

"What does that mean, Denise? What do berries have to do with it? I thought your wager was for dinner," Eugene queried as he gathered the last of their trash.

"Never mind. It's a black woman's thing," Denise replied with a quick snap of her fingers.

Chuckling under his breath, Tom commented, "And you are one sweet berry."

Shaking her head and laughing happily, Denise slipped her arm through his. As their colleagues dispersed to Union Station and waiting cabs, they walked toward Tom's car. The old, comfortable wreck would take them safely home and to another case.

COMING IN MARCH 2002 FROM ARABESQUE ROMANCES

__WHEN A MAN LOVES A WOMAN
by Bette Ford   1-58314-237-1 $6.99US/$9.99CAN

Successful designer Amanda Daniels is desperately afraid her hasty marriage to rancher Zachary McFadden will lead to nothing but heartbreak. She agrees to give their union a try for one year. To her surprise, Amanda finds the fiery sensuality between them creating a fragile bond that grows stronger every day.

__SURRENDER TO LOVE
by Adrianne Byrd   1-58314-291-6 $6.99US/$9.99CAN

Julia Kelley's abusive husband has been murdered . . . and she's afraid she might be next. Penniless, she hits the road with her six-year-old daughter, only to have her car give out in the middle of a small town. Julia's sure her luck has turned from bad to worse . . . until handsome mechanic Carson Webber comes to her rescue.

__WHAT MATTERS MOST
by Francine Craft   1-58314-195-2 $5.99US/$7.99CAN

If there's one thing that mezzo-soprano Ashley Steele knows, it's that the demands of love and career don't mix. She's already seen her first marriage destroyed by her dream of singing all over the world. So why—just at the moment she's poised to become an international star—is she about to let a gorgeous horse-breeder steal her heart?

__PRICELESS GIFT
by Celeste O. Norfleet 1-58314-330-0 $5.99US/$7.99CAN

Burned by an ex-fiancé, professor Madison Evans has poured her life into her work. The only thing she wants when she arrives at the small Virginia coastal island is peace and quiet to finish her book. But from the moment she encounters antique dealer Antonio Gates, Madison finds herself swept up in sudden, breathtakingly sensual desire.

Call toll free **1-888-345-BOOK** to order by phone or use this coupon to order by mail.

Name_____

Address_____

City_____ State_____ Zip_____

Please send me the books that I checked above.

I am enclosing	$_____
Plus postage and handling*	$_____
Sales tax (in NY, TN, and DC)	$_____
Total amount enclosed	$_____

*Add $2.50 for the first book and $.50 for each additional book.

Send check or money order (no cash or CODs) to: **Arabesque Books, Dept. C.O., 850 Third Avenue 16th Floor, New York, NY 10022**

Prices and numbers subject to change without notice.

All orders subject to availability.

Visit our website at **www.arabesquebooks.com**.